Happy Birthday

Erlon paced again, rubbing his face with one hand, now. "I'm not the kind of person you should be getting close to. It's like I said. You come to me with a straight life and a clean history. I'm proud to be seen in your company. I'm proud to be your friend. It's not the same with me."

"All right." She shrugged. "You're older. You've had tough times and had to do what was necessary to get through them. You kill people for a living. I can handle that." She spun to face him. "But tell me what it is you won't tell me!"

"Jameta, I can't. Some day I may be able to, but at the moment, I don't know what to say, and I just can't. Please believe me, my past makes me the wrong person for you. Some day you will discover that. So it's better if we don't start. Can't you take my word for it?"

"No, I can't. I don't take anyone's word for anything. Not when it's this important. You tell me what's put the burr in your boot."

"Or...?"

She threw up her hands. "Or who knows what! I refuse to get into a fight with you about it."

"This isn't a fight?"

She stared at him. "Oh, no. This isn't a fight. This is a heated discussion between friends. It's only a fight between lovers when there's enough love to need one. And that's not what's happening here!"

She tried to say more, but the lump in her throat choked her, and she spun and strode out of the warehouse. As she turned the corner, she glanced back. He was standing, hands at his sides, staring after her.

She shook her head. *Well, happy birthday to me. Good thing it isn't really my birthday. Because it isn't. It isn't happy at all.*

The Trouble with Tents

Gordon A. Long

AIRBORN PRESS

Delta, B. C.

The Trouble with Tents

Gordon A. Long

Published by
ᴀɪʀʙᴏʀɴ Pʀᴇss
4958 10A Ave, Delta, B. C.
V4M 1X8
Canada

ISBN: 978-0-9952687-2-2
Printed by CreateSpace

Cover background image by Debra Ellis on
    <cognitive liberty.net>
Cover model – Nova Long

More from Gordon A. Long

Other Titles Available at Smashwords and Amazon

"Out of Mischief" World of Change Book 1
"Into Trouble" World of Change Book 2
"Mountains of Mischief" World of Change Book 3

"Zoysana's Choice" Book 1 of the Petrellan Saga

"A Sword Called...Kitten?" Romantic Comedy with an Edge
"The Cat with Many Claws" Sword Called Kitten Book 2

"Why Are People So Stupid?" Social Humour with a Point

Look for Gordon's books, selected reviews, poetry and short
stories at <airbornpress.ca>

Gordon's opinions on humanity are at the
"Are People Really That Stupid?" blog

Find his weekly reviews and his ideas on writing at
"Renaissance Writer"

Contents

Thanks to all my beta readers for their tough love.

Have the will to speak your opinion and the intelligence to wait until you have one.

– Zelfana ofthe Aine Tolbè

1.   Chase

Jameta stood in the stirrups so that just her head peeked over the top of the ridge. One hand smoothed the warm hair of Doe's neck, the other keeping a light tension on the reins. "Easy, now, girl. I don't like what I'm seeing down there."

Her horse, well-trained and steady, made no response.

Jameta waited, looking out over the crest. The scree below her tumbled around the roots of the scattered pines that cloaked the hillside. Farther out the mountains sloped down to rolling hills, and farmsteads dotted the forest. It was a beautiful area. *If only the people could take the hint.*

Down among those trees an unpredictable scene was playing out. A grey-coated official of the People's Republic of Ferbodin rode jauntily along as if enjoying the late spring day. Two mounted soldiers trotted behind, single-shot rifles slung over their shoulders.

Around the next corner of the trail a scruffy man sat on a pony that was equally decrepit, its hide matted in clumps of shedding winter hair. At the leader's back a large group of similar men sat their horses among the trees, giving off the signs of controlled boredom. There was something...wrong about those riders, but she couldn't quite put her finger on it. Maybe their polished weapons ...

"What do I do now, girl? It's too late to go down there and warn him, too far to shout." There was nothing she could do. *I hate this. Anyone else on the caravan would charge down there and help out. Not me. The bandits would look at me and laugh.*

She shrugged to herself. "Well, this is his country, not mine. Maybe he knows what he's doing."

Then the official rounded the last corner. *Ah. He knows exactly what he's doing.* He raised his hand and his escort halted, bringing their rifles to the ready. The bandit – if that's what he was – trotted his horse forward. Only two of his men followed him. When their horses were nose-to-nose, the leaders stopped and began to talk. In a rather friendly manner.

Aleria and Roeble are going to find this very interesting. Jameta reined Doe gently around and walked her away, eyes scanning the surrounding hills. Only when they were a good half mile from the meeting did she lift Doe to her swift, smooth lope, and they hurried back to the caravan.

The Caravan Master was on the lead wagon seat as usual, Roeble Cloet's sturdy pony ambling alongside her at the speed a loaded cart horse could manage all day.

Jameta pulled up on the other side. "We're about to receive a semi-official delegation."

Aleria glanced at Roeble, raising her eyebrows.

The trader shrugged. "Not something I expected, but this is Ferbodin, after all. There's the scheduled inspections, then there's the unscheduled inspections and after that the unofficial inspections, sliding rapidly towards the illegal inspections, demands for bribes and outright thievery. And I'm only talking about the government officials."

"My guess would lean toward the latter end of the scale." Jameta pointed a thumb over her shoulder. "There's a man in government greys back there having a cosy chat with forty-three scruffy-looking characters whose choice of weapons far outpaces their sense of style."

"Shit!" Aleria craned her neck back. The caravan was spread out in its usual formation, wagons far enough apart to minimize dust. She stood up, bracing her knee against the jouncing seat, and gave a shrill whistle. When she had the attention of the following drivers, she shouted and made the signal to close up ranks. The sound of the order being repeated faded away down the line.

They pulled into a straight stretch of road, and Aleria stood again to see that the last wagon was in sight. Then she signalled again, and Cavick, the lead driver, snapped his whip above the backs of his team. They lurched into a tired trot, and all the wagons behind picked up the pace. Dust boiled away from the straining hooves, an increasing cloud that drifted high on the breeze.

"Where's Lavan?"

Jameta gestured. "Off to the north. He won't be far."

"If he heard my whistle he'll be here soon. I want both of you on our back trail."

"I'll circle left, try to pick him up. If I don't see him, I'll go out alone."

"Just be careful. I want information, not a hero."

Jameta rolled her eyes. "Yes, boss. I got it."

"I can't say it too many times."

Jameta raised a hand and turned away. *But you do say it.* She trotted along the caravan to find Erlon. "I'm going back to check on

2

the enemy. I'll swing north to pick up Lavan if I can. If he shows up, send him after me."

"Was it Pavenkov?"

"Too far away to tell, but Pavenkov rode out in our direction after the meeting, and the leader of this bunch was riding a dark-maned bay."

Erlon spun Rogas, his big gelding, and paced beside her. "They might be just a bunch of bandits, but if they're attached to Pavenkov they may be more organized. Watch for outriders."

"Thanks, Erlon." Jameta reached up and brushed her knuckles down his cheek, then kneed Doe to a gallop. She knew that Erlon worried about her, but he did her the honour of not harping about it. She glanced back to see him sitting his horse, unmoving, his hand covering the cheek she had touched. *I really ought to marry him, if we survive this one.*

She concentrated on her path. *If I can get him to look at me twice, that is.*

The trees were open here; she made good time, but there was no sign of Lavan. Settling more firmly in the saddle, she headed south and moved, slowly now, towards the approaching enemy. When she got back to the wagon road she turned left and rode along for a while, but she felt exposed, so she cut into the forest on the right-hand side and went looking for a vantage point.

A rocky knoll soon presented itself. Ground-tying Doe tight against a small cliff, she slipped up to the top and squirmed out to where she could look around. The Dalmyn caravan was throwing up a dust cloud that boiled above the trees to the west. East along the road was another cloud, much smaller, filtering up through the trees. *Good. They're not galloping yet.*

Back along her trail she could see a horse trotting after her. The distinctive white eagle feather in the rider's hatband made her grin. *No missing Lavan.*

What she saw next wiped the smile off her face. A horseman on a shaggy pony was ambling along through the forest right below her perch. *Outrider. Damn! Any moment now he'll see that cloud of dust we're kicking up.*

Without further thought Jameta slithered down the rock, dropping onto Doe's back from above and kneeing the startled horse into a trot. *If I can keep him occupied...*she calculated the scout's course and set herself to cross in front of him. Sure enough, she

3

caught a glimpse of a surprised face and an open mouth. She kicked Doe into a gallop, and the rider followed.

As soon as she had outpaced her follower she started to look for Lavan. *He ought to be about...there he is!* Relief coursed through her as she reined her mount in his direction.

He made no comment when she galloped past him, merely turning his horse to run alongside.

"Scout. Right behind."

Lavan looked over his shoulder. "Honey trap?"

"Sounds good. On the road."

"Aye." He hauled his reins to the right and disappeared into the brush.

Now she slowed, allowing her pursuer to catch up as she angled towards the wagon trail. Soon she saw thinning trees to the right and cut towards the road. Rapid hoofbeats behind brought her head around. *At least he doesn't have a rifle or a bow.*

She slowed her horse further, and the scout began to overtake her on her right side.

He waved his sword in a threatening manner. "Pull up, Darkie. I wanta talk to you."

She did not answer but swerved back and forth, riveting his attention so that he did not notice Lavan until it was too late.

The Dalmyn outrider pulled up beside the little man, his rifle cocked and aimed. "Sheath the sword."

The other rider looked up at the two enemy towering over his short pony, glanced at the road behind him then put away his weapon. "Whataya want?"

"Keep riding."

As they galloped forward, the scout swore; he had seen the dust cloud ahead. He looked around, checking angles and spaces through the trees.

Jameta grinned over at Lavan, his rifle aimed across his saddle bow, then frowned down at their prisoner. "Don't try it. Our horses are faster than yours, and Lavan will shoot you down before you can turn. Pull out front a ways. You're going on a little ride with us."

The scout's mouth turned down, but he rode along without comment.

They passed the tail end of the caravan, wagons bouncing along the rugged road, the remuda strung nose-to-tail behind the third wagon from the rear. When they reached the front they reported in, and Aleria held a quick conference on the run.

"Where are they?"

"Back on the road a couple of miles. They weren't putting up much dust yet. We brought our little friend along in case he told tales."

Erlon slid up between them, cutting the prisoner out of the group. "Should we kill him now?"

Aleria glanced at Roeble. The merchant shook his head. "He might be an innocent peasant going to visit his ailing grandmother. We can hardly kill him out of hand."

The Dalmyn Caravan Master shrugged. "Aye. And his grandmother might be visiting with my grandmother, but I doubt it. Erlon?"

"Yes, Ma'am."

"No removing heads so early in the day in a foreign country. Keep him until we see the border. Then put him off his horse and turn him loose."

Jameta frowned. "But he called me 'Darkie.' That's rude."

Aleria laughed. "He's hardly going to call you 'Blondie.' And we're much too civilized to kill him for his taste in women."

The big soldier leaned over his victim, his hand fingering the sabre that hung from his saddle. "Hear that, friend? Play nice and you get to live. No name-calling. Especially the dark one. She's sensitive."

The enemy scout had forgotten his sense of humour. He nodded with a sour glare and rode along, his shoulders slouched.

Aleria stood up and checked the wagons, then sat again. "All right. The frontier ought to be around the next corner. Or the next one. In any case, those bandits will be after us full tilt any moment. Do we dare play the normal dance at the border post?"

Roeble shook his head. "If they've been meeting with Pavenkov, they might have friends up ahead, too."

"Hmm." Aleria stared ahead. "The Ferbodin border guards are pretty reliable."

"You mean once they're bought, they stay bought?"

"Exactly. And we pay them well every time we come through. As long as we get there before Pavenkov shows up to throw his political weight around, they shouldn't be a problem. I hope."

5

2.   Border Bandits

The border was three corners ahead. When they came within sight, Aleria called her riders to her again.

"Listen up. From here on, we're in trouble. We're in a hurry, we're desperate, we keep looking over our shoulders. Act scared."

Lavan grinned. "That oughta be pretty easy. We are scared, aren't we?"

"Yes, but only of what's behind us. We're happy to see the soldiers at the border, right? Eyes and rifles pointed at our back trail. This is an acting job, folks. Do it right and we might get out of this with everyone alive. Erlon, you go first and prepare them. Jameta, you're lightest and I'll need a ride. Stay with me."

She snapped her fingers at an idea. "Lavan, turn the remuda loose and send them ahead."

He frowned at first, then nodded and spun his horse towards the rear.

At Aleria's signal Cavick laid his whip on the backs of his team. Startled by this rude treatment, they leapt into a gallop, and the whole caravan stampeded toward the border post, where the guards were jumping to their positions. Jameta loped Doe alongside the bounding wagon, alert for trouble from other directions.

Erlon brought his horse to a sliding stop in front of the fortification, pointing back along the trail and shouting. As the lead wagon wrenched to a stop the Ferbodean commanding officer was just striding up, a frown on his face.

"What is going on, here?"

"Bandits, Citizen." Aleria jumped down from the wagon and ran up to him. "A whole lot of them. Back along the trail, coming this way fast."

Now her wagons were piling in, loosely grouped, the horses stamping and steaming. The officer's head went from side to side, trying to see everything. His frown was getting deeper.

As he opened his mouth the remuda of spare horses galloped around the wagons, leaping the gate in ponderous bounds and rolling off up the pass.

"You've got to let my wagons through, Citizen." She waved her satchel. "All the paperwork and fees are here. Let me get my goods and people to the safety of my border."

"But what if…"

She gestured back along the trail. "See that dust cloud? There are about twice as many of them as there are of us, including all your soldiers. If we're gone, they'll have no reason to bother you. If we stay, you'll have to defend us." She stepped closer, her hand brushing the pistol at her belt. "We have to go through, Citizen. You understand that, don't you?"

Aleria opened her satchel and grabbed the papers. "Here are the proper forms, all filled out, just like they want them," she fanned the sheets out, "signed and stamped by the proper officials." She pulled out a second parcel. "And here are the fees, including a bit of extra for your men because of this problem." She glanced over her shoulder at the approaching dust cloud. "You can send a team to check our goods at the Galesian border post once the bandits get bored and go home. I'll wait for you there."

The guard Captain nodded. "We could do that…"

"Now, may I go? I want to prepare our border guards in case the bandits decide to keep coming."

The officer weighed his options. The plump parcel of "fees" in his hand and the shiny Double-S rifles brandished by her guards decided him. He signalled his men to open the gate, and the wagons filed through, breaking into a laboured gallop again up the steepening pass.

The soldier glanced at Aleria, then at the approaching cloud of dust, his bribe weighing down his hand. "What would you like me to do, Citizen?"

"Nothing. You've done all you can. I doubt they'll bother you when they see my plump little caravan getting away. I'd leave the gate open and let them through, if it was me. Of course, you will do what your duty tells you."

He straightened at that and saluted. "Good luck, Citizen Dalmyn. I hope this will not discourage you from further trading."

Aleria smiled and swung up behind Jameta, who urged Doe to a gallop after the departing wagons.

"All right. Now we have to deal with our own border."

Jameta concentrated on the rough road under her horse's hooves. "Why?"

"Because…go left of our wagons…our soldiers have been out on the frontier too long, and I sometimes wonder whether some nasty Ferbodean ideas have been seeping into their greedy little minds."

Now Doe had brought them to the front of the caravan as they approached the border post. Jameta pulled up beside Erlon and slowed her panting horse.

Aleria glanced back along the trail. "We've got time, now. Let's go in there with snap and decorum. Thoughts?"

The guard Captain pointed. "If they attack, the post covers the north side of the pass. That open area to the south side is the problem. They'll take a few shots from those new cannons in the fort, but whoever's left will rush right on through, and we can't outrun them. But if we line the wagons in overlap position we can plug the whole pass and keep them out."

"Excellent. Give the order. I'm off to speak to whoever's in charge." Aleria slapped Doe's rump with her folded gloves, and the horse sprang to a gallop again. Jameta held her mount back to a decent pace, saving her energy in case of need.

She let Aleria down in front of the fort, where Galesian soldiers where bustling around, rolling their new toys forward in a businesslike fashion, the long barrels poking over the wall.

The Major strode out, his hand on his sabre hilt. "Well, my Lady. Have you brought guests home with you?"

"Unwelcome ones, Sir. About forty of them, and I doubt if they'll stop at the border."

He rubbed his chin. "What sort are they? Bandits, I presume? Why would they dare to approach a border post?"

"Because I'm not sure they're bandits. This stinks of diplomacy." Aleria shrugged. "They aren't soldiers in uniform, but they're too well organized to be bandits."

Jameta thought that over. "But if they're official, they won't attack a Galesian border post. It would be tantamount to starting a war."

"Which is why they don't look official. Just bandits, could be from any side or no side. If they can overrun this post and the Ferbodeans come in to "help" us because we aren't able to maintain our position, who knows where the border might end up when it was all over?"

The Major's face blanched. "So I have a major diplomatic incident on my hands. What the hell do I do, now?"

Jameta smiled down from Doe's back. "Fortunately for you, you have a diplomat to handle it. Aleria, do you still have that letter of marque the king gave you?" She watched the Major's face lighten.

"No, I had to give it back to his Majesty after the last mission was over. But I still have his trust." She faced the officer. "The only way this incident will become a problem is if they overrun this post and get into Galesia. Your fort defends this side of the pass. My wagons and my Sustained Shot rifles can handle the other side."

The Major looked across the pass with a doubtful frown. "That's a wide space. Can you cover it?"

Jameta pointed to the line of wagons, overlapped so that each team of horses was protected by the wagon in front. Shiny gun barrels poked out from behind the wheels. "Our men are very good shots, and you have an idea of the power of our weapons, since you store them for us while we're inside the realm."

Aleria flicked her fingers up towards the fortifications. "And tell your men to aim down if the enemy gets between us. No sense in shooting each other. And keep those nasty cannons pointed down the pass."

The Major's back straightened. "Exactly. We'll handle this mob, don't you worry, ladies."

Aleria nodded as if dismissing him. He headed back into the fort, shouting orders, and she walked alongside Jameta. She looked down the empty pass, then glanced at the horse. "No sense in burdening poor Doe any more. That was a hard ride."

Jameta tried to grin and make normal conversation, in spite of her distress. "She's not so fast uphill with a double load, especially after that little race. Come with me for a run some day. I've never been able to figure out whether Brownie is faster, because I don't have a good rider who's light enough to make it an even go."

"I'll take you up on that if we get out of this one."

This sent another frisson of fear coursing through Jameta, and she glanced down the pass. Then she looked again, and terror choked her. Three leading riders pushed their tired horses up the hill, strung out along the trail. A larger, tighter group appeared around the last corner. "Here they come!"

Aleria sprinted towards the wagons. "Get your horse in with the remuda and stay there, so I know where to find you. Stilet will need help if there's shooting, and the remuda will handle better if you're there." As Jameta passed her, she called out. "And keep your stock back against the rocks, behind the other horses. If we need to get a message out, I want you in good shape to take it."

Jameta frowned but could say nothing; her fear would not allow it. Obediently, she dismounted and led her sweating mount behind the wagons to safety. She whistled for Brownie and switched her gear to the fresh horse, then filled the anxious wait by rubbing Doe down with a cloth from her saddlebag.

"Well, aren't we the cool one?"

She turned. Lavan was dismounting, sliding the rifle from his saddle scabbard.

"I'm not cool at all. I'm trying to find something to do that keeps my shaking hands from showing."

He nodded. "Nothing wrong with being scared. Just be planning your escape route."

She was beginning to catch on to Lavan's technique. *No sense worrying about what can't be changed. Look around for possibilities.* Checking the pass to see that the approaching mob was still a fair distance out, she slipped up on Brownie's back and nudged her along the wall of rock, looking for an alternate route. *If they make it through, the road would be a bad place to run.*

The rock was broken on this side of the pass, and large boulders lay strewn where they had fallen from the mountainside above. She spotted a well-used animal trail and urged her mount down it. It was a tight squeeze between the boulders, but Brownie was a slim horse, and by lifting her feet from the stirrups Jameta was able to make it. The trail wound away to the west, and soon she was out of sight of the frontier. At this point she began to feel very alone. She turned back with a shaky grin to herself. *I like it when my feelings direct me towards obeying orders.*

When she came down out of the rocks the so-called bandits had gathered in a group, and their leaders sat their horses in the van, talking it over. From a distance, one of them looked a lot like Pavenkov, although he was no longer wearing his grey coat. It was definitely the same horse as he had been riding in the forest.

For the moment she was snug enough here, but as soon as the shooting started she would move down to the safer position behind the remuda as she had been ordered.

Erlon's voice carried, not loud but calm and clear. "The first volley into the rocks beside them. I want ricochets buzzing all over. The second volley immediately after into the ground at their feet. Then they'll know they're up against Sustained Shot rifles. If they still attack, shoot to kill. Horses or men at a distance. Once they get close enough, try for the riders."

There was a mutter of assent from his men. No fuss, no running around. Everyone ready to do his duty. Jameta tried to feel reassured.

The leader of the Ferbodeans raised his sword and called out. His troops lifted their horses to a trot.

Erlon's voice rose. "First volley before they get to the gallop. Ready...Fire!"

A wall of sound blasted out, and Jameta discovered her mistake. Brownie tried to rear in the tightness of the rocks, banging her rider's leg painfully against the granite. Wrestling the horse down, Jameta pushed her back to the remuda, her breath coming in gasps as the second volley rang out, closely followed by another from the fort across the pass.

The trotting horses milled in confusion.

She craned her neck to see through the wagons. It looked like two animals were down, and several men. *I guess the soldiers are not so strategic. They're shooting to kill already.* Then the "boom" of a cannon drowned it all out, and an empty swath appeared in the mob, horses and men falling like wheat before a scythe. She could actually see the cannon ball, bouncing off the ground and bounding away down the canyon.

The leader had swung his horse around and was now facing his men, looking back over his shoulder at his enemy.

Oh, no. Erlon, no!

The guard Captain stepped out from behind the wagons, his rifle at his shoulder. He paced forward, then stopped and shot. As he levered another round into the chamber he stepped ahead, then stopped and fired again. Each time an enemy soldier fell from his horse.

Then Erlon stopped, his rifle still ready. "Hold it right there."

Jameta's nails dug into her palms, her breath coming tight and fast.

The leader spun his horse to face the soldier.

"You move, you die. Tell your men to ride back a hundred paces and dismount." The rifle cracked again, and chips flew from the saddlebow in front of the enemy leader.

The man cursed, shaking his hand as if it stung.

"Tell them."

The Ferbodean turned and shouted to his men. They milled around, uncertain, but finally moved away and dismounted, forming a suspiciously straight line. *Those are no regular bandits.*

"Now get down and walk towards me."

The enemy hesitated, then shrugged and dismounted, stepping forward.

Erlon signalled, and Aleria appeared with Roeble, striding ahead, her pistol holstered but her drawn sword in her hand. After a moment the postern door in the fort opened, and the Major marched out. The group met in the middle of the pass and their voices dropped so that Jameta could hear no more.

But the exchange was obvious. The enemy leader was into his spiel, gesturing and grimacing. Jameta grinned. *A lot of noise from someone who is outgunned and outmaneuvered.*

In the middle of this tirade Aleria sheathed her sword and raised her voice, cutting him off. "I'll give you two choices, Citizen. One, you get on your horse, turn around and go back to your men and ride away. If you don't prefer that, you get choice two; Erlon boots you in the butt a couple of times, then dances you back to your men by shooting your bootheels off. In choice two we wait one minute and then start shooting to kill. In case you didn't figure it out, the first two volleys were only warnings."

The leader snarled and tried to stare Erlon down. *Rather difficult, since he has to look up to do it.*

"You're lucky you haven't actually done anything wrong on Galesian soil, Pavenkov, because none of your fake bandits fired a gun, and you didn't make it across the border. I suppose the Major, here can find a reason to arrest you anyway, and our courts will deal with you."

That was the final straw. With a curse, the man swung onto his horse, jerked its head around and rode back towards his men. As he approached they swung up into their saddles. He said nothing, but rode through them and back down the trail. They formed up in pairs and followed, exactly like a cavalry troop on maneuvers. A smaller group came back and began to deal with the wounded and the dead.

Now we know for sure they aren't bandits, in spite of the small, scruffy horses. She giggled to herself. *Maybe that's all the Ferbodean government can afford for their cavalry.* She choked down the next giggle as it rose towards hysteria at the back of her throat.

Once the Ferbodean customs team had trundled up and done their bureaucratic job, the Dalmyn guards lined up to turn their Double-S rifles over to the Galesian Border Patrol. Aleria watched it all with a sharp eye.

"That's eight rifles in perfect working order and 1,420 rounds of ammunition out of the original 1,500."

"A peaceful trip."

"No action besides target practice. Until the end."

The Major scrawled his signature on the paper and turned the clipboard towards her. "Exactly as you say, my Lady. And problems with the weapons?"

"My lads have been keeping them in tiptop shape, but that's a dry and dusty land over there. It wouldn't hurt your men to practice stripping them down and oiling them. They'll last better that way."

"Oh, we do a lot of that." The Major grinned. "Soldiers need to know their weapons."

Aleria nodded. "These Mechanicals take 'maintain your equipment' to a whole new level. You keep a sword or a bowstring dry, and it's always there for you. One grain of sand in the wrong place, and an eight-shot rifle's no better than a club."

"I make sure the men know it."

"Well, have them ready for the next time."

"Don't you worry, my Lady. When will you need them again?"

"Could be a month, could be five. But make sure there's a good store of ammunition at all times, too."

"Of course, my Lady. You can count on it. We'll see you on your next trip, then."

"I will count on it."

Jameta watched this exchange, saying nothing. Later, as the caravan drove away from the frontier, the Wagonmaster waved her over to ride alongside. "What did you think?"

"I think he was happy to get those weapons back."

Aleria shrugged. "Price we pay. Normal citizens are still not allowed Mechanicals like that inside the realm."

"There was something..."

"Yes?"

"Something about the ammunition. He jumped too heavily on that. Defensive, I thought."

"I trust your instincts. We'll have to be careful about the ammunition in future. Now let's move along. We've still got several days to go, and summer is on its way."

3.   Debriefing

Seven hot, dry days later, the triumphant Dalmyn/Cloet expedition rolled into the Dalmyn Cartage yard in Kingsport. Wagons were off-loaded in an atmosphere of jubilation. It had been a profitable trip with an exciting ending. *And nobody dead. That really helps.*

Once everything was packed away and the horses pastured out, the men rolled off to the Falcon to celebrate. Jameta was in the stables straightening her gear when Aleria showed up. "Knew I'd find you here. We have a visitor, and I want you to talk to him."

"Certainly. Who is it?"

"Just an old friend."

"You want me there when you report to Raif anCanah?"

"That's it. You have been useful on this trip, and you would be more useful if you had a better idea of our political objectives."

"Well, I live to be useful. Lead on."

Aleria regarded her. "You do, don't you?"

"What, live to be useful? I suppose. What good are you if you aren't useful? Easy answer. No good at all."

"I never looked at life that way. Don't you have time for being useful to yourself? Doing what you want to do?"

"Oh, I usually manage to slip in a little of that."

Aleria grinned. "The handsome Erlon is otherwise occupied. Raif is up at the office. Let's go."

"What will he want from me?"

"I'd like him to hear your story about that almost-attack."

"Your wish is my command, O Caravan Master."

When they got to the yard office the clerks were tiptoeing around. Raif had commandeered the foreman's workroom and was leaning back in his chair, his hat and gloves on the desk, his polished bootheels propped beside them. He jumped to his feet when the women entered, striding over to envelope Aleria in a firm hug. He gave Jameta a more decorous greeting.

"So, ladies. Sit down, sit down." His hand swept the room. "I'm sorry my office doesn't have the proper amenities, but I wanted to get the information as soon as you got in."

Aleria sat, her head on one side. "You're in a hurry. Is this youthful enthusiasm, or do we have a political crisis?"

"A bit of both. We are trying to formulate policy and we don't have much to go on. There are all sorts of theories floating around, so I thought I'd grasp at the straws I have."

"Before others start twisting them to their own ends."

"Nail on the head. Let's start with those bandits. Jameta? I gather you spotted them."

"I was led to them."

"By that Pavenkov character."

"That's right."

"And what set you on that trail?"

"Well, my Lord, I'll try to explain. I go along to all the meetings to represent my family, and frankly, to get all the experience I can."

"Fair enough."

"But I don't have any function. I sit back and watch and listen."

Aleria grinned. "And then afterwards, she tells us what was going on under our noses, but we were to busy to notice it. Very handy."

"I see. And what was going on this time?"

"Nothing I could put my finger on. But it was different."

Raif glanced at her. "What made it different?"

She composed her thoughts. "I'll be honest, my Lord, I didn't like him."

"There's nothing different about that. Nobody from Galesia likes Pavenkov. I doubt if many in Ferbodin do either. I've never met the man, and I don't like him." He raised a hand. "I'm sorry. Go ahead."

"I didn't trust him. I know. The rest of you don't either. But I picked up on his expression when he was asking about our route. He wasn't telling the truth."

"You can tell when someone's lying?"

"I don't think that's possible unless you know them well. No, it meant more to him than he wanted us to think. There was an urgency...hard to explain. So when he left, I decided to see where he was going. When the caravan pulled out, I waited. And guess what? He came out, got on a horse and cut into the woods on a path parallel to the road. This made me more suspicious, so I kept an eye out. Sure enough, a few hours later I saw a Ferbodean officer over to the south of us. Couldn't be sure who, but I thought I recognized that horse Pavenkov rides. When I saw the so-called bandits I thought he was in trouble, but I soon realized it was a friendly meeting."

"And why weren't they bandits?"

"In the first place, they didn't act like bandits. In spite of the shaggy little horses. They were too...still. Too patient. They sat or

15

stood without moving. With good posture." She threw up her hands. "I don't know, my Lord. It's too difficult to figure it out afterwards. I looked at them, and a voice in my head said, 'Those aren't bandits.' That's all I can tell you."

"You're doing fine, my Lady. I'm sure your intuition is keen. It's just that I can't go to my superiors and say, 'She felt they weren't bandits.' Wouldn't go over well."

Another thought came to her. "Oh, and they were riding strange horses."

"You already said that."

"No, I mean strange to their riders. You know, when you watch a horse and rider, you can tell if they're familiar with each other. They're...sort of...comfortable? If they're strangers, there's a whole lot of edginess. Getting things straight."

"It's not something I ever thought much about, but I suppose you're right. If I'm on a strange horse, it's not the same as one of my regulars."

"Exactly. So I put together a bunch of people who looked like bandits but weren't acting like bandits, on bandit-type horses they weren't familiar with..."

"...and you came up with a troop of cavalry soldiers made out to look like bandits, including bandit horses."

"Then Pavenkov met with their leader, and they had a friendly chat..."

"And you were right. The Galesian guards also noticed their military bearing. So your analysis is that there was a troop of disguised cavalry under the orders of a Ferbodean high official that chased your caravan across the border and attempted to cross into Galesia after you."

"I wouldn't exactly call that analysis, my Lord. But it's an accurate guess."

He laughed and looked at Aleria. "Sounds familiar?"

She grinned. "Some of us don't use the kind of analytical skills the military prefers, but we come up with a reasonable approximation of the truth, nonetheless."

"Good enough. It jibes with our other reports, and if both of you are agreed, I'll present it that way to the king."

"You think their main objective was to overrun the border, don't you? My caravan was only a convenient excuse."

"Much thought I hate to suggest that your brilliant device to get through the frontier wasn't necessary, it's a possibility we have to consider."

Aleria frowned. "And I wasted all that extra bribe money?"

"Oh, I'm sure it will sweeten them up for next time."

"There will be a next time, will there?"

He shrugged. "These border games don't affect the realities of commerce. They need our trade, and we need theirs. In fact, I can tell you right now that you'll be back there within two months."

"We will?" The two women exchanged glances.

"I realize you haven't had time for a debriefing, Aleria, but I've been meeting regularly with your father and Joem Cloet, and we have the basics sketched out. A trip through Ferbodin with enough trading to keep them happy, and then a little junket out the other side to see what's happening in the desert beyond."

"And Roeble and I will be leading it?"

He shrugged. "That's up to Kensel and Joem, but I somehow doubt they'll change the players on a winning team. The Dalmyn and Cloet bank accounts are going to be very happy with the results of your latest run."

"What would you know about that?" Aleria frowned and stared into his eyes.

"I have my sources."

Jameta grinned. "At the border post."

Aleria turned the frown to her.

"A messenger passed us the following day, remember?"

"Right. I wasn't having suspicious thoughts at the time."

"I wasn't suspicious either, until just now."

The young lord looked at her a moment, then at Aleria. "I see what you mean."

Jameta regarded the two of them. "And what sort of comment was that?"

He shrugged. "Aleria told me about you. I'm just starting to get the idea."

She tossed Aleria a quick glare. "What has she been blathering about?"

He smiled. "Nothing to your disadvantage." Then he became serious. "It's my duty to know what's happening and who's making it happen. When I find someone who doesn't fit the pattern, I look closer."

"I'm not hard to understand. Ask Aleria. I'm a simple girl from the North, doing my best to be useful. She was just saying that as we came across the yard."

"And if that's all you were, you'd still be in the North, being useful."

"So you've got the two of us written into the story as anTollen the Lion and his faithful companion Dudge from the old legend, have you?"

"Something like that. Now we have to decide which one is the knight and which one the peasant."

"We switch back and forth: even and odd days. I get the odd days."

Raif nodded. "Whatever works. With Roeble and Erlon, you're the best we've got."

Aleria ignored this repartee. "So we're out on a big one this fall."

"Soon as the heat of summer is over. You don't want to be out in that desert, this time of year."

"I'd have to agree. Our recent little chase wasn't fun in that heat." Aleria pulled at her collar. "Speaking of which, is there anything else? I could use a bath and a chilled wine."

He rose. "No, no, I'm sorry to keep you from a well-deserved bath." He turned to Jameta. "Notice, I did not say 'desperately needed bath.' I'm being pleasant, because you are both entitled."

"It is gratifying to be treated as we deserve, my Lord." She grinned. "Especially this time."

"Well, I'm sure we'll be seeing more of you in the next little while. Come over and see our wonderful offspring. I can play the proud father, and Mito can use the distraction."

"Thank you, my Lord."

He glanced at her once more, dropped a hand on Aleria's shoulder. "Good to have you back."

She placed her hand over his. "Good to be back. I'll be over tomorrow."

"I'll tell Mito. She's dying for your stories." He nodded to Jameta and strode out.

"And that's it?"

Aleria shrugged. "You could write it down while it's fresh in your mind. Not right now. Go home and take a rest. Someone from Raif's office will want to talk to you. If they think any of this is important they'll sit you down and try to get every ounce of information they can. If that happens, the only advice I can give is, don't let them put words in your mouth. It doesn't do the king any good to give him stories slanted to suit the objectives of his underlings."

"I'll remember that."

"Please do. The politics at home are worse than the dangers of the road." The Caravan Master leaned back on her chair and regarded Jameta. "So, out on a real adventure this time. What do you think of that?"

Jameta shook her head. "I'm not sure, Aleria. I've been doing fine on these trips through civilized territory. I'm not sure I'd be an asset in wild country. Too much of my technique involves talking to people. It wouldn't be much good to me in the middle of a dozen charging desert bandits."

Aleria nodded. "We should talk to Erlon about that little problem."

"Yes, the safety of the caravan is his responsibility."

"And like it or not, so are you. Where are you headed now?"

"I'm off to Lord Dennal's. The Twins are expecting me."

"I don't see enough of them. We'll have to get together." Aleria stood. "Are you staying in the city long?"

"If I'm going out with this next expedition, I suppose. Otherwise, I might as well go back to Oudonsford and get to work again."

Aleria laid a hand on her shoulder. "Being useful."

"That's right."

"You pulled your weight on this trip."

"Thanks, Aleria. It's good to hear that." *But what about the next one? What do they expect an unarmed, frightened messenger to do on a long-range caravan?*

4.   The Twins

The anDennal mansion was in the "Crescents" area of the city. It overlooked a beautiful park with a lake in the middle and gardens all around, where people loved to drive and walk on pleasant summer evenings and feastday afternoons.

As a servant bowed her through the ornate front door and carried her saddlebags to her bedroom, Jameta contrasted this with the Dennal house above the coal-port at Oudonsford and considered the advantages of her new position.

After her bath she regarded her meagre selection of dresses, hanging lonely in the huge armoire. *No sense dressing up. I can't compete with those two.* She shrugged her shoulders and put on the one decent gown that she owned, aside from the Samnian silk one her mother had woven for her.

When she came downstairs Gita and Hana were relaxing in their private drawing room. Jameta hesitated just inside the doorway. *Go on in. They invited you here, after all.*

"Well, here we have her." Hana, the taller and slimmer of the two, cocked her head to one side. "Our little cousin, now a famous caravan outrider."

Gita frowned, planting her stocky body in front of Jameta, looking her up and down. "But we simply must take you shopping."

Jameta smiled. "I admit those dresses are impressive. Is this your daily wear, or did you put on a splash to keep me in my place?"

The Twins exchanged a glance. A smile spread across Gita's face. "Well, that didn't take long." She turned to Jameta. "Do you know what a bird bet is?"

"Of course. The drivers play that silly game all the time."

"Do they? The bargemen do, too."

"And this is apropos of...?"

"We had a bird bet on. I got put in my place first. I lost."

Jameta turned to Hana. "Do you want your turn now, or shall we keep you in suspense for a while?"

The taller girl flopped back in her lounging chair and waved a languid hand. "I'll do my best to make it not worth the effort. You two whale away at each other all you want."

Gita took a stance beside her equally ornate lounger. "She's trying to be a spoilsport for her own protection. I demand equal treatment. We are twins."

Jameta took a more formal seat, a heavily embroidered armchair. "I tell you what. Why don't we wait until she deserves it? I'm on my mettle in cases like that."

Gita sat down with a flounce. "I suppose I don't have any choice."

Jameta regarded each of them in turn. "I don't understand it. Everybody else thinks I'm a friendly, pleasant person. You two act like I'm your favourite contestant in some kind of social battle. Why did you invite me to stay?"

"You're family. But you're also the best entertainment we have." Gita turned to her sister. "We should take her out and show her around. Can you imagine her with Envelune?"

Hana shook her head. "She'd ignore Envelune completely."

"Why would I ignore this person?"

"Because she isn't worth it. She's a girl that went to school with us. She's not very smart and she doesn't usually cause any harm. She just opens her mouth without thinking."

"You're right. I don't think it's fair to take advantage of people like that."

Hana's eyebrows rose. "My, you have grown up. I don't recall you being so discriminating in the past."

Gita sat up straight and pointed. "There! She's done it. She has treated you in a demeaning way. I demand satisfaction."

"Gita, I refuse to be a performing horse to do tricks on demand."

The smaller girl's mouth turned down.

"I tell you what. I'll keep her in suspense and hit her when she's least expecting it. How's that?"

The other's face brightened. "That's more like the Jameta we know and anticipate."

Hana regarded her with narrowed eyes. "I hope you've grown up past pushing people into the river."

"Oh, yes. I only do that in a social sense, now."

Hana nodded slowly. "What was that about, anyway? It was the second year you rode down the river on the log rafts with us. The year before, you were such fun. Then you went silly."

"Oh, that was Aleria."

"Aleria? Wasn't that the first time she came with us?"

"Exactly. The first year we had all that fun, swimming and playing in the water. I was so looking forward to it the second year. And then this prissy society girl shows up, and suddenly it's childish to have water fights and run around screaming. She wants to have swimming races and diving competitions – which she always won – and sit around talking about stupid things. So I pushed her in the water."

Gita grinned. "You could have at least waited until she had her bathing dress on."

She shrugged. "It worked, didn't it? We had all the screaming and chasing my heart desired."

"But why did you push us in, too?"

"I couldn't very well push the guest in alone, could I? That would be rude."

Hana sniffed. "You were a real pest that summer."

Jameta smiled, thinking back. "Remember the day we swam ashore?"

"You mean the day Aleria chased you ashore. Was she angry!"

Jameta's grin widened. "By the time she got to the shore she was too tired to be angry."

Gita held up her hands. "The one who was really put out was the sweeps Captain. He was ready to anchor the raft and row to shore in the skiff."

Hana laughed. "But Mother told him not to. 'Let them be. They'll catch up.' That's what she said. We were astounded! That didn't sound like dear Mother at all."

Gita grinned, but her eyes narrowed. "That's not all she said."

The other two looked at her.

"She said, 'They'll catch up. At least the one that survives will.' I didn't understand what she meant, but I do now."

"You do?"

"Of course. The two of you are still at it. The battle to see who's the herd boss or the lead mare, or whatever you call it."

Jameta opened her mouth to protest, but then she closed it. *That would explain a lot of things, wouldn't it?*

"Care to tell us the deep thoughts?"

She smiled at Gita. "Deciding to agree with you."

The smaller Twin clapped her hands. "Well, there you go. If Jameta agrees, I must have said something intelligent for a change."

Hana waved a hand at her sister. "You always were the first one to sniff out a battle. Before it started, even."

"Well, it's a boring life." Her head turned to Jameta. "Maybe I should come with you on the next expedition."

Jameta considered that idea for the two seconds it deserved. "Have you thought about the unpleasant details? No baths, no functionaries..." she paused dramatically, "...no maid to do your hair."

"Oh. Perhaps a shorter trip, then."

"Yes." Hana grinned. "Like across the city to the beauty shop."

After that Jameta was busy refereeing a pillow fight that threatened the furniture.

5.   Frustration

The following day, Aleria and Jameta were dressed in more appropriate clothing for two Ranked ladies on a hot summer day in the city. Except neither of them would stoop to a side saddle. Aleria swung up on her mount and reined out of the Dennal stable yard. "All right, Jameta. The trip's over, and I can ask. What's between you and Erlon?"

Jameta pulled Brownie alongside the Dalmyn Caravan Master and met her eyes, then shrugged. "Nothing."

"Nothing? Last summer you told me you were going to make a play for him. You asked me if I cared, and I said it was fine with me. Now you've had ten months. We've been out on three missions: two inside Galesia and one to Ferbodin. The pair of you spend most of your time together. Hell, you're even finishing each other's sentences like an old married couple. But I've never seen him kiss you or put his arm around you. I guarantee he isn't sneaking into your tent at night. He may be a good hunter, but I've got sharp eyes, and we do share the tent. What is going on?"

"What I said. Nothing."

"Why? You lost interest? He never had any?"

"It's so hard to tell. It seems like he does. We're...well, we're such good...*friends*."

"Oh, my, that's the killer. Last thing you want to be with a man is friends."

Jameta shrugged. "I like him. He's fun to be with."

"You love him?"

"Probably. A little bit, for sure. But..."

"So he's the problem."

She couldn't bring herself to say it. She nodded.

"Shall I go and kick his butt?"

A pang of horror shot through Jameta's body. Without thinking, she reined Brownie against the other horse, forcing a sudden stop. "No! No, don't you dare do anything like that."

"Just offering." Aleria steered her horse around Brownie and continued. "After all, what are friends for? So what's the problem with him?"

"I've been trying to figure it out. I think he thinks he's not good enough for me."

24

"What, the Ranked thing?"

"Mostly, but there's something else, as well."

"Such as?"

"I can't put my finger on it. But there's something about him not being worthy."

"He's one of the worthiest men I know. Trustworthy, noteworthy," she raised her eyebrows, "bedworthy…"

"I couldn't agree more. But he won't discuss it."

"Let me get this straight. He's done a dishonourable deed in his past, and that stops him from falling in love with you, because he's too honourable to dishonour you."

"That's about it."

"I think he needs someone to kick his butt."

"Yes, well, thank you, Aleria, but if anybody's going to be touching his butt it will be me. You hear?"

Aleria held her hands up. "Loud and clear." Her brow wrinkled. "And more forceful than I'm used to from you."

Jameta lowered her eyebrows. "I'm willing to talk to you about my problems and maybe even take your advice, but I draw the line at letting you pry inside Erlon's personality and mine like those new head-doctors they have up at the University."

"You know, there's something about you…"

"You're still doing it."

"That's what I do. I'm always thinking about people and how they react. I have to. It's my life." She pointed a finger again. "And I haven't been able to figure you out. You've been trained to run away. You're afraid at times. That's expected. But then you go and do things. Dangerous things."

"I do what I have to. But I'm still scared."

Aleria regarded her. "You might be very, very brave, but your courage is way down inside. Not like Lavan's"

"Oh, poor Lavan."

"Why, 'Poor Lavan?' He's brave enough. He never shirks his duty, no matter what."

Jameta shook her head. "As you say, it's on the surface. He spends all his time trying to be brave. I'm not sure it works like that."

Aleria shrugged. "Well, I suppose different people have different ways. I trust both of you and I wouldn't want to say who is the bravest. Stupid conversation, anyway."

"I'd agree. Shall we stop?"

"Aye. Let's go back to Erlon. He's more fun."

"We will not go back to Erlon. You just want to talk about parts of his anatomy you're supposed to be keeping your hands off. Which you will. Right?"

Aleria chuckled. "Well, you keep at him until he comes clean on whatever burr he's got in his boot. Once you've got him married, you can relax. I'm a moral person. I don't fondle my friends' husbands. Honest!"

"Hah! You've only got one friend who's married, and I somehow can't see you messing around with Lord Raif anCanah."

"Shows what you know. Raif and I have a very complicated relationship. Did you know he raped me, once?"

Jameta frowned, trying to remember. "But that wasn't the story I heard. I thought it was...are you making fun of me? If you are, that is the most twisted..."

"No, no, he didn't. He only pretended to. Haven't you heard that story?"

"Do I want to?"

"I'll tell you some time, out on the road when we're bored."

"Does that mean I'm coming along?"

"It's not my choice to make. I would like you to settle your relationship with my guard Captain, but that's not enough to keep you from joining us." She reined her horse to a stop and faced Jameta. "I will ask you not to interfere with each other's duties with silly love games. The situation will be too serious for that sort of distraction. If you want to move into his tent, go ahead. But don't be chasing around the campsite for stolen kisses."

Jameta shrugged. "We've kept it sane for the last ten months. I don't see it changing any time soon."

"Fair enough." They moved on. "Anyway, I'm more worried about your lack of ability to defend yourself."

"You are?"

"Oh, yes. That peaceful stuff you got all your life from Uncle Arjan is great as far as it goes. I like the idea that the message is more important than the messenger's pride. But out on the long caravan routes you need to be able to survive as well." She pulled her horse up at an intersection. "Say, how would you like to learn to shoot?"

"Shoot what?"

"Whatever you like. You should at least be familiar with a Double-S rifle."

Jameta made a face. "I don't think so."

"Oh, come on. Why don't we go out to the shooting range and try a weapon or two?"

"I don't know of any shooting range."

"The Army has one just outside the city."

Jameta stared at her friend. "But that's for the soldiers. An average citizen doesn't go onto the Royal Army base and say, "Can I play with the guns for a while, please?""

Aleria grinned. "I'm not an average citizen, but now that you mention it, I don't say 'please' often enough. You're right. They're being very helpful, and I should be more polite. But if you want to shoot, we'll go and shoot."

"Where is this range?"

"Down at the end of the street, there."

"So that's where we were going all along?"

Aleria chuckled. "Can't put anything past Jameta anDennal, can we?"

Jameta considered that comment worthy of ignoring.

* * *

The rifle was a disaster. Aleria broke into helpless laughter before Jameta had fired the first shot. "You're not supposed to wave at people before you shoot them. Point it and pull the trigger."

"It's heavy!"

Aleria calmed herself. "All right. You're never going to shoot one of those free standing. Come over here and lean it on the rest."

That went better, but the noise was terrible, and after five shots her shoulder felt like it was broken. "Aleria, I have now fired one of these things. I hit the target every time. I try to pull the gun against my shoulder tight and everything else you say, but it still hurts too much."

The older girl nodded. "That's fine. I thought you should have a chance to fire it in case you're called upon to shoot one in an emergency. You know how it's done, and that's enough. What about a pistol?" She drew her sidearm from the shoulder holster under her flimsy summer jacket. It was a slim, black object, not much more than a barrel with a handle.

"This is a hand-made single-shot Quarter. It's about the only thing legal to carry inside the realm, because it's not rated as a Mechanical. You break it to load it, like this." She pushed a lever aside, and the barrel hinged down. She put a brass cartridge in, clicked the barrel back in place and aimed down the range. "You have to be careful with these, because the act of closing the barrel cocks the firing pin." She shot, making a reasonable hit about an inch out from the upper staff of the cross. Then she opened the gun again, and the spent shell popped out, falling to the floor. "Want to try one?"

Jameta took the weapon in her fingertips. She closed it and opened it a few times to get the feel. Then she took the cartridge Aleria offered and pushed it into the chamber. It slid in easily. She closed the gun. "Now what?"

"Well, the first thing you don't do is wave it around."

"I wasn't. I was pointing it down there."

"And that's the right thing to do. Point it where you're going to shoot or at the ground."

"So, I just shoot?"

"The sights are the same as a rifle. Use both hands. Firmly but not too tight. There's not much kick, and if you keep your elbow straight it will only kick upwards."

Following instructions, she aimed at the target and squeezed the trigger. There was some kick, but not much. "I hit the card!"

Aleria glanced down the range. "Yes, you did. If that had been an enemy, you would have nicked his shoulder. Good enough for your purposes. Does that work for you?"

Jameta regarded the weapon. "I suppose. It's not as loud and it doesn't kick. What was that you said about a quarter? A quarter of what?"

"The size of the bullet. A quarter of an inch across."

"I see. And what size are the Double-S rifles?"

"They're Thirds."

"A third of an inch across. Does that make a lot of difference?"

"It's not so much the size of the bullet as the weight and the amount of powder in the shell."

"I could probably figure that out if I wanted to."

"The quarter is not very powerful, but I'm told it will kill a man if you hit a vulnerable spot, like the eye or throat."

Jameta's imagination shrank away from the thought of aiming a gun at a man's eye. She firmed her posture. "How do I get one of these?"

Aleria smiled. "I think you're ready for a stroll to a different side of town."

"What side?"

"The side where I spend my spare time. Here, take a few more shots, and we'll go for a drink."

Jameta took the shells Aleria offered and lined them up on the counter in front of her. Methodically, she loaded and fired each one, getting the feeling of the gun, the idea of aiming, the technique of breathing so that her hands were steady. When she had fired ten bullets and got three within the cross, she nodded. "I think I want one of those."

"Right. Let's take this rifle back and go downtown."

They returned their equipment to the soldier in the weapons room, thanked him politely and went outside to their horses.

Once they reached the city centre, Aleria turned to the left, towards the river.

From her position on horseback, Jameta could see down into the alleys and over the fences. "I've never seen this street, but I've been here before."

Aleria raised her eyebrows.

"There are a couple of places like this in Oudonsford, right along the water in the old part of town. I'm always going down there to pick up stuff from the blacksmith shops. Nobody ever bothers me."

Aleria shrugged. "Nobody ever bothers me, either, but I wouldn't come down here alone at night."

"So, where are we having tea?"

"Well, there is a tea shop, but I don't think they'll sell you a gun, there."

"Oh. We'll be going to Jems' bar, then. The Falcon."

"You know about that? Of course you do. Lavan would have told you."

"That's right. And Juli and Geran."

"And you pay close attention."

"Information is my business."

"Good." Aleria led the horses to a ramshackle excuse for a stable behind the tavern and swung open the back door. They stepped into a low, dark room. The windows, not overly clean, let in a hazy light. In spite of the bright daylight outside a pair of lamps cast a glow along the back wall. In their light a pretty, heavyset girl with long, curling black hair was leaning on the bar. When the two entered her head came up, but she did not move.

Aleria flashed two fingers and led the way to a table near the window. The barmaid nodded.

While their order was coming Jameta looked around the room. "So this is the Falcon. About what I'd expected. Not a patch on the Angry Log in Oudonsford."

"A smaller version. Same function, though. Ale, food, and information. Sometimes entertainment, if you like fights."

Juli brought two small mugs of light beer and plunked herself down in the third chair at their table. "Good to see you. Brought high-class company for a change?"

Jameta frowned, but Aleria chuckled. "This is Jameta, and yes, she is Ranked. How can you tell?"

The girl leaned over and fingered Jameta's kerchief. "Nobody around here wears nothin' like that. In fact, I never seen cloth like that, ever. Where'd you get it?"

"My mother. She's a weaver."

"A better weaver'n any in this town." She turned back to Aleria. "And she's a dancer. Nobody else moves like that."

It was Aleria's turn to be surprised. She turned to Jameta. "Are you a dancer?"

"Well, sort of. I mean, we all dance."

Juli grinned. "Sure you do. You've gotta be onea the Dennals, right? Ain't many around with hair like that. There's a whole passle of you lot up in Oudonsford. Cousins of the anDennals down here. Came over from Samnia a couple generations back. My guess, you still keep a lotta the traditions alive. Your braid, your kerchief. So you do that Samnian dancin' stuff." She waved her hands over her head in a graceful twirl of fingers.

Aleria chuckled and Jameta closed her mouth.

"Juli had a different education than you or me. I told you this place dealt in information. This is her university, and I'd say she earned her degree."

"So, can she help us with our other problem?"

"Yes, but perhaps she shouldn't."

Jameta frowned. "So you brought me down here for...?"

Aleria held up cautioning hands. "Let's put this straight. Juli, I'm getting Jameta lined up with a little helper for when we go out with the caravan next month. She likes my single-shot Quarter."

Juli nodded. "Aye, but you come to the wrong place. There's no sense a lady like you gettin' nothin' illegal. Too much hassle. You got other things to think about. Lemme see." She stared at the ceiling. "Hmm. A Quarter single-shot? Young Lady anTahl has one, if she didn't sell it to Envelune what's-her-name, which I told her not to do, because that girl ain't got the brains not to shoot her foot off. Sorry if she's a friend of yours, but..."

Aleria grinned. "No, that jibes with my opinion."

"Right, then. So go and see Lady anTahl. Tell her I sent you, and you know about the shells."

"What do I know about the shells?"

"The odd one's a dud. Got wet or somethin'. So don't buy her shells. Get those from Stawek the blacksmith down the road here. He's doin' good these days, what with the Mechanical rules easin' up. Got wagonloads of steel 'n' iron comin' in from Domaland every day..."

"...and other things as well." Jameta was beginning to catch on.

"There ya go. One beer, and we tarnished your mind already."

Aleria finished her drink. "Thanks, Juli. Anything else?"

The black-haired girl frowned in thought. "Nothin' goin' on right now. Lotta talk about the Ferbodeans, but nothin' more than the usual mouthy stuff about trimmin' their toenails with cannon fire. Nobody really knows nothin'. What I hear, I'll pass it along."

"How's Geran doing?"

"Workin' up north for the Canahs right now. Bear problems, if you believe it. Pay's good and the contacts are better, but I dunno. Bears? That's dangerous!"

Aleria chuckled. "Don't worry. Duke anCanah has two old mountain men who know their bear hunting. I was talking to Raif about it. Warm spring last year. Too many weak cubs survived. So this year there's a lot of youngsters pushed out and looking for territory. The hunters needed a few extra hands. I bet Geran's happy with the weapons."

"Oh, yes." Juli grinned. "Special dispensation for Mechanicals because of the danger to life and limb of the local population. Double-S rifles."

"I was just firing one of those."

The barmaid regarded Jameta. "Didja like it?"

"Not really. My shoulder's still sore."

"Ya gotta hold it tight." She reached out and squeezed Jameta's shoulder. "Helps to have padding."

Aleria rose. "Well, we could stay gossiping all day, but we have illicit weapons to buy."

Juli shook her head. "That one's legal. You'll hafta file the papers."

"Well, since we're going out of the realm with it, we shouldn't have any problem."

"As if you ever have any problem with that sorta stuff."

Aleria slid a coin across the table. "Dalmyns do everything to the letter of the law. You know that."

"That's right. And you always know which letter to quote." Juli scooped the coin and nodded. "Nice to meetcha, Jameta. Drop in any time you wanta gossip a bit."

"I might do that."

They turned away, but the barmaid's voice brought them back around. "Nice horse. Ever race it?"

Jameta considered. "Maybe."

"Aye. You come back and talk to me. We got stuff in common."

Aleria slapped Jameta on the shoulder, turning her around. "It's bad enough having Lavan riding with this bunch. I don't want you caught up in it, too. Another time, Juli."

"Another time, ladies."

Jameta allowed herself to be moved out the door. "My horses are faster than Lavan's."

"Don't tell Juli that. They won't let a woman race, and yours might not be so fast with the extra weight on them."

They mounted and jogged into the street. "Still, it might be fun to try."

Aleria looked back over her shoulder. "See? I was right. We start you thinking about being brave, and suddenly you want to take on the world. Calm down. I want you and your beauties alive and healthy a month from now."

"So do I. No racing. I promise."

"Don't promise me. I have nothing to do with it."

"You always do that, don't you?"

"What?"

Jameta pushed her horse up beside Aleria. "You pretend that you aren't telling people what to do."

"But I'm not!"

"Of course you're not. But if they do anything else and it goes wrong, then it's all their fault. Very smart."

"And that's why we're taking you along on this trip. You read people. I've decided to make a merchant out of you."

6. The Perfect Gentlewoman

Jameta was in the middle of a great to-do when Aleria arrived to pick her up for tea at the anCanah residence.

"Come on in and join us, Aleria. We're discussing the border situation with Ferbodin. Gita thinks we should send the Royal Army in."

Aleria looked at the smaller Twin. "Are you out of your mind?"

"Why, Aleria, I was counting on your support. My diplomatic sister is teaming up with my too-intelligent cousin to try to persuade me that those idiots will listen to anything but a very loud cannon. With grape shot."

Aleria sighed. "And now we see why a diploma from the Young Ladies' Academy has nothing to do with the diplomatic service." She turned to Jameta. "Whatever got them on that topic? You haven't been stirring the pot, have you?"

"Who, me? I like political discussion. I was only asking..."

"Oh, I know what you were doing." Aleria turned to Hana. "I think I liked her better years ago, when all she did was push us off the raft into the river."

Hana nodded. "I agree. At least then she was smaller than us."

"But I don't have time to give her the argument she deserves. We're on our way to the anCanah mansion, and it doesn't do to show up late at the Duke's invitation."

Jameta tried to remember. "I thought we were visiting Raif and Mito."

"Ah, but we are entering the den of the Head Lion himself. What if he decides to drop in?"

"You think he might?"

"He does all the time. We're moving into unsure diplomatic territory and what we do could have serious effect on Galesian foreign policy. He might well want to have his oar in those waters."

Gita laughed. "Actually, he has a soft spot for Aleria, and he always comes around when she visits."

The other woman blushed, but no one remarked on it, so Jameta filed it away for later observation. They went outside, where Aleria's carriage was waiting.

So this is a formal occasion, in spite of all the "just friends" talk.

* * *

The Duke did put in an appearance. They had just seated themselves in a beautifully appointed sitting room. Mito was performing the ritual of the pouring of the tea while the rest of them laughed at her enthusiastic assumption of matronly duties. A maid entered and slipped over to her, bending to speak softly.

Lady anCanah's smile grew as she listened. Then she nodded. "That will be wonderful, Millée. Bring another setting, please."

The maid curtseyed and exited with the same inconspicuous speed.

"We are about to have company. I apologize, but it's unavoidable, I'm afraid."

"You're damned right it's unavoidable. I do still own the house, no matter how much of it is taken over with drying nappies." The Duke of anCanah strode in, a smile on his face. He went straight to Mito and bowed over her hand. Then he approached Aleria.

"Am I allowed to make proper greeting, my Lady, or have you rolled in some sort of egalitarian nonsense in Ferbodin?"

Aleria looked heavenward for support and offered her hand.

He bowed over it with perfect grace. Then he made a show of dropping it and staring at Jameta. "Aha! But there is new competition for the title of 'Most Exotic Visitor'."

Mito sighed. "My Lord, this young lady is a recent addition to our circle and an important ambassador from a new ally. Perhaps you could restrain your enthusiasm, or at least your sense of humour."

"But of course, my dear." He turned to Jameta. "I am pleased to make your acquaintance, Lady anDennal. I do hope a perceptive young woman such as yourself will ignore the familiar pleasantries that might otherwise sound like familial discord."

"Of course, my Lord Duke. I am aware of the liberties allowed family and the closest of friends. It is pleasant to observe such intimacy in the home of the powerful. It speaks to a depth of understanding of the human condition, no matter the Rank."

He regarded her for a moment and then nodded. "An astute observation for one so young."

She took her time answering. "I would prefer my thoughts to be appreciated for their worth, my Lord, rather than for the age of their presenter. Or lack of age, in this case."

"Your point is well taken, my Lady."

She inclined her head. "Aleria tells me that our next enterprise may have repercussions at higher levels."

"Aleria is an astute diplomat," he glanced across the table, "or, at least in the process of becoming one. Do you have ambitions in that direction?"

She smiled. "I do not have the connections or the training for that position, my Lord. I merely wish to use my talents in any way that may benefit my family and my kingdom."

"A laudable and mature approach."

"My Lord might wish to rephrase that."

"Ah. True. A laudable approach for any loyal subject of his Majesty."

"You are too kind, my Lord."

He laughed. "A concept not often expressed."

"False modesty, my Lord? Or do you prefer it that way?"

"I wouldn't dream of answering that question."

"And I wouldn't dream of pushing for an answer. But I did not come here to indulge my curiosity about the Exalted class. Would you say that our main problems will come in Ferbodin, or farther east?"

He thought a moment. "The main political issue will always be Ferbodin, of course, because its borders touch ours. Perhaps 'chafe against' would be a better term. Farther east the concern is mainly commercial, and there we bow to the expertise of the Cloet family. Raif, you would have more on that."

His son nodded. "The area east of Ferbodin is dry land inhabited by nomad tribes who mostly trade in livestock: horses, cattle, sheep, goats. Farther east is the true desert, where they use camels. However, their lands have mineral wealth, and we would be very pleased to find a way to work with them, if we could avoid conflict with the Ferbodeans. And the Domalian mining companies."

Jameta shook her head. "I do not understand the Ferbodean form of government. They supposedly have a parliament elected by the people, and it controls the realm. But it doesn't seem very able to control anything. Its own officials run their own businesses, often in direct conflict with their official positions. How can a realm function like that?"

Raif nodded. "I have little experience over there, but I suggest you take a look at their common folk. If the leaders are getting very rich, it probably means that the rest of the population is paying for it."

"Which means another revolution is coming."

Lord anCanah shook his head. "And that is the last thing we need on our borders. We have our disaffected groups here as well. If the unrest were to spread, and these rebels were to join forces, it could lead to chaos. Our economy is not strong as it is…"

"…and the Domalanders have always regretted allowing us to create our independent little realm on their doorstep." Jameta met the duke's eyes.

"Precisely. Only one mountain range…"

"My Lord, much as I dislike interrupting this fascinating conversation, I must observe that your tea is getting cold." Mito hefted the ornate teapot. "Jameta may also be hungry."

"Quite right, my dear. And those scones you keep persuading the cook to make are not to be missed."

Jameta allowed herself a polite smile as one of the most powerful men in the realm busied himself with passing plates.

Once they were all settled again, the talk ranged among the others as well, and Jameta contented herself with listening. When the duke rose to leave, she maintained her perfectly correct demeanour, and he responded in kind.

When he was gone, there were looks around the table that she could not miss. She refused to let them have all the points in the game. "Easy to see how his Grace has such a reputation as a diplomat."

Aleria glanced at her, then at Raif. "Why do you say that?"

"He puts everyone at their ease with such simplicity."

Mito's eyes twinkled. "You noticed that, did you?"

"Well, if I am to assume that was his intention. I'm sure if his motives had been otherwise, it would have been obvious."

Raif chuckled. "I believe you have just called my father simple and obvious."

She glanced at him. "Techniques only to be used by the very confident."

Aleria's hands slapped the table. "All right, give it up. We've got business to discuss, and I can't stand all this fancy dancing around. Jameta, in this room you say what needs to be said."

"I thought I was doing a decent job of that."

Aleria shook her head. "I know, I know. It had to be done. But from now on will you forget the social foofaraw and treat this as a planning session for our upcoming expedition?"

"Most certainly, my Lady." She straightened her posture. "Raif, what do you consider the most likely source of conflict with the Ferbodeans? What do we need to avoid?"

He grinned. "Well, that's a problem, because what Roeble has been doing is exactly what we're worried about."

"Dealing with the so-called People's Market, I suppose."

"That's right. The main flaw of the People's Government is that their attempts at complete control of the economy don't work. So there are surpluses and shortages, and someone is always eager to take advantage of those problems to turn a profit."

"And good transportation is an advantage."

"Precisely. So as long as you buy things and take them out of the country, leaving good Galesian gold behind, the government doesn't care who you buy them from. However, if you start buying surplus products cheap in one corner of the country and selling them high where they are needed..."

"Then we're running afoul of the government and competing with the racketeers who run the People's Market as well. Which leaves us with few friends."

"And if the Ferbodean government gets the idea you've been sent by the Galesian government to foment trouble..."

Jameta looked around the table. "Why is the king allowing us to go in there at all?"

Mito gave her gentle smile. "Because some of his most loyal supporters, namely the families in this room, want him to."

"That's not the only reason." Her husband steepled his fingers. "Galesia is interested in plain old trading, politics aside. We don't care who we trade with. Our economy needs markets. Dalmyn and Cloet are the best producers in that respect, and we are confident that Aleria and Roeble will continue to bring in more business. And where you lead, others will soon follow. The inclusion of the Dennal family is an experiment. Transportation is a big part of the trading business."

"But we concentrate on water transport..."

"Ah. You haven't had your briefing from your...what, your uncle? Second cousin in the third generation? I can't keep track."

"No, I haven't. I've been living at his house off and on for several months, but I don't think he sees me as important enough to talk to."

Raif frowned at Aleria, then at Jameta. "I'm going to leave that to you two. I'm sure your families can figure it out. If anDennal wants in, he needs to learn who the rest of his new partners trust."

"And you trust me?"

"I've only met you three or four times. Aleria trusts you, and for the moment, that is sufficient."

Jameta grinned. "Well, according to you, I've managed to insult your father twice, so I shouldn't have much trouble impressing my uncle in a similar manner."

Mito poured more tea. "I'm sure you'll do fine. Now, would you like to meet the Crown Prince and Princess? I believe I hear their dulcet tones."

Squalls were drifting through the corridors, and women were rushing back and forth. Soon two beaming nurses entered, each carrying a lace-wrapped bundle. Raif took one, and the nurse plopped the other on its mother's lap.

"How are they?"

The older woman dropped her smile, all business. "They slept for three hours, my Lady, although Himself had a restless hour in the middle. My Princess was good as gold."

Raif unwrapped his bundle, revealing curly blonde hair, chubby cheeks, and a winning, if toothless, smile. "She's always your Princess when she's quiet."

"Right you are, my Lord. And when she starts ranting and throwing things, I'm reminded whose daughter she is."

"Oh, really? I don't recall hearing that Lady Mito ever did anything like that."

The fussing and playing was a pleasant change from business and allowed Jameta to see this new young power clique in a different light. Her final analysis was that it had little to do with politics. *Rather, it has everything to do with politics, but they don't care. They'd be close friends anyway. I never had friends like that...*

The adults amused themselves until the babies lost patience and were sent back to their nurses. After a round of conversation, Aleria and Jameta called for their carriage and left.

The horses hadn't moved three steps before Aleria rounded on her.

"What kind of game were you playing?"

"I don't know, yet."

"You don't know? You're messing about with one of the most powerful men in the kingdom, and you don't know?"

She shrugged. "He hasn't placed me, yet. Once he does, things will get more comfortable."

"And aren't you even a bit uncomfortable?"

"Not particularly." She regarded Aleria. "Oh, come on. I watched him with you and Mito. He's a pleasant man who rarely gets the opportunity to let down and enjoy himself. He treats Mito as the mother of his heirs should be treated. Their repartee may sound like joking, but from what I hear you were the only one who treated her with proper respect before he and Raif came into her life. She responds by becoming the perfect mother of his heirs. The basis for a wonderful relationship, I'd say. Each provides exactly what the other wants."

Aleria was staring at her. "I'm almost afraid to ask about the duke and myself."

Jameta took a moment to decide. Then she shrugged her shoulders. "I'm going to take you at face value, Aleria. I'm going to assume you really want the answer."

"What do you mean? I wouldn't have asked the question if I didn't expect an honest answer."

"How to put this...? Between a man and a woman, no matter what their ages, there is always a certain amount of – what should I call it? – amatory strife."

"Amatory strife. I've never heard of that term before."

"That's because I just thought of it. Most people don't seem to be aware of it, but it's there. The assumption that, should circumstances be right, there might be a relationship between the two. Don't you notice that?"

"Not especially. You can't possibly think that every man is walking around considering his chances of bedding every woman he sees." She paused. "Wait a minute, you may be on to something, there. But not every woman thinks like that!"

"Why would women be that different from men?"

Aleria opened her mouth, then closed it. "Are you trying to get me onto another topic so you don't have to answer my question?"

"Oh, no. I'm trying to get you in a mood where you'll accept it."

"Is it that rough?"

"Not if you agree with my premise. Many of the conventions of our society are tools to deal with that strife. You and the duke use every trick at your disposal to persuade everyone that there is no great amatory strife between you."

"What?" Aleria shot upright. "Between me and the Duke of anCanah? That's ridiculous!"

"Precisely. It works very well, doesn't it? I am in awe at the ability of humans to find ways to cope with the uncopable."

"Uncopable? You made that word up, too!"

"I might have. But I seem to be doing all right, aren't I?"

"In what respect?"

"I answered a difficult question with complete honesty, and you haven't even thought about biting my head off."

"Why would I...? Oh, yes. I see." Aleria leaned back against the cushion and looked out the window. Twice she turned and looked over at Jameta, then her attention went outside again.

Good. You need to stop seeing me as the brat that pushed you off the logs, years ago. Not that you didn't deserve it, but still...

7.   Birthday Present

Jameta strolled into the wagon yard where Aleria was supervising the loading of cargo, doing her share of the work, as usual.

"If you want it done right, you have to do it yourself?"

The Wagonmaster grinned as she peeled off her gloves. "Something like that. Helps me keep in condition."

"So, what have you two got me down here for?"

"Us two?"

Jameta sighed and pointed.

Erlon lounged in a corner of the yard, unoccupied.

"What?" Aleria was doing too good a job of looking innocent.

"Erlon is standing around doing nothing. Erlon never stands around. He's waiting."

"Maybe he's waiting for you."

"Maybe he is. And maybe you are, too. Call him over and let's have it out."

"Have what out?"

"Oh, that's the plan, is it? You're going to pretend I started the fight. All right. I will." She turned and gestured to Erlon, who sauntered over and stood, smiling down at her.

She propped a boot up on the lower fence rail and frowned at the pair of them. "Look, you two. I know that you think you should follow Uncle Arjan's requests and keep me out of violent situations. Aleria, I know your theories about how messengers aren't supposed to be brave. And Erlon, you only want to protect me. I don't mind that."

She hitched her belt up and stood firm. "But I've learned a lot in the past few months. Yes, it's a good idea to be able to run. I still practise. On my horses, on my feet. But being able to twist out of a few grapples isn't good enough to defend myself. A Quarter pistol with one bullet is pretty useless. I've been applying Lavan's techniques as well."

Aleria grinned. "Oh, no. She's learning bravery from Lavan."

"No, I'm not learning how to be brave. I'm learning how to use my cowardice wisely. When I'm scared I don't only sweat and shiver. I plan ways to get out of the situation. And every scrape we were in on that last trip, most of my escape routes involved a path through men with weapons. I'd get cut to pieces.

"I'm tired of Aleria mother-henning me all the time. And I don't like to think Erlon is spending time worrying about me instead of his duties. Either I have to learn to defend myself properly, or I have to stay home." She glowered at Erlon. "No matter what you say!"

Aleria chuckled. "That rather makes it easy, doesn't it?"

She frowned. "It does?"

"Yes. I'm pleased to hear you say it. I think you're right. Your duties within the realm all happen in places where the laws of the land hold sway. So, your training is appropriate. Even the loggers, miners, and teamsters you deal with have a sense of decency. But now that we're going into places where the law is not in control..."

"Exactly my point."

Aleria shrugged. "So train yourself."

"I can?"

"I'm not your nursemaid. I've done my best to keep Uncle Arjan and Lord Dennal happy, but if they're going to allow you to come with us..."

"Allow me!"

Aleria raised calming hands. "Easy, easy. I didn't say they wouldn't. I'm not saying they're happy about the situation, but they understand the benefit to your family of having a representative along, and you're here and you're willing. And mostly able."

She turned to Erlon. "You have your orders. Find her a way of defending herself and train her up on it. This last trip was a ride around the park. Once the summer's heat drops off, we're headed out on a real doozy."

Erlon's eyes opened wider. "We are? I hadn't heard anything..."

"No, you hadn't. But now you have. You've got a month and a half. I'm heading up to the Trench, and I expect progress when I get back."

"Mixing business with pleasure?"

Aleria grinned. "Kolwyn and I have a mine to attend to."

"Give him our regards. If you remember."

"Don't worry about Kolwyn and me. You have your assignment. Get to it." She slapped her gloves on her thigh, raising a cloud of dust. "Now, I've got more important things to do." She strode away, calling to Lavan to "Get over here and make yourself useful."

Jameta stared at Erlon. "Well. That was quick."

He grinned. "That's Aleria. Once her mind's made up, she doesn't waste time asking for opinions."

She regarded him. "But since this is me, what's your opinion?"

He shrugged. "I do what I'm told around here. But I didn't like the way things were either. It reduces my effectiveness as a leader when part of my mind is worrying about you."

Her heart sank. "Does that mean you don't want me to come?"

He stood. "No. It means that you and I have to take a walk."

"A walk."

"That's right. We're going on a little shopping trip."

"What are we shopping for?"

"Birthday present."

"It's not my birthday."

He tucked her arm through his and strode out of the wagon yard. "Can't you let a man be a tiny bit romantic?"

She smiled up at him. "Pardon me. It happens so rarely, I sometimes don't notice."

"If I get made fun of when I do, it's not likely to happen often, is it?"

"Oh, I wouldn't make fun of you. Not until after you've shown me how to defend myself."

"You're not making this easy for me."

"Yes I am. What's this present?"

"Jewelry."

"Jewelry? How will that help me protect myself?"

He patted her hand. "Have patience, my dear, and all will be revealed."

"Fine." She relaxed and strolled beside him. *I don't care what he has planned. I've got him to myself for the afternoon.* She began to watch where they were going, trying to place the tea shops in the area. There weren't any.

"Where, exactly, are we finding this jewelry store?"

"I didn't say it was a jewelry store."

"I see." She didn't see, but he was looking too smug, and she wouldn't give him the satisfaction of rising to his bait. She strolled along, looking into the windows of the shops.

It wasn't the jewelry-store or tea-shop part of town. Half the buildings along the street were shop fronts, and the others were open workshops: farriers, blacksmiths and a whole lot of armourers. The air vibrated with blows of iron on iron. Every second window was jammed with swords, knives, spears and various protective wear. Helmets, greaves, cuirasses and armlets filled the stalls in front of the workshops. *I'm getting the picture. I wonder what I'm going to end up with? A steel coat?*

She glanced up at Erlon, but he was interested in the ironmongery that surrounded them. "What is this place?"

"The locals call it 'Armourer's Alley.' Has a ring to it, don't you think?"

"Haw, haw. I get the joke. Is this smoke getting to your brain?"

"Right this way, my Lady." He led her to a grubby store that leaned against a huge workshop, from which smoke and steam rose in clouds. She coughed and pulled her neckerchief over her nose. "I hope you didn't think you'd solve all your problems by choking me to death."

"No, that would start a whole new set. Come on inside."

He pushed the door open, and she stepped into a room full of shiny metal. Suits of armour, chain mail and an olio of plate metal fought for space with cases of swords, axes, and daggers. The whole back wall was taken up by a rack of pole arms, each one different from the others.

"What is this, a museum? Nobody uses this stuff any more."

Erlon shrugged. "A bit of a museum, a bit of a junk pile. But this is where I always come." He looked around. There was no one in the store.

He picked up a dagger from the counter and used the hilt to bang on a cuirass hanging nearby. "Hey, Farian! I'm stealing all your merchandise. Better get out here!"

A growl issued from the depths of the shop. "If that's who I think it is, he'd better have a good excuse for disturbing my nap!"

A stooped, cadaverous figure emerged from the gloom. If the state of his hair was any measure, he had indeed been sleeping. He scratched a long, furrowed cheek and regarded them. "What's this? Brought a lady slumming? Sorry, the dancing bear doesn't seem to be in a performing mood today."

"Farian, this is Lady Jameta anDennal. She's looking for a birthday present."

"A birthday present, is it? And who might it be for?" He leaned closer, and the odour of mint wafted towards her. "A young man, I suppose?"

She smiled. "No, it's a present for me. From him." She pointed a thumb over her shoulder.

For the first time, the wrinkle-edged eyes opened fully. "Well, fancy that. A birthday present for a lady in my shop. What is the world coming to?" He regarded her. "And what sort of present would interest such a dainty as yourself?"

Erlon leaned forward and put a hand on the counter. "I was thinking about a set of vambraces. Not too heavy, but businesslike."

"Vambraces. Now, that's a practical gift. Let me see, let me see..." a cloth tape measure appeared in his hand, and he whipped it around her forearm: first up near her elbow then down at her wrist. "Hmm...woman's arm."

"Are we surprised?"

"Very seldom, and it doesn't help." He stared up into her eyes. "Woman's arm is a problem, girlie. Men don't have arms like that. At least, not the type of men I make weapons for."

Erlon sighed. "The proper term of address is 'my Lady,' Farian. She's Ranked."

The armourer straightened and glanced down at her. "An arm like that...? Too long and not thick enough for most of my wares. Let me see, now..." He dove into a bin and pulled out a metal tube with a hinged flap at the bottom. "Give me your arm, now dearie. Yes, that measures well enough. A bit of alteration..."

He slipped her arm into the guard. The hinge ended up over her wrist, and the flap protected the back of her hand. She slipped her fingers through the strap and flexed her wrist.

Erlon was shaking his head. "No, no, Farian, you've got the wrong idea. She isn't a gladiator. This is for everyday. Something light and comfortable that looks good enough to wear, but strong enough to turn a sword."

"Oh my! Why didn't you say so? Decoration is our second line of business." He led the way to a small counter in the corner of the shop. Jewelled daggers, fancy scabbards and objects she couldn't begin to recognize were piled haphazardly about.

"I think I remember...ah, yes. Here we are." The forearm guards he pulled out were of beaten bronze, but simple in design. An embossed eagle graced one, a lion the other. Otherwise, there was a rolled flange top and bottom, and that was about it. But the detail on the motifs was exquisite, and the bronze was so polished she could see her face clearly.

She held out her arm, and he opened the guard and snapped it in place.

"Now, that is a piece of jewelry, my dear. Look at the shine!"

She lifted her arm, regarding the lion. "I don't especially care whether they shine or not. Will they work?"

Farian raised his eyebrows at Erlon. "Do I detect serious intent, here?"

"As serious as can be. The only reason we want them pretty is so she can wear them in the greatest variety of situations."

"They are a tad loose. Tell you what." He snapped the guard open again. "You need a pad. Leather, a touch longer, with a raised seam on the outside to keep it in place. Suede or chamois to soak up the sweat. We could glue it in."

He wrapped her arm in the cloth that had covered the vambraces and snapped it back on.

She swung it experimentally. "That feels much better. It doesn't slide around at all."

He nodded. "There we are, then. Perhaps my Lady would like a pair of matching greaves?"

She laughed. "I have leather chaps for riding in cactus country. I don't want to be walking around weighed down like a steam wagon."

"How about a nice bronze helmet? No lady of fashion can be seen on the battlefield without one of my made-to-match helmet and vambrace sets."

"Sorry, not in a fashion mood today. These will be fine. A great birthday present." She turned to Erlon and laid a hand on his shoulder. "Thank you so much."

"Well, now." Farian leaned his elbows on the counter and beamed at them. "Isn't that sweet? You can kiss him in private later."

She glanced at Erlon. Sure enough, he was blushing.

"May I put the other one on?"

"Of course." He pulled out another cloth to wrap her arm. "You can practise out back if you like."

Erlon smiled. "We'll wait for a more private spot. I know you. If I had Jameta out there working against my sword, you'd have half the neighbourhood cheering and making bets."

"You do me wrong, my friend. Privacy is my password."

"As long as it doesn't get in the way of a good story."

Their talk rambled on, and Jameta found a small space of empty floor. She swung her arms around, getting the feel of the weight. They certainly were light, but her arms swung with more power. She thought about how to block a sword. She tried to picture deflecting one...*but if it slides off, it cuts my wrist or elbow. Of course, that's why the flange, top and bottom.* She could see that these would be useful, but they would take a lot of training. *Well, unless I go full-on attack and get a sword...I can imagine. Between Aleria and Uncle Arjan, there would be fifty fits of feathers flying. I guess I better go with what I've got.*

46

She turned back, having given Erlon enough time to pay the bill discreetly. "Thank you for your help, Farian. I'm sure there are jewelry stores uptown that could learn from your approach to your customers."

He grinned and winked at Erlon. "Got yourself a real diplomat, there, boy." He unsnapped the braces and laid them back in their cloth.

Erlon took her arm and spun her around. "And I'm getting her out of this place before you start working your wiles on her."

"Wiles? Hah! I'm headed back to my nap. Come back in five-six days for the finished items." He disappeared behind the curtain, and they stepped out into the street.

After they had gone a block, Jameta looked up at Erlon. "Why did you say you didn't want to go in there? He was sweet."

"I didn't say I didn't want to. I said I didn't like to. Do you know what I paid for those?"

"It's a present. I'm not to know."

"Well, it doesn't matter, because I didn't pay anything."

"What? Those must be worth a fortune. The workmanship! I was worried that they would cost too much."

He shook his head. "That's why I don't go in there unless I have to. He always gives me whatever I want. Won't take a penny."

She regarded Erlon for a moment. "Saved his life, once, did you?"

"Not really." He shrugged and tightened his lips. "I stood up for him when no one else would."

"And that's all?"

"He felt the need for support. My backing gave him the confidence to make a good move. And here he is today. So he feels he owes me...no, not that he owes me. He just wants to give me things."

"I'm not surprised." She slipped an arm through his and squeezed. "Sometimes you're a very nice person."

He flexed his arm in her grip. "When I'm not killing people for a living."

Jameta looked up at him. "If you could find another job, would you stop?"

He shrugged. "I'm very good at what I do. I'm not especially good at anything else I can think of. So it's a pointless question."

"But you didn't answer it."

"Because..."

"Right. Pointless question. I'll ask another one. What do you like about the job you have?"

"That's easy. I like to travel. I like to be a leader. It's very flattering to have my opinion accepted without question by experienced people in my field of work. Scary, but flattering."

"Hmm. Yes, you don't want to be wrong too often, do you?" She took his arm again, and they strolled on. "Well, I don't know how effective those arm guards will be, but I'm certainly pleased with the look. A person could wear them."

"They're perfect for you. Most vambraces are simply to protect from a chance hit. These have that rolled edge, top and bottom, to keep a sword from sliding off and slicing your arm. They're better for an actual blocking motion." He swept his arm in front of his face in demonstration.

"And that's what I'm going to do?"

"That's right."

"And you're going to teach me."

"Sort of."

She turned to face him. "What do you mean, 'sort of'? Here I go out into dangerous territory with the best fighters in the realm, and my best-trained trainer is telling me he's going to do a half-baked job of training me? I might as well resign myself to staying home."

The truth of her statement sank home to her, and her shoulders drooped. "In fact, this was only a silly dream, wasn't it? There's no possible way I could ever learn enough to protect myself in the time we have."

She looked up at him. "I won't go and be a burden. I won't have the mission threatened and men killed because of protecting me when they should have been doing something else."

He nodded. "That's a good attitude, but let's wait and see. When I said 'sort of,' I meant that nobody does the type of fighting you're trying to do. So there's no one who can say, 'Do this,' and it will be right. That doesn't mean I can't help you train. It means you have to do a lot more of it yourself."

"I've been making my own way all my life." She smiled at him. "Having someone to help will be more fun."

8.   Tea and Philosophy

When they entered Farian's shop six days later it was empty again. Erlon was looking for a hammer, but Jameta stopped him. "Don't wake the poor man up. Show me weapons."

"You want to look at weapons?"

"If I might have to face them it wouldn't hurt to understand them. In fact, it might hurt a whole lot less."

"Good point." It didn't take him long to find what he wanted. "Swords. This case has most of the regular ones. The curved sabre is a cavalry sword. The curve is made for slashing at infantry from a running horse. The one that looks similar but is shorter and straighter is a cutlass: naval sword. Good for close quarters work. Now, you notice this thinner sword..."

"She'll never remember any of that. She has to have it in her hand. Feel the weight, try the swing. Here, girlie..." Farian lifted the hasp.

She reached out and stopped him. "No, that's all right. We were filling time in case you wanted to finish your nap."

"Who said I was sleeping?"

"Nobody."

"But you..." His eyebrows went up. "But you don't say anything you don't mean, do you?"

"I try to be specific."

"As you should my dear. As you should." He took her arm and led her behind the counter. "But now, because of this special occasion, I will award you a boon that few of your gender ever receive."

"Isn't that nice?"

"It is, now that you mention it. But, as I said, special occasion. You can bring him if you like."

"I suppose I should. I wouldn't want him to think I was stealing his friends."

"But isn't that the wonderful point about friends? You don't have to steal them. You can share them. Come."

She glanced over her shoulder at Erlon, who gave her no indication of what was ahead. Turning to the front, she followed...

...and walked into her mother's drawing room. Or something very similar. A subtle blend of high-quality Galesian furniture, made from the exotic hardwoods of Sheldit by fine craftsmen, but covered in beautiful silk draperies in the patterns of the East. Her eye was

49

drawn to a couch, upholstered in deep red velvet, heaped with gold-tasseled cushions. "My mother has one like this!"

"Ah, I am gratified that my effort has struck a chord. Perhaps my Lady would sit there?"

She smiled at him. "With pleasure." She plopped herself down like she would at home, plumping the cushions until she had them just right.

"Would my Lady like tea?" He raised a finger. "No...chai."

"Make it chai, my dear Sir."

Her host bustled off, and Jameta gazed around the room. "That's a tiger skin!"

Erlon was standing at the door, a bemused look on his face. "I can't think of any other animal quite that big with stripes."

"Well, come in and sit down. Who would have thought that Farian would have taste like this?"

"He doesn't."

She stared at him. "What do you mean?"

"His personal taste does not run in this direction."

"But..."

"I won't spoil his fun. Wait and enjoy."

She wasn't going to get any more than that, so she leaned into the big, soft cushions and decided to enjoy herself. "This is so beautiful!"

"I am pleased that my Lady sees fit to recognize my small talent." Farian placed a tray on the low table in front of her. It contained the familiar paraphernalia for a full Samnian chai treatment. He lifted the lid of the pot, gave the contents a final stir with the whisk and poured a long stream of caramel liquid into the dark blue glass mug. With a flick of his wrist, he spread cinnamon on the top of the creamy mixture and offered it to her.

She took the cup in both hands as she was supposed to, brought it to her nose and inhaled. Then she smelled it again, glancing at her server as she did so. He rewarded her with a satisfied smile.

She sipped, tasted, then sipped again. "This is wonderful. My aunt Dennal would kill for this." She drank more, then returned to the reality of the room. "Erlon, aren't you having any?"

The guard Captain strolled over and slid into more upright seating, a heavy teak chair with carved armrests. It creaked as he sat. "No, I'll wait for something more appropriate."

His host did not disappoint him. Farian brought another tray, this one with a simple, clear glass and a squat, dust-covered bottle. He pulled the cork and sniffed it, then poured a light amber liquid into the glass and presented it to Erlon.

With an expectant smile, the soldier lifted the glass to the light. It shone clear. He sipped, then rolled his eyes back. "I keep searching, but it's never as good as this."

"Precisely, my friend. And if it ever is, I assume you will bring me back a bottle." Farian sat in the only chair in the room that was different in style from the rest, with a higher seat and stiffer back. It had been disguised with a patterned throw.

"That I will." Erlon took another sip, then raised his glass towards Jameta. "But your chief guest is confused at your taste."

Their host turned to her. "As I expected. The mere experience is not enough for my Lady. There must also be the analysis, yes?"

"If you mean I'd love to know what's going on…"

"I'm sure you would." He steepled his fingers and his eyes rolled towards the ceiling. "Let's put it this way. When you go to tea with young Lady anCanah, what do you expect?"

Jameta shot a frown at Erlon. *How did he know that?* Erlon gave a negative shake to his head. "I expect to be treated in perfect style."

"Exactly. But whose style? I will answer you. In her style. You are visiting a perfect gentlewoman, and you expect perfect gentility."

"I would think that is normal."

"True. Unfortunately true. But don't you think that such a display is rather selfish on the part of the hostess? Oh, I don't mean that Mito anCanah is a selfish person. But it has occurred to me that a truly thoughtful host might instead wish to create a display that would suit his guest instead of himself."

"You mean you change your décor to suit the person who is visiting?"

"My Lady, you abandon subtlety."

"But surely that is a great deal of trouble."

"Of course. That is the point, is it not?"

"And you do this for all your guests?"

He grinned. "In truth, I have few visitors who deserve such treatment."

"Then I had better settle in and enjoy this to the maximum degree, hadn't I?"

"It would gratify your host."

She grinned back and took another sip, settling back into the cushions with a long sigh. "How long to I get to stay? A day? A month?"

51

"Until you tire of luxury, my dear lady, and return to your life of action and usefulness."

"How well you know me." She raised her head. "But you don't know me. Has a little bird been twittering?"

Erlon took on a hangdog look, but his friend laughed. "Only the basics, my dear. The rest I see for myself."

"Hmm."

Farian raised a finger. "The moment requires a change of subject." He rose and left the room, coming back with a bundle wrapped in pink silk and tied with crimson cord, two huge tassels hanging from the complicated knot. With one hand he slipped the tray of tea equipment to the opposite end of the table and with the other he swooped the present in front of her.

She tried not to fumble with the knot, but her hands would not cooperate. She looked up in embarrassment to catch a smug glance between the two men. She bent back to her task.

The vambraces lay nestled together, their bronze sheen picking up the lamplight. Curving around the inside and slightly overlapping with a stitched curl at the ends, the deep brown leather pads glowed in the reflected light.

She raised one. "These are beautiful!"

Farian nodded. "I thought the colour matched. There is a touch of red when the sunlight hits it. Like in your hair."

"Red? In my hair?"

"Now, Erlon did tell me that. You have to look at it from the right angle, but it's there."

"Oh." She slid the guard onto her arm and clicked it into place. "It fits perfectly."

"I had hoped it would. In a while they will loosen up, but I am counting on you growing into them."

"I scarcely think I'll be growing any more."

"A month or two on the trail with the amount of practice you will need? I think your muscles will respond."

She clipped on the mate. "I don't care. These are beautiful. Thank you so much."

"And to go with them..."

"Wait. Erlon gave me these. There wasn't any mention of..."

Again the cautioning finger rose. "Ah, but this is from me." He lifted a second package, corded like the first.

This one opened easier. Inside was a vest of the same leather. It was of plain design, with four bronze catches down the front, matching the clips on the vambraces. She stood up and slipped it on. It felt rather stiff. She fingered the fabric.

"I thought you might notice. There is a certain amount of steel mesh in the shoulder and down the front. Not for serious battle, perhaps, but useful in times of need."

She tucked her arms in, admiring how the bronze warmed the leather. "But they're so wonderful together!"

"Precisely. If they match, you will wear both more often. Hence you will be safer. The designer has worked his magic."

"And the designer is you."

He made a small flourish with his hand.

She opened her arms and hugged him. His body felt lean and hard, all sinew and bone.

He returned the grasp, laughing. "Hah! My ineffable charm works its wonders."

She released him and turned to Erlon, who seemed to be finding this quite amusing. "Well, stand up and get your share."

He stood obediently, and she pulled him tight, taking care that her arm guards did not dig in.

Their host clapped his hands together. "Now we must turn to serious things. Please sit once more."

Mystified, they did so, looking at him expectantly.

Farian took an orator's pose. "My two friends are going on a dangerous journey. I have done what I could to ensure that they are physically protected. But I fear another danger. It is here that they must prepare themselves." He touched his temple. "It is in their minds that they might fail."

Erlon shook his head. "A common topic of discussion in our business, Farian. How can one prepare for the unpreparable?"

The armourer shrugged. "My job is easy, is it not? Regard the offensive weapons, build something to guard against them. The mind is more difficult to predict, yes?"

"It is."

"But the advantage with the mind is that it is the opposite of armour."

Erlon frowned, but Jameta was following. "Outside and inside."

"Exactly. Because armour protects from the outside, even the smallest chink can allow a fatal projectile to enter. The strength of the mind comes from the centre."

"But can't there be chinks in the mental armour as well?"

"Bah. The image breaks down. The mind is not a shell. The mind is...indescribable. Its firmest strength is at the centre. Its weak areas are on the outside. There may be many attacks, and even wounds to the exterior, but as long as the core is strong, the person continues."

Jameta held up one finger. "Are you telling us that we are not strong at the core?"

"Hah! Straight to the crux of the matter. Of course you are strong. But you could be stronger. And so you will listen to an old man who has seen much and endured much, who but for the help of one friend in his moment of weakness would not be where you see him today. I hope to return that favour."

Erlon grinned. "That would be nice. Then you'd stop giving me things."

"No I wouldn't. I feel no sense of obligation. My motivation differs greatly from that."

"I know."

"So, now I come to the words I have prepared. Words I have thought long and hard about. Ideas that come from the gathering of information. At which I have a small talent." He slid into his chair and regarded them.

"Jameta, look at this man beside you. What do you see?"

She took him at his word and looked, trying to see Erlon as at a first meeting.

"Big, strong, handsome, friendly. Confident. A good man to have at your side, no matter the nature of the fight."

"Exactly. And not much more. With this man, what you see is accurate. But you have not finished. What do you see at the core?"

She thought. *Not what I want to see. What I really see. What is causing me all this trouble.* She pulled her eyebrows together. "Diffidence."

"That is all?"

"No, I also see loyalty and intelligence and humour and many other wonderful things. But the diffidence is the key. He defers to others as a habit. It makes him easy to work and live with, because he will not take a stand unless he thinks he must. But he also defers when he should not."

"I would have to agree. And we will deal with that later. Now it is your turn." He turned to Erlon. "What do you see?"

Erlon's worried face relaxed. "In some ways the opposite. Slim, beautiful, intelligent, less delicate than she looks, friendly, but with

54

an edge. Confident, perhaps to a fault. A good woman to have at your side, no matter what the fight."

"And the core?"

There was silence. Finally Erlon threw up his hands. "There's something...I can't say."

"Exactly. And neither can I. And neither can her family or her friends. But there is something. Look at the facts." He pointed a finger. "Here is a young lady who does what she shouldn't, and everyone lets her. Can you imagine? A slim young Ranked woman, unarmed, riding her horses through the northern forests, confronting the weather, the animals, the people, and all on her own! Who could allow such a thing? Does her family not care?"

"Of course they care. But I didn't give them any choice."

"Nonsense. Your family is very traditional. The women rarely make a name for themselves outside the sphere of the family business and home. Yet last summer your uncle sent you on a dangerous mission with a dangerous person, a situation in which you could have died several times. And since then, you continue to move in these circles.

"Now here you are, about to go on the most perilous caravan journey taken in many years. A girl with no defence except these trifles and the fleetness of your horses. Why are you allowed to do this?"

She shrugged. "Uncle Arjan didn't want me to go, and it hasn't quite been decided yet..."

"This has nothing to do with Arjan. If Lord Dennal wasn't prepared to let you go, you would be in Oudonsford right now, trotting messages between the miners and the loggers."

Her heart sank. "It doesn't sound very smart, does it?"

"And you are very smart."

"You don't think I should go, do you?"

"Nonsense. It isn't me. It's you. You don't think you should go."

"What?"

He did not answer, and she thought about it. "You are saying that I haven't learned any of the skills and knowledge to go on an important journey like this. I have wangled my way into the situation by manipulating people, who let me have my way because it's too much bother to fight me."

"Exactly." He turned to Erlon. "Diffidence, yes?"

They both looked at Ferian.

"Diffidence. You think your presence here is due to your skills at maneuvering people, skills that will do little good when you face the dangers of the unknown. You think you are here under false pretenses, that once real danger threatens you will fail yourself, your family and those who count on you."

She sighed. "Yes, I suppose when I think about it, that's exactly it. I shouldn't be going on this expedition. What made me think I should even try?"

"Do you know your uncle, Lord anDennal, very well?"

She frowned at this sudden change of topic, but strove to give an honest answer. "Not well. He's always friendly and polite, but he's not very...approachable."

"But you have respect for him?"

"Of course! He is a very astute businessman, a wonderful head of our family. We are all employed, most of us are happy, there is little strife. We have strong allies. Yes, he is a wonderful man."

"Doesn't make mistakes?"

"I've never heard of one."

"Except for you."

"Me?"

"Yes. This wonderful, intelligent man, this striking leader, has allowed himself to be completely fooled by a sly young lady who will go out and fail in a spectacular way, and bring the whole family into disrepute with important allies. Yes?"

"But..."

"And what about Erlon? You think he's completely stupid? Fooled by a slender figure and a beautiful face?"

"Well, no, but..."

"And inside there's a sly, scheming, selfish, spoiled girl who only wants to grab everything she can get her hands on."

"No! That's not true! I..."

He rose and stood over her. "Don't think you can fool everyone like that. You can't. And especially..." the deep blue eyes bored into hers. "...you can't fool me." He held her in his gaze, then straightened.

"At least not completely." He returned to his chair and relaxed into it, regarding her. "And now we get to the point of this conversation. What is it, down at the core of Jameta? I doubt if anyone is sure, and especially not you. Your family sees it, of course. Lord Dennal is a very astute man. He knows more than anyone else." He grinned and flapped a hand. "Erlon...well, he's in love, so he doesn't count. Completely unreliable. But I have rarely known him to make a mistake where people are concerned.

"Yes. There is an element at your core that gives you the sure knowledge of the rightness of your actions. I sincerely doubt that it is a false security developed because everyone lets you have your way all the time."

"But you were just saying I have the opposite problem. You're saying I'm too diffident."

"Exactly. Delicious irony, is it not? You have the confidence of everyone around you, and the only person who is unsure is yourself."

"Hence this lecture?"

"This little chat."

"And what am I supposed to take away with me, that will help me survive what the next few months will throw at me?"

"I don't know."

"You don't know?"

"How could I? I am not mending armour, here. If I were, I'd find a chink and put a patch on it. This is more like nurturing a plant. I don't know how the plant is going to do it, but I've just now scattered a bit of manure around the base and I'm leaving it up to nature to do the rest."

"Wonderful." She glared at him. "Don't think I missed the reference to bullshit. But I do understand that if it's going to do any good it's up to me to figure it out."

"Exactly." He grinned. "And now I believe you are ready to give up luxuriating, and go out and be useful again?"

"Right. I certainly paid for my brief rest."

"I find the rest one deserves is more refreshing."

"Which means you're going to have an especially fine nap today."

He stood, yawned, and stretched. "I do believe you are right."

They rose as well, and Jameta clipped on her arm guards. "I'm going to get used to these."

"Appropriate to the section of town. If Erlon gets in any trouble, I'm sure you can talk him out of it."

She rolled her eyes at the double meaning, and stepped closer. "I would like to thank you again for everything. All the protection." She tapped her temple. "Of both kinds."

He opened his arms. "It was all my pleasure, my Lady."

Once again she felt the wiry strength of the man, and wondered how old he really was.

Erlon, too, clasped his friend in an embrace, and they made their way back into the shop. Farian stopped in the doorway, looking back into the sitting room. "The couch with all the cushions is comfortable. I might keep that for a while. You must come and sit on it again."

"I'd like that. Maybe in a few months I can come back and tell you how wrong you were."

He smiled, but his eyes were bleak. "Oh, no, my dear. If I'm wrong, I'll know. Because you won't be back."

Without another word he ushered them to the front door and stood watching them walk away. Jameta glanced back as they rounded a corner, and he was still there. He blew her a kiss, finished with a flourish of his hand and turned inside.

Jameta and Erlon paced the street in silence for several blocks. She glanced up at him. "Were you expecting that?"

"Not a whit. I've always thought him rather clever, but that was…"

"…wise."

"Yes, that's it. He is very good at collecting information. But how he puts it together…"

"He said you were in love."

"He did. If it were true, that would make things more difficult, rather than better, don't you think?"

"I can't see it." She looked up at him. "Why can't you be more wise, Erlon?"

He shrugged. "Too diffident, I suppose."

She sighed. "And I have to be more confident about…?"

"Being confident, I think."

"But there is one thing that came out of that whole thing loud and clear."

"Yes. He thinks you should go. Apparently Lord anDennal thinks you should go. What's stopping you?"

"Do you think I should go?"

"Don't ask me. I'm much too diffident. I never disagree with my superiors."

"Erlon!"

"Yes, yes, I think you should go. Farian is right about one thing. There is something in you that makes all the little reasons seem meaningless."

"But you're in love, and your logic is flawed."

"Well, there you are. You can't blame it on me. Make up your own mind. As if you haven't already."

"I have?"

"Look at you. Swinging down the street in your swordsman's vest and arm guards. Have you noticed how much room everyone is giving us? You're ready to go."

Then his smile faded. "Now we have to find a way to prepare you to defend yourself."

"I guess we'd better get training."

"Fine. So, when will we have our first training session?"

"What are you doing right now?"

He glanced down at her dress. "I'm out with a young lady who is dressed for a tea shop. I sort of thought…"

"Not with these things on my arms! What would they think?"

"They do come off."

"But I have to get used to wearing them. Let's pick up a kebab at the street merchant's stall and go back to the Dalmyn yard. We'll find an empty warehouse. I don't want anyone seeing my first awkward attempts."

"Neither do I…ouch! I never thought of those things as offensive weapons."

She flexed her arm. "Neither did I. But I'm figuring this out myself, remember."

"Well, don't figure it out on my shoulder. That hurt."

"Good. Then you won't be making fun of me, will you?"

9.   Training Dance

They found a warehouse with only a few sacks of something-or-other piled along one wall.

"Plenty of room here."

She looked around. "I have no idea how much we need, so I'm taking your word for it."

"I prove my worth already."

"How do we start?"

"Usually with a warmup. Do you know any?"

"No, but I can improvise."

"Fine. You do your warmup, I'll do mine." He lifted the practice wand he had brought, stepped over to one side of the floor and began a set of ritual movements with it.

She watched for a while, wondering what to do. *He's so graceful. It's like a dance...dance! I can do that.* She began the moves of a dance she had known since childhood, an old pattern that apparently came from the hill people of western Samnia. *Or something like that. Who knows where folklore comes from?*

When she had finished Erlon was still working, so she moved into another old dance, the Path of Light. This one was supposed to be connected to her family, back in the mists of time when they worshipped their ancestors. She rather liked it, and the weight of the metal gave her arms an extra swing. She went through the pattern a second time with even more energy, and when she stopped she was thoroughly warm and panting. She turned to see Erlon watching her.

"What are you doing?"

"I'm warming up like you told me to." She mopped her brow. "I think I'm quite warm, now."

"No, the movements. What were you doing?"

"It's a dance called Path of Light. An old Samnian folk dance, popular with my family. It's about making a path through the jungle. Pushing things out of the way."

"I don't think so."

"It's my dance. What do you know about it?"

"That's not a dance. It's a fight pattern. Those are swords and daggers you're parrying. Here. Do that move from near the beginning where you push aside, then step forward and bring your knee up."

60

"You mean this move? I push aside the branch that stretches over the trail. I hold it aside, and then I step high over a log. It's a dance."

"No," he imitated her move, "that's where you brush his lunge aside, reach forward and grab the quillon of his sword, then bring your knee up and break his wrist to disarm him. It's a training pattern. Where did you learn it?"

"I told you. It's an old dance pattern handed down in my family for generations. Where did you learn it?"

"I learned it from a guard I worked with in Domaland. Dark-skinned fellow. Long, black hair."

"Samnian."

He shrugged. "Might have been."

"So you're telling me that my family has been training its women to be fighters for all these generations?"

"Could be. It has all the standard moves in it."

"I can't think why. We have always been less warlike than most Galesians. That's why we went into shipping on the river. It's a rather safe occupation."

"If you don't consider the river."

"Yes, but you don't fight the river. You flow with it."

He grinned. "Do the part where your wrist waves."

"You mean this one?"

"I can't see a better example of moving with the flow."

She shrugged. "So how will this help me defend myself?"

He gripped his practice wand. "I have an idea. Do all your dances have patterns?"

"No, sometimes we just dance. We make it up as we go along."

"Great." He hefted the wooden sword. "Dance for me."

"What? Now? With no music?"

"Sing if you want to. Don't follow a pattern, don't think, just dance."

Jameta frowned at him, then peered around the warehouse to be sure there were no spectators. "This feels strange, but all right." She raised her hands above her head and closed her eyes. The music moved in her, the flow of the dance. She started with her fingers, weaving in one of the old, old patterns that she had learned as a child. The feeling began to flow down her arms, into her shoulders. She began to sway, bending first one knee, then the other. Soon the emotion took over her whole body. She opened her eyes and moved, stepping slowly in an arc.

He followed, circling outside her, his sword at the ready. As she turned to face him, he slid forward, his sword lunging at half speed towards her. Her hand came up and brushed it aside, and she spun away. He followed, his weapon swinging in a short arc aimed for her head. She shot her arms upward, and the blade glanced off her vambrace.

Allowing the sword to continue its path, he brought it around and under, striking upwards, now.

She reached down and guided it past her, lifting the blade and ducking under to come up behind him.

His attacks were speeding up now, and she increased the tempo of her dance. He tried a series of lunges, which she avoided by swaying her body to one side and then the other. At the third lunge she spun in, her body rolling along the blade towards him, her hand sweeping up to brush his throat as she passed. Then she was away again, her feet moving in quick-time, and she intertwined a series of sharp arcs that swept the space between them, turning away a run of jabs from the tip of his sword.

He grinned and swept the sword low. She leapt over it, her knee grazing past his crotch as she closed then spun away. But he caught her wrist with his free hand as she passed. She laughed and spun harder, twisting her arm in one of the breaks Aleria had taught her, and her hand flew from his grasp.

He was not smiling, now. He attacked in earnest, his sword slashing at her from all directions. Jameta was no longer dancing, caught up in the rhythm of the battle. She could see how to direct her movements, and she created a choreography of violence, her hands reaching, jabbing, clawing. Now he was on the defensive, his sword swinging in short arcs to protect the space around him.

She could feel by the pattern. *Soon...soon...*it was too quick for thought. In a blinding instant of clarity she knew where it would all end. His sword swept...*once, twice, and then...*

...as the heavy practice wand swung down at her she froze, body braced, her arms crossed above her head. Her wrist guards caught the weapon just at the hilt and held it suspended for long enough to seize one quillon and pull it down behind her as she ducked under and twisted up inside his arm, her back to his chest. Now all she had to do was crouch and lift...

...it didn't work. His other arm came around and clasped her. Jameta heaved upward, but he was too heavy. She stopped, leaning against him. She could feel his chest heaving, smell the sweat that slicked his arm, tight under her breasts. "Well, I almost had you."

He chuckled. "I think you still do."

She leaned away and reached up to run a hand down his cheek, looking up sideways at him. "That was rather fun."

His sword hand dropped until his arm encircled her waist. "That was rather difficult. It's a good thing you weren't armed. You'd have killed me about five times." He looked down at her. "Of course, you are armed, aren't you?"

She turned in his grasp. "Nothing but what I was born with."

"Hmm. And grew into."

She slid her arms around his neck. "You never kiss me."

"Um...no, that's true. I don't think I should."

"Why not? Don't you want to?"

"Of course I want to. You think I'm made of stone?"

She squeezed the muscle that ran along the top of his shoulder. "No. Well-tempered steel, perhaps." She raised her face to his. "I think you should kiss me."

Instead, he closed his arms around her in a soft hug, his cheek against hers. He held her that way and then released her.

She stepped back. "That wasn't a kiss."

"No, it wasn't. But I had to do it. I've been wanting to for a long time."

She dropped her arms, anger building in her chest. "I don't understand. We like each other. We spend all our time together. Everybody thinks we're...together. But we're not, because you treat me like...like a little sister or something. I don't want to be your little sister!"

"Now you're angry at me."

"You're damn right I am. We're two adults, and you're playing a childish game and I don't understand it!"

He sighed and ran a hand down his face. "But I don't know what to do."

"We've been through that already. I told you what to do."

He smiled at her. "Yes, you did. You certainly aren't shy, are you?"

"I'm a shy as the next girl with strangers. I'm dealing with you right now, and you're more than a friend. At least I thought you were."

"Well, I didn't do a very good job, then. I was trying to act like a friend."

"And you don't want to be more than that?"

"I didn't say that. I don't think I should try to be more than a friend."

"I can't go out on this journey with you until we get something straightened out. That would be even worse! And I want to go. But I want to get us straight even more than that. So there we are. I've said everything I can. It's your turn now."

She stomped over and sat on a pile of sacks and stared at him.

He paced back and forth, running his fingers through his hair roughly as if he wanted to tear it out in handfuls. Finally he faced her. "I don't want to sound like I'm complaining, but this is easy for you. You have a straight and simple life. You've never made mistakes. You know what you want and you only have to reach out and get it."

"I'm not getting much of anything at the moment. I can't even get a kiss from the man I love."

He raised a hand in warning. "I don't think you should be tossing around words like 'love.' You don't know me well enough. You don't know where I came from, what kind of life I've led. It's bad enough that you're Ranked and I'm not. There are other things as well…"

"I wish you wouldn't go on about that Ranking business. I am Esteemed, the lowest rank. My father has the same grandfather as Arjan, the head of the Dennal family up in Oudonsford. And Arjan is only the younger half-brother of the real Lord anDennal down here. Who has the same grandmother, but a different grandfather. I think. You see? I don't even know. It's not that important. Nobody's trying to marry me off to anyone, and there's nobody to marry me to if they wanted. I've got all sorts of value to my family, but only because of what I've done and what I can do. If I want to get married to anyone, I can do it. Don't use that as an excuse."

"It's not a matter of Ranking. I've told you that."

"Then what *is* it a matter of?"

He paced again, rubbing his face with one hand, now. "I'm not the kind of person you should be getting close to. It's like I said. You come to me with a straight life and a clean history. I'm proud to be seen in your company. I'm proud to be your friend. It's not the same with me."

"All right. You're older. You've had tough times and had to do what is necessary to get through them. You kill people for a living. I can handle that. But tell me what it is you won't tell me!"

"Jameta, I can't. Some day I may be able to, but at the moment, I don't know what to say, and I just can't. Please believe me, what is in my past makes me the wrong person for you. Some day you will

64

discover that. So it's better if we don't start. Can't you take my word for it?"

"No, I can't. I don't take anyone's word for anything. Not when it's this important. You tell me what's got the burr in your boot."

"Or...?"

She threw up her hands. "Or who knows what! I refuse to get into a fight with you about it."

"This isn't a fight?"

She stared at him. "Oh, no. This isn't a fight. This is a heated discussion between friends. It's only a fight between lovers when there's enough love to need one. And that's not what's happening here!"

She tried to say more, but the lump in her throat choked her, and she spun and strode out of the warehouse. As she turned the corner, she glanced back. He was standing, hands at his sides, staring after her.

She shook her head. *Well, happy birthday to me. Good thing it isn't. Because it isn't. It isn't happy at all.*

10. Lord Dennal

Her meeting with her uncle was more formal than any of the others. She had been in his house for ten days, had spoken to him at mealtimes and during the evening social time, but never to any serious purpose. However, after breakfast on the following morning he beckoned to her. "Perhaps you and I should have a chat."

"Of course." She gave him her most gracious smile. "My calendar is yours to fill."

He smiled in return. "Right now?"

"I always like to get the work done before I go to play."

"A good attitude." He nodded. "There is work to be done."

He ushered her into his personal office, a large ground-floor room overlooking the park. Ignoring the work area, he led the way to a pleasant alcove with windows on three sides. Two chairs were angled to the best view, and a small table in front of them held a pot and two steaming cups of chai. *So this was already planned.*

She sat and looked out at the gardens, enjoying the summer sunshine and the dark green of the trees, speculating how long it would take him to get to the real point. She sipped the chai, registering its complex aroma.

"This enterprise is new for us."

"I gather it is."

"Kensel anDalmyn was quite forceful when we discussed it. He feels the East is the future of both our houses. He has not led me wrong before."

She leaned forward and set her cup down. "Yes, he said as much down at the yard yesterday. Galesia has to expand. Our economy demands it. We can hardly branch out into Domaland. Any expansion is more likely to come the other way, should our realm weaken further. Aleria and Kolwyn's iron mine has started us in the northerly direction, towards Aesmark. The Cloet caravans are the most convenient southern method."

"Exactly. You listen when Kensel speaks."

"I don't know him well, but I like him. He treats me like an intelligent adult. Puts me on my mettle to prove him right."

Her host laughed. "A fine technique." He hitched forward and turned towards her. "How do you see anDennal fitting in with his plans?"

"I don't. We're water transportation."

"Perhaps anDalmyn considers us important for our heritage."

"Ah. Samnia. But we're not going that far on this expedition."

"And I hope we never do. It is not spoken of in our family because it is an unpleasant memory, but our departure from Samnia, all those years ago, was not the most genial."

"I have pieced enough together to know that."

"We have no desire to return to the land of our ancestors, and the land of our ancestors might have even less desire to receive us."

"I hadn't heard about that."

He shrugged. "There is no information. It was too many generations ago. But the instructions have been passed down. Stay away."

"And thus the problem."

"Exactly. If Kensel thinks our Samnian heritage is going to aid his enterprises in the East, I'm afraid he will be disappointed."

"Does he know this?"

"He has not opened the topic, and it would hardly be in my interest to disillusion him."

She nodded. "You're playing, 'You didn't ask, so I didn't tell you.' Standard merchant technique, to be used with great discretion between friends."

"And thus our chat. I'm not asking you to lie to anyone, but I want you to be aware of the situation."

"May I act as I feel appropriate?"

He regarded her. "It could place you in a situation where your loyalty to your family runs afoul of your feelings for your friends."

"In that case, I must be frank with you, my Lord. I feel that a lie of omission is a poor way to treat allies. Thus, while my loyalty to my family supersedes all, I might consider it best for my family to be frank with our allies, rather than the other choice."

He nodded. "You may find it guileful, but I am happy to give you the responsibility for that decision. That leaves me with no choice but to accept whatever you do."

"I am flattered that you would see it that way, Uncle. Guile aside, few would place such responsibility on one of my age and experience."

He smiled. "I am glad you brought up this matter, although I did not feel it appropriate to mention it. You come highly recommended from many directions. The lukewarm approbation I receive from farther north is rather a recommendation than otherwise."

Lukewarm? I'm going to shoot Uncle Arjan next time I'm home. Well, maybe only in the foot. "It is?"

"Oh, yes. We've been hearing stories about you for years. Even my daughters sing your praises in a mildly negative way. It has occurred to me that anyone who could cause that much concern without ever having done anything wrong must have some kind of talent."

"Thank you, my Lord." She regarded him. He had a stern look, and the sharply trimmed beard gave his face a hawkish demeanour. But his eyes had kindly wrinkles, and his daughters adored him, if from a distance. On impulse, she took a chance. She grinned. "I suppose I inherited my wiles from a member of the family. Perhaps it was you."

There was a pause, and then he laughed. "I begin to see." He glanced at her. "Calculated risk?"

"Yes, my Lord. I have heard about you, as well."

"Fair enough."

"So you will approve my presence as the Dennal representative on this expedition."

"I thought that was obvious."

"Just making sure. It's a big responsibility."

He shrugged. "Not really. I have no specific expectations of gain from the enterprise, so sending someone like you is an appropriately low risk."

"Why, thank you for your concern for my welfare."

He laughed, but then turned a serious face to her. "But anDalmyn has a reputation for coming up with new ideas, and that daughter of his...I have been watching Aleria all her life, as well. She is a formidable force, and will become stronger as the years progress." He paused. "If she survives."

Jameta let that thought sit for a moment.

"So my assignment is to keep my eyes open for a place where Dennal talents can be of benefit to our allies. As long as it does not include contact with Samnia."

"Precisely."

"And to try to keep Aleria alive. Perhaps the more difficult of the two."

"Do your best. She is a valuable ally. But not family."

"I understand the distinction."

They sat sipping chai in silence for a while.

"May I ask a personal question, my Lord?"

"As long as I am free to answer or not."

She nodded. "You watch people, don't you?"

"As do you."

"I have always been small and weak, with everyone around me bigger, rougher and more aggressive. I have found it a useful survival technique."

He looked out the window, taking another sip. "I have always been a leader, and none dare confront me. I, too, find it a useful technique."

"Perhaps a family trait, then."

"Perhaps." He finished his chai and stood. "Thank you for your time, Jameta. A productive meeting, I think."

She stood as well. "It is good to have my position clear, my Lord. It allows me to do the best I can for my family."

"I have no doubt on that score." He turned towards the door. "And what have you planned for the day?"

"I am going for a session with my trainer. He is working on my defensive abilities to prepare for the dangers we face."

"Ah, Erlon the Loatan, is it?"

"Yes." She hoped she wasn't blushing.

"A formidable man. In high regard with the Dalmyns, I gather?"

"Very. For his fighting and his other abilities as well."

"And more than your trainer?"

Now her face burned. She stared at him, speechless.

"My daughters." A small grin. "Terrible gossips, but useful." But he still regarded her, waiting for an answer to his question.

"...perhaps, my Lord."

He slapped her on the shoulder. "Don't worry, Jameta. Arranging marriages was another thing we left behind us in Samnia."

Then he squeezed her shoulder again, turned and looked down at her. "You are so...so unlike my daughters."

With that, he turned and walked away, leaving her standing, confused, in the middle of the corridor.

11. The Roan

The day before they left Kingsport, she went out to the Dalmyn horse ranch to bring her stock in. She and Maddoes looked them over "from poll to pastern" as the old teamster said, but only for the form of it. She had never seen her mounts in better shape. When the two had finished their inspection and stood gazing at their charges in satisfaction, she glanced over. "So, Maddoes. You're not coming with us to far climes unknown?"

The old teamster shook his head. "I don't wanta go that far from home. Got m'grandkids, now. Their father got killed, and m'daughter needs help."

She elbowed him. "And you don't have enough teeth left to chew the camp cook's steaks anymore."

He grinned. "Naw, that ain't it. Tell the truth, I can't do the long trips. I get so stiff by th' enda th' day, I c'n hardly walk for half a hour. I do that for a coupla weeks, I c'n hardly get outa the sack in the mornin'. So I stay around here on the short runs an' help out with the horses out to the farm, y'know?"

"Anything we need to know about the horses for this trip?"

He shrugged. "Sendin' the best, is all I was told." He glanced at her, and a sly grin appeared. "Don't tell Aleria, but the Roan's goin' with you."

Jameta frowned. "The Roan? He hardly counts as one of the best, does he? He only gets along with about three of the other horses."

The old man shrugged. "He's too feisty around here. Different sitiyation out there." He swung an arm to the east. "Out there, you might want a little morea that."

"Hmph. Aleria might not see it that way. He bit her last month."

"Aye, well, she stuck her arm in where she shouldn'ta. He never meant to bite her, only that other horse, which deserved it. But will Aleria let them work it out? Oh, no, she's gotta be in the middle of it. So she got bit."

Jameta matched his smile. "That's Aleria. Always in the middle of everything."

"Right. And she got a lesson. Don't know if she made it a lesson, though."

"What do you mean?"

He shrugged. "It ain't a lesson if it ain't learned, is it?"

She regarded him, but no more was forthcoming. "I suppose. And I won't tell Aleria about the Roan. But don't you think she'll notice?"

He grinned. "I'll slip him into the remuda at the last minute. She'll be up with the lead wagon. Keep an eye on him, will you?"

"I'm certainly not going to let him bite me!"

"That ain't what I mean. You watch him. You're the horsewoman. You might find him useful."

She shrugged. "Oh, there's something I've been meaning to talk to you about."

"U-huh?"

"You used to tell us there are slavers in Ferbodin. I've been there, and there's no such thing."

"There ain't, hey?"

"Nary a one."

"Well, what if you was wanderin' around Ferbodin mindin' yer own business, and some guy grabbed you and took you to the police. The police paid him a 'commission.' Then you got put in front of a judge and charged with 'unproductivity,' or some such word. Of course, you got convicted, so they sent you to a camp where you worked for the government for a year or five, and all they gave you was yer clothes, yer food, and the shackles on yer legs. You may not call that slavery, but I know what to call the guy what sold you."

"Oh. That."

"Oh, yes."

"Happen to you?"

"I never went to Ferbodin but on a job with Dalmyn."

"I don't intend to, either."

"Good. I never heard of any women in them camps. Which ain't a good thing, I don't think. Not for women, anyhow."

"No, neither do I."

* * *

So Jameta had her equipment, her marching orders and an unsettled mind as the caravan made its way across Galesia towards the mountain pass that led to Ferbodin and the East. It was mostly the same crew as the last trip, so they slipped easily into their travel routines, leaving her mind leisure to wander where she wasn't sure she wanted it to go.

She had just turned Brownie out for the evening graze after the first day's travel and was cleaning her tack when Aleria appeared from the direction of the remuda, fuming. Jameta waited until the string of curses had wound down, then looked around mildly. "Something wrong, Aleria?"

The Caravan Master glared at her. "You knew, didn't you?"

Innocence seems the best policy, here. "Knew what?"

"Is this his idea of a joke? Because if it is, I'm going to kick it right back up his..." Aleria waved her hands in frustration.

"Aleria, what has got you so upset? Is something wrong with the horses?"

"Something wrong? SOMETHING WRONG! That damned Maddoes has sent the Roan with us! That's what's wrong."

"What's wrong with the Roan? He's one of the best pullers we've got. Remember that mudhole outside of Kasnel last month...?"

"Oh, sure, he can pull. If you can get another horse close enough for them to pull together. Do you know that he bit me?"

"Oh, yes. Maddoes did mention that. He said it wasn't a lesson if nobody learned anything."

"Well, that gods-bedamned Roan better have learned not to bite me."

"I think Maddoes was talking about you."

"Me? What are you yammering about?"

She shrugged. "He didn't say. You know Maddoes."

Aleria regarded her for a moment. "So you knew he was coming. The two of you cooked this up between you."

Jameta grinned. "Don't make it sound like a conspiracy on the part of the world to thwart you. He told me that going so far away from home we might find a horse like that useful."

The Wagonmaster chewed on that for a while. "I can't see how. More likely to cause more trouble."

"We might need his muscles some day."

"If he doesn't spend his whole time trying to dominate his partner."

"He'll be better when we leave the wagons behind and use packs on the caravan trails."

"If he doesn't use the opportunity to dominate all of them."

Jameta shrugged. "Then we'll put him at the front of the train, and everyone will be happy. If someone shows leadership, the best thing you can do is let him lead."

"He isn't a 'someone,' Jameta. He's a horse."

"Same thing."

"In your twisted world...no," Aleria raised a cautioning hand. "Don't go into your usual rant about how horses are better than people. At times I even agree."

Jameta shrugged. "He and I get along all right."

"Yes, well, take a look over there. You might not be so happy."

She regarded the horses. The Roan was standing between Doe and the rest of the remuda. Whenever she moved towards the herd, he pushed her back. When Brownie tried to join her, the Roan's head came up and his ears flattened. Brownie lowered her head and turned to trot a few steps away, then went back to grazing.

"Up to his usual tricks. He only wants a friend." She whistled. Doe raised her head and trotted towards her mistress. The Roan placed his muscular shoulder in her path. She paused.

Jameta whistled again. The Roan's head came up and he looked at her, ears forward. Doe slipped under his chin and trotted towards the two women.

The Roan thought this over. Just as Doe reached Jameta and nosed her hand for a treat, he trotted to them, his head and tail up, his ears slightly back.

As he came up behind her the smaller horse shifted, the tip of one rear hoof raised from the ground. The Roan thought better of his approach and circled around to the side, nosing up to Jameta for a treat as well. Very politely.

"See what I mean?"

"How did you do that? He thinks you're the boss."

Jameta shook her head. "You're boss of a lot of people, Aleria, and you always think that way. Horses don't."

"What do you mean? There's a lead stallion and a lead mare in every herd."

"The stallion's job is to protect the mares. He doesn't boss them around unless it is necessary to get them to run from danger. If you ever watched, the lead mare never pushes anyone around. She leads. They don't follow because she makes them. They follow because they have learned that she usually leads them somewhere to their advantage. Food, water, safety."

Aleria frowned. "So the Roan comes to you because...?"

Jameta held out her hand. "Oat cakes with molasses. I keep them in my pocket all the time. He's learned that if he approaches me politely he gets a cake. So he does. Don't you, laddie?"

She reached up and took one ear in each hand. She twisted them back and forth, causing the horse to roll his head around. Finally, he snorted and pushed his nose against her chest, driving her back a few steps. She came forward again, slapped his neck, and fed him another biscuit.

Aleria shook her head in disgust. "You're taking extreme liberties with the nastiest horse in the caravan. Why?"

She slapped the Roan's neck again and rubbed under his chin. "I'm getting him used to having his ears played with so it's easier to get a bridle on him. But I think he's lonely."

"Lonely? That hammerhead is just a poor lonely soul in need of friendship? You must be joking."

Jameta fed one biscuit to each horse, then tapped their cheeks, turning them back to the herd. When the Roan hesitated, she held out an empty hand. He snuffled it, blew a snort, then pirouetted after Doe.

The two women strolled towards the fire. "I was asking Maddoes. The Roan was intended to be a breeding stallion. He should have been perfect. But when he was about three years old they realized that he was far too ornery so they gave up on his bloodline and gelded him."

"That's pretty late, isn't it?"

"If they didn't do something he would have been completely useless."

"And it didn't work."

"It calmed him down. At least he doesn't challenge stallions all the time. But he didn't grow up with a herd, so his horse skills are dreadful. So he's lonely. I think that's why he hangs out with Doe. The only difficulty is Brownie. If I could get him to herd up with both of them it would be better, but horses can't count past two. It gets too complex for them."

Aleria clapped her on the back. "Sort of the same as humans. That's why a marriage tends to be a very small group."

Jameta laughed. "Yes, I can see a marriage of three being a problem."

"Yes. I can't see sharing a man with anyone."

"Oh, that kind of marriage." Jameta grinned. "I was thinking of hooking up with two men."

Aleria pretended to mull that over. "Yes, I think I can see that working better."

Their gales of laughter brought heads around the fire turning their way.

"Which two do you want?"

At the continuing laughter the men turned their attention back to their suppers, shaking their heads.

Roeble looked up from his plate, grinning. "Women are good for an expedition. Livens up the party."

Aleria nudged Jameta. "Are you going to tell him, or should I?"

Jameta shrugged. "Why bother? He's already married."

They broke into laughter again.

12.   A Box of Rocks

Jameta rode beside Aleria's wagon as they approached the border post.

"Why do we have to leave those rifles at the border? The realm is full of Mechanicals these days. You and I are carrying Mechanical pistols. What's the point?"

Aleria sighed. "It's a concession to the old moss-backs that don't want change. No normal citizen is allowed to have a Double-S rifle within the realm. There used to be similar rules about crossbows, but nobody uses them anymore. So we have a set of rifles that we store with the Royal Army post at the border. The understanding is that they can use them for training and in case of emergency. When we leave the realm, we pick them up and take them with us."

"It sounds like a stupid idea."

"I told you where it came from."

The lead wagon pulled up at the border post, and an unfamiliar officer with a Major's bars stepped out to meet them. When Aleria introduced herself cordially he responded in kind, but Jameta could see that something was wrong. *Here it comes...*

"I have a request, Lady anDalmyn."

"Yes, Major?"

"Could you leave us a couple of boxes of your ammunition?"

"I don't think so. We're going into unknown territory, and the Double-S rifles are our main source of firepower. Why would you need the ammunition?"

The Major shook his head. "Our old single-shot rifles use the same shells, and you're leaving us short."

"Leaving you short? Why? We have an arrangement. These are our guns and ammunition, stored here at his Majesty's pleasure, for the Royal Army to use inside the realm only in case of emergency. Do you have any emergencies planned?"

The officer's face reddened. "No, I mean you're taking all the good rifles and almost all of our ammunition."

Jameta watched the tension in his shoulders, the way he held his hands, tight against his body. *There's something else going on, here. He's not telling us everything.*

"How can that be? Doesn't the Royal Army provide you with ammunition?"

"They do, but you know bureaucracies. It's never enough."

Aleria grinned. "I have to agree. But don't worry. You're not going to have any emergencies as long as we're over there." She flicked her fingers to the east. "All eyes will be on us, I'm afraid."

"Hmm. Well, I suppose…" Finally he gave the order, and five soldiers appeared, each with a small, square box.

Aleria glanced at them. "Right. Five boxes, five hundred rounds each box. Thank you, Major Lucapa." She waved a hand, and five guards stepped forward, each taking a box of ammunition to his assigned wagon. "I gather you've been keeping your men in training. Any problems with the rifles?"

"Um…oh, yes. One of them has been jamming. I sent it back to Headquarters."

"So we only have seven?"

"That's right, my Lady." He shrugged. "Nothing else to do."

She grimaced. "Can't be helped." Then she slapped her eight-shot Third pistol, belted at her hip. "I'll get more practiced up with this."

"You?" The Major frowned. "You shoot, my Lady?"

She looked up at him. "Everyone in this caravan is an expert shot, Sir. Our lives may depend on it."

Everyone except me.

As if Jameta had spoken, Aleria's eyes turned to her, and a thoughtful frown passed across her brow. Then she turned back to the Major.

"So, if that's all, we'll be on our way."

"Just sign the release, my Lady, and everything will be fine."

She signed the clipboard he handed her, and the two women returned to the caravan.

Roeble was waiting. "What took so long?"

Aleria glanced back, then shook her head. "Talk about it later."

Roeble raised his eyebrows at Jameta, but she could only shrug her shoulders. He turned to his horse and mounted.

Aleria climbed up on the lead wagon, Cavick cracked his whip and the caravan lined out down the pass.

Jameta pushed Brownie up alongside. "What was that all about?"

Aleria shook her head. "What were you getting from him?"

"He was too reluctant about the guns. And then too slack with the rest of the inspection. It's not as if he could persuade us to leave him our guns."

"It wasn't so much the weapons as the ammunition."

"Yes, I got that, too." Jameta grinned. "You think he's been shooting away his portion?"

Aleria frowned. "Or selling it. I told you last time we came through here that I smelled the stench of bribery. Now we know who." The Caravan Master straightened. "And speaking of bribery, are we prepared for our next encounter?"

"As you ordered, my Lady." She hefted the satchel. "The main bribe, the extra bribe, aaaand...the emergency bribe, just in case."

Aleria shook her head. "One of the benefits of foreign travel. Discovering the quirks of everyone else's system. And paying for them. Give it to Roeble. That's another caprice of these revolutionaries. In spite of their 'equality for all' rants, they still like to deal with a man."

Jameta made a sympathetic face and trotted Brownie back to where Roeble was riding beside the wagon that carried his personal equipment. "Your pay packet, Sir."

The merchant hefted the satchel. "Seems heavy. Are we expecting more trouble than usual?"

She shrugged. "I seem to remember a bit of rough road the last time we visited. Aleria thinks we may have to smooth things over at the border in case we need to slip on through like that again."

He grinned. "Aleria learns fast, I'll give her that." He bounced the weight in his hand again. "Anything I don't give away, I get to keep?"

Jameta scowled. "You're in Ferbodin now, Citizen. All assets apportioned equally to everyone."

"Excuse me, Citizen. The glories of the People's Government had slipped my mind." He slung the strap over his shoulder, and they approached the border.

The wagons drew up in good order, and a team of officials stepped smartly out, clipboards in hand, pencils sharp; the teamsters removed the tarps and the Ferbodean agents began their work. Roeble and Aleria patrolled the caravan, alert to any hitch.

And any official with sticky fingers as well. Jameta pushed her horse up beside a wagon so she could look down into the box, where an agent was opening a crate of Domalian kitchenware. He had been scrutinizing a knife, but when she appeared he frowned and put it back in the crate, closed the lid and applied his official stamp. After that, Jameta was more vigilant in her observations.

The boxes had been loaded for ease of inspection, but once each box was cleared and stamped the teamster nailed it shut and repositioned it to a safe travelling spot. It took most of the morning, but it was still short of noon when the last paper was stamped, the last "tariff" was paid, and the caravan rolled happily on towards its destinations in foreign lands.

As soon as they were out of sight of the border, Jameta rode up beside Aleria. "You remember about the ammunition? I paid special attention."

"To what?"

"When they were inspecting it. Which they didn't, not properly. They just opened the lid and glanced in. And when the teamster put one of the boxes back in the wagon? It rattled."

"Rattled? Are you sure? Why would a box of ammunition rattle? Maybe it was poorly packed."

"And maybe not."

Aleria sighed. "Which wagon?"

"Koama's"

"Roeble is up ahead with Erlon. Tell them why we're stopping, and that I'm sorry to spoil their fun." She raised her hand, and the long caravan ground to a halt.

Jameta trotted ahead to inform the other two. When they got back to the third wagon, Koama had already pulled his ammunition box out of the load, and Vracha was levering slats off with his box hammer. Soon a row of gleaming brass circles rewarded their eyes.

Erlon leaned down from his saddle. "That looks all right."

Jameta shook her head. "That box rattled."

"That row isn't going to rattle. It's perfectly packed." He nodded to the guard, who lifted out the tray of ammunition.

Underneath was a layer of packing cloth, and under that...

Erlon and Aleria swore in unison. Roeble made a disgusted sound. Everyone else stood agape.

Finally Aleria gave voice to their feelings. "That son-of-a-bitch. That conniving, thieving, swindling, double-dealing, deceitful son of a crawling snake! Rocks! He's sold off our ammunition and sent us out on a dangerous journey with a box of rocks!" She looked around the circle. "Oh, that's funny. That's a great joke. When we run out of ammunition we can throw rocks at the enemy!"

Jameta frowned. "I don't understand. How did he think he would get away with it? I suppose if we didn't run into trouble we would never need the second layer of shells and we'd bring the ammunition back to him and never notice."

Erlon moved his horse nearer and dropped a comforting hand on her shoulder. "He knew how far we're going on this junket. If we did run into enough trouble to need the second layer, we probably wouldn't make it back, so he'd still be safe."

Jameta's mind was already on the trail ahead. "So what do we do? Do we go back?"

Aleria's eyes slid to Erlon. "We did bring a lot of shells."

"First we check the other boxes. If we still have half the load, I'd be satisfied to go on. We might be able to buy more in Ferbodin, but they'll cost."

Roeble frowned. "I hate to be running back and forth through the border with boxes of ammunition. If there's half, we still have over a thousand rounds. That seems like a lot."

Erlon shrugged. "That's the problem with Sustained Shots. They run through ammunition like miners through beer."

"I suppose." Roeble nodded slowly, thinking. "So if there's less than half, we send a party back to the border and take all the damned ammunition he has there, and let him figure out his problems on his own." He laid a restraining hand on Aleria's shoulder. "And you don't go along, because killing is too good for him."

Jameta was trying to remember. "I think there's a precedent for this. If a senior officer is found in dereliction of duty, his immediate junior is allowed – no, expected – to relieve him of his post."

Aleria snorted. "Unless the next in line has his hand out as well."

Roeble shrugged. "Let's get the lids off and check those other boxes before we execute half the Royal Army."

The guards had already been at work, and soon all the boxes were open. It was not as bad as they expected; only three boxes had been tampered with. The other two were full, and a careful check, including a few test shots, made Erlon as certain as he could be that they had a reasonable store of good ammunition, and that the rifles were in working order.

The leaders looked at each other. "Are we all right to go on?"

Roeble nodded. "If you think so, Aleria, I'm fine with it. Erlon?"

The guard Captain reached over his shoulder to pat the hilt of his sword. "We never had that kind of weapon before and we always made it back."

Aleria grinned. "That's the spirit. Jameta, what do you think?"

"I'm just a messenger with a toy gun. Why should I worry?"

"Yes, we'll be talking about that, too." Aleria raised her voice. "Nail them up, pack them down, and let's roll this caravan."

The men sprang to their work, and soon the wagon train was moving again. Not so happily, but moving nonetheless.

13. Klodzo

The next day they received one of those semi-official visits that were the norm in Ferbodin. A grey-coated bureaucrat, escorted by a sergeant and four soldiers, trotted towards the caravan, stopping their horses in the middle of the road.

Jameta was scouting off to the side, and she watched Roeble ride up beside the lead wagon and speak to Aleria. Then the wagon moved forward until its horses were nose-to-nose with the official's mount, a familiar bay with dark mane and tail.

By the time Jameta approached, the discussion was over. The official turned and trotted down the road, his soldiers behind him. Aleria, with a sour look on her face, ordered the caravan onward.

Jameta swung alongside. "Pavenkov?"

"None other. I'm surprised he dares show his face."

"He must have better backing than we thought. Change of plans?"

"Huh! We have been invited to attend a market. Klodzo."

"And that's not good?"

The Wagonmaster shrugged. "We are expected to hit a couple of the smaller government-sponsored markets. It's good for our relationship with officialdom. We were just hoping for a larger centre of population. Klodzo is in poor farming country. Pavenkov says he has a new official position direct from the central government: calls himself the 'People's Commissar for Trade,' an excuse to put away bribes if I ever heard one. But he says he's got supporters and policy backing him, and it may even be legitimate. Whatever the truth is, he wants us at the next market? We go there."

Jameta shrugged. "So we go there. Part of the deal."

"It's likely a complete bust, but that's not the problem. The size of the bribe he wants is. Roeble figures it's way out of line for the size of the fair, so he bargained. Half now, the rest when the trading is over. Pavenkov didn't like it, but it's a reasonable request, and he's asking more than his superiors would allow. So we have a compromise."

"More of the learning process."

"An expensive lesson, I'm afraid."

Up ahead, the official was turning off the road onto a rutted path that led to a village of scattered, thatch-roofed houses.

Aleria shook her head. "This is going to be wonderful."

The Trouble with Tents

Once they were set up, Jameta surveyed the market in front of them. They had a prime location: a wide space at the end of a T-junction. But the view wasn't pretty. The local merchants didn't have much to sell, most of it in poor condition. The awnings were patched and tattered. The footing was slippery. A few customers paced the lanes, but they had little money. Down at the other end of the aisle Citizen Pavenkov was strolling along, snacking from the food vendors. She saw no money changing hands.

She busied herself with arranging their goods in an artistic display.

"Jameta." Roeble's voice was low.

She glanced at him without moving her head.

"Get rid of the jewelry."

She looked up. Pavenkov was heading their way, munching on a mungy pastry that left grease on his fingers and flakes all down the front of his soiled grey coat. She tossed a cloth over the jewelry and slid the case out from under it, slipping it into a nearby pack. Then she smoothed the cloth down on the table and laid out a row of kitchen implements on it.

Pavenkov reached them, wiping his hands down the sides of his coat. "Very nice, very nice." He leered at her and picked up a small knife. "Is the metal good?"

"Best Domalian tempered steel, Citizen." *The bastard is going to put it in his pocket.*

Sure enough, he lowered his hand as if he had forgotten it, and began to paw over the rest of the goods with his other hand.

"Perhaps the Citizen would like to have it as a present to his wife?" Roeble's voice came over her shoulder, and she slid aside.

"That would be very kind. She would appreciate it."

"We would be pleased. Only the one, though. If you wished more, we could arrange to take the cost off our fee, perhaps?"

"No, no, the one is fine. Thank you, Citizen."

"It is our pleasure, Citizen. We are happy to be here, taking advantage of your government's good will."

Pavenkov nodded with an insincere smile, pocketed the knife and strolled away.

She turned to Roeble. "Do you have to do extra penance?"

"What do I have to atone for?"

"Such blatant lies."

He shrugged. "I'm a merchant. Special dispensation."

"I'm so glad. To think your soul might be endangered by dealing with such as that."

"If I was going to endanger my soul I might as well go for broke and slit his throat."

"Ah, the advantages of a strong religious belief."

"A few prayers might do our pocketbooks more good than anything I can think of, right now." He rolled his eyes heavenward.

"Should we change our merchandise?"

"A good thought. Take off anything expensive and bring out those trinkets we had planned to give away to the tribesmen further east. I tossed them in this morning, just in case."

She complied and then watched in awe as the trader skillfully determined how much these poor folk could afford and adjusted his prices accordingly.

It was a dismal day. Jameta, used to chatting up the customers and learning about their lives, was completely frustrated. "They won't talk at all."

Roeble's lip twisted. "In this society, you don't tell anyone anything. A quarter of the people here are government spies, another quarter are government employees and about ninety percent of them would turn you in if you said anything of interest: for money, for advantage or to protect themselves from getting lumped in with dissidents."

"And what about the other ten percent?"

"They're honest people keeping their heads down and trying to survive."

Jameta glanced at the coins a ragged woman offered, shrugged and pushed the tin pot across the counter. The woman's face lit up. *I suppose that might have been too generous, but what the hell.*

So, at the end of the day they had a poor report for Pavenkov. He came around as Aleria was clipping the last buckle on the Roan's harness before they backed him in and hitched him to the wagon.

Roeble looked up from lifting the singletree aside to make room for the horse. "This was a pretty poor excuse for a market."

"Yes, yes, I understand." A frown crossed his pock-marked brow. "It is the weather. First it is too hot, and then it rains. Everyone stays home."

"Well, the ones with money must have stayed home. We made much less than we had hoped."

"But you did promise the government's percentage."

"Yes, I did, and here is the remainder." He handed the official a drawstring bag.

Pavenkov spilled the coins out on his hand. He looked up, frowning. "This is not enough!"

Roeble tilted his head. "It's exactly the percentage we agreed on."

"You must have made more than that." He jingled the coins in his dirty hand.

Roeble stepped closer. "Citizen Pavenkov, if we are to do business together, there has to be a certain amount of trust. If you do not trust me to report my earnings accurately, you will not allow me to come here. If I do not trust you to put on a good market where I can make an honest profit, I will not return. I have given you more than this market was worth, but I am willing to consider it payment for the opportunity to learn."

The official stood speechless for a moment. Then he raised his hand. "Take your bourgeois filth out of my town." He slapped the Roan on the rump, hard.

The Roan's rear foot twitched. Jameta watched in horror as it swung forward, paused and drove back, catching the unfortunate official in the stomach. His body was lifted across the road, slamming upright against the wall of the building opposite. He fell face down in the dirt and did not move.

Roeble ran across to the man, ran a finger down the front of his neck and held it there. "He's still alive." He stood. "Get that horse hitched to the wagon."

Jameta finished and swung into her saddle. "We're just going to leave him?"

"There are people nearby. He's going to wake up with a hoofprint-shaped bruise. No one can accuse us of attacking him with a horseshoe. The longer we are gone, the better."

"What about the money?"

Roeble picked up the purse from the ground and slid it inside the coat of the injured man, who gave a groan. He returned and swung onto his horse. "We pay our debts."

There was no sign of Erlon, so they headed back to their camp in the gathering darkness. Soon hoofbeats approached from behind them. Roeble's head came around, but Jameta smiled at him. "That's Rogas. Know his gait anywhere."

Soon Erlon jogged up, slowing when he noted their easy pace. He pulled in alongside Jameta. "You left a bit of a hornet's nest back there."

"Is he still alive?"

"Alive and aloud."

"Did he say anything about the money?"

"I didn't stay long, but he wasn't making much sense. Said a horse kicked him."

Jameta grinned and poked a thumb over her shoulder. "He stood behind the Roan and slapped him, hard, on the rump."

"That explains a lot. Also why Pavenkov was so breathless."

Roeble chuckled and kneed his horse to continue. "If he didn't say anything about the money, that's good. The only thing that could go wrong is if someone found him and stole it before he came around."

"So, double guards and an early start, tomorrow?"

"I'm afraid so."

"Did we make any money?"

"Enough to cover the bribe plus a tad more."

Jameta smiled to herself. Roeble was being a merchant. *We sold a bunch of stuff we had planned to give away for free. Of course, that might mean that down the road we have to give away something we planned to sell. Trading is a complex business.*

Roeble called an informal meeting over their evening cup of wine.

Aleria was still chuckling over Pavenkov's short flight with the sudden end. "Nobody deserved it more than that bastard. Did you know he propositioned me?"

Erlon's head came up. "He what?"

She flapped her hand at him. "Oh, calm down. It wasn't anything overt. But he left the door open, I could tell."

Jameta made a face. "I felt like that, too. Guaranteed that little present never got to his wife. If he has one." She turned to Roeble again. "So, was it worth the effort?"

"Besides seeing that slimy bastard fly across the road, we didn't get much satisfaction. But we did make something, and since we didn't want to go there at all, we can call it a win."

Jameta frowned. "I have a question. The situation with that Pavenkov bastard. He's a government official. How much trouble are we in due to what happened?"

"A good point. We have friends in high places, or we wouldn't be here at all."

"Which means we have paid bigger bribes farther up the line?"

"Not entirely. The people in power have a stake in keeping the country running. A few of them even believe in their form of government. And they need our trade. So, by demanding such a large fee for such a terrible fair, Pavenkov has made it difficult for us to trade. If he had a lot of clout in this district, he might be able to rouse trouble for us. But I don't see it that way. I think he's very small beer, and if he dares to put up a fuss, it will draw attention to his actions. So he'll take his huge bribe and his tiny paring knife and consider himself lucky."

"In spite of the Roan?"

"He won't want that story spread around."

Aleria chuckled again. "First time I ever thought that horse was worth something." She glanced at Jameta and raised her hand to stop the outburst. "And the mudhole at Kasnel."

"What about Hungry Hill?"

"Don't push it. I still think he ought to be sold for dog meat."

"Couldn't get any money for him. Too tough."

Aleria looked up at her. "Do you always have to have the last word?"

"Not at all. You go ahead."

Aleria made an inarticulate growl and stood. "That was an early start this morning. I'm for my cot."

As the others trickled away, Jameta caught Erlon looking at her. She made a "what?" gesture. He rolled his eyes and turned away to check on the guards.

She strolled towards the tent. *If she's going to find things to needle me about, she'll have to pay the price. But I do have to share a tent with her for the next two months. I better be nice for a while.*

14. Fair Trade

So they left the town of Klodzo bright and early. Erlon and the guards patrolled widely all day, but no one disturbed their journey. Once they were well away from Klodzo, the leaders held an informal meeting around Aleria's wagon.

Aleria looked up at Roeble. "What's our plan for the next official market?"

He let his horse amble along for a while. "We don't know whether Pavenkov has any support in the capital, but any of the next few towns will have a market. And without Pavenkov, we ought to do better." He let his horse amble along for a while. "Dealing with local authorities this time. The profits won't be much higher, but they'll be happy to see us." He grinned. "The bribes ought to be less."

Aleria nodded. "Any ideas?"

"Remember Ancenis?"

"Was that the town we didn't stop at on our way back last time?"

"Yes. We noted it as a possible for the future. We are now in the future."

"Ancenis it is. How far?"

"I'm not sure. Jameta?"

"About a day's travel." She saw the map in her mind's eye. "We have to cross that pass with the groves of elm trees, and then there's that pretty stretch where the road winds through those meadows along the river. Remember, we had trouble with the ford? The river will be much lower, this time of year. We should get across tonight. There's a good campsite on the other side under the cottonwoods."

Aleria shook her head. "I'll take your word for it."

Jameta grinned. "Why would I lie?"

Aleria shrugged. "And after that?"

The merchant tipped his head from side to side. "We went to Klodzo because the government sent us. We have proved our willingness to cooperate, and the result was rather embarrassing for them. The next time I will take a firmer stance, and they will know they can't send us to somewhere like that again. So, yes, we will be good little traders and put on a show. Ancenis will help. However...Erlon, do you remember Nad Desnau?"

"The big People's Market where all the government officials showed up, out of uniform."

"That's the one. Where they cleaned us out of gold jewelry."

"Let's keep our ears open. They might have moved it, but it will be in the same area. We'll be there in about three days." He glanced at Aleria. "What do you think? One more from the official list, and then one to pay for it all?"

She grinned. "The king can't expect us to do this out of the goodness of our hearts. A bit of cash coming in wouldn't go amiss."

Roeble nodded and turned to Jameta. "Is that fine with you?"

"I bow to your expertise, Sir.

* * *

Ancenis was a much more tidy and pleasant town, and the officials were pleased to have a caravan of such status at their little market. They made a bit of a celebration of it, and as a result the buyers were in a receptive mood, and all went well.

Until Pavenkov showed up.

Fortunately, it was late in the day. The crowds had tapered off, and Roeble had already gone to discuss percentages with the mayor of the town. Jameta and Lavan were just about finished packing up their gear when a Jameta raised a warning hand. "I hear horses."

"What do you mean? There's horses all over the place."

"Listen. A party of horses, moving at a trot. Very close."

They stared around. The hoofbeats slowed, but the horses came on.

"They're coming into the market."

Lavan frowned. "Nobody rides a horse into the market. It's not done."

Jameta tossed her head. "And here comes somebody who does what he likes."

In the direction she indicated several horsemen appeared, walking their mounts through the narrow aisles of the market, a grey-coated official on a bay stallion in the lead. He pulled up in front of their stall and stared down his nose at them.

"So, here you are."

Jameta gave him her best merchant's smile. "Good afternoon, Citizen Pavenkov. What can I sell you?"

"What are you doing here?"

Repressing the quick answer that came to her, she widened her smile. "What do you mean, Citizen?"

"I didn't give you permission to trade here."

"Oh, I'm sorry. There must be a misunderstanding. You told us that the officials wanted us to stop at a few of the local markets." She brightened. "So here we are! Isn't this a pleasant market? Such a pretty town." She flung her hand to the east. "That bridge is such a work of art. Look at the carving on the parapet."

He made a "Hmph!" deep in his throat. "Yes. It is a credit to the People and their Government."

She continued to smile at him. The bay stallion stirred, and he corrected it with a sharp jerk of his wrist. "I hope you have done well, here?"

She shrugged. "It is only a small town, but the Citizens have been welcoming, so we kept our prices low in appreciation. At this stage in our trading, the good will of the people is more important than turning a large profit. Roeble Cloet is making his report to the mayor at this moment."

"Ah. Thank you, Citizen." He wrenched his horse's head around and pushed through his soldiers. Their horses backed out of the way, crushing several stalls in the process. Then the whole group rose to a trot and mashed their way out of the market, leaving a trail of broken goods and sullen faces behind them. Ignoring the looks sent her way, Jameta continued packing.

"Well done."

She glanced at Lavan. "Not much choice."

"Still, you handled him perfectly. You're like a duck in the rain, you know."

She stopped and stared at him. "I can't wait for the punch line."

"No, I mean it. All his antagonism slides off you like water, and you keep on as if it never happened."

She tossed him a grin over her shoulder as she went back to packing. "It does seem to disconcert him, doesn't it?"

Later, in their campground, they discussed the development. Aleria did not mince words. "That scruffy son-of-a-bitch is following us. What does he want? To destroy our trading?"

Roeble shook his head. "Perhaps to get his share of the profits. He tried it today, but he was too late. The money had already changed hands and was out of sight."

Jameta nodded. "It's more than that. Ever since we backed him down at the border he's determined to make our lives miserable. From the sound of it, he does have government backing, but he's using that mandate to indulge his personal animosity."

89

Aleria sighed. "So the bastard's going to follow us for the whole route. What do we do about that?"

"Certainly no more trading." Roeble frowned. "At least, not at the government markets. We've done our 'good little Citizens' act."

Jameta glanced at him. "You're still thinking of Nad Desnau?"

"We'll have to play it by ear. If he's nowhere in sight we should risk it. If he's around, it wouldn't be fair to the other traders, and it would get us in their bad books if they thought we brought him. Erlon? What do you think?"

The big swordsman shrugged. "Apart from picking him up one dark night and dropping him off a high cliff…"

"Could you do that?"

He grinned. "Aleria, you are indulging your bloodthirsty side. Think of the consequences."

"Only if we got caught. Could you make it look like an accident?"

Roeble waved his hand between their faces. "We are traders. We don't murder government officials just because they don't like us."

Aleria's bottom lip came out. "Roeble, you're not much fun."

"No, but I make a lot of money. If you want that sort of fun, bring a different sort of party."

15. Unfair Trade

It was a rare lull in the bargaining, and Jameta brought Roeble a cup of chai from the little brazier they had set up. He accepted it, pushed his stocky body back on the stool, sipped, and sighed.

She went to arrange the goods on the table, making a pattern in the cheaper jewelry that led the eye towards the case of gold at the centre.

"That's very good."

"Thank you. Presentation is more important than most people think."

"You are right. And not only for trade goods."

"May I make an idle comment on that topic?"

"Please do. I find your idle comments worth listening to."

"I am under the impression that you and Aleria are equal leaders on this expedition."

"That is true."

"At the beginning, I wondered. Aleria runs everything. She makes all the decisions. Oh, she consults in a very Alerian way, but no one ever argues. And you sit back and say little. It seemed strange at first."

"But now?"

"Now I begin to understand. You know this business. Your decisions are clear, your reasoning is logical, and you have brought us through some tight spots."

"So far, so good."

"Yes. And I have confidence for the future. You and Aleria are a well-matched team."

"We are. Different abilities, different areas of responsibility. She takes care of the local politics and the transport as she is supposed to, and I take care of the trading."

"And you share the diplomacy, because half is politics and the rest more trading."

He nodded. "And don't forget the others on the team."

"Yes. Erlon fits in too, doesn't he?"

"Yes. In another group, he would be too...I would call it diffident. He doesn't push himself forward very much. But with Aleria making most of the travel decisions and listening to his opinion, it works out well. And then there's you."

She sighed. "Yes. Me. How do I fit in?"

He grinned and gestured towards her display. "We all contribute as our talents dictate."

"Thank you ever so much. You brought me all this way to set up your tables?"

He became serious. "It's more than that. I would sooner have you with me for the selling than any of the others. Especially the smaller items to the poorer folk." He glanced at her. "Although you do tend to be charitable."

"Oh. I wondered about that."

"Yes, it's always an argument among merchants. The ones who sell for lower prices often make more money, because word gets around and they get more business."

"But we have a finite amount of goods to sell, and something we sell cheap here, we might get more for farther along."

He nodded. "You're getting a grasp of the business. But we have to freight that object, and perhaps we will pick something up instead that we can make more money on." He glanced at a woman who was fingering the household items.

Jameta went to serve her. When she turned back to Roeble he was smiling.

"And then there's the most clever part of it."

"Am I going to like this?"

"Not at all. Really smart merchants sell their low-priced wares for lower prices, because their reputation spreads around. And what do you think they do, then?"

She stared at him. "They sell their expensive goods for more?"

"Exactly, Citizen. And now you know why I have you here. I've been using your soft heart as a heartless marketing gimmick."

"Well, I am heartbroken to be so used."

"Such is the learning experience of the real world, my Lady."

He glanced up the alley between the tents and rose to his feet and grabbed the jewelry case. "And right now, you're going to pack as much of our goods as you can, as quickly as you can. Most expensive stuff first. Then prepare the horses."

She didn't even look around but began to pack, her heart pounding. As she worked, Erlon appeared with the two other guards. He shouldered her out of the way. "I'll finish this. Get the horses. Now you know why we didn't bring wagons today."

Happy for a task she was good at, she slipped out the back to fit bridles and tighten girths. As the men brought the filled packs out, she tossed the ropes back and forth, two of them cinching up a packsaddle in a third of the time it took a single packer.

As she tied the lead rope to the last horse she could hear a ruckus starting at the far side of the market. Men shouting and horses squealing. Their big awning swept out of sight, and Erlon and Roeble appeared, bundling the stiff canvas into an awkward clump, which they tossed across the last horse's back and lashed roughly in place.

Then the three of them swung into the saddle. Roeble took the lead and Jameta followed with the pack animals, threading through the hodgepodge of corrals and shacks that dotted the back alleys of the market.

When she looked behind she could see Erlon riding at the tail with his rifle in one hand, his eyes turned backwards. The two guards jogged along on foot at the rear, their rifles at the ready as well.

Finally they broke into the open to join a muddled stream of horses, riders, handcarts and pedlars with packs that flowed away from the market into the surrounding woods. Now their progress slowed, and one of the guards trotted forward to take up position at the shoulder of Roeble's horse.

The merchant knew what he was doing. Soon a path cut off from the main crowd, and he took it, winding up among the rocks and over a low pass into the next valley. At the crown of the gap they held up, and Erlon came to the front.

"It's yours from here, lad. If they're smart enough, they might have someone waiting on the escape routes."

The guard Captain pointed down the trail. "Sartek, scout ahead. I'm behind you. Birlik, take the tail. I don't expect the soldiers to get through that mob any time soon, but it could happen. I don't like to hamper you, but this could be a legitimate government raid. We don't want to shoot anyone unless we have to."

Both guards nodded and moved off. Erlon looked at Roeble. "Any ideas?"

"Have to agree. This can't be bandits, and we might be the main target. If we get caught, we'll be arrested, not murdered. This will be a propaganda coup for the reactionaries. Of course, they'll steal our goods as well, but we might get to keep our horses."

"Any point in dropping our loads?"

"Too much chance someone else would get them. There's always jackals around when the lion hunts."

"Right, then." Erlon tossed a grin to Jameta. "Away we go."

He kneed his horse into a fast walk, and they moved off down the trail. The Roan pushed up beside Brownie, and Jameta flicked the end of the halter rope across his nose. "Now would not be a good time to misbehave, partner."

He snorted and eased back. Soon he was pushing forward again. This time she whacked him, and he squealed and reared. Brownie danced when the pull came on the saddle, but this was an old game, and she settled at once. Jameta turned and scowled at the big horse. "Stop it. I have other things on my mind."

His flattened ears rose.

"Good." She turned her attention to the surrounding forest and hills, and they rode on.

It was an uneventful trip back to the caravan, although twice they pulled off as a troop of horsemen thundered past, and several times they were the ones barging down the trail while a group of pedlars huddled aside to let them by.

They had just finished unloading the packs, and Jameta and Stilet were rubbing down the sweaty horses when loud voices approached. She looked around to see Pavenkov, Roeble, and Aleria approaching, two Dalmyn guards and three grey-coated soldiers in attendance.

The official strolled up and planted himself in front of her, fists on hips. "So. Been out today, have you? Carried a load, perhaps?"

Jameta raised her eyebrows and said nothing.

"Where were you?"

She nodded, once. "Good afternoon, Citizen. It is a rather warm day. Surely Citizen Aleria has offered you a cool drink?"

"I am not here for a cool drink, little girl."

"Oh. I apologize that I am not in proper attire to change your mind." She gave him a gracious smile. *He's focused on the horse. I'll go there first.* "I was too busy dealing with a troublesome pack animal."

The official stepped forward. "You are trying to rub out the evidence that he has been wearing a pack saddle."

She frowned. "Why would I try to do that with a sweaty pack saddle sitting beside him? He has been under a saddle today. What is there to hide?"

"That is what I would like to know."

She glanced at Aleria, who was watching with polite interest. *So it's up to me. Fair enough.*

"Would the Citizen like to speak of horse training...I wouldn't do that."

94

The man had stepped forward, reaching out towards the horse's shoulder. His hand hovered, and the Roan's ears lowered along his neck. "And why wouldn't you?"

"Because that is why he is under saddle in the heat of the day, Citizen. He is a bothersome horse and requires training."

"Oh, I don't think he'll give me any trouble." The hand descended in several firm slaps. The horse's ears stayed back, but he did not move his head, his upper lip twitching.

Jameta shook her head. "As you wish, Citizen, but you have been warned."

The man spun on her. "And you have been warned, Citizen. Don't lie to me!"

She regarded him, her head tilted to one side. "Why would I lie to you about a difficult horse? Surely if I wished you harm I would have done nothing and let you take the consequences as you did the last time you met him. I am impressed at your skill at handling him, but he remains a difficult horse that will not walk properly in tandem with the others. He's fine in front, but he will not follow. So I train him in the heat of the day with a heavy load, to take the fire out of him. Perhaps I have been successful, today." She shrugged. "Or perhaps you are very good with difficult horses. In any case, I am satisfied with my day's work, and I thank you for your assistance."

He grunted. "I think you will find that I am quite competent with difficult horses." He turned to the others. "As I am with difficult people. If I find that you have been overstepping your mandate in any way I will bring the full weight of the law of Ferbodin against you."

Roeble stepped forward, taking his cue from Jameta. "Of course, Citizen. We are merchants. We have no intention of breaking the time-honoured customs of your country. It is our intention to fit in, because that way we will profit the most. If you would like to see our manifests, please come this way."

"I have no interest in your manifests. I know merchants. They will all be falsified anyway." The official signalled to his soldiers. "Come. The smell of camel dung disgusts me."

He turned and strode away, his soldiers marching in formation behind him.

Roeble turned to Jameta. "We were discussing earlier?"

"Excuse me? Oh, that."

"Exactly. If I hadn't seen it with my own eyes..." He shook his head. "He storms in accusing you of lying, and the next moment you're talking about his talent with difficult horses, and I never did notice when the subject switched."

Aleria chuckled. "She's been doing that since she learned to talk. Her family is in despair over her, but before they can take any action they find themselves on a completely different topic."

Roeble turned to Jameta. "Which reminds us that we, too, have things to discuss, but not out in the hot sun. Would you finish up with your troublesome horse and join us in the shade of my tent?"

She nodded. "I'll have to settle him. That man frightened him, and he's not in a good mood. Once I get him picketed out, I'll be there."

Aleria glanced at the big horse. "You mean he sometimes isn't in a bad mood? How do you tell?" Then she lifted a finger to Jameta. "Don't say whatever it is you're thinking."

Jameta grinned. "May I think of something else, if I hurry?"

"I'm not waiting around to find out. Get that monster calmed down and let's talk about the other monster."

Jameta turned to her work, rubbing and murmuring to the sweating horse, and the others walked off, talking in low voices.

The meeting outside the merchant's tent was more comfortable, physically at least. Each of the caravan leaders owned a light canvas chair, and they perched them in a half circle under the awning in front of Roeble's tent and relaxed while he played the host.

When everyone was settled with a cool drink he sat and looked around at them. "I think our course is set."

"Then lay it out for those of us with less experience in this business." Aleria took a sip of her drink, then raised her head to regard him. "Did I ever mention that it can be useful to have you along?"

"Not often enough. But this is the way I see it. Pavenkov is after us. For whatever reason, he's decided to use us as examples or victims or whatever. I don't think there can be much doubt about what happened today. He raids the market where we are selling, and then immediately turns up at our camp, asking more than pointed questions."

Jameta frowned in thought. "And whether he was after us or not it doesn't matter, because all the other free traders will suspect that's what happened."

"That's right. The market rarely gets raided. We show up for one day, and there's a raid. You don't succeed at underground trading if you believe in coincidences."

Aleria nodded. "So we might as well keep moving."

"I think we should make one more stop, though."

"The main market in the capital." She finished her drink and slapped the empty cup into her palm. "We could go there."

"For several reasons. First, it would be good politics to show up where everyone who wants us there can see us. Second, I need to consult with my supporters. While I'm on the road I can't do that, even inside their realm. And third, it's a big market, and we'll make a lot of money there, where Pavenkov won't be able to bother us."

Aleria. "I like your logic, my friend. Erlon?"

"The politics are up to you, but I can't help but think we'll be safer in a more central area. These freelance rogue politicians can always do better where no one else is watching them."

"Jameta?"

"I would like to go with Roeble when he talks to his supporters." She turned to the merchant. "If that would be allowed."

"I don't see why not. You are a Ranked person in your land. Your family is in good odour with the king. I can use that."

"Use what you like. It would be good for me to learn how that end of the business works."

"I would appreciate your company. We are all agreed, then?"

Aleria handed him her cup. "If we're on the road tomorrow, I have things to do this afternoon." She strode off, leaving the others to share a chuckle.

Jameta rose as well. "And I have horses to see to. Thanks for the drink, Roeble. Refreshes the body and the mind."

He smiled up at her. "It refreshes the body, but there is alcohol in that stuff. You only think your mind is refreshed."

"I appreciate the warning. I'll stay away from the Roan until I sober up."

16. Politics

The Ferbodin Central Market was situated in the courtyard of the castle of the pre-revolutionary rulers of the country. In deference to the climate, the inside of the fortress was a huge five-sided open courtyard with a shady arcade running around the perimeter. Stairs led to an upper story, where a wide walkway encircled the battlements, fitted with awnings all round.

And every square foot of the interior was used for selling. In the central plaza, posts had been set up, creating a grid of tight alleys with stalls on either side, the goods sitting, lying, and hanging everywhere. Not a finger-width of space was wasted.

Jameta strolled through, admiring pyramids of bright-coloured spices, herbs, and fruits. One section was nothing but hats: woven, knit, straw, wool, of all colours and all shapes. Another was given over entirely to shoes. Floor to ceiling and strung from the rafters. Shoes everywhere. She had to turn sideways to follow the winding aisle through the muddle.

"Oh, look at that cloth!"

"Which one?" Erlon was staring at the wall of fabric in front of them. Hundreds of bolts of cloth of all fabrics and colours.

"That one. The shot silk. My mother made me a dress like that last year. Almost the same colour, even."

He grinned. "Can't wait to see you model it."

Then baskets of all shapes, materials and sizes. Pottery. Metalware. Fabrics. Candies, vegetables, and meats. There was even a section of dolls.

That one was creepy. She turned to Erlon, shuddering. "Look at all the eyes watching us." Then one of the faces loomed forward, and she jumped, then realized it was the merchant, stepping out to offer her wares. She grinned sheepishly and turned away.

"Do you know where the jewelry section is?"

Erlon glanced pointedly at her vambraces. "Your real birthday is coming?"

"No, no, I don't want to buy anything. I want to see how our goods compare."

"All right, then. I think..." his head came up, searching, "that way."

The lavish display of beads and gems had her shaking her head. "How can we compete with this?"

"Novelty. These are permanent shops. They're here the whole year. Every woman of any degree knows them all, has checked their wares and is bored with them. Our display is in a section of the market all our own with new and interesting goods. We'll compete, don't worry." He tossed a hand. "Plus there's the wholesale trade."

"What's that?"

"Roeble has bales of expensive cloth and crates of Mechanics that he doesn't sell himself. The local merchants buy the lot from him and put it out at their own stalls after we're gone. That's where some of our support comes from. Word gets around. Our goods are new and different. As long as he keeps his prices up while he's here, then the merchants he sold to can up their prices even higher when there aren't any of our goods left."

"Works for me. And it leaves us with empty horses, to buy from the producers here, and take farther on?"

"That's how it goes."

"I remember now. As long as we don't try to sell it inside Ferbodin."

"That's right. We pass through and leave our foreign goods and our foreign currency behind."

She grinned up at him. "My learning goes on apace. Can we go to the food area now?"

"I was thinking that way myself. Anyone can find it. Follow your nose."

The cooking space was filled with a miasma of steam and smoke, as everything possible to eat – and a few things that looked impossible – were baked, fried, boiled and served completely raw.

"Is that what it looks like?"

"You mean the ox eyes or the prairie oysters?"

"Do I assume you eat the ox eye raw?"

"I gather so. One crunch and then swallow. It's a great delicacy."

"And an aphrodisiac?"

"How did you know?"

"Hmph. All those ghastly things that turn your stomach but people pretend are delicacies are always aphrodisiacs. It's a great way to sell them to old men whose brains are declining in concert with their sexual powers."

They returned to the camp to find Roeble waiting for them, dressed in his best robe. "Let's go, Jameta. The schedule got pushed. No, don't bother to change. Let's give them a show." He glanced at Erlon.

"I wasn't planning..."

"You look fine. Come."

He strode off across the camping area towards the blocky cement building that backed on the old castle wall but towered several stories above it.

"That's the seat of government?"

"The Ferbodeans don't believe in the frippery of royalty or the ostentation of the bourgeois."

"They seem to believe in grey. In many aspects of life."

"I'd have to agree."

They entered an ostentatious-enough set of doors at the front, and a bowing underling led them up a curving stone staircase to the second floor. He somehow knew all about them, because he brought them to a large meeting room, ushered them in and announced their names.

Jameta followed Roeble, wondering what to expect. She slowed in the doorway, feeling Erlon's comforting presence at her shoulder. They stepped forward.

The room was dominated by a circle of tables. About twenty men sat on the perimeter, with no indication of who was in charge. Behind each cushioned chair a double row of benches teemed with grey-suited aides and secretaries.

Right in front of them one chair was empty. Roeble stepped forward and made a small bow. "I apologize, Citizens, but another of our party wished to accompany me to this important meeting. She is of Rank in my country. Perhaps...?"

The man to the left of the empty chair rose, bowed and turned to the benches of his neighbour. There was a hasty shuffling, and he sat in the front row.

Jameta gave him an especially gracious smile as she took his chair. Roeble sat as well, and Erlon stood between them, sliding his cavalry sabre out of sight behind his hip.

An older man from across the circle rose. "We welcome the representatives of our trading partners to the west, the Galesians. It is with great anticipation that we look forward to their wisdom, which has aided us so successfully in the creation and fulfillment of our latest Plan for Prosperity..."

As the official rambled on, Jameta scanned the other faces around the table. *Since their compatriot is saying nothing, it might be interesting to see where they direct their attention.* Which at the moment seemed to be just about everywhere.

Then Roeble spoke, with his share of empty phrases about cooperation and mutual benefit.

So far, so good. Who's going to say something important?

No one was. As they rambled on, each speaker brought up points from his own agenda, but none of it had much to do with trade. She heard about education of minority groups, government aid to flood victims, if she understood correctly, the difficulties of reading cattle brands. Finally something noteworthy: the transportation of coal. She listened to that one in case there was information Dennals could use, but it was all about tonnage and production projections that would be grossly exaggerated.

Finally Roeble was allowed to get a few more words in, but he did not embark upon their problems, only congratulating the earlier speakers on their accomplishments and commiserating on their troubles.

After he finished a break was called, and various groups huddled together while tea and trays of dainties circulated.

Roeble leaned over to her. "How are we doing so far?"

She glanced around to see if they were being observed. "Watching the food disappearing, I'd guess that we're a good excuse for a serious raiding of the larder."

He seemed about to answer, but glanced at her and said nothing. She continued to scan the groups, trying to place who was talking to whom.

When the meeting resumed, it seemed that progress had been made. A portly gentleman with a full beard addressed Roeble directly.

"It is my impression, Citizen Cloet, that Galesia is changing its policies on Mechanical devices, is it not?"

"That is true, Citizen. And we are thus open to trade in a wider variety of goods than previously." He went on with lists of equipment that was being brought in from Domaland, including the machinery the Dennals were using to load their coal barges.

As he talked and various people responded, the pattern began to emerge. The table was divided into three camps, as far as she could calculate. The ones to her left were the agricultural lobby. Those to Roeble's right were manufacturers, and those across the table were extractors of raw materials: mining and lumbering.

During a short break, she leaned over to Roeble. "Are we a threat to their factories?"

"Many of them, but not this group. These are the progressives. They are willing to change, to create new products. Our problem is to get them to understand that the quality of their goods must match up to the competition from outside the country."

She nodded and went back to her task.

Talk rambled back and forth, and a picture began to build in her head. Oblique references, eye contacts. Then she had it.

The next time Roeble glanced her way, she laid a hand on his arm. He leaned closer.

"Do you want to move the meeting along?"

"I have said all I can."

She kept listening. Soon it came time for the Galesians to speak, and she flicked a finger. He turned to her.

She smiled at them and raised her voice. "Citizens, as a newcomer to your nation I have listened with great interest to your discussion. It will take much thought and many days of discussion with my compatriots to grasp the totality. However, if you would indulge a beginner, I would find it useful to hear the opinions of Citizen Druzhba on the topic of trade with Galesia. Perhaps specifically the free movement of our goods across the borders between your provinces?"

There was dead silence.

"Please forgive me. I did not wish to force Citizen Druzhba to express opinions which he may not wish to express, or which he may not even have..." She allowed her eyes to stray towards the dapper little man with the goatee who sat across from her at the junction of the manufacturers and the miners.

He awarded her with a cold smile. "Perhaps if the young Citizen is as naïve as she suggests and she were to hear my opinions, she would find them difficult to understand. But perhaps not."

"I put myself entirely in your hands on that matter, Citizen."

He nodded and glanced at another man across the room, who took up the baton, and the orchestra played its complex tunes again.

But not for long. It seemed that everyone who wanted to had made his point, and all had enjoyed the products of the baker's oven to their satiation. Roeble proclaimed his satisfaction with the information he had received. A representative of each bloc again welcomed the Galesian delegation and wished them good trading on the morrow.

And that was it.

The three were escorted with all due deference to the huge double doors and dumped ceremoniously on the street again.

As they strolled back towards the caravansary, Jameta stole a look at Roeble.

He seemed to be trying without success to keep a straight face. Finally he glanced around to see that they were not overheard. "Well, did you enjoy the circus?"

"Few of the acts were entertaining. I thought the overall quality was reasonable, though."

He burst out laughing. "All right. We can stop talking in circles. Why Druzhba?"

She feigned nonchalance. "Perhaps because if our new trading enterprises are successful, he will be the next Grand High Poo-Bah or Premier Minister, or whatever substitutes for a king in this place."

Roeble glanced over to see if she was serious. "You think so?"

"What I think matters little. They think so."

"Hmm. I don't know much about him. He's relatively new. Slipped up from the ranks two years ago. I'd say he was a behind-the-scenes sort."

"He certainly wasn't putting himself forward, today."

"He didn't say a word."

"In case you didn't notice, neither did anyone else."

"I'd have to agree. Well, we'll find out this evening."

"We will?"

"I dropped enough hints."

"Did you? I'm sorry, I wasn't listening that hard."

"My dear, I am disappointed. I thought you went there to learn from my demonstration of my diplomatic skills."

"Oh, but I did. I thought you did a marvellous job. You just didn't say anything."

"Hmm."

She looked over at him. "I didn't step out of line did I? Of course, I did step out of line. On purpose. But within acceptable boundaries?"

He mused while they walked on. "I think you struck the right note. I got the feeling that everyone had a chance to play his solo before you closed down the performance."

"That's nice. They seem an earnest lot. I'd hate to take their fun away."

He grinned. "They all ate well. I think most of them will consider it a successful afternoon."

"Well, we have performed one charitable deed today. Those were good pastries."

"Yes, that is one export the Ferbodeans could make money at. Their chefs."

As they approached the camp, Jameta looked up at Erlon, striding at her side. "You haven't said much."

He looked down at her and shook his head. "Nothing to say. I've stood guard at a few of those meetings, and I find the conversation very distracting, so I stop listening. I watch how they sit and who they look at, trying to discover the power blocs and the alliances. See if anyone is going to cause trouble. I look for secret tip-offs and people that act out of character to the group. People walking too fast, that sort of thing. Dangers. That's what I'm there for."

"And what did you see?"

"The same as you saw. Three groups. I didn't realize they were product-oriented until Jameta tipped me off. Miners and loggers are divided among themselves. The agriculture lot are solid. The manufacturers are hard to tell. Uneasy truce, perhaps?"

Roeble nodded. "That tallies."

"So what are we going to do?"

Roeble turned to her. "Nothing. We have done what we came to do. It is their move, now."

"But what if they don't?"

"Ah, rash and impetuous youth. We will make progress when we make progress, and we will stay right here until we do. Why such a rush? This is a wonderful place to explore. The food is good. Wait to see how much trading we do tomorrow."

"But we have an agenda. We have to get out east and fulfill our purpose."

"And the passes start snowing up in about four months. Do you have a fancy ball scheduled?"

She reached out and hit Roeble's shoulder, causing him to stumble. "I saved you from a further hour or three of crushing boredom this afternoon, and this is how you repay me?"

"And how do you know I wasn't playing a deeper game, and you cut it off in the middle?"

She looked at him in horror. "You weren't were you? You said..." Then she growled and turned to Erlon. "The next time you need a practice dummy for your sword demonstrations, I nominate him!"

Laughing, they entered their camp.

Aleria wanted only a brief rundown on their success. When Jameta expressed surprise at her disinterest, she shook her head. "Roeble and I each do our jobs and don't bother the other with the details. Any leader who tries to do everything will end up doing a bad job of all of it." She grinned up from her portable writing table. "But you can give me your impressions as well."

Jameta shrugged. "Nothing to bother you with. I imagine the king's council meetings back in Kingsport are pretty much the same. Everyone trying to get his agenda put forward, and nobody listening to anyone."

"And everything else happening in the undercurrents. At which Roeble says you're a natural."

"I suppose so. Erlon does the same thing, but he's looking for evidence of trouble."

"And he's the only one of the party that we wish a complete lack of success."

"But only if he's correct." Jameta shuddered at the thought of him being wrong. "Roeble says we will get a response tonight."

"I certainly hope we do." Aleria shuffled the papers in front of her. "We've gone out on a limb, here."

"We have?"

"Yes. We can handle ourselves against bandits and rogue bureaucrats. What we can't deal with is a change in government policy. If the wrong faction gets power we might as well go home. Assuming we can get there without being used by somebody to score political points."

"Then I hope we get a response. What do you expect? A visitor or an invitation?"

Aleria glanced up. "Bird bet?"

Jameta considered. "It's easier to move one of them than several of us. Visitor."

"I'd have to agree. Give me two-to-one?"

"You're on for a penny."

* * *

Jameta won. Just at dusk Erlon gave a brief whistle, alerting the camp that something was up. The leaders strolled over to the entrance. Three grey-clad Ferbodian bureaucrats were strolling up the street towards them. As they passed, one of them slipped aside

105

while his companions continued along the passage, entering a bar nearby.

The Galesians strolled back to Roeble's tent and filed inside. Roeble lit two more lamps, and they all took seats and surveyed their visitor. Once he removed his cap, Druzhba turned out to be an unassuming fortyish man with brown eyes and thinning hair. His goatee was neatly clipped, as was his speech.

"I am pleased you came, Citizen Cloet." He turned to Jameta. "And brought your so-intelligent apprentice."

She inclined her head. "Citizen."

He turned back to Roeble. "What can I do for you?"

"Pavenkov. What can you tell me about him?"

The man sighed. "A nation can go two ways. Forward or back. It can never stay still."

"Ah. And Pavenkov is part of the 'stay still' faction?"

"That is correct. This group has warmly feathered nests and they fear the slightest wind."

"Do you have any advice?"

The little man gave a wry smile. "Do what you do best. Bring trade and prosperity to our two nations. Soon these reactionaries will be lost in the dust behind us."

"We can agree on our long-term goals. Any short-term advice?"

"Do not kill him on Ferbodean soil. I could not protect you."

"I knew that."

"We continue to work against his cadre. Overt actions on his part might bring them into disrepute."

"So if he's caught wiping out a trading caravan, his people will lose votes in the next election?"

The smile returned. "You understand our system well. I hope you are not required to aid us in this way."

"As am I."

"Is there anything else you need?"

"Once we leave here, we head east."

"We have interests there. Several mines run by a business consortium from Domaland. They would appreciate a visit and might be useful if you need assistance. Your trading permits will vouch for you. Other than that, you are free to trade with anyone who will deal fairly."

Roeble grinned. "And trade more carefully with those who do not."

Druzbha rose. "I should go. The less time I am away from my familiar routine, the less likelihood of a chance meeting with the wrong person."

They rose as well. "Thank you for visiting."

"I assume you will stop in on your way back?"

"The road home leads past your door."

By now it was almost dark, the street revealed by splashes of light from shops and taverns. They strolled along, their visitor in the middle. When they passed the bar, he slipped aside and was gone. By mutual consent they continued, enjoying the warm night and the exotic smells and sounds. After a while Roeble stopped. "Well, much though I am enjoying this, we have an active day tomorrow. Sunup to sundown. Money to be made."

They turned and strolled back, parting outside their tents.

When Aleria and Jameta were alone in their tent, the older girl sat on her cot. "Interesting day?"

"Yes. I quite enjoyed it."

"Sounds like you did well. What do you think of him?"

"Hard to know, isn't it? He's the only one to talk straight to us, and he didn't say much."

"He confirmed that nothing has changed. That's all we needed. Contact has been made. Our plans continue."

"Our problems are our own?"

"As usual."

Jameta slipped off her boots. "A good day, then."

"A good day."

"And you owe me a penny."

A grunt was the only reply.

17. The Road East

Five days later the Dalmyn caravan wound through the early-morning crowds of the capital city and out to the open plain. The loads were different. Gone were the bales of cloth, the heavier Mechanicals. Now the wagons were laden with cooking utensils, many of Ferbodean manufacture. Robes and other clothing sewn in Ferbodean mills. Anything modern factories could supply that primitive living required. But no extra guns. Everyone agreed on that. Erlon enjoined the guards to take special care of their Double-S rifles, and they repacked the ammunition in flat packages, deep in the packs.

And salt. The medium of currency in the desert was salt, and every wagon carried a block. Every member of the expedition had a ration.

Jameta was on Brownie, who cantered ahead, anxious to be moving after days in a sparse pasture. Lavan seemed equally eager to range.

She glanced at him loping along beside her. "Enjoy yourself? I hardly saw you."

"Oh, you might say that. I kept busy."

"Doing what? You weren't in the market."

He shifted in the saddle to turn towards her. "You worked hard, Jameta. Everyone says what a good seller you are. But I was working too. Did you see the tribal horses?"

"How could I miss them? They certainly are pretty little ponies. They carry their heads with such pride. A reputation for speed, as well."

"Oh, yes. Did you see the races?"

"Only one. They did look fast. I doubt they'd match Brownie, though." She patted the neck of her tall, slim steed. "And what else did you do, other than watch races and think about buying horses?"

He shrugged. "A certain amount of social interaction was necessary for my credibility."

"You win or lose?"

"Lost, of course. Winning wasn't the point, and I'm not familiar with their games. I consider it money well spent."

"And the rest of the time?"

"I admit to enjoying the entertainment. Some of it was…" He glanced at her. "You wouldn't have been interested."

"You never know. I'm a dancer myself, as you may have noticed."

Lavan snickered. "I don't think your training sessions with Erlon would go down very well in that crowd. Your dress covers too much." His face was browned by the desert sun and wind, but the blush still showed.

"Well, that's as it should be, then."

He rose in the stirrups, gazing ahead. "And now we're off into real adventure. Up until now we haven't really been anywhere. Only from one capital city to the next. Where's the adventure in that?"

She made a face. "I didn't find it boring."

"Oh, it wasn't easy. Don't get me wrong. But this…" He swung his hand to the southeastern horizon where the arable plain faded into the purple-brown of dry mountains ahead.

She smiled. "I feel it too. I may not be so keen as you are, but I'm glad I came."

He grinned. "Can you imagine what it will be like? We'll be sitting in the Falcon, and I'll say, 'Jameta, remember that tribe we met down along the Hasi Bel River?' The clothes they wore!"

"And I'll say, 'but Hasi means river, so you just said the River Bel River' and we'll all get a good chuckle at your expense."

He frowned. "How do you know that?"

"Because my family speaks Samnian. 'Hasi' is the Samnian word for river."

"You never said you speak Samnian."

"You weren't listening."

He frowned, his eyes rolling up and to the side. "Oh. Your family speaks it."

"That's right. My grandparents always spoke to me in Samnian because they wanted me to learn it. So I understand it pretty well. However, being a rebellious twit, I always answered them in Galesian, which got their goat nicely and gave me all sorts of attention I didn't deserve. Now I wish I'd done as they asked."

"I'm sure you'll catch on."

"If I find anyone that speaks real Samnian. These tribes probably have a related language, so who knows how much I'll be able to communicate?"

"Still, it's an advantage."

"And we need all the advantages we can get. This won't be easy, Lavan. It's just as likely you'll be sitting in the Falcon saying,

'Remember that girl, Jameta? Yeah, too bad she got in the middle of that tribal battle. For once her horses weren't fast enough to save her.' And then you'll all have a drink in my honour."

He was silent for a moment, but then he grinned. "Ah, you're a spoilsport. We'll do fine." He scanned the terrain. "I'm going to sweep out to the right. Why don't you take the left?"

"Sure. But don't trample a farmer's crop. It takes a long time to grow them out here."

He nodded and turned his horse away, and she kneed Brownie out across the dry prairie.

* * *

The Ferbodean border guards did not show the diligence of their compatriots to the west, and the halt was minimal. Jameta looked around as they pulled out.

"What does this tell you?"

She glanced at Erlon, pacing along on his big gelding beside her. "Their minds are on other matters. An attack from the east. Horsemen."

"And what makes you say that?"

She indicated the wide field of ditches and spikes that the caravan was forced to wind through. "Infantry would spread out and clamber through. Horsemen would have to gallop up the road. Right here, they'd be in a tight group charging straight at that cannon port. Then they turn sideways to the wall, where the riflemen can pick off individuals."

"And how would you attack it?"

"I'm the messenger, remember?"

"Perhaps you should expand your area of expertise."

"If you want someone vying for your job."

"I'll take the risk."

She looked at the fortifications with renewed interest, but had come to no conclusions when the road straightened, and they continued out onto the plain.

They travelled for days, the road getting narrower and the terrain more arid. Once through the mountain range they came upon what Roeble said was their first "real" desert. Spindly, thorny bushes poked up here and there from dry, sandy soil. Ribs of rock pushed up, and the double track became a wide single trail, though still heavily used. Every once in a while they would meet or overtake a herd of goats or sheep, and long strings of horses passed every day in both directions. The farther into the desert they went the more caravans they met. Caravans transporting food: dates, millet, dried meat, dried cheese, butter. Caravans transporting garments, indigo turbans, leather products, ostrich feathers. Caravans transporting salt to be used for exchange against other products. But most of all, caravans of horses. Often nothing but horses. Sometimes the odd camel, but camels were only needed where the sand started, several days to the east.

18.   Ambivalent Reception

The first mine was a half-day loop off the caravan route, at a spot where a stream burbled out of a low range of hills to the east.

They pulled in at dusk to be welcomed personally by the manager: a tall, handsome man with a clipped moustache, an erect military posture and an upper-class Domalian accent. A pistol in a worn holster rode at his hip. He introduced himself as Gwaller Rees, greeted them warmly and allotted them camping space inside the perimeter fence, a high barbed-wire enclosure patrolled by men on foot with SS carbines.

Jameta looked around with interest. Her delivery duties often brought her to the open-pit coal mines of Galesia, but this deep-shaft mine was altogether different. The compound centred on a tall derrick with a huge pulley at the top. Cables ran from a shed that bore all the evidence of a steam engine inside, up to the pulley, then straight down into the clump of shacks around the mine head. Cables also ran to a horizontal track that carried the ore away to a mill, where another steam engine set up a rhythmic thumping. From there a conveyor spread a pile of rubble out over the plain to the west. Where it left the compound the water of the stream was an oily yellow colour. Smoke rose from several smokestacks, and soot lay everywhere.

Aleria regarded the area and pointed. "We're not too concerned with safety. Could we camp over there?"

He shrugged. "Be my guest. I suppose you'd find this a tad noisy."

"A tad. Does it stop at night?"

"From midnight to four. We're running two shifts."

Roeble looked around. "Any trouble getting fuel for the engines?"

"There's a coal mine twenty miles north." The manager pointed to a trail of double ruts that wound away over the prairie. "The road is the problem. This desert soil is so fine, the wheels cut down to bedrock with a couple of rains. So the coal has to be brought on horseback and the concentrate has to be taken to the Ferbodean border the same way. That's what makes this such an expensive proposition. If the ore wasn't so rich, we'd never turn a profit."

Roeble grinned. "As long as you're making enough to buy our goods, we're happy."

The manager indicated the row of small houses along the upwind side of the compound. "The miners' wives will be happy, that's for sure. Lots of money and nothing to spend it on." He grinned. "Which I shouldn't be telling you."

Aleria matched his smile, nodded and strode off to give orders. Leading Doe, Jameta followed.

The Caravan Master slowed for Jameta to catch up. "What do you think?"

"Gwaller Rees? Ex-military. Seemed genuinely glad to see us. I hope he's a good engineer."

"Why do you say that?"

"Because he's too open to be a good politician."

Aleria nodded. "Makes it easier for us." She waved a hand in front of her nose. "Horrible place to make a living."

Jameta elbowed her. "I'm sure he thinks the smell of horse droppings is just as bad."

Aleria turned to give more instructions. Jameta busied herself with the horses.

They set up tables at the edge of their camp, and soon a trickle of women and children left the compound, their eagerness barely concealed. Jameta regarded the women as they shopped. They seemed a friendly lot, bantering with her and each other. Their clothing was of decent quality and looked spruce and bright despite the soot that drifted around on the wind. The children acted free and cheerful, running happily off to play with the toys she gave them.

"And you'll get more'n their worth because of the givin'."

Jameta grinned at the tall, gaunt woman. "You've cleverly seen through my pathetic ploy. Now can I overcharge you for this knife while you're feeling so pleased with yourself?"

"Hmph. What kinda knife is this?"

"Only the best steel from Domaland, Ma'am."

"Domaland? I've gotta come six hundred miles from home to buy onea our own knives?"

"And get overcharged for it as well." Jameta imitated a miner's accent. "Ain't that life?"

The woman grinned and got down to serious bargaining.

That evening the caravan leaders were invited to dine at the mine manager's table. Jameta confided to Aleria that she'd rather eat in the single men's dining hall.

The Caravan Master regarded her. "I doubt if Erlon would appreciate that."

"He would if he came with me. They have the best cooks in these places. It keeps the men happy."

Aleria grinned. "Maybe the manager has his own chef."

"Maybe we'll be lucky and they bring the food from the dining hall."

They were luckier than that. Gwaller's wife, Jeppa, was her husband's opposite. Short and stocky, she could have come straight from a farm, and she cooked like it. The food was fresh, well-spiced even to Jameta's taste, and plentiful.

Afterwards, they lounged in the sitting room with good brandy swirling in their glasses, and the talk ran to politics. Rees was interested in the Galesian view. "We don't hear much from you folk. What brings you out this way?"

Roeble sipped his drink. "We are businessmen looking for new markets. There is nowhere else to expand. To be honest, we hope that by passing through Ferbodin we can gradually induce them to expanded trade."

The manager snorted. "Wouldn't expect much. Their government is so messed up, they can't even manage to build a road across their country."

Aleria frowned. "I thought they were good at road building."

"I didn't say they couldn't build roads. I said they couldn't organize the building. Give me a team of Ferbodean craftsmen and I'd have a good permanent surface built from here to the Galesian border inside a year."

Jameta smiled at him. "I note that you don't plan to continue into Galesia."

He regarded her a moment, then returned the smile. "Not politic, my dear. But your roads are fine. It's your mountains that are the problem."

"Don't we know it."

And the talk turned to engineering, which Jameta didn't understand, but she listened anyway, picking up anything useful that drifted her way. When the opportunity came for an opinion on distances and travel times, she contributed what she could.

In all, it was a pleasant evening, and the Galesians strolled back to their camp in a mellow mood.

* * *

The next morning it all changed.

Aleria strode into camp shortly after breakfast, her shrill whistle echoing off the nearby hills. Soon all were gathered around her. "Listen, now. We're breaking camp. On the road in an hour. Do it right, but do it smooth. One hour." She flicked her finger in a circle and the crew bustled away. Nobody ran, but every step was purposeful.

The leaders waited, eyes questioning.

Aleria shrugged. "I just got called in to meet with Gwaller Rees. He was very nice, very polite, thanked us for our visit, praised our wares, but he suggested that we should move on. We were a distraction to the men, production targets are high, perhaps the presence of women..."

Jameta made an explosive sound. "They have their wives and children in the camp!"

"...and all sorts of other polite nothings. These people were happy to see us come. They have enjoyed our company and bought our goods. A sudden change like this, and we're getting a message." She lowered her head and raised her eyebrows. "...oh, yes, and he suggested that the route south was better travelling this time of year."

Roeble nodded. "So, whoever or whatever is coming in on the west road, we don't want to meet."

"That was my interpretation."

Jameta remembered. "I heard a horse come in from the west about sunup. Sounded tired."

"Let's pack." Roeble turned and strode off.

Jameta glanced at Lavan, and they headed for the remuda. On impulse, she saddled the Roan. Three-quarters of an hour later, the caravan was on the move.

19. Pavenkov Again

They regained the main caravan route and turned southeast again. It was only an hour later that Jameta pulled the Roan to a halt and regarded the route ahead. "What do you see over there?"

Lavan stared ahead. "Haze of dust, just beyond that little rise."

"That's what it looks like to me."

"And I doubt if the road twists around that far to the right."

"So there's something big or fast that shouldn't be over there."

He shot her a grin. "Might be a flock of sheep."

"Might be something more harmful."

"Shall we take a gander, as Erlon says?"

Jameta looked down at the Roan. "Well, I did want to tire this fellow out so I could train him."

Lavan tossed a hand to the west of the trail. "Push him up over the shoulder of that knoll. If he's still feisty when you finish that climb in this heat, he might still be good for a battle."

"Don't start a battle for the Roan's benefit. He'll be getting above himself."

"I'll do my best. Let's go."

Heeling their horses forward, they passed the guard Captain as they approached the lead wagon. He tossed his head, indicating the dust cloud, and they nodded and set their mounts to a gallop.

"You take the road. I'll go around from the other side." Jameta reined off the trail and allowed the Roan to slow to a trot. She kept her eyes open for outriders, but saw none.

Staying off the high ground, she cut along the shoulder of the knoll that hid the source of their concern. The other side was more open, and there below her was the cause of the disturbance. About thirty riders, trotting up a trail that slanted off towards the main roadway. Even from this distance their horses looked tired. Heads down, tails drooping in spite of the flies, they ambled along, their riders slouching in their saddles. *They've been riding fast in the heat. To get ahead of us.*

She spotted Lavan over near the front of the enemy but could think of no way to attract his attention. *There's no need. Somebody has to warn the caravan, and that's me. He'll cover my backtrail if he can.*

116

She spun the Roan around and trotted back the way she came, her eyes searching her surroundings. Once behind the hill, she kicked her steed into a lope. "Now's the time to be fast, my boy."

The horse sprang ahead and settled into his ponderous pace. Soon they were at the caravan, and Lavan was just coming into sight around the far corner of the road.

"What is it?"

"Thirty-two riders on tired horses. My guess is they hurried to get ahead of us."

"How armed?"

"I didn't take time to get close enough. Maybe Lavan has more"

He pulled in right behind her, and his report was not reassuring. "They look like what I'd expect the local tribesmen to be. All covered up. Horses like the tribesmen we see going by. Long-barreled muskets, swords."

Aleria glanced up at Erlon, who had joined them. "If they have anything near the speed we've heard, it doesn't matter how tired they are. Laden wagons can't outrun them."

"Leader's on a big bay with dark mane and tail."

"Any guesses who that will be?" Aleria looked around but got no takers.

Jameta was thinking. "If it's Pavenkov he'll come forward alone."

"You think so?"

"Yes. He'll play the official, try to stop us, get a bribe, whatever works. Can we do anything?"

"We don't have much choice. We can circle up anywhere, but that gives them a chance to rest their horses. They can out-wait us. We have to keep moving, they don't."

Roeble nodded. "Best to keep moving, then. They might let us past."

"Aye. And maybe they'll hand out mugs of ale as we go by." Aleria nodded to Cavick, and he snapped his whip. The horses leaned into the traces, and the caravan moved out.

Sure enough, around the next corner a mass of horsemen blocked the road. Except for five in Ferbodean grey, they wore turbans and robes that covered them and flowed down across the backs of their graceful horses, which seemed to have already regained their interest: heads up, ears searching. Several paces to the front stood a big bay with dark mane and tail. A familiar figure in a grey coat and peaked cap sat there, looking down on them. Aleria pulled her wagon right up to him before she signalled the stop.

Pavenkov urged his horse alongside the team so he could look down on Aleria.

As they neared, Jameta regarded the man's horse. She shivered in sympathy at the look of the bit, with long lever arms and sharp spines on either side. She didn't want to see what nastiness was inside the horse's mouth.

"And what have we here?"

Aleria looked up at him from her wagon seat, taking her time. "Good morning, Citizen. A bit out of your range, aren't you?"

"Not at all. Ferbodin's area of influence extends much farther in this direction than you might think."

"Oh, it's an area of influence, is it? I suspect the tribes whose traditional grazing lands cover this area may have other ideas."

"Hmph. Primitives with no idea how to use the land."

"Seems they've been doing all right for a thousand years or so." She shifted on the seat to face him squarely. "But I didn't come to discuss history. I came to trade. What can I sell you?"

"Sell me? You can open your packs and show me you're not carrying any contraband."

"I see. And what would constitute contraband?"

"That's my business. Open the packs and we'll see."

"You know something, Citizen Pavenkov? It doesn't strike me that you have much right to stop me out in the middle of somebody else's country and paw through my packs to see what's worth stealing. I'd say that kind of action slides very close to banditry. And neither my company nor the Ferbodean government takes a real shine to that kind of activity, within your borders or outside them. So I will decline your offer. Will you please ask your men to move off the trail?"

"My men will move off the trail when I tell them to..."

"And I'm asking you to tell them. Is there something about that idea you don't understand?"

The Ferbodean was about to answer when a clicking noise stopped him. Aleria's Third pistol was pointed straight at his chest.

Jameta reined her mount aside to be clear of any firing and slid her hand onto her own gun. The Roan had other ideas. His ears were back, and he kept trying to sidle around the wagon to get near the Ferbodean. Jameta held him in, leaning forward to whisper in his ear. "I don't like him either, but now isn't the time."

Aleria's mein did not change. "Why don't you pull in alongside me here, and we'll stroll over to your men. You can ask them politely to remove themselves from the public road. Then we'll go on our merry little way, and you can go back to where you have the authority to act in such a high-handed manner."

She moved her aim up to his face. "Now."

He snarled and wrenched his horse around. Blood appeared on its lips, and it tossed its head in pain but obeyed, swinging in beside Aleria's wagon.

Cavick pulled ahead, and the caravan followed, staying in tight formation, the guards patrolling either side. Erlon was out to the right, keeping his rifle in sight and maintaining a clear field of fire. Jameta slid out just to Aleria's left for a clean shot at Pavenkov. The Roan also had a view of his enemy and he settled into the position, ears still back, the whites of his eyes glinting.

When they reached the mounted troops, Pavenkov made a sweeping motion with his hand and the men pulled aside. The caravan marched down the lane between the double line of horsemen like monarchs on parade.

Once the last horse had cleared, Aleria's pistol disappeared. "There you are, Pavenkov. That wasn't so difficult, was it? Off you go. And if you think a pitched battle against half a dozen Double-S rifles and assorted other weapons is a good idea, then today you are lucky. Here we are."

He cursed and jammed his spurs into his steed's torn sides and galloped over to his men, who swarmed around him.

Aleria signalled the wagons to continue and stared back along the caravan, with Jameta at her front wheel and Erlon curving in from his flank position.

"What do you think he'll do now?"

The guard Captain glanced over his shoulder. "Not sure. There's a little pocket in the rocks up to the right that's defendable."

Aleria turned. "Spread that up the line will you?"

"Right." Before she left, though, Jameta paused. "Those men aren't cavalry."

Erlon glanced back again. "They are not."

Aleria looked back. "Maybe we're still too close to Ferbodin for him to try anything completely illegal."

"Nice thought, but it doesn't bode well for the future." Jameta went to do her task, keeping an eye on the mob milling behind them. But Pavenkov had other plans. He trotted his men off up the trail towards the west.

The caravan settled down to its walking pace.

The Trouble with Tents

Now they travelled deeper into the desert. Roeble's map came out more in the evenings, but Jameta and Lavan found it harder to reconcile what it said with what their eyes told them of the terrain.

The road was becoming rougher as well. In places they had to harness the Roan to each of the heavier wagons to pull them through deep washouts. Here, Jameta was pressed into service, as riding him bareback was the best way to control him, instead of trying to run alongside in the uneven footing with driving reins. But he pulled willingly, and there was no talk of biting or domination around the campfires at night. Besides, he was too tired.

After two days of this, Aleria looked harried. "Roeble, we've got to get rid of these wagons."

"That we do. The river's the obvious place."

"Is it?"

"The ferrymen will be happy to charge us to look after them, since the river will be too low for their ferries to work."

"How far to the ford?"

They hauled the map out and decided, as near as they could make out, that it was only two more days.

Aleria grunted. "As long as we don't have a hill like the one down into Oudonsford, we'll be fine."

Roeble grinned. "Then we'll be fine. The land is flat, and from what I've heard the river valley isn't deep at all."

20. Attack

It was the third day away from the mines, and they were passing through a low but rocky range of hills. The weather continued hot and dry, and the wind from behind was pushing the dust over all of them. It was the kind of day that everyone hunkered down in the saddle or on the wagon seat and endured. Except Erlon, who was out patrolling the immediate area as usual, and Levan, who was out of sight on a similar mission.

Jameta had just reported in to Aleria with nothing to say, and Doe was strolling along beside the lead wagon, snatching a bite of grass where she found any.

Aleria looked around, her nose wrinkling. "I don't like this canyon. Smells of ambush." Her head came up. "What the hell...?"

Jameta looked back. There was trouble with the remuda. A horse reared, dust erupting. A familiar horse. Her heart sank.

"And the Roan picks now to put on a scene? We don't have time for this. Jameta, get over there."

Jameta pushed Doe to a gallop along the line of wagons.

At the remuda, Stilet was wrestling the Roan out of the line. "He's putting up a hell of a fuss. Keeps wanting to turn back!" The Roan's ears were pinned to his neck, and he kept staring back along the trail, his nostrils flaring.

She slipped off Doe and tied her hackamore rope to the last horse in line. "You got the big saddle?"

"Right away." He handed her the Roan's lead rope and dragged the Roan's saddle and bridle out of the wagon.

They stood aside and rigged him as the last wagons went by. He had calmed as they worked, but the moment she swung up on the saddle he turned back along the road again. She looked down at the wrangler. "If he wants to go back, I should go back. He's caught a scent of something he doesn't like, and I think I know what it is. You go ahead."

Stilet jogged after the departing wagons, and she gave the Roan his head.

He fired up to a gallop, straight up the trail. The dust of the wagons had faded away, and now she could see. The path was straight and flat here, so she let him run it off. "Just to that next bend,

Hammerhead, and then we're heading for the caravan, no matter what bee bit your butt."

They rounded the corner. Down the road a mob of men trotted towards her. They were too closely packed to count, and the moment they saw her they surged into a gallop.

She hauled on the reins and her horse spun on his hind legs. As his forefeet hit the road, terror drove her heels into his sides, and he leapt ahead.

"All right, lad. We found out what the wind was bringing you. Let's see how you run."

They thundered up the road, soon catching up to the tail of the caravan. As she neared, she imitated Aleria's shrill whistle and swung her hand in the signal to close up. "Go, go, go! Enemy behind!" She pulled out and galloped beside the wagons, urging them to hurry as she passed.

By the time she came alongside the front wagon, everyone was watching her anxiously. Roeble was galloping on the other side and Erlon was pulling in from point.

"Riders after us. Twenty or thirty. Coming fast."

Erlon looked at the canyon walls "No room to circle up here. Keep going." He kicked his horse to a gallop back along the line.

Aleria shouted over the rattling of the wagon and the pounding hooves. "We have to find a wider spot to circle. Let's move!"

Away they went. Jameta loped alongside Aleria's wagon, her place during an attack. "There were no grey coats, but Pavenkov has to be back there somewhere. The Roan does't put up that kind of fuss over locals."

"That bastard probably sicced them on us to teach us a lesson." Aleria stared around. "Well, it isn't a lesson unless somebody learns it." They were coming out of the canyon, now, and the walls were sweeping away, but boulders scattered over the rugged valley floor, and there was still nowhere to get off the road. Looking back through the dust, Jameta could glimpse the riders catching up.

Aleria stood up in the bounding wagon and looked around. A wheel hit a hole, and she dropped, grabbing the seat to stay aboard. "This is useless. They'll run us down and cut us apart like wolves on a herd of deer. Look for somewhere flat, even if it's small."

Jameta raised her eyes and pushed the Roan forward. Freed of the dust, she could see the enemy better. They were almost up to the last wagon. She sent her horse lunging down the trail. Then, ahead and to the right, she saw what they were looking for: almost flat, free of boulders, just off the road. She reined up in front of it and waved. Aleria waved back, and leaned over to shout to her driver.

Then there was another shout. Lavan, his horse flat out, raced up along the wagons. She urged the Roan back, reaching the lead wagon just as he did.

He pounded alongside, his horse lathered. "We've lost a wagon!"

"What?"

He indicated back along the caravan. "Fourth from the back. He stopped. No idea why."

"Shit! That's Vracha. He doesn't even have a guard." Aleria looked at Jameta, who pointed to the spot ahead. "Right. We'll circle up."

The lead teamster hauled on the reins and the wagons pulled off the road, curling into a tight defensive circle. Jameta caught a nod from Aleria and reined the Roan back along the line.

Erlon pulled in beside her. "What?"

"We've lost a wagon. Vracha stopped. Don't know why."

He winced and pulled his rifle from its scabbard. On the other side of the wagons, Lavan was doing the same. "You follow, but not too close. If we get into trouble, I want the message to get back."

She nodded and edged the Roan in behind Erlon's slower steed.

Back along their track they could see the wagon, circled by a mob of horsemen. As they galloped nearer the bandits closed in, jumping from their horses to swarm over the load.

Erlon cursed and slapped his horse with the ends of the reins. He swerved over beside Lavan. "Don't shoot straight ahead. Turn sideways."

Lavan raised his eyebrows but nodded. They thundered on.

About the time the bandits looked up from their loot, Erlon eased to the right. Lavan mirrored his move, and they opened fire. There was a scurry towards horses, and robed riders began to flood away from the stream of bullets that tore into them.

Then, over the rattle of rifle fire, there came the "boom" of a musket. Erlon's horse hesitated, then slowly, ever so slowly, began to fall, his head going down, then his forelegs. His shoulder plowed into the ground, throwing up a cloud of dirt and dust. The rider arced forward, and Jameta winced as Erlon's head aimed for the hard prairie soil.

Then he tucked into a ball, his rifle safely across his middle, and somersaulted, coming up standing. He shook his head and checked his rifle, peering down the barrel. Then he raised the gun to fire again.

Now the enemy riders had taken stock and realized that only two guns faced them, one on the ground. Their leader harangued them, and they circled around, gathering speed and nerve for a charge. Erlon's head swivelled. He was too far from the safety of the wagon, not close enough to Jameta for a pickup. He turned to face the charging horsemen, slapping a fresh cylinder into his rifle.

Jameta could count. There were still about twenty horsemen. Eight shots in that cylinder. His sword was sheathed on his saddle, several paces away where the wounded horse was struggling to rise.

She charged.

She dug her heels into the Roan's ribs and raised her voice in a wordless scream of anger, despite the fear constricting her breath and twisting her guts.

The call echoed from her left, and Lavan swooped in as well, curving around the enemy to strike at their flank as they rode past him.

Faced with this triple attack, the bandits faltered. Erlon's steady shooting was taking its toll.

If Jameta hadn't been so frightened she would have grinned. Despite his wild attack, Lavan was making little difference, aiming left-handed from a galloping horse, and she was unarmed, but the bandits didn't know that. She urged her mount to further exertion and yelled again.

The leading bandits hesitated, sitting back in the saddle, tightening their reins. Then they cut left, slipping down behind the bulk of their horses for protection from the gunfire and peeling away. One man on a limping horse followed more slowly.

Lavan shouted in glee and pulled his mount to a stop as the bandits fled. He raised his rifle, pointing between his horse's ears, and fired a parting shot.

The animal dropped to its knees.

The surprised rider fell forward, ending in an ungainly sprawl at the feet of the Roan, who had just pulled up, snorting and stamping.

Erlon jogged forward. "I believe I mentioned not shooting straight ahead."

Lavan got up and stumbled to his horse, which was clambering to its feet, shaking its head and snorting.

"He's probably deaf right now. Don't worry about him. Check your rifle for dirt in the barrel. Then get Rogas. He's back on his feet, so he might be all right. Jameta. The driver."

She reined her horse over to the stranded wagon. It sat atilt, something dragging underneath inside the slanted right rear wheel. The driver lay sprawled on his stomach across the seat, his spear driven into the ground in front of the wagon box. As she rode up he stirred.

Jameta hoped the Roan would ground-tie as she dropped the reins and jumped onto the wagon. Vracha was groaning, blood pouring down the side of his head and drenching his shirt. She took a closer look and her stomach lurched. A sword slash had glanced off his skull, removing the top half of his ear, and spent itself on his shoulder, which curled in at an awkward angle.

Erlon vaulted up a moment later. "How bad is it?"

"Banged head, cut ear, broken collarbone, I'd say. Lots of blood. We need to tie this up."

Erlon had his dagger out, stripping the driver's shirt away. "You keep watch. Lavan!"

The rider jogged over.

"How's Rogas?"

"Bullet in the shoulder. Went in, didn't come out. He can walk, but slowly. Bleeding is almost stopped. Wound's dirty."

"My kit off the saddle. Then leave him and get back to the caravan and report. Tell them we've got a broken rear axle and we need a stretcher. And..." He scanned the surrounding canyon. It was empty. "...two more rifles."

"Got it." Lavan brought the kit, mounted and galloped away.

"What can I do?"

"Sit behind him and pull his arm back into normal position. I've got to patch the wound before I strap the shoulder. Quicker we do this the better. Once he wakes up fully, he's not going to be a happy soldier."

With deft fingers the guard Captain folded a pad from the torn shirt and used it to hold a patch of clean cotton on the shoulder wound. Then he tore long strips and twisted them in a figure eight around the wounded shoulder, across the man's back, and around the good arm. When he tightened it, the shoulder was pulled back into its proper position, and Jameta could feel the collarbone slip into place under her fingers.

By the time he finished, the patient was groaning with every touch, his head weaving in confused agony. Erlon took a quick glance at the head wound and shrugged. "Not pretty, but as long as his

125

skull's all right, it won't kill him." He fashioned a bandage from the remnants of the shirt and fresh cotton from his kit.

Meanwhile, Jameta had been keeping her eyes on their surroundings. "Here they come."

His head snapped up. "Who?"

"Sorry. Our people."

"Thank you. Keep an eye out for anyone who tries to cut us off from the caravan."

The wounded teamster was trying to sit on his own, so she stood on the wagon seat, her knees supporting his back, and kept watch. The only tribesmen in evidence were two bodies bleeding into the sandy soil nearby.

The rescue party showed up and dove into their work with little conversation. They used a lever to lift the wagon level and put a temporary clamp on the broken axle. Others retied the sword-slashed tarp to cover the load again. Lavan dismounted and checked the draft horses. The stretcher-bearers eased the driver off the wagon and started off to camp with him.

Relieved of that duty, Jameta joined Lavan at his task, then reported to Erlon. "No damage. The off horse may be favouring one hind leg, but we won't know until we start moving."

He nodded. "Then let's try it. Ready, boys?"

Cavick nodded. "Go slow. That's not going to last long, but we don't wanna unload the wagon."

"You want to take it?"

"No, I'll walk behind and keep an eye on it. Droser'll drive if you got better things to do."

"Thanks." He handed the reins to the driver who clambered up.

Jameta jumped to the ground and went to Erlon's horse, which was standing, head down, dirty blood soaking his chest and leg. She took his reins and urged him forward a step, watching his movement.

She looked up as Erlon approached. "He's putting weight on the leg, and there's no more blood. If he can do it, I'll walk him beside the wagon. You take the Roan."

He lengthened the stirrup leathers and swung up on the horse, who tossed his head but then was still. Erlon glared down at her. "What the hell were you doing?"

"I was attacking."

"Jameta, you didn't even draw your pistol."

"I forgot." She shrugged. "There was no choice. When your horse went down...no choice." She looked up, tried to smile. "It worked, didn't it?"

"I suppose." He sat, looking at her.

"So, shall I lead him with the wagon?"

He jerked his head. "Huh...? Oh, yes. We need to get him to the caravan." He scanned the area. "No counterattack. I doubt if there'll be one, now." He gave a lopsided grin. "You rather scared them."

"Your rifle and Lavan's wild attack scared them. I was just the comic relief."

"Hmm." He firmed his hold on the Roan's reins and looked down at her. "You and I need to talk."

"That will be a change."

"Yes, maybe it will." He pulled the reins more sharply than necessary. The Roan complained with a snort but trotted off obediently.

When the halting procession reached the circled wagons, Aleria was pacing out in front, Roeble standing calmly, waiting, muscular arms akimbo. Erlon jogged forward to report, and Jameta led the wounded horse through an opening in the circle.

Stilet appeared immediately. "Lotta blood, there."

"Took a musket bullet. He's walking decently, though. With a limp."

The wrangler regarded the drooping animal. "Straight from the front?

"No, slightly from the left, I'd say."

Stilet moved to the side, glancing at her.

She watched him, trying to remember. "Whoa. From about that angle. Erlon was cutting right to go around them." She grinned. "And keeping his rifle barrel away from his horse's ears."

"Hmm. That can be tough in a straight charge. I hear Lavan learned sumpin' today." He ran his hand over the leg beside the wound. "Range?"

"About a hundred yards, I'd say."

"Musta missed the bone. Smaller horse, it woulda gone right through." He felt around the back of the horse's leg. "It's in there somewhere. Might not cause any problem if it don't get infected." He wiped his hands on his pant legs. "I'll wash him up, put on a bandage if I can get one to stay that high on his shoulder. We won't be goin' far tonight. If he can walk tomorrow, we'll take him, If he can't...?" He shook his head. "Rogas is a good mount."

She nodded, a lump in her throat. *Erlon loves that horse. They've done a lot of miles together.* She went to find the guard Captain.

Erlon was where she expected him: patrolling the outer perimeter. "How is he?"

"Stilet says the bullet is probably not too far from the surface at the back of the leg. If it doesn't infect, we leave it. We'll see how he is tomorrow."

Erlon's face remained stoic, but she noted the relaxing of his shoulders.

"Any action?"

He shook his head. "We're only a few miles from El Sibh, where we cross the river, but with the broken wagon and the wounded horse, it will take more than a day. Vracha would appreciate a smooth trip as well, and the roads aren't great. We're fine here for the night. We can dry camp. There's lots of water soon."

"Fair enough. Are you staying on my horse?"

He looked down at her. "He's your horse now, is he?"

She shrugged. "You can borrow him until yours heals up."

He leaned forward and patted the Roan's cheek. "I may take you up on that offer. He's a decent ride."

"I'm the one that's been telling everyone that, remember?"

He straightened. "Until he bites someone, we'll all pretend he's a reformed character." He reined the Roan around and trotted off along his beat.

She went and saddled Doe. *My duty is on patrol, no matter what.* When she came out of the circle of wagons she trotted over to the Roan and turned alongside, looking up at Erlon for instructions.

He returned her gaze longer that necessary. "Where are you off to?"

"Thought I should take a ride around before sundown. Anywhere special?"

He checked the area then pointed. "The only problem spot would be that low copse of trees over there. I wouldn't go in. Circle around it and look for tracks."

"I'll do that. Then I'll sweep west and north."

"Good. I'll send Lavan south. Can't see the bandits coming in from the river. Too many people at El Sibh."

She raised her eyebrows but said nothing.

"All right. I'll send him east as well."

She nodded and rode out. It was a tense patrol, and she fought to keep her mind on her work. Thoughts kept creeping in, distracting her. *What does he want to talk about? What did I do? I don't even know if it was good or bad.*

She kneed Doe to a trot, remembering her training. *They could be watching. Change course, change gait. Don't be predictable. Go left when the normal thing would be to go right. Play with their minds. Muddle their thinking.*

Jameta finished circling the grove, the trees hardly tall enough to deserve the name but thick enough to hide a man on foot. She concentrated but found no tracks. Bringing Doe up to a lope, she headed west, waving to Erlon as she went by. *Easy scouting where it's so flat and bare.*

Then she remembered. The week before, Erlon had snuck into camp over what everyone thought was flat prairie. Later he took them out and showed them the small dips, stands of grass and dry water channels that criss-crossed even the flattest stretches.

She watched more carefully, but nothing attracted her attention. She circled outside the scene of the afternoon's battle, noting the direction the bandits had come from and departed to. She resisted the urge to follow their trail. *Not without several rifles behind me.* Then she realized; the bodies were gone. She stared around, but saw nothing.

As the sun sank into the desert haze she turned and headed back to camp, satisfied that nothing stirred in the immediate vicinity. She reported her lack of information to Erlon, and he nodded. "Lavan just came in. Same thing. I guess we put the fear into them."

"The fear of what?"

He grinned. "That's a good question. Doesn't matter at the moment. As long as they leave us alone."

"I'll bet on that bird. Supper soon?"

He shrugged. "I don't interfere with that end of things. I eat when I'm fed."

"Good policy. I remember Aleria's rule. He who complains cooks the next meal."

They rode around the caravan in companionable silence. She glanced over at him. *Any time now.*

He cleared his throat. "I said we would talk."

"Yes, you did."

"Now isn't the time, but we will." He turned in the saddle and looked down at her. "But there's something I do have to say right away."

Here it comes. She looked up at him.

"You can't do things like that."

She had no response.

"Jameta, I mean it. That was completely foolhardy, charging those men, unarmed. They had swords and guns. I know they're only those old flintlocks, but as my horse found out, they're very effective."

"I had to go. You were on the ground with eight shots. Your sword was too far away. Lavan had...what...three shells left?"

She had never seen Erlon angry. "You were unarmed!"

She tried to smile. "You can't argue with success." She raised a hand to stop his response. "Erlon, you must understand. There are times when you can't turn around and ride away, no matter how smart it would be. Have you ever felt like that?"

"...well..."

"In other words, yes."

"Yes, but I was well armed and the person I was rescuing was more important to the expedition."

"Exactly. I was riding the biggest, nastiest horse in the desert, and so far my usefulness to the expedition hasn't been huge. You, on the other hand, will be needed more and more." She shrugged. "It's an easy calculation."

"No! This isn't a calculation. You did something you should never have done because of your emotional attachment to me!"

"That's right. And nothing I hear or see from you makes me believe that it was a mistake. So you can argue till your skin turns blue, or scream and yell, but it won't change my mind." She watched the emotions play on his face. "Or you could stop avoiding whatever it is you're going to tell me one day before we both die of old age."

"I'm not avoiding it." He sighed, and the tension went out of him. Now his voice was calm. "I'm being very careful, here. The next month could make all the difference to this enterprise. I don't want to change anything that might jeopardize that. That's why Aleria trusts us not to have problems."

"Like you and I having a huge blowup because of something you did in your long-forgotten past."

"Exactly. We can't afford ourselves the luxury."

"But once we start for home?"

"Then it's business as usual, and if you want to boot me off the caravan, it won't be a problem."

"What do you mean, boot you? The caravan needs you a lot more than they need me."

"I'm beginning to wonder."

21. A Social Slip

They made the river at noon, two days later. Jameta walked Doe beside the remuda, Erlon's gelding limping behind them. Up ahead the road wound in easy loops down a wide valley and came out at water level where the remains of an ancient town spread along both sides of the stream. Only a few of the ruined buildings were occupied, now. The rest were drowned in a mat of refreshing greenery that stretched as far as she could see, up and down the river.

Adobe houses thatched with mats of reeds stood in compounds with low mud walls. Broken stone pylons and disconnected arches, the remains of an ancient bridge, stepped across the wide, shallow stream. On the hill above, the vacant windows and tattered walls of a fortress crumbled back into the dirt from which they came.

She let Rogas splash down to the water to drink and sat looking around. Roeble's horse was drinking nearby.

"Welcome to what used to be El Sibh."

"This was once an important place."

Roeble shrugged. "You run into this all over. Whole towns or cities, empty and ruined. No idea why. River course changed, climate changed, politics changed..."

"What's that over there? Out in the river? A bunch of small islands, or what?"

He grinned. "That's where we're going." He reined his horse back to the road, and she followed.

"You won't tell me?"

"Oh, no. I'm going to watch you discover it for yourself. That's much more fun."

She nudged Doe ahead. "Then stand back." She grinned back. "I'll try not to disappoint."

As they rode closer she continued to stare. A curve of the river created a backwater, and the surface was covered with small, flat islands, each one walled up above the water with a fence of interwoven sticks. A reed hut occupied one end of each, and the rest of the area was given over to yard and workspace. Huge woven baskets dotted the yards, storing...*whatever needs to be stored, I suppose.* Pudgy flat-bottomed boats were pulled in alongside, and Jameta saw a few of the same paddling between the islands. A woman was inching along in a completely round boat, moving ahead by pulling the paddle through the water towards her.

"How can they live there? Doesn't the river flood?"

"They must move onshore in the spring. The structures look temporary."

"Why would anyone stay in a place like that?"

"For safety. Which is why we'll be leaving the wagons here."

"Is the river shallow enough, or will we float them out?"

"It must be shallow. From the dung piles, I'd say they put their cattle on the islands at night."

Jameta regarded the stocky trader. "You've never been here before."

"No, but I have heard the stories and seen similar in other places."

"I understand why you travel. This is fantastic. I've never seen anything like it."

"Once in a while you see something that makes up for the last ten days of dust and heat."

She grinned. "If it was next door, you wouldn't appreciate it."

"Huh. If I didn't make such a good living this way, I'd be happy to look much closer to home for my entertainment."

"I don't think so."

He turned to her. "You don't."

"No."

He raised his eyebrows. "You make a sweeping statement like that, and you're not going to give me any more?"

"Only if you want me to." She grinned at him, challenging.

"You're using merchant tricks on a merchant. You always meant to tell me, but now you're being coy."

She shrugged. "I find it gentler to speak about people if I first get them to ask my opinion. They accept it more readily."

"And why is it important that I accept what you're about to tell me?"

"The fact that I'm on the river side, and it's a three-foot drop from the road into the mud?"

"All right. I've been sufficiently set up. Please, O Seeress, tell me my innermost thoughts and desires."

She tossed him another grin. "I have no idea of your innermost thoughts and I'd like to leave your desires out of it, but if you didn't enjoy this, you wouldn't be doing it. I don't mean you have to enjoy it all. I'm talking about the whole idea. The merchant traveller, returning with exotic goods and more exotic stories from faraway lands." She glanced sideways. "And staying out of the way of your wife for large chunks of time."

He stared at her. "So it's my relationship with my wife, now? What do you know about that?"

"Nothing but what Aleria tells me."

"Which can't be much. She's only met Delestra a few times."

"You know what I'm not hearing?"

"What do you mean?"

"When I say something that touches a delicate spot, I can tell a lot by what the person doesn't say. If it's an honest person, what they don't deny is often as telling as what they do deny."

"Ah, but you're dealing with a merchant."

"An honest one. At least with his friends. We are friends, or we wouldn't be having this conversation."

"And if we weren't friends, we soon would be, because I don't think I'd want you for an enemy."

"And I feel the same way about you. So there."

"What do you mean, 'So there'? You sound like you just won an argument."

She grinned again. "I lost track of the score. It sounded like a good time to go for the win."

He leaned back as if to get a wider look at her. "You do this for entertainment?"

"Are you entertained?"

He shook his head. "This has been a longer trip than I had thought it was. I've jumped the wagon tongue already."

"Jumped the wagon tongue?"

"It's an expression we use for someone who has been on the trail too long and has lost his sense of perspective."

"Ah. Like a horse that gets over the tongue and into the other horse's space."

"Exactly. Quite often that's exactly what people in that state do. Mentioning no names at the moment."

"Well, don't worry. You haven't intruded on my space in any way. I'm sure you're fit to pull for many a long day, yet."

* * *

The trouble with tents is that sometimes you hear things you shouldn't. Or at least that others don't want you to hear. *Or maybe they want you to hear, but they didn't want to be the one to tell you. I have to remember I'm dealing with devious, intelligent people, here.*

In any case, what she heard between Roeble and Aleria later that evening was...instructive. She had been walking around to the front of the tent she shared with Aleria, intending to go inside, when she heard voices. Not wanting to intrude, she hesitated, just long enough to recognize Roeble's deep tones.

"Where did you find her?"

There was laughter in Aleria's response. "Jameta got at you, did she?"

"You already knew?"

"No, but the symptoms are always the same."

There was silence, and Jameta wondered what to do. She was about to go forward when Roeble spoke again.

"Aye, she got to me. Flipped me over, rolled me around, then slapped me on the shoulder and told me I was fine."

"Sounds serious."

"It wasn't. It was all perfectly polite. Friendly, even."

"That sounds about right."

"And she does this to everyone?"

"No." Aleria chuckled. "Only people she really likes."

Jameta had decided to leave, but the conversation ran on.

"Why do that to your friends?"

Aleria was silent a moment. "It's the only way she has of making sure you aren't afraid of her."

"Afraid? Of little Jameta?"

"That's right. Afraid."

"Oh. Yes, I see what you mean. But after that little chat, aren't I more likely to be afraid of her than not?"

"I don't think so. If you've been through what I think you have – and your description was so apt it must have been like that – she has just picked you up and twirled you around to show you how strong she is, and then put you back on your feet and patted you on the back to show that she's your friend and she would never harm you."

"You're serious."

"I am. In case it hadn't come to your attention, she has a dangerous ability that few people have..."

Voices came from behind the next tent, and Jameta fled, her cheeks burning. *People who listen around corners never hear good of themselves. But I wasn't around a corner. I should have gone in and faced them from the beginning. Do I act like that? But we were only chatting. I didn't mean...*

...all right, Jameta. What did you mean? You said what you said. Nobody twisted your arm. He was being a perfect gentleman, and you – how did Aleria put it? – picked him up and twirled him around.

She turned back to the tent, where the trader was just coming out.

"Roeble, I must talk to you."

He looked at her, frowning. "Is something wrong?"

"Yes, and I want to right it. Can we take a walk?"

They strolled past the guard and out into the moonlit desert. After a moment, he stopped. "We have to stay near camp. What is it?"

"Roeble, I want to apologize. I went too far this afternoon, and you have a right to be upset."

"I'm not upset."

"Well, I know you aren't, but you are, aren't you?"

"Now, that one surpasses even my wife at her worst. What's wrong?" He turned to get her face clear in the moonlight. "Were you listening around a corner?"

"No. Well, yes. There wasn't a corner. I was only going to come into the tent, but then..."

"Ah. Then you heard us talking about you, and you didn't know whether to come or go, so you did nothing. Which is usually worse."

"Exactly. And, as I should have expected, I didn't hear much good about myself."

He chuckled.

"I don't find this funny. Oh, I can see why you would. But I don't." She stared out into the moonlit desert. "Why do you find this funny?"

"The irony of it. I gather you do this to other people all the time. You've now had it done to you, and you don't like it so much, do you?"

"I don't." She turned to him. "Oh, my feelings aren't hurt, or anything like that. But until I heard what Aleria said, I didn't realize what I was doing."

"You didn't?"

"Well, yes, but not in those terms."

He chuckled again. "But now I apply what you said this afternoon. There are certain things you are not denying."

"Exactly. Roeble, it's important to me that you understand this. I'm just as hard on myself as I am on everyone else. Harder. I know my own weaknesses better than yours. And the problem is, I forgive everyone else, because a weakness is a cause, not a choice. It makes you what you are, and it's not your fault. But I don't seem to be able to apply that to myself."

"You're pretty hard on yourself."

"I'm cynical about my own objectives. It has a good result. I try to act correctly because I'm always looking over my own shoulder. But sometimes, I...forget. I get chatting with someone I like, whose strength I respect, and I forget that they might be hurt by what I say."

He slapped her on the shoulder and turned her back towards the camp. "Well, I wasn't hurt by anything you said. Surprised, but not hurt. I didn't see any intent to hurt, so I wasn't bothered."

"There wasn't any attempt to hurt. I promise you that."

"Right. No attempt to hurt. Maybe a little showing off at my expense."

"No!...well, maybe."

"Fair enough. We all need a chance to show off now and again, and if our friends have to take the fall...well, if they're good friends, they should be willing."

"And are we still friends?"

"We have tested each other. We have found strengths and forgiven weaknesses. Our friendship should be stronger. And if my wife, the gods love her, heard me saying such a thing to a young, pretty girl...well, let's just say a winter caravan to Aesmark would be a good alternative to life at home."

"Would I like your wife?"

"Probably. She would like you a lot. Similar sense of...well, hers isn't always humour. You'll have to come visiting when we get home. She was much happier about me going out with Aleria once she met her."

"And having Ranked friends doesn't hurt? Even only Esteemed ones like me?"

"There is a little bit of that, yes. Do you blame her?"

"I shouldn't. The ones who pull the Ranking system down are those who have it and worry too much about it."

"I'd have to think about that, but coming from your perspective, that's a good point."

"In other words, you don't agree, but it's better if I think that way, so you're not arguing."

"Precisely." He laughed and clapped her on the shoulder again. "And next time I stab you in the back, I'll make sure I'm not in a tent."

22. Out of the Frying Pan

So the Dalmyn horses emerged dripping from the ford of the Bel river, their wagons left nestled together on an unused island by the western bank, looked after by Vracha and Rogas, who were both already making friends among the local boatmen.

The trail was less distinct on this side of the river: more a wide swath trampled down by the many herds that passed. As the caravan gained altitude the sere desert claimed them, and the green of the river valley faded away.

They moved even more cautiously, now, with riders ahead, behind and on the flanks when they could. Guards were doubled at night, and the horses were kept in a portable corral, made with iron rods driven into the ground and ropes tied along the tops. In this climate, the enclosure was moved twice a night to allow the animals better grazing.

Jameta had become even more watchful, so she was pleased, four days later, that she spotted the tribesman before he saw her. She sat her horse in a thick stand of young pines and watched him amble down the trail, unaware of her presence. He was a nondescript young man, dressed in ragged robes, on a mount that didn't look like much: plain and brown and rather spindly. She suppressed the urge to follow him. Better to heed her training and head for higher ground for a better look. She reined Doe around and headed back towards the caravan, pleased with her craft.

Until she saw the second rider above her. He didn't see her, likewise riding along about his own business. She cut down the hill again, walking Doe quietly on the soft pine needles.

There was another rider across the valley. Farther back, but going the same direction. She swung Doe around, but the map in her head told her that the other two riders had her hemmed in. *There will be one behind, of course. I'm being herded! So much for my skills.* She suppressed the urge to run. *Think first. What's going on? They could have attacked, but they didn't. So they want me somewhere. I can go along with that for a while. If I run, we'll never find out what they want. Save that for a last resort.*

The sound of her heart beating filled her head as she rode along. Every time she slid to one side or the other there was a rider, just behind her, moving at her pace. She kept careful watch, but the valley was wide and open. She could still get away any time. *They must know that. What do they want? A meeting, I'd guess.*

They came around a bend in the valley and it became clear. There, in the middle of a wide clearing, was a man in a grey coat on a large bay horse. He was sitting still, reading a map. Or pretending to.

No surprises so far. Now, what does he want? She checked that her pistol was loaded and loose in its holster and rode forward.

He looked up as she approached. "Good afternoon, Citizen. Out for a ride?"

"Checking the area for varmints, bandits, and other riff-raff."

Pavenkov smiled, his rotten teeth spoiling the effect, and turned his horse. "I'll ride along with you. It's pleasant to have company, don't you think?"

"It's always nice to have the right type of company."

"Perhaps you would like to visit my camp?"

"No, I have my duties to attend to. If I were to be late, people might worry."

"This area isn't safe for a young woman alone."

"Why would that be?"

He shrugged. "All sorts of nasty people about." He reined his horse in beside Doe. "A sweet young lady like you needs protection."

She played along. "Oh, I don't think I'll have any problem. My horse is very fast."

"You're not riding that big roan today."

"No, he needs his rest like all the others. And I need mine. He takes a lot of concentration."

"Yes, problem horses do. Like problem people."

She glanced up at him. "Is there a message there for me?"

"There might be. What are you up to?"

"I'm not up to anything. I'm scouting for the caravan."

"You know what I mean, girl."

The bay nudged over, and she allowed Doe to slip aside.

He looked down at her. "Your group made questionable contacts back in the capital city. And now here you are, driving off into territory you have no business visiting. That's enough to make a loyal Ferbodean citizen such as myself suspicious. What trouble are you stirring out here?"

Jameta gave him her most innocent smile. "Not much, as I'm sure you already know. There aren't any people to make trouble with. In fact, I'm not sure we're going to get much trading. If you ask me, we should just go to all the mines and trade with them. They're civilized people. We haven't met any of the natives, yet, but any I've seen don't look like they have much money. We can hardly drive a herd of goats home, now, can we?" She frowned. "Do you know, we were attacked by bandits a few days ago? A whole tribe of them, it looked like. Have you seen any bandits around? Or maybe it's a tribe that doesn't like trading."

"You Galesians have a lot to learn about the desert. These tribes are an untamed element. Likely to take offence at anything. That raid was probably only a warning, telling you they don't want you in their territory. If they wanted to they would have wiped you out."

"I doubt if there were enough of them."

"Possibly a bunch of disaffected young men, looking for fun." He waved his hand at his own escort. "There are plenty of those around. Enough to cause your caravan a lot of trouble."

"Perhaps we should turn around and go back, then."

He glared down at her. "That would be a very good idea. Why don't you suggest it to that woman who leads your caravan?"

She allowed her face to fall. "I already did. Aleria's not interested. She says there's markets out here somewhere, and we're going to find them." She gave him a winsome glance. "Do you know where the markets are?"

"I can tell you there isn't a market in the direction you're going."

"Oh, that's good, then. Thank you. I can tell Aleria, and maybe she'll decide to turn back." She lifted her reins. "Thank you for the information, Citizen Pavenkov. I'm sure we'll see you again." She clucked to Doe, who jumped to a lope so quickly that they were far down the trail before the man had time to react. Jameta glanced over her shoulder, but the Ferbodean was just sitting there, glaring after her.

She scanned the woods, but the outriders were gone. Eyes alert, she galloped back to the caravan to report.

When she had finished, Aleria frowned. "What did he want?"

She grimaced. "Besides me taking a little visit to his camp? He asked me what we were really doing out here. Either he thinks we've come to cause political trouble, or he wants us to think that's what he thinks. If that isn't too complicated."

"No, I understand. He didn't give anything away, then."

"He suggested that the group that attacked us were freelancers looking for trouble and loot. But he's out there, too, shadowing us."

Aleria gave a flat grin. "Here comes Erlon. I don't envy you, telling him what happened."

Erlon pulled up, riding a smaller horse. If he was missing Rogas, he didn't let on. She told her story, with predictable results.

She cut him off before he got started. "Calm down and use your brain. I was never in any danger. Nobody got close enough to stop me. The only thing they could have done was shoot my horse, and then you would have heard the shot and come and rescued me."

"It's rarely that easy."

"But he has showed his hand. We know where he is, and what he's doing. We'll be even more on guard."

He gripped the hilt of his sword, his face thunderous. "You can be sure of that."

* * *

The following day they reached the point where the main caravan route turned south and a smaller branch headed straight east. Jameta, Roeble, and Lavan reached the junction first and sat their horses, waiting for the slower pack animals.

Jameta gazed south, memorizing the skyline, then squinted east, where the thinner trail disappeared in a dusty haze. "What's that way?"

Roeble tossed a hand. "The Horse Fair is two days in that direction. It won't start until the heat lessens even more than this. A month or so, I'd guess. If the timing is right, I want to drop in on our way home."

"Are horses important to us?"

"Not very, but there is much more to the Horse Fair than just horses. Any trader who is anyone will be there. The opportunity for contacts is not to be missed."

She rubbed her hands together. "I'm always ready to look at horses."

He grinned. "Just be careful you don't run into a dealer with more smarts than you have."

"Don't worry. I still prefer my own."

He tilted his head. "Loyalty. A good quality."

"Right up there with diligence." She looked south. "And now we have a new direction to scout. Lavan!"

His head came up.

"Which side do you want today?"

"I'll take the west side." He grinned. "Looks smoother."

"Then I expect you to go farther and be back sooner."

"Yes, boss." He glanced at her. "You've been hanging around Aleria too much."

"That's it. Learning how to be a leader."

"Just what I need. Another woman snapping orders." He kneed his horse ahead.

They trotted together and parted where the scant forest closed in on the trail.

Erlon had taken a wider swing around the rear of their route, and he caught up when they were eating the noon meal. "We're being scouted. Tribesmen again. And not just Pavenkov's little cadre."

Jameta felt a chill go down her spine. "What does that mean?"

"Difficult to tell. If we're going through their territory, they may be only checking up on us."

Roeble shook his head. "Or Pavenkov wants to see which way we turned at the junction."

Aleria frowned. "If Pavenkov has decided to attack us, he'll do a better job of it than that rag-tag bunch that Jameta shooed off."

"It has to be Pavenkov, with a bigger troop." The trader looked at Lavan and Jameta. "Any evidence on our flanks?"

"I didn't see anyone to the west." Lavan scratched his head. "Jameta?"

She frowned. She didn't feel like speaking. She still shook when she thought about the last skirmish. *And the next one is going to be worse.*

Erlon looked around the group. "From this moment, we're at war. Nobody goes outside the sentries at night, because their rifles will have a shell in the firing chamber, and we don't want any accidents. Nobody except the scouts leaves the caravan for any reason during the day. If anyone stops, we all stop."

"Unless there's an ambush."

He nodded to Jameta. "And that's where we come in. There will be no ambush. We stay in touch with each other and Aleria. We change mounts more often. We don't turn aside to investigate anything without backup. If you disappear, we assume an attack." He grinned. "So even if you die out there, you will have saved us simply by not coming back. I hope that's some consolation."

Jameta was feeling cold and dizzy. She gulped and focused her mind. *You will not embarrass yourself and all your friends. Concentrate!*

"Any questions?"

He stood. "Fine. Jameta, you have the fastest horses. I want you to range a bit farther in front, both sides. Lavan, you're at the back. Stilet, keep making a circle within sight of the wagons. I'll be doing the same farther out. Best we can do."

"Erlon."

He turned to her. She tried to keep her voice level.

"You haven't eaten."

"Oh. Right. Sorry. I sometimes forget, when I'm having fun." He dropped a hand on her shoulder and left it there, warm and heavy and comforting. "Thanks for taking care of me."

"When are they likely to attack?" She made it sound casual, practical, hoping her voice didn't waver.

He glanced at Roeble. "I can't see them attacking while we're camped. They must know about our firepower. We're much more vulnerable while we're strung out on the road."

Roeble shrugged. "There's always the traditional dawn raid."

"I'd like to see them try that one."

Aleria stood and stretched. "It all depends on what they want."

"That's right. If they're just tribesmen, they'll hit us during the day, cut a few horses loose and disappear with the loot. If it's Pavenkov, he'll be happy to hit us in camp. Kills more of his men, but keeps us together for a massacre."

Jameta turned down the corners of her mouth. "Well, the answer to my question boils down to, 'Any time they like.' Thank you for the information."

He grinned. "Couldn't have said it better myself."

She knew that the joking was a way of draining the tension, but she still didn't appreciate it. She sought the comfort of her real friends.

But the horses were edgy, too. Doe and Brownie were ganging up on the Roan for a change, and he was pushing the rest of the stock around. She saddled Brownie, checked that her pistol was loaded and started out.

To her inexperienced eye, it was a poor area for an ambush. True, this was not so dry as the real desert, and there were trees and shrubs, but no groups of trees on the valley floor large enough to hide a group of mounted men. *Assuming that they'll be mounted. I should have mentioned that to the others. If they're led by Pavenkov, they might not use nomad tactics. Erlon will think of that.*

Jameta rode through the skimpy forest, trying to look in all directions at once. She used every high point she could, keeping off the skyline, staying dead still for long periods: everything that Erlon had been teaching her. She found nothing.

Farther along, the ridge to her left closed in on the road and grew higher. *Up there would be a great place to see everything. Or to be ambushed. Should I go that far without backup?* She scanned the area thoroughly. *There is less cover for an enemy scout. If I follow that little forest of trees up that wide draw, I can stay hidden. I'll take it slow because of the dust.*

Eyes and ears straining, she started up the little valley. It was steeper than it looked, so she got off and helped her horse, stopping often to look out over the caravan route. Under the trees the slope was less, and she made good time. When she reached the top, she tied Brownie with a single rein in a slipknot and crawled up to the crest, finding a rock to slide in beside.

The valley spread out before her. The caravan looked such an easy target, sprawled along the trail, a cloud of dust announcing its presence to all.

She took the time to search every dip, every clump of trees. There was nothing moving as far back and as far forward as she could see. *Well, that's good. I wonder...*she turned and looked over the ridge.

The hills stepped ruggedly down away from her, a series of rocky ridges that stretched out to the east. The valleys between were greener than those along the caravan trail, with trees showing their tops above the ridges. Farther out there was nothing but haze, although the ground seemed lighter and smoother. It was too misty to tell. She filed that away as a fact to report and crept back to her horse.

Once again she moved with utmost care, and by the time she returned to the trail she knew she had been gone long enough. She took a short swing to the right on her return, but curved in to the front of the train as soon as she got close.

Aleria rode at the front, her pistol in her hand, watching Jameta pull up. "Anything to report?"

"Nothing moving as far as I can see. That ridge is closing in on us from the east."

"What's on the other side?"

"The land's a little greener, and it slopes away to the east. Then...I can't tell. It's very hazy out there. Flatter. Could be lighter in colour."

Aleria aimed her pistol at a bush, held it steady as she rode past. "Sooner or later we're going to get to the real desert. Sand dunes."

"That could be it. Of course, I've never seen a real desert."

"You have that experience to look forward to."

"I look forward to seeing it. From a distance."

"Couldn't agree more."

Jameta looked back along the caravan. "Horses coming. Two of them. Fast."

Aleria glanced over her shoulder. "If there's an attack coming, is there somewhere defendable nearby?"

"The ground is getting smoother, so there aren't any canyons we could hole up in. I made it up to that ridge through a wide draw that's full of trees."

"Do you think we could get over and not be seen?"

"If they weren't too close."

"We'll keep that as an option."

Lavan galloped in, his horse lathered and blowing, the rider in a similar state. "We've got trouble."

Erlon soon caught up. "This looks like the real attack. There's about fifty riders behind us, coming straight down the trail. They're a ways back but catching up. Jameta, what are the options ahead?

Jameta quailed at the thought that her inexpert opinion could mean life or death, but she kept her chin up and her voice firm, describing their possible escape route.

Erlon didn't ask any questions, waiting only long enough for the last packers to catch up and hear their orders. "This needs better horse control than fighting ability. Split the caravan. Everybody on foot leads two pack animals. Stilet, take the rest of the remuda. Lavan, change horses and go back. Catch us the other side of the ridge. Jameta, take Doe and the Roan behind Brownie. The last thing we want is a horse battle in the middle of this.

"We need to spread out so we don't raise a column of dust. Make your way up through that little forest, cross the top in those rocks and meet on the other side. Aim for that crag sticking out. If you're not through the forest when the enemy passes, hide. If they spot us, the rifles will hold the ridge while the rest get away."

The caravan started out in the new formation. Reaching the draw they turned aside, and Erlon stayed behind to clear all evidence of their passing from the trail. Meanwhile the crew tugged their charges up the steep draw to the sheltering trees.

Jameta came last, keeping the Roan out of the way of the other animals. Her two light horses, unencumbered, clambered up easily, but the big packhorse was carrying the heaviest load, and the ground continually broke away under his hooves.

Once in the safety of the forest, Jameta looked back. The Roan's deeply gouged trail pointed an accusing finger straight towards her. She waved Erlon ahead, tied her charges to a tree and went back to brush sticks and leaves over the worst of it. As she made her way higher, she could see the dust cloud of their enemies approaching. It was too late to get over the ridge, so she moved the horses into the deep shade of the trees and hoped they would stay still.

Sure enough, the attackers galloped along the trail, passing the caravan's exit point without a glance. She counted fifty-two of them, all on frisky desert horses except for the second man in line: a taller individual, dressed in robes like the rest, on a bay stallion with dark mane and tail. *And we know who that is. Now he's trying to hide, is he? I can guess why.*

After the danger was past she untied her horses and led them away through the trees. It was a difficult scramble because of the rocks and uneven footing, but finally they were clear of the forest and over the ridge. She swung up on Brownie's back and trotted towards the spire of rock. The whole caravan was waiting for her.

"Everyone here?"

"We are now." Aleria peered up at her. "What happened to you?"

"We had a bit of trouble getting up to the trees. I went back to sweep our trail, then had to wait while they went by."

"Get a count?"

"Fifty-two. And you know who the leader was."

Aleria nodded. "No surprise there. What's wrong with the Roan?"

She looked back, "The Roan? What's wrong with him?"

"He's limping. Near foreleg."

"Drat. He might have pulled a muscle climbing that hill. He's load is pretty heavy and he slipped around a lot."

"Well, I hope he's up to it. Once Erlon gives the all-clear we move."

Erlon was loping down the hill from behind. When he got there, he pushed to the front and faced them. "We're not out of the woods yet. We need to go farther east." He turned his horse and moved on.

They all followed, downhill now, through the rocks and into a jumble of canyons. Jameta kept scanning their surroundings. She began to see openings ahead, and soon clear sand was showing more and more on their left.

They came down out of the rocks and stopped, confronted by a blank expanse of dunes, reaching out until they faded in the haze. To left and right the rocks also tapered off, leaving them stranded on a point of land with nowhere to go.

Lavan's horse scrabbled on the rock as he panted down from behind. "They've turned back. Once they start looking, they'll see where we left the trail. Can't help it."

Aleria looked at Roeble, then Erlon. "Anywhere we can fort up?"

He stared left, then right. "This place is too exposed. I think there's another canyon over..." He stopped.

A rider appeared, right where he was pointing, trotting out of the rocks and onto the sand. Behind that rider was another. And another. A shrill whistle sounded from the left. They turned to see a second file of riders appearing as if emerging out of solid rock.

They rode the proud horses of the desert nomads, their tack festooned with tassels. The men wore tattered robes that covered them from head to toe, only their swarthy faces showing. The two lines paraded out, the leader followed by a standard-bearer.

"I hope that's not what I think it is."

Roeble shook his head. "It's a horse skull with horsehair tassels."

Jameta grinned shakily. "Glad of that."

The two lines met, and the riders turned their mounts as one to stand on the top of the dune regarding the caravan impassively. Their horses stopped prancing and stood like rocks.

Erlon reined his mount to the side. "Pull the pack animals against that rock face over there. Those on foot set a guard around them. Those of us on horse will charge the centre the moment they attack. I'll lead. Aleria and Lavan, stay as close to me as possible. Jameta, behind me, between them. Save your pistol for the first one that breaks through."

Jameta watched the leader of the tribesmen. "Erlon?"

"What?"

"Look at him."

"I am. I don't like what I see."

"I do. He's not going to attack."

"And you can tell that."

"Look at how calm his horse is. He's holding his sword out and down. He's watching us, not firing his men up." This man's robes looked new, and the stock of the long, slim rifle slung on his back swirled with inlays of mother-of-pearl.

"Well, you can watch him right back." Erlon had his sword in one hand and his Double-S rifle in the other. "I'm getting ready for the charge."

23. The Tolbè

"He's waiting for us to make the first move. Maybe we don't have to fight." Jameta kneed Doe one step forward, held out empty hands and raised her voice. "We do not come to fight."

The leader frowned and stared at her, leaning his sword across his saddle in front of him. He said something that sounded vaguely familiar.

I may be making progress. She shook her head. "No. No fighting." She tried again, in Samnian this time. *No fight. Trade.* She gestured to the pack horses. *No fight.* She made a "down" gesture with her hand.

"I don't think this is working, Jameta..."

She focused on the tribal leader. "Give me a chance. He's listening, at least."

The man raised his voice in a high, wordless yodel that rang through the rocks.

Erlon gripped his sword and pushed his horse in front of hers. "Here it comes. If things go wrong, duck into that crevice to the left."

"But..."

His brows lowered. "Not everybody wins every fight, Jameta. Be ready to run. That's an order." He turned his back and faced the man in front of him...

...who was busy sheathing his sword. The tribesman smiled and raised his voice to call an order. A wave of movement swept down the line, riders relaxing, horses stirring again.

To Jameta's surprise, she could understand him. She tugged at Erlon's shoulder. "Erlon! He just said, 'Come to me.' I didn't catch who, but that's what he told them."

He half-turned, keeping his sword pointed towards the tribesman. "What?"

"I can sort of understand him. He's speaking something like Samnian. He's called his leaders to him."

"Look." Aleria pointed. "Here they come."

Three riders separated themselves from different points down the line of prancing horses and trotted towards the centre.

Roeble shrugged. "This has all the signs of a parlay. It would help if we can can actually talk to them."

Jameta raised her eyebrows to Aleria, who gestured her forward. "Give it a try. Can't hurt."

Erlon frowned and raised an arm, barring her way. "Can't hurt anybody but her."

"Better if you go along with her. But sheathe your sword. They did."

"You're the boss, Aleria. Please don't be wrong."

She grimaced. "Do my best."

They kneed their horses forward. To Jameta's dismay she found herself in Erlon's favourite spearpoint formation. With herself at the tip. Stamping on her fear, she urged her dancing horse forward, finally settling her right in front of the leading tribesman. She looked into his face. He seemed amused.

What language do you speak? She tried in Samnian.

Ah, Pretty Horse Lady is Samnian.

That's right. I speak Samnian She gestured. *Not well. Not fast.*

"What did he say?"

She turned to Erlon. "He knows I'm speaking Samnian. He called me...Pretty Horse Lady, I think."

Erlon glowered at the man. "What did he mean by that?"

She slapped him on the arm. "Either that I'm the pretty lady who owns the horse, or I'm the lady who owns the pretty horse, I suppose. I don't speak Samnian that well, and he's talking a very strange version of it. Stop acting threatening and let me do my job." She pointed backwards.

He frowned at her, but reined his horse back while she slid forward.

The tribesman was openly grinning. *Pretty Horse Lady and White Warrior...* She did not understand the remainder of the sentence, but his hand gesture made the meaning obvious.

She tried not to blush. *Yes, we are, so you watch yourself!* She backed her horse a couple of steps to slide in beside the big soldier again.

Now the man laughed outright and tossed a comment to the men behind him. They laughed as well.

"What was that all about?" Aleria pushed up on the other side. "We seem to be having all sorts of fun, here with a battle hanging over us."

Jameta shrugged miserably. "I don't understand enough. As far as I can figure, he said something like, 'My mother's going to like this one,' and they all thought it was terribly funny. No, sorry, it was 'mother-in-law,' I think."

"He doesn't look so happy, now."

There was a whistle from the left, and the tribesman's head came up. He looked both directions and pushed his horse forward. *Pretty Horse Lady is not safe here. There are enemy all over that hillside.* He swept his hand in a half-circle to the north. *Many enemy, with that Ferbodean animal. Come.* He reined his mount around.

Roeble nudged his horse forward. "I don't need a translation. This is the first guy that's been friendly enough to laugh in the presence of strangers. Let's go."

Aleria signalled to the wranglers, and the pack train lined out along the sand, a file of ragged tribesmen on either side.

Once they were clear of the rocks the leader pulled his horse aside and gestured the caravan to go ahead. They did so, but Aleria and Roeble stopped, so Jameta stayed. Erlon, with a warning frown, rode on at the head of the train.

As the individual horses passed, the tribesman regarded each one. When the Roan approached, he made an exclamation and trotted his horse alongside, looking down.

Jameta pulled up on the other side of the packhorse. "Sore shoulder." She rubbed her own shoulder, swung her arm in a circle and winced as if in pain.

He nodded, and rubbed his arm, but lower down, just above the elbow, at the back.

She gave an "Oh, I see," expression.

He gave the Roan one more glance and turned to Jameta, *If there is trouble, cut the girth.* He mimed cutting the strap.

I understand.

He nodded and went back to his perusal of their stock.

She rode back to their little group. "What's in the Roan's pack?"

"Mostly trade goods. A couple of tents." Roeble shrugged. "I caught that exchange. He's not carrying anything worth risking a good horse to save."

Jameta grinned. "You think the Roan is a good horse?"

"I don't care if he's a bit snarky with the other horses. He carries his share of the weight."

"Which he may not be doing at the moment. I think he's only got a pulled muscle. If he doesn't have to gallop with a full load, he'll be fine."

At that moment Stilet trotted up. "What's the problem, Aleria?"

"It's the Roan. Our new friend suggests that if there's trouble, we cut his pack loose."

Stilet nodded. "He's loaded pretty heavy today, but the sand is level and hard. If he don't overdo it he oughta be fine."

"Well, let's hope he doesn't have to overdo it." Roeble scanned the surrounding hilltops. "If he does, we may have more problems than a lame horse."

Aleria regarded their escort. "I'm not too worried. This is a doughty bunch, well armed."

"And they belong here. Pavenkov and his bandits might have found us easy pickings, but between our rifles and these rightful owners of the land, I doubt if anyone in this area would dare bother us." Roeble clucked to his horse and followed the Headman at a trot towards the front of the caravan.

Jameta glanced at Aleria. "I hope you're right."

"So far we have been."

"Let us take heart from that fact." She kneed Doe to a trot and moved ahead to the relative safety of Erlon's presence.

The tribesmen's camp was on the flat sand at the edge of the desert. Behind the tents the rocks began, piled in an ascending jumble to the low mountains where the caravan route lay. Sheep, goats, and horses grazed on the tough grass and shrubs in valleys between the hills.

As they pulled in they passed a well. Jameta rode closer. The circular stone-clad shaft dropped into darkness. A crude windlass system stood over it with a copper bucket hanging on the rope.

The leader sat his horse, tall in his saddle, while they scanned the camp. "I am Sfisef. Welcome to the tents of the Aine Tolbè."

About twenty dark-brown tents huddled against the rocks, their backs to the open sand and the bright sunlight. At key points, woven mats of reeds tied to poles made windbreaks. There were few people about, mostly older men sitting in the shade of tents and a few children playing. These broke off their activities to stand, wide-eyed but unafraid, as the foreigners filed in. No one shooed them away.

Just inside the closest valley mouth the nomads dismounted, the Galesians following suit. Sfisef gestured an area for the visitors, and the packers began to unload, picketing the horses on a long line further up the valley where the sparse grass afforded feed. Then the men opened the packs and began to set up camp.

While they were working Aleria, Roeble, and Jameta were received at the Headman's tent. It was similar to the others in the encampment but larger, constructed of long strips of woven wool, striped in various shades of brown. The roof had three ridgepoles, highest in the centre, tapering down to below head height at the edges. Three sides were enclosed, but the side facing away from the wind and the sun was open.

Aleria nudged Jameta. "You'd think with one open side there'd be no privacy, but look at that." With the sun in their eyes and the bright sand all around, the interiors of the tents looked inky black.

Once Sfisef brought them into the shade they could see that the tent was divided into three rooms. He escorted them to the one on the right. *Men's room. Public.* He flipped his hand towards the other two, the middle one of which contained a loom. *Women's room and cooking.* Sure enough, in the third section a woman was mixing something in a cloth laid across a hollow in the sand. A little girl was swirling sand in a bowl. At first Jameta thought she was playing, but then she realized that the girl must be cleaning it with sand.

That seemed to be the extent of the guided tour, and they sat in a circle on the carpet in the public section. Sfisef looked around at the group, slapped his knees, and smiled. *So, you have trouble with the Ferbodeans too, do you?*

Jameta nodded. *Traders must move, must trade. Ferbodeans say no move.* She grinned. *We move. They not happy.*

*Ah. The Ferbodeans don't want us to move either. But what can we do? If we stay here, the flocks will run out of food, the well will dry up and then we will die. The Tolbè must move. It is our life. *

She translated this to the others. "Sounds like we have something in common."

Roeble nodded. "See if you can find out what they have to trade."

She turned to the Headman. *My leader asks about trade. What do you need?*

What do you have?

She laughed. *Yes. Tomorrow we show.*

You need horses, cows, goats?

Not today. Maybe a goat to roast tonight?

No, no, you are guests of the Tolbè. Today we chased away the dreaded Ferbodeans and their traitorous allies. My men showed themselves at the top of that ridge you crossed, just as the enemy were starting up the steep spot. They turned and ran like sheep when a bear passes. Tonight we will celebrate! He glanced at her. *Unless you want to buy a horse?*

She laughed and translated. "I don't think there's going to be any trading today. Not unless we're looking for a horse."

Roeble chuckled. "That sounds about right. These people will bargain for horses at any time – day, night or in the middle of a sandstorm. But regular trading takes time. I think tonight we should relax and enjoy ourselves."

Aleria nodded. "Except for a guard or three."

Jameta turned back to Sfisef. *Is there ceremony? We bring gifts?*

He tossed a hand negligently. *No, no. You are here, you have been greeted well, I hope?"*

Tolbè chase Ferbodeans, traders well greeted. Thank you.

He rose. *Very good. You will want to set up. We eat after sunset, when it cools.*

The group stood as well. *Until sunset, then.*

They strolled across the camp to where the teamsters were finishing the setup. They had taken a hint from the nomads and put the tents in a close-fitting arc with their doorways facing inwards and their backs to the desert.

The canvas tents of the visitors attracted no end of wonder, with a steady stream of people strolling by as the crew was setting them up. The ground alternated between rock and pure sand, making tent pegs a problem, which the men solved by using the nomad trick of putting a heavy rock on every rope.

Erlon came to meet them. "Several women are driving sticks into the ground, out back, there." He gestured behind the tents. "I couldn't see what they were doing, but I didn't want to interfere."

Jameta took his arm. "Then let us go for an afternoon stroll."

By the time they arrived the women had finished driving a line of sticks into the sand in a great curving arc close behind the tents. Now they were bringing rolls of woven mats, which they were tying to the sticks.

"Ah. A windbreak." Erlon stepped up to a veiled woman and made a slight bow. "May I help?"

She looked up at him, laughed and slapped his hand away from the mat. *No, no, no. Not men's work. Go hunt, herd, fight somebody.* The other women laughed merrily and went on with their work.

Jameta tugged Erlon's arm. "You've been put in your place, I'm afraid. This is women's work, and you've been told to go and play with the other men."

"Oh. My feelings may be hurt, but I'll appreciate that fence if the wind comes up."

Jameta called a general thanks, and they wandered around to the picket line. The nomads had various corrals and pens in valleys nearby where the stock was put at night. The traders carried a heavy rope with loops spaced down it. They anchored both ends to large rocks, tied each horse separately and fed them their portions of grain. The animals would be set to graze wherever the nomads wished for the length of their visit in the Tolbè camp.

The Roan, of course, was at the end of the line, with Doe and Brownie between him and the rest of the horses. Jameta checked her stock first, then moved over to him. Erlon hovered nearby while she worked on the injury, ready to step in if needed.

She held out a biscuit. "How's it feeling now, lad?"

He took the treat and allowed her to feel his leg up and down. There was a quiver when she pressed one muscle, but otherwise no reaction. She slapped his shoulder. "I think you'll be fine."

She grabbed his underjaw and pulled his head around to face her. "And you're going to be nice to Doe, aren't you?"

His ears came forward, and he pushed at her with his nose.

She laughed and gave him another biscuit. Then she turned to Erlon. "I have to make up more of those treats. He's using more than the other two combined."

"Whatever keeps him happy."

24. Business Problems

The feast that evening was pretty much what Roeble had led them to expect. They ate with the men of the tribe, served by young women. In rather scanty attire, and no veils. The few women they had seen around the camp had been well covered, some of them with veils as well. Most of the servers seemed shy, but one of them, an especially pretty girl with an enviable figure, introduced herself as Medlili. She stayed in attendance on Aleria and Jameta all evening, not saying much but listening intently.

The festive meal did not last long, and soon everyone was in bed. "They sleep early and wake early, I suppose."

Aleria yawned and stretched. "I'm looking forward to a decent night's sleep. Haven't felt so relaxed since...I don't know when."

"They're a pleasant bunch, aren't they?"

"Yes. Proud, but in a good way."

"Like their horses."

Aleria yawned again and rolled over. "You go to sleep dreaming of horses. I'm going to dream about rolling around in all the gold and jewels we're going to trade for."

Jameta giggled. "And all the men are going to dream about Medlili."

"I wonder what that's all about...?"

"I think she understands Galesian."

Aleria turned over to face her. "Why do you say that?"

"She was listening too hard."

"I suppose I could figure out what that means, but I'm too tired."

"So am I. Happy dreams."

* * *

By the following evening, Roeble was shaking his head in frustration. Jameta was shaking hers with fatigue. They returned from their third session of talks with Sfisef and the other men with nothing to report. "I can't figure it, Aleria. We talk, and we talk and it seems we're getting somewhere but they won't commit to anything. These are nomads, travellers. They make half their living buying and selling. They will trade for individual items gladly. But they won't make any kind of promises or deals for the future. Maybe it's their way."

The other Caravan Master shrugged. "I'm not getting any negative feelings. They certainly are friendly enough. The kids are curious, and the parents don't stop them from interacting with us. I always take that as a good sign."

"Maybe it's because I'm not translating well enough." Jameta wrinkled her brow. "I don't understand them half the time."

He patted her hand. "It's not that. I've made deals with people with a lot less language in common than you have with them. No, I've run into this before, and it's not communication. When I get blocked like this, its cultural." He tossed a hand in a careless gesture. "Or else it turns out I'm talking to the wrong person, and he doesn't have the authority. But I don't see that here. Sfisef is the Headman, no question of that."

Jameta thought back to their meetings. "Then why does he always go into that darker tent over there when we finish?"

"He does?"

"Yes. Directly there, every time. And, if I remember correctly, he comes from there as well."

"It could be his home."

"No, his tent is the fancy one over there where we met the first time. The dark one has walls on four sides, and there are always women going in and out."

Roeble's eyes took on a thoughtful look. "Well, there's something strange going on. I'm willing to accept any explanation. But who could the Headman be reporting back to?"

Aleria grinned. "The Headwoman?"

His eyes widened, but then he shook his head. "I doubt it. This society has all the trappings of a rigid patriarchy. Look at their dress." They paused to watch a woman stroll by, swathed from head to foot, only her eyes showing. "Her beauty completely controlled for only her husband to enjoy."

Jameta met Aleria's eyes, and they both grinned. "Maybe she's completely controlling her beauty so nobody gets a look at it unless she says so."

The merchant's head tilted. "I never thought of it that way, but you're right. A woman in one of those veils is pretty much in charge of herself, isn't she?" He shrugged. "It's something to think on, but I'll have to leave it to you two. I'm not likely to make any progress."

Jameta had been thinking. "I might be able to get a line on this. That girl that always serves us at meals? Medlili?"

Roeble grinned. "The one with the curves? I could hardly miss her. Strange, isn't it? Some of their women so hidden, others so free in what they wear? I wonder if it's a caste system."

Aleria shook her head. "I don't think so. Look at that girl that lives in the third tent over. With skin that light, she has to be part Ferbodean or another race. But she's dressed like all the other girls and she seems to move freely."

Jameta snapped her fingers. "That's it. Girls. You don't see any older women dressed like that. Let's keep our eyes open. I'll bet we find that the older a woman is, the less we see of her."

Aleria nodded. "Could be. I can't figure how that would work, but who can tell?"

"Simple." Jameta shrugged. "The men are talking to our men, waiting for us to talk to their women."

"Then why haven't they said so?"

"I have no idea. Cultural?"

Roeble nodded. "The meeting of strangers for trading is always guided by rules. Often a gift is involved. Sometimes valuable, sometimes only symbolic. Whoever is seen to be at a disadvantage is expected to present it."

Aleria stared at the dark tent. "So the Headwoman is sitting in there wondering why the hell we haven't showed up with the gift. She probably thinks we're holding out. Waiting for her to cave in and give one."

Jameta frowned. "Or maybe it's a test. We have to figure it out."

"How do we do that?"

"Easy. We ask."

"Just ask?" Roeble shook his head. "I wish it was that simple. Most of these rituals have their basis in need. Protection, power, whatever."

Jameta threw up her hands. "I don't know anything about it, but why make things difficult if they don't have to be?" She started for the tent. "What are they going to do, chop my head off?"

"They might."

She glanced over her shoulder. Aleria looked serious. *Now, that's just ridiculous.* She decided not to respond and kept walking.

By the time she reached the tent there was a young woman waiting for her. *They were watching us.* She bowed as she had seen equals bow. *Is Medlili here?*

The girl bowed in return and stepped inside, dropping the flap.

Jameta turned to gesture helplessly to her friends and waited. Not for long. Medlili arrived, pulling the flap closed carefully behind her. *Pretty Horse Lady.* "How good...nice? To see you."

"I knew you spoke Galesian."

"Yes. I learn."

"We say, 'How nice to see you.' It is nice to see you, too." She repeated the phrase in Samnian. "Would you walk with me?"

The girl nodded, and they turned together to stroll along in front of the tents. After they were far enough in the open for privacy, Jameta began. "We have a problem."

"Yes, we do."

"We wish to trade."

"We know."

"But we cannot."

"Of course you can."

"We do not know the rules."

"Ah. I thought yes. What rule?"

"We must speak with your Headwoman, yes?"

"It is usual."

"How?"

"You ask."

"Who do I ask?"

"Proper family person."

"I have to ask the proper member of her family? Who is that?"

The girl's lip twitched. "Favourite granddaughter is good choice."

Jameta frowned. "You?"

"Me."

"You? That's it? I only have to ask you?"

Medlili shrugged. "Honoured guest asks lowly granddaughter to speak to Headwoman. Granddaughter asks mother. Mother asks Headwoman..." The girl made a wheel movement with her hand.

"And the Headwoman tells her daughter to tell the granddaughter that we can talk." Jameta laughed. "That's it?"

"Very good...hold...?...grasp?"

"I have a very good grasp of diplomacy. Why didn't you tell me?"

"Good chance to practice Galesian. Much work needed."

"Oh, you're doing fine."

"Pretty Horse Lady is...good...?...nice?"

"Either one will do. Can we go and do this now? The men are getting tired of talking around and around." She made the wheel motion.

"Ah, men love to talk. No hurry. But we go now. Come." The girl turned and moved with a long, free stride towards the black tent. At the door she stopped Jameta with a gesture and slipped inside.

Looking around, Jameta saw Aleria lounging outside their tent. She raised a hand, giving a success sign. Aleria ducked back into the tent and came out with her best jacket on. Jameta looked down at her own sweat-stained blouse and leather vest and decided it was too late.

By the time Aleria arrived, Medlili was back, a smile on her face. "Headwoman would be honoured to speak to *Pretty Horse Lady* and *Sword Woman.* Come." She swept the curtain aside, and they entered the black tent.

Jameta had expected the dark tent to be hot, but it wasn't. She looked up at the eaves, where daylight showed in regular slits. She leaned over towards Aleria. "The ventilation must be sophisticated."

Aleria elbowed her. "Forget the science and worry about translation."

"Yes, boss."

They passed through an outer room that contained only woven storage baskets and a loom with a long, narrow swath of striped cloth on it. The colours were beautiful, and Jameta would have loved to investigate, but Aleria forged ahead.

Behind the next curtain was a luxurious lounge. The walls sparkled with mirror-studded tapestries, and the floors were covered with intricate weavings. They filed across the back of the room, regarding the group that awaited them at the front.

The centre of attention was a woman totally covered in dark robes, who lounged on a low divan, surrounded by pillows. The only part of her that showed was her eyes, which were heavily made up in shades of purple and black. A similar divan sat opposite, and Medlili motioned Aleria to sit. She indicated a short-legged chair to Aleria's left for Jameta, and took one in a similar position beside the Headwoman.

The only other person in the room was a fully clothed woman to the Headwoman's right, although this woman's veil was flimsy enough to show her facial expressions, and her clothing was striped in shimmering colours.

Medlili glanced at her grandmother, took a deep breath, and began. "My grandmother, Zelfana, Headwoman of the Aine Tolbè, welcome... honoured visitors to tent...to her tent." She gestured to the other woman. "Also my mother, Hajira, daughter of Zelfana."

Aleria smiled and nodded to Jameta.

Aleria anDalmyn of Dalmyn Cartage, and I, Jameta anDennal of Dennal Shipping, pleased to...to...attend.

The Headwoman leaned over and spoke to her granddaughter. Medlili nodded. "My Headwoman has...interest. Your people. Who...I know not how to say. No offence, please. Who is married?"

Married...married together?

Medlili smiled. "Yes. Married together. Tolbè woman travel with husband."

Oh. No. No married.

"Not at all?"

Jameta glanced at Aleria. *Not now.*

The Headwoman stirred, and a heavily ringed finger pointed at Jameta. She spoke and chuckled and the mound of clothing shook.

Medlili frowned and spoke at length. Finally Zelfana gestured with her finger. Medlili gave in and turned to Jameta. "Not to offend, please?"

Jameta threw up her hands. "Medlili, I will not be offended." *Not offend.*

The Tolbè woman smiled. "My grandmother says...*Pretty Horse Lady* soon have husband." She regarded Jameta and raised her hand way above her head. "*White Warrior?*"

Jameta felt her face grow hot. *Maybe. Your grandmother...wise.*

"Grandmother say love not hide well."

Very wise.

The Headwoman made a sharp gesture.

Medlili grinned. "We work now. My Headwoman wish to understand families."

Yes. Jameta pointed. *AnDalmyn, anDennal,* she gestured in the direction of their tents, *Cloet.*

Three bejewelled fingers appeared from the folds of the veiled woman's robes, along with a terse question.

Three families, two women?

Jameta nodded. At least she didn't have to translate that. Her head was beginning to spin. She had already spent several hours translating for Cloet, and there was only so much she could take.

Positions? AnDalmyn. Aleria, Daughter. She raised her hand high. *Dennal. Jameta. Cousin.* She held her hand lower, wavering back and forth. *Cloet. Roeble. Son.* She raised her hand again. *First son.*

The robes stirred as the Headwoman straightened. A frown wrinkled the bridge of her nose. She copied the hand gesture, and spoke directly to them. *Man?* She had a deep, soft voice that resonated.

Jamilla nodded. *Son.* "Oh, dammit, what's the word?" *Wise.* She tapped her head and nodded judicially. *Son very wise.*

The older woman nodded in turn, and the outline of her body relaxed. *Ah. Wise son. Good.*

Jameta turned to Aleria with a grin. "We seem to have that straight. I gather it's all right to have a man as a partner, as long as he is useful. I told her that Roeble was wise."

Aleria shared the smile. "I got all that. You don't need to talk. Your hands are very expressive."

Jameta felt her face warm. "Oh, that's nothing. Only dance training."

"What kind of dance is that?"

"Remember, like Juli was talking about back in the Falcon. Folk stuff." She made a few simple hand passes. "Samnian."

There was an exclamation from the robed woman. Medlili's voice took on more animation. "Dance? You dance?"

"Oh. Yes, a little." She mimed small. *Little.*

"You dance."

"What...now?" Her eyes shot to Aleria's in dismay.

A brief chuckle from the folds of cloth. *No, no. Later. Eat, drink, dance.* The woman gestured to her granddaughter and said something too rapid for Jameta to follow.

The girl smiled. "My grandmother...happy. Very happy. She dance, too." She glanced at the older woman. "Not now. Too many...births?" She mimed pregnancy, and they both nodded.

"She loves dance." The girl made a hand pass similar to Jameta's. "I dance, too." Her eyes fell in modesty.

"Wonderful."

The jewelry-covered hand flicked out. *Sword Woman dances?*

Jameta turned to translate, but Aleria shook her head. "I caught that." She met the Headwoman's eyes, then nodded. "I dance."

Medlili's eyebrows rose. "You do?"

"Oh, yes. Does my Lady wish a demonstration?"

Jameta communicated this to the Headwoman, who indicated the space of carpet in the other half of the tent.

Aleria strode over to the centre of the carpet and stood, dead still, until all eyes were drawn to her. Then she drew her sword and saluted.

Of course. A sword drill. Jameta glanced at the tribeswomen, who were rapt in their attention.

Looked at from this new light, the sword drill was a rather impressive dance. Graceful, forceful, with increasing tempo and a build of emotion to a cathartic end. When Aleria finished the final, triumphant lunge and stood, panting lightly, Jameta caught her eye and tapped her fingers to her palm in soft applause.

The old woman burst into gales of laughter.

Aleria stood, her sword sagging to the carpet, a questioning frown on her face. "Was it that bad?"

Jameta turned an enquiring glance at their host. The woman said something to her granddaughter and roared with laughter again.

The younger woman's skin darkened, and she frowned at her grandmother and spoke sharply.

The veiled woman seemed to make an effort to control herself, but the odd chuckle escaped.

The girl turned to Jameta and Aleria. "That was...rude. Very rude. My grandmother is rude old woman. I...apology." She bowed her head. "Deep apology."

To Jameta's relief, Aleria grinned and turned to the Headwoman, gliding forward and making an upthrusting motion with her sword and her hips, a question on her face.

The older woman nodded fiercely, sputtering into laughter again.

Aleria nodded. "Not much doubt what she's on about. You don't use a sword and hang around with a bunch of men without hearing that joke." She rolled her eyes. "Over and over again."

Jameta found herself blushing. "I suppose not."

Aleria sheathed her sword. "So, if we've got that out of our systems, what's next?" She returned to her lounge.

In response, the leader calmed and straightened under her robes. She turned her head to Jamilla. *Business?*

As you wish, Headwoman.

Is good. She looked to her granddaughter and indicated the back of her neck.

The girl's eyes widened, and she stared at her grandmother.

The woman snapped her fingers, an impatient command.

The girl shrugged and stepped behind her, loosening the veil and removing it in a ritualistic sweep.

The face that was revealed was remarkable. Fleshy and lined perhaps, but carrying the remnants of a great beauty. Fine eyes were framed by prominent cheekbones, the nose long and straight. Her mouth was generous, and a set of even, though lightly stained, teeth showed in her smile.

The girl folded the veil with care and laid it on her grandmother's lap. Then she turned to the Galesians. "It is not...right. Not...fair. Talk business and hide face."

Aleria grinned. "Does that mean you think our people must be very honest?"

"Oh, no." The girl shrugged. "Men don't cover face. Better liars."

Aleria shook her head. "Great. So because we don't cover our faces, they assume we are better liars. Why would they want to do business with us at all?"

Jameta shrugged. "Maybe they need our goods?"

"Let's hope so."

After that it was easy. At least for everyone else. For Jameta, and probably for Medlili too, the negotiations were a blur of words and ideas that left her head spinning and her energy drained. Once the talks widened to include Sfisif and Roeble and the topics of conversation broadened to defence and regional politics, she felt completely drained and had to beg for a break.

"Aleria, I can't even remember how to speak Galesian any more, and I'm sure Medlili feels the same. Can we stop now and do more of this tomorrow?"

The Caravan Master glanced at the other girl. "What do you think, Medlili? Time for feasting and dancing instead?"

"Oh, yes, Sword Lady." She made one of her fluid gestures. "Work body. Rest head." She turned with a question to her grandmother, who responded with a sharp comment about duty and honour and lazy young women.

Aleria shook her head. "You don't need to translate that. I'm getting tired as well. It's been a long day. I'm hungry, and I'm tired, and you," she pointed at Jameta, "are becoming completely useless. We're finished." She made a chopping motion, but then swayed her hand gracefully towards the Headwoman. "If my Lady desires."

The old woman stared at Aleria a moment, then gave a "Hmph" sound. She flicked her fingers in a gesture that dismissed all youth and weakness, then looked to her left and made a beckoning motion.

An unseen person folded back the inner wall of the tent, and a line of girls and veiled women entered carrying platters and napkins. They placed the food in the centre of the carpet and the older women sat while the girls knelt behind them. Medlili replaced the Headwoman's veil. Formalities had resumed.

Erlon appeared and sat beside Jameta. "I seem to have been invited for supper. Are we making progress?"

She laid a hand on his shoulder. "You are in the presence of Zelfana, Headwoman of the Aine Tolbè. Are you impressed?"

He grinned. "I suppose I must be. I can't see anything but her eyes, so it's difficult to tell."

She slapped his arm and withdrew her hand. "Don't be rude. And remember what Roeble said. Never assume someone doesn't understand you."

"Good point."

The Headman grinned at Jameta. *This is good. It is not often I feast with my mother-in-law. The best food, the best entertainment...* He made awkward dancing motions with his hands.

Zelfana snorted. *Men? Dance? Hah!*

The man winked at Jameta, reached for a chicken leg and shrugged. *Good food, anyway.*

The meal was excellent, some dishes reminding Jameta of her mother's favourite recipes. She was more used to eating with her fingers than the rest of the caravan people, so she relaxed and enjoyed ignoring all the talk around her and just eating.

25. Dancing

When the dancing time came, it turned out that only the best of the women performed. First two younger girls did a folk dance that dealt with domestic duties and herd husbandry. Then Medlili performed a steamy commentary on the more intimate elements of human interaction, to the great appreciation of the men.

The girl folded herself down beside Jameta as the applause fell away, delicately mopping her brow, a proud smile on her face.

"I hope you're not expecting dancing like that from me!"

Medlili pointed. Another woman, quite old from the density of her veils but dressed in a flashing robe that accentuated her mature figure, was taking the floor. "Now you see real dance."

Which they did. Who knew what the story was, but there was everything of the human condition: passion, love, sex, agony and perhaps a death, although it was hard to tell. The applause was heartfelt after this performance, and the dancer took her place beside the Headwoman with a dignified curtsey. Once she had regained the familiar position, Jameta could tell that she was the same woman from the afternoon, but in a different costume.

"My mother."

"Of course. Who else could have taught you so well?"

The music became louder, the string players twanging away with abandon, the drums thumping out a heady rhythm, the horns wailing. Medlili stood, taking Jameta's hand. "Come. Join us. It is fun."

Several younger girls stepped out on the carpet and began to move in familiar patterns. With a private grimace towards Aleria, Jameta joined in. She held back at first to see how the others interacted, what kind of moves they made, but they grabbed her hands and hauled her into the circle, and she had no choice. Then it was nothing but fun; this was not for show, not for the audience, but only dance for the joy of dancing. She threw herself into the patterns with abandon, twirling and sweeping with the rest, blending with the rapture of the music and exhilaration of the companionship.

When the music slowed, then stopped, Jameta returned to her place, her heart beating, sweat beading her brow.

Aleria passed her a napkin. "That looked like fun."

"Oh, can those girls dance!"

"You don't do so badly yourself. I'm envious."

"Why didn't you join us? They would have loved it!"

Aleria tipped her head towards the old woman in the veils. "She would have loved it, anyway. Her girls showing me up for the awkward clod that I am. No, you maintained the honour of our troop, and I was pleased to observe. Here, have a cup of this beer. It's sour but refreshing. I don't think there's much alcohol in it."

Jameta sipped the light brew and turned to watch the rest of the room. It seemed the festivities were over. The old woman was talking to her daughter and a couple of the elders. Medlili and the rest of the girls were tidying up.

She turned to Erlon and Roeble. "Feeling left out?"

Roeble grinned. "I'm glad our friend in the turban was here or I'd have felt completely out of place. That was definitely a women's celebration. Of what, I'm not sure."

"Womanly things, I suppose."

"It seemed so, but not completely. A privilege, in any case."

"Yes. I don't know much about trading, but it seems to me that we have done well with these folks."

The merchant rolled his eyes. "Done well? Being allowed to join in a private feast with the Headwoman and her family? Believe me, I have rarely been so lucky. If we don't make trading progress out of this, then there was nothing to trade."

She grinned. "There's always something to trade."

"Exactly. Let's see how it goes tomorrow. I hope you sleep well tonight."

"I plan to fall into a coma the moment my head hits the pillow, but why do you mention it?"

"Because sometimes after a session like that you fall asleep from the exhaustion of it all, but just as often you lie awake with all those new words spinning around in your brain."

"I gather you have done this before."

"Many times. A familiar experience for merchant travellers."

She sighed. "Well, I hope I sleep well, too, then." She scooted closer to Erlon and leaned against his firm bulk.

The Headwoman barked an order, and Jameta turned to see Medlili approaching with a steaming mug.

"My grandmother says need drink. Sleep well. She says needs you sharp tomorrow."

Jameta shared a glance with Roeble and reached for the cup, but Erlon's arm was longer. He took the drink and sniffed it.

"What's in this?"

The girl shook her head. "Nothing...how would you say...strong. Helps sleep."

He sipped and raised his eyebrows. "Tastes good."

"Then don't keep it for yourself. It's for me."

He grinned and passed it over. It was a pleasant drink, like the chai they drank at home on special festivals, with hints of cinnamon and nutmeg, maybe lemon. Jameta drank a larger sip, allowing the warm fluid to drift down her throat. She leaned against Erlon, and his arm supported her. She continued to drink, the noise of the room washing over her, snatches of conversation in different languages mixing in her head. *I am so tired. I should...*

The next thing she knew it was morning.

* * *

She woke when a stray shaft of sunlight slanted into her eyes. She yawned, stretched, and tried to roll over. There was a large, heavy object next to her. She turned to look. It was Erlon, lying with his hands behind his head, watching her.

"What?" She gazed around. Erlon's tent. "Why am I here?" She pushed to a sitting position. "Aleria said..."

He pulled her arm from propping her up and tucked her back beside him. "Aleria said to look after you, because we weren't sure about the effects of that drink."

"Oh...what were the effects?"

"You were tired, both body and mind. You dropped asleep so fast I barely caught you. Medlili said all you needed was a warm, safe place to sleep. My tent was the safest I could provide. And you slept. Task accomplished."

"But you...I...did you stay awake to watch me?"

"Not for long. You were sleeping peacefully, so I did the same. It was rather pleasant. Especially waking with you cuddled up next to me. I could get used to that...no, don't squirm away. Sorry, I shouldn't have said that. But it was. And I could."

She relaxed against him. "I suppose it was. It's just that..."

"Stolen pleasure. Against the rules. Isn't it fun to cheat and get away with it?"

She slapped his arm. "Don't be mean."

"I'm not. I'm being pleasant. Enjoy it while you can."

They lay there in comfortable silence for a while.

"I suppose we have to get up."

"Now who's being mean?"

"No, but we must. They'll be meeting again, and I have to be there."

"Of course you do. But you have to be at the top of your game, and Aleria the Caravan Master has decreed that you rest as much as you can. Arguing with me is not resting, so stop."

"I bow to the expertise of the Master." She turned and laid her cheek against his chest. Even relaxed, the muscles bulged. "I could get used to this, too."

"Don't get any ideas."

"I wouldn't think of it." She snuggled in. "Not any new ones."

"Do you think this is a good idea?"

"You and me going out on these expeditions, where we're together all the time but forced to stay apart? It can't be a normal situation."

"Probably more normal than you think, though a bit extreme, I admit. At least it gives us a chance to get to know each other. With all our wrinkles."

"I don't have any wrinkles."

"Yes, you do. Both figurative and literal."

"What?"

"Can't say. That would be arguing."

She pushed him away. "Go on. Show me."

He took her hand, straightened her fingers. "See? Wrinkles all over your knuckles."

"All right. What about the figurative ones?"

"Umm...you snore."

"What? I don't snore!"

"You're arguing again. And you do. Rather quietly, I admit."

"Nobody ever complained before."

"Perhaps it was the fatigue and the drink, but you were definitely snorking along for quite a while, there."

"Fine. Snorking. If that's the worst you can come up with, you're not doing too well."

"On the contrary, I'm doing very well."

"If you're doing so well, can I ask you a question?"

"Ask anything." He settled himself further. "I might even answer."

"All right. Where did you get your education? You toss around expressions like 'figuratively and literally' as if they were completely normal to you."

"Ah..."

"Well?"

"Well…easy to explain, but difficult to get there, do you see?"

"I don't see. It sounds to me like you're ducking the question as usual. If you don't want to answer it, say so."

"No, don't pull away like that. I will tell you. I promise. But it's a long story, and now may not be the time."

"When will it ever be the time?"

He sighed. "Soon, obviously." He squirmed around to face her. "Look, Jameta, I've never told anyone at Dalmyn any of this before. It's hard for me, and it might affect my relationships with everyone. But I will tell you, because you deserve to know."

"But not right now."

"That's right. Not right now." He swung his feet off the bed. "It's rather simple, when you think about it. If you and I are going to have a longer-term relationship, then I obviously have to tell you, even if it's harder to tell you than anyone else. But if we aren't, then I don't have to tell you, because it won't matter."

She sighed and clambered to her feet. Then she looked down. "Where are my clothes? How did you find my nightgown?" She frowned at him. "Who put it on me?"

He grinned. "That, I don't promise to tell you. Stew a while."

"You are coming very close to creating an argument."

"True, but you are awake and rested, and I am now getting your mind alert for your coming toil…all right. Don't look at me like that. Your clothes are on the chest, over there, and I'll go outside while you change. But one thing…"

"What?"

He reached for her. "One last chance for a little cheat."

She grinned and stepped into his arms. He held her there, her head on his chest, and she could hear his heart pumping, slowly and steadily. She looked up. "Isn't your heart supposed to be going 'pitty-pat' right now, with the love of your life here in your arms?"

He shrugged and pulled her back tighter, resting his chin on the top of her head. "It doesn't feel like that. It feels comfortable and…right."

She gently extricated herself. "And that is the most dangerous of all, isn't it?"

"Yes, I suppose it is."

"Then you'd better go outside while I change. I trust you, but I don't necessarily trust me."

He ran a finger down her cheek and leaned down and kissed the same spot. "I don't trust me either."

He turned and brushed the tent flap away.

At once Aleria's voice rose. "Oh, there you are. Is she awake?"

"Awake and rarin' for battle. Sharp as a snee."

"No problems last night?"

"Nothing until we woke up this morning."

"You need to explain that."

"Not really. Ask her if you want to."

"Do you think I should...?"

Jameta snorted and raised her voice. "The trouble with tents is that out of sight isn't out of hearing."

There was silence outside, then a soft chuckle from Erlon. "Sharp as a snee, and rarin' for battle."

"Good. I'll see you both at breakfast."

"Coward." He chuckled again. "She's worried about who put her in her nightgown."

Aleria laughed. "You didn't tell her?"

"You said you wanted her sharp."

Jameta laced up her final boot and stepped out into the sunlight. "Here I am. Sharp as whatever a snee is, and primed to do battle, especially with certain people."

Aleria looked her up and down. "Good. Come on. Let's see what's on the menu for breakfast."

26. An Unfortunate Family Tree

It took two days to finalize whatever it was that Roeble was setting up. Jameta had a blurred idea of products, quotas, price guarantees, quality checks, but it all blended together in the search for the right word, interpreting a turned cheek, a tilt of the head.

In between, though, there was time to sit with Zelfana and watch her dispense leadership, justice, and wisdom. Time to talk to Medlili about Galesia and the way of life there. And to tell about herself and her family's connection to Samnia.

This revelation brought a frown to the girl's smooth brow. "Denali family of Samnia? I know this."

"You do?"

"Yes. Is old story. I will ask."

The following day Medlili caught her after lunch. "My grandmother has decreed. Story time today."

"Is 'story time' what it sounds like?"

"Old story. One old woman remembers. Story of Denali." The girl's smile faded. "Sad story. But must tell. All must hear."

"Everyone? Does that mean the men are invited?"

"Headwoman says everyone."

It didn't take long to arrange. Roeble once more exclaimed at their good fortune in being accepted so deeply into the hearts of these people. He chuckled. "And they aren't doing it for advantage in negotiations. The trading is over!"

There was a fair crowd in the Headwoman's tent, with all the family leaders and their husbands joining the occasion. An old woman in deep black robes stood forward, and Medlili knelt with the Galesians to translate.

The speaker bowed to Zelfana, then posed, and a young woman slipped out and removed her veil for her.

Aleria leaned over. "Story telling needs an honest face, I guess."

Jameta grinned.

The storyteller began to chant in a singsong voice, her body swaying in time to the rhythm of the poem, her hands describing the action in expressive gesture. Medlili translated as fast as she could.

"A long time ago...maybe four hundred years...the Aissa invaded Samnia. They were fierce warriors, wonderful horsemen from the plains to the far north. Ruled with iron fist." The girl's face brightened. "Oh, I know this. Two tribes in Samnia. The Denali were first family of the Aissa tribe, who took over land of Beni Ksabi. More Benis than Aissas, different religion. Now same culture and language, but never...together." She interlaced her fingers. "Marriage forbidden. Government positions...Aissas only. Still very fierce. Story says soldiers went...mad in battle, fight no matter what, even injured to death."

Aleria nodded. "Berserkers. It's an old story."

The old woman paused, staring at them. Medlili reddened, then made an apologetic bow. The story teller continued.

"Ah, makes sense, now. Denali king a hundred years past. Much worse. He was what you say, berserker? Yes, in politics too. Ordered a hundred..." she listened to the chant a moment, "...no, a thousand Benis killed for one man...um...let shadow fall on king. Benis fought Aissas leader. Killed much of family. Story says rest fled far off."

The story teller stopped, and there was a hum of approval and thanks.

"And that is end of story."

Aleria turned to Jameta. "Any of this sound familiar?"

Jameta nodded. "It jibes with my family's lore." She had to smile. "Of course, our tale is that a group of fanatics arose and slaughtered the innocent but popular king, and our poor remnant of the royal family were forced to flee in the night with little more than the clothes on our backs."

"And more than a few jewels sewn into the lining of your coats."

"Aleria, how cynical of you! But we were certainly able to set ourselves up in Galesia quickly."

Roeble frowned. "But you wouldn't be telling us all this only for entertainment."

Medlili nodded. "Trader very smart. Jameta has big problem."

"I do?"

"Yes. Aissa tribe very low in Samnia, now. Beni Ksabi still angry, still afraid. All members of Denali family killed. Much hate."

"You mean because of my name, people will hate me?"

"Might kill quick, and none punish."

Roeble winced. "And who are these people? These Beni Ksabi?"

"Today rulers of Samnia. Also tribes between here and Samnia. All Beni religion." She swung a hand around. "We are Beni religion. Not so strong. You are safe, here."

Jameta looked at the Headwoman. "Ask her what she thinks we should do."

Medlili had a quick conversation with her grandmother. Then she turned to the Galesians. "Pretty Horse Lady must not go further south. Too dangerous."

Jameta felt her cheeks go hot. "We can't stop now. We've been through all this hardship and danger to get here, and we're so close..."

"Pretty Horse Lady stay here. White Sword Lady goes on with Trader Man and White Warrior."

"But I'm their translator. As we get closer to Samnia, I'll be able to understand the people even better!"

Aleria laid a hand on her shoulder. "It doesn't matter that much, Jameta. We were planning to go without a translator before we discovered your ability. Your safety is much more important."

"But..."

"But this was going to be your chance to be useful to the enterprise. Well, you've been very useful already, and now we'll have to do without you."

Jameta felt her dreams tumbling. She remembered Lord Dennal's instructions. A lump rose in her throat as she thought of what she would say to him when she returned and told him that she had failed.

Medlili was hovering close, and they turned to her. "My grandmother has also idea..."

"Yes?"

"You need translator, yes?"

Jameta took in the girl's hesitant posture, her glowing eyes. "You! She's offering you to go in my stead."

Medlili shrugged. "No danger for me. Same religion, almost same language. My two brothers come, protect me." She took Jameta's hand, led her towards the Headwoman. "Trade granddaughters, yes?"

The older woman's bejewelled hand rose from her veils. *The Pretty Horse Lady will visit with me awhile. You will teach me about Galesia.*

Is what you want?

The woman released her hand and made a seesaw motion, her graceful gesture an echo of her early life as a dancer. *What I want means little. It is what the Great God wills. You will stay. You have no other choice.*

Jameta bowed and grasped the old woman's hand briefly. *Thank you, Headwoman.*

Then she turned to Aleria. "But what if I didn't tell anyone my name...?"

The Caravan Master smiled. "It's still too dangerous, not only for you, but for all of us." She waved a hand towards Medlili. "And she really wants to go."

Regarding the other girl's anxious face, Jameta sighed. "I suppose you're right."

Aleria slapped her on the shoulder. "Think of it as a chance to learn another culture. By the time we get back, I expect you to be speaking their version of Samnian perfectly."

"How long will you be gone?"

Aleria glanced at Roeble.

He scratched his cheek. "Hard to say. Not more than a month. The summer is moving on, and the rainy season is no time to be trekking with heavy loads. No, I'd say one month, maximum, and all the gods are willing."

Aleria snapped her fingers. "And that's a solution to the Roan's problem as well."

"How so?"

"He's not healing up fast enough to go on. I don't want to lose him, but a month's rest would put him back in his normal fettle, and all Roeble's gods protect us."

Jameta forced a grin. "You'd be happy to lose him. Fine. I'll stay here and pretend to be a good little tribeswoman. I'll exercise the Roan up into fighting trim. You go out in the sand and the rocks and the dangers, and I'll lie here in a comfortable tent in luxury."

Roeble was looking past her at the Headwoman. "I'm not sure you'll get the luxury part."

Jameta turned to regard the old woman, who beckoned to her. She went forward hesitantly. The woman pointed to a cushion beside her. Jameta sat. That ringed hand appeared, patting her on the shoulder firmly enough to push her down in the seat.

She regarded her party. Medlili made a sympathetic face.

It seemed very suspicious. "What's the problem?"

"Well, I am favourite granddaughter..."

"And that's not completely a good thing?"

The other girl shrugged. "Sometimes..."

The firm old hand patted Jameta's shoulder again, and she looked up. *Don't worry. We will get along fine.*

She patted the wrinkled knuckles. *Favourite grandmother.*

The old woman laughed. *Good granddaughter.*

27. The Ancient Curse

For the first while following the departure of the caravan Jameta was awash in the new culture. She felt battered by all the differences, and the longing to speak Galesian was a deep ache in her. But the days passed and her loneliness eased. A lot of her time was at Zelfana's side, learning the skills of tribal leadership, which turned out to be an exhaustive training. *If this is how Medlili works every day, she's going to be some kind of diplomat when she's done!* She took over Medlili's duties in the cooking area, or as many of them as she could manage, under the firm eye of Hajira. She also took dance lessons with the younger girls, an activity she enjoyed immensely. Hajira was a wonderful dancer and a good teacher, and Jameta felt her skills improving.

As she got more comfortable with the language she spent more and more time with Amguid, the old storyteller, who had taken it upon herself to teach the new "granddaughter" the lore of her people. She was particularly insistent that Jameta learn the saga about Tamdjert, a minor hero who didn't do much except make an important journey to somewhere. Jameta had given in and was beginning to get the plot straight when she began to recognize places in the story. A particular ridge that cut off sharp like the nose of a huge, reclining sleeper. A valley that divided and joined again. *This is the route to the Ferbodean border. She's teaching me the caravan route home!* At this point, she threw herself into her studies with more enthusiasm.

The nomads were aghast at her ignorance of the desert, especially its dangers. Sand traps that could swallow rider and horse. Snakes and scorpions. Dust storms and sand storms and moving dunes that could travel twenty yards in a day. She took it all in, schooling herself and her horses as the men insisted. *Just in case.*

She also joined the women on their foraging expeditions, where it was brought home to her how strange this land was. The caravan, with its noise, its large numbers of animals and people and its store of food had insulated her from the realities of life in this arid place.

The desert was filled in equal parts with food and danger. Jameta threw herself into the study of this environment, aware of how useful the knowledge could be in an emergency. The women scorned the pack of emergency rations she carried on her saddle. Dried meat was exactly that: dry. In the desert, food that needed water to wash it down was useless. Mare's or goat's milk was the usual drink. All cooking was done in buttermilk, to save water. She learned to cook unleavened bread laid bare on top of the coals of a tiny fire. Dust off the ashes, and it was very tasty.

She foraged with the women and rode with the men, racing Doe and Brownie against their fine desert steeds. She was pleased at the results, because depending on the terrain, her mounts did well. In the rocks and bush of the hills the smaller, more agile horses could leave her behind, but give them a straight, firm road, and the long legs of her beauties left the fastest desert horses gasping.

The Roan was another matter. Big, heavy and slow by the standards of the other horses, he still dominated them in the pasture, standing with his head over the withers of many of the stallions, even. All but Sfisef's stallion allowed this familiarity with little upset. With Al Mudarib, the Roan minded his manners. Most of the time.

Jameta was checking his leg one morning when the Headman appeared.

How is he?

I think...good.

Completely healed?

I think so.

Would you like to try him out?

Yes, yes, I would. When?

Come with me. I have a short ride to look into a problem

Good...but I have...problem. Erlon left big saddle at El Sibh.

Ah. You have no saddle big enough?

I don't think mine...

The Headman measured the big cart horse with his eye. *I have exactly the one*

You have? I thought...all horses small here.

My father was a big man. He rode a big horse. Not this big, but... He ran a hand over the horse's back. *I will bring the saddle. You get ready to ride.*

She glanced around. *I am ready, I think...*

He shook his head. *I never leave camp without my sword.* He indicated her bare forearms.

Oh. Yes, I should...

Fine. I will be right back.

Thank you, Sfissef.

She went into her tent and pulled on the vambraces. They fit snugly. *Hmm. I'm gaining weight or muscle. Maybe both. Food's good, work's hard.* She considered the vest. *This is only a quick jog to check out the Roan's leg. I doubt if I'll end up in a pitched battle.* Then she thought about what Sfisif said and put it on in spite of the weight. Over the days of heat and sweat the leather had conformed to her body shape, and now it fitted like a second skin. *Which is not an advantage in this heat.*

Smiling to herself, she topped up her waterbag and returned to the picket line. Sfissef was just arriving with an interesting saddle. It was bigger than the ones she had seen in camp and had a higher cantle.

Do you think this will fit?

I will try. She slung the saddle over the Roan's broad withers, slapping his shoulder when he shied from the unaccustomed feel. The girth system was more complicated than she was used to, but it resembled a packsaddle, having breastcollar and breechband to keep it from sliding forward or back.

Strong saddle. What is this? She flipped a long strap attached to one side of the pommel.

The Headman shrugged. "It's a fighting strap. Our horses turn quickly in battle. They often fight with their feet."

She tugged once more at the cinch, then swung into the saddle and wiggled around. *I see. Too wide for me.* She laid the strap across her thighs and cinched it down, not too tight. *Feels better. Shall we go?*

He reached up and took the end from her. *Fold this back through the ring. In an emergency, you pull...so...and the whole thing comes free.* He mounted and kneed Al Mudarib alongside. *How fast can we go?*

She shook her head. *Not too much. I think leg is good. Maybe not.*

He nodded and trotted his steed out of camp, heading up along a tiny stream that wound its way down the rocks to die in the sand.

It was a beautiful morning, as the full heat of the sun had not burned off either the dew or the cool of the night. The Roan was happy to be out: his neck arched, his ears scanning in all directions. He even allowed Al Mudarib to lead without more than a half-hearted nip towards his hindquarters, which Jameta headed off with a twitch of the reins.

She decided it was a good time to practise her Samnian. Her inability to communicate was crucial, and the men used a different vocabulary from the women she spent most of her time with. *Where...do we...are we going?*

There's a good view up here, and I can see what I want to see. Can your horse climb this trail?

She looked where he gestured. A narrow path wound up between the shrubs and exposed rocks. It didn't look too steep. *Injury...over, I think. We go his speed.*

Fair enough. He turned his horse up the trail, and she signalled the Roan to follow.

He would allow the smaller horse to lead, but he was certainly not going to let it get too far ahead of him. His nose overlapping the stallion's rump, he surged forward. Jameta chuckled and held him in check. She watched his movement, conscious of the feel of his gait, but there was nothing: no hesitation, no favouring of the leg.

He is good.

Fine. We will be at the top, soon.

The scrub began to thin, with more and more rocks sticking up through the sparse grass that scattered across the scant soil. The footing became rockier, and the Roan's steel shoes clacked and slithered. The unshod stallion danced up the track, and Jameta winced at her steed's rough gait. Then she grinned. *Cultural differences between horses, I guess.*

They had reached a spot where the bones of the mountain, ground smooth by erosion, sloped gently to the skyline. As he topped this rise, the Headman held out a restraining hand to her and slowed his horse, edging forward, standing in his stirrups so he could see over the top. Then he spoke a word she had never heard before. It sounded like a curse.

She eased the Roan up beside him and looked to where he pointed.

A column of horses wound through the scrub, heading along a well-used track towards the Tolbè camp. Sfisef swung his hand to the right. Closer to camp a line of his tribeswomen, coming home from gathering, strolled down the same trail.

Who is that?

It looks like the Aine Lareba. Travelling, see?

In the rear of the column heavily laden cattle and horses plodded, and far behind a scattered herd of sheep and goats grazed along. Once Jameta knew what to look for, she could spy bright dots of fabric spread out across the countryside: women gathering firewood and whatever food they could glean.

This... problem?

He shrugged. *They should not be here in summer. This is our territory now. Perhaps the dry weather pushes them? But what if they come to fight? Maybe it is a problem, maybe not.* He mused a moment, then made up his mind. "I'm going for help. Quickly. You stay here and watch.*

Watch? No more?

He indicated her big, clumsy horse, her lack of weapons. *What else? If they attack, come and tell us.*

She nodded, the familiar helplessness like a ball of fire in her gut. *I must learn to fight. I could do something!*

He spun his stallion and clattered back down the trail: no longer graceful, but much faster than when they climbed it.

She turned to analyze the scene below. The vanguard of the other tribesmen, in no hurry, was slowly catching up to the women on the ground. As she watched, a cloud of dust scurried back towards the intruders. It must be an outrider, bringing news of the quarry ahead. *Now we will see how they react.*

It didn't look good. The approaching horsemen swirled out into a long front winding through the scrub forest, and she could see the glint of drawn swords. Around the next bend in the valley, the Tolbè tribeswomen strolled on their way, unaware of the danger easing up behind them.

I need to be closer.

Jameta pushed the Roan to the edge of the cliff and searched the hillside below her. *There! Over to the right. That ridge comes out above our people. I think we could...*she kneed the horse ahead, and he took the plunge, sliding and pawing to keep his balance. He made the first steep pitch and trotted more easily down through the thickening forest, headed for the vantage point. A huge plume of dust rose behind them, but it couldn't be helped. Her need was too strong to worry about details.

When she reached the open ridge again, the whole scene lay before her. The enemy riders were at a trot, now. As she looked to the right, she could see the reason. The Tolbè women had become aware of their peril and were streaming down the trail, some sprinting ahead, the older ones trailing. Three dots of colour – *must be an older woman with attendants* – were lagging far behind.

Farther off towards camp was the rescue party, a column of riders galloping at full speed along the trail. She only had to watch a moment to know they would be too late.

Again her impotence burned at her. The Roan shifted under her, agitated by her uncertainty. She held him back, but it did no good. As she pulled on the reins he half-reared, snorting. The urgency in his manner came through to her.

We must do something!

Reaching down, she yanked the fighting strap tight across her thighs, clamping her legs to the saddle. "All right, Hammerhead. You want to go, let's go."

She jammed her heels into his sides. Startled, he took the edge of the drop-off with a bound and landed far down the slope in a slither of pine needles and gravel. The last thing she saw before she dropped in among the trees was a trio of horsemen splitting from the approaching enemy line and cutting towards her. *Good enough. They might be surprised.*

The Roan dodged down the hill, slipping to his haunches on the rocky spots but rising gamely again and surging forward. Branches slapped at her face and trunks scored her knees. Thankful for her forearm guards, she protected herself as best she could, allowing the horse to choose his own path.

They hit the open valley floor at full gallop as the leading attackers caught up to the lagging trio. The old woman was down on the ground, and two girls stood over her, bravely brandishing short daggers. Swords held high, five enemy tribesmen galloped forward, laughing and cheering to each other.

She watched the scene in helpless dismay as her mount thundered towards them. *I'll never make it in time. I can't watch this. I have to do better! Come on, Horse! Faster!* The frustration built, and a white-hot anger clawed at the edges of her mind. It surged in rhythm with the Roan's bounding gait, and she could feel it taking over her whole being, a red haze covering her sight.

And then everything changed. The helpless anger slid aside, and a great calm came over her. Time seemed to slow, and she could see everything, calculate angles, assess threats. A wild scream arose, and she registered that it was from her throat and that of the Roan as he surged forward, his ears flattened into his mane.

The heads of the attacking tribesmen turned as one, and they straightened in their saddles, hauling their mounts around to face the new threat.

Too late. As they turned, their horses off balance, the Roan was among them, his hulking shoulders knocking the first two spinning. In his next stride he reared and plunged forward, steel-shod front hooves slashing at the back of another horse, pounding it into the dirt. She hauled right on the reins and he pivoted on his forefeet, his rear hooves driving into the side of the next enemy, the cracking of bones and the howls of pain from both rider and horse rising above the tumult.

The final rider had time to ready himself, and his nimble steed ducked the juggernaut's charge. But the sword slash came in dream-like slowness, and she fended it off with an easy warding gesture of her metal-covered arm. Then the Roan was turning, and she felt her body strain as he switched ends and attacked with his teeth, shredding the haunch of the enemy stallion that screamed and fled, rider clinging for life. The force of the turn laid her out along his back, arched over the high cantle, and she wrenched herself upright again, ignoring pain, her eyes scanning the scene.

During this brief battle the other enemy horsemen had converged and were rushing at her from both sides. In an eye-blink of calm, she assessed the situation.

Away in the depths of her head a small voice was trying to get her attention. *This is not normal, Jameta. What are you doing?*

She pushed it aside. *We have an enemy to conquer. Where are those tribesmen when I need them?*

The answer came in the high yodel of the Aine Tolbè, and a stream of horsemen galloped out into the open behind her. Shouting and waving them on, Jameta turned on the approaching enemy. The line to her right was packed more densely, and she chose that direction. The Roan needed no urging. Their battle cries blending, they charged into the mob of horses and men, piling up a wave of falling animals and scrambling riders in front of them, a mass that tangled with each other, some with their backs turned trying to flee, others fighting their way forward.

In a tremendous leap the Roan vaulted from the back of one falling horse completely over the next, sweeping its rider aside with a slash of his teeth. Then he was in the middle of them, kicking out front and rear, spinning to kick again. And all the time Jameta urged him on, her yells of rage driving him to further exertions.

And then the Tolbè closed in behind her. There was a volley of musket fire, and Lareba riders fell like wheat before a scythe. Now Jameta was flanked by men with flashing swords, and she charged down the line of enemy, who by now were concerned only with getting out of her path.

Once again, the small voice whispered. *You must control yourself. This is not right.*

The ecstasy of the battle swept her away. She thundered on, the Roan screaming and striking in all directions.

Then there was only one more enemy before her.

A tall woman stood on the trail, her sharp digging stick protectively raised, a basket of food scattered at her feet. A small, tousled head of hair and a tiny round face peered over her shoulder from a bundle slung on her back. Her mouth contorted in fear, the Lareban held her ground as the beast surged down on her.

Jameta wrenched on the reins in desperation, and the Roan slid to a halt, raising a hail of gravel that covered the woman. An indignant wail rose from the child as dirt splashed its face. The woman slung the baby forward, gentle fingers brushing the dust away.

Jameta sat on the heaving Roan staring down at the tender scene. The rage faded; the world took on its normal colours and sounds. She peered around. Her arm-guards were cut and dented, her forearms bruised beneath. Her body ached as if she had been twisted in half and jammed back together.

She looked down. The Roan's hide was streaked with sweat, gore and strings of saliva. A shallow slash ran at an angle along his near shoulder ahead of her knee, and blood trickled from the lower end.

The baby's cries died to whimpers.

Is it all right?

The mother glanced up. *Dirt in his eyes.*

Crying... help.

I hope so.

Then the woman remembered to be afraid. *Who are you? What do you want?*

Jameta shrugged. *I am called Pretty Horse Woman. Your men...attack our people.*

The tall woman frowned. *That is a pretty horse?*

Jameta laughed. *No. This one is pack horse.*

This brought forth a smile. *A pack horse? And what do the warriors' horses look like in your tribe?*

Same to yours. She waved her hand towards the mounted men milling around behind her. It seemed that the battle was over. She remembered, now. *Your men make big mistake. They attack our women.*

They did what? The Lareban stood even taller, and her eyes blazed in the shadow of her shawl.

Attack. Old woman and children. I stop them.

The other sniffed. *Stupid men. Come. I have words for them.*

By now the baby was making mewling sounds. The mother opened her shawl, slung the child around to her breast and strode forward. Jameta and the Roan, quiet now, followed.

When they reached the open the mob of men stood staring at each other, swords in fists, but slanted down. Most were still mounted. Jameta's tribesmen were holding their muskets at the ready: not pointed at anyone, but dangerously close to it.

The woman shouldered between them. *What is going on? Outoul, what have you done?*

A young man who was keeping his left arm tight against his body with his right hand frowned and bowed his head. *They attacked us, Headwoman.*

Her hand flashed towards the old woman, sitting comfortably on a rock, now, her two granddaughters fussing over her. *They attacked you?*

The lad's head went up, and he stared at Jameta, perched on the Roan high above him. *The Warrior Woman attacked us. She killed both Idlés and Dragon. She crushed Edjelet's leg and several of Panther's ribs. I think my arm's broken. Look what she did.* He had no use of his arms, but he gestured with his chin down the line, were a path of bodies, both men and horses, writhed in pain or lay splayed in the awkwardness of death. Nearby a man stood over a struggling horse, tears in his eyes and a dagger in his hand.

Jameta turned her head, knowing what must come next.

The Headwoman strode over to pick up the pieces of a sword, lying in the dirt a few feet from the old woman. She glanced around at the torn prairie soil. *This looks like your sword, Outoul. There was a battle right here.* She turned to the old woman. *Are you well, Grandmother of the Tolbè?*

The old lady waved her hand in a dismissive gesture.

The spoor is clear. The woman strode back to the young tribesman. *Outoul, you have done an evil deed here today. We need help, not enemies. And now what have you done?* Her hand flashed towards Jameta. *You have wakened an ancient curse, and our reward is that it has been visited upon our tribe. Five-six good men killed. Many horses injured.* She stared him down. *There will be a Speaking on this."

The youth slunk away.

The tall woman turned to the Headman. *This is a mess, Sfisef of the Tolbè.*

He nodded. *Why are you here, Ilamane? This is not the Aine Lareba season for this path.*

The drought and the Ferbodeans. Both have been pushing us. We hoped to pass through without trouble. We did not expect to see you this far north at this time of year.

He winced at her unspoken question. *Us too. The drought and the Ferbodeans.*

They regarded each other, shaking their heads.

With your permission, we will leave, now. May we cross your lands to the west, to reach the Valley of the Hasi Bel?

He nodded. *If you will travel in peace, you may go in peace. You will meet the Aine Hasisna there.*

We have dealt with the Hasisna. We must again, no matter the cost. Until the weather changes and the Ferbodeans are put in their place...

I am forced to agree. The rains we cannot affect. One day soon we will deal with the Ferbodean menace. Will you help us?

The woman laughed. *If the Warrior Woman walks amongst us again, we would follow her unto the Edge of the Darkness.*

They both turned and looked at Jameta, who raised her hands in defence. *I only understand part. I don't know what you say.*

They both nodded sagely, but she had the feeling they were agreeing about something other than what she had told them.

The tribeswoman nodded. *It is decided, then.* She slipped her baby around to her back again. *We go. Headman, I wish you cool streams and fertile valleys until we meet for a more deadly reckoning.*

Cool streams and fertile valleys, Headwoman.

The woman walked over to the Roan and laid a hand on Jameta's knee. *I wish you peace within yourself, Pretty Horse Lady. It may not be easy to find.*

Jameta smiled as much as she could, then wiggled her fingers at the shiny dark eyes peering up at her over the woman's shoulder. She was rewarded by a loud burp.

The Headwoman of the Lareba chuckled, but then her face dropped into sorrow. She shook her head and strode away; her people began to gather their wounded and their dead to follow her.

The Headman looked up at Jameta. *It seems the myths of your family have come to reality again.*

Jameta shook her head. *I...don't understand...* The impact of what had just happened was beginning to strike her. Her whole body felt shaky, and the sounds and images of the battle swarmed through her mind.

Sfisef also reached up, but his hand fell on the Roan's neck beside her leg. For once the horse did not react. *Perhaps now is not the time to worry about understanding. For now, the Aine Tolbè have much to thank you for. You must speak of this with Selfana at a later time.*

An image of the canny eyes of the veiled woman passed through Jameta's mind, and warmth suffused her. *Yes. I must speak with Zelfana*

But until that time... he turned and said something to one of the women, and she pulled off one of her veils. He handed it to Jameta. *Please wear this.*

Why...?

Power. You must display your new strength. It would be false to do otherwise.

She thought about that. *I suppose.* She knotted the cloth behind her head, sliding it around until it felt comfortable, chiding herself. It's not as if I've never worn one. Then, I thought it was a quaint folk custom. Now I want to hide behind it.

28. Traders Return

As the days went by Jameta became used to the veil. It only got in the way occasionally, and it certainly changed how the Tolbè treated her. Or something changed it. Now, when she sat with Zelfana in council the Headwoman would turn to her with a question about how some detail of life was dealt with in her tribe. Once in a while she understood the question clearly enough and had something to contribute.

Hajira was particularly comfortable in her presence, now, treating her with the casual equality of sisters. Now they danced together, each practicing the other's ideas, each learning from the other, discovering with glee that Jameta's family dances had echoes in Hajira's lore.

It was the same with Zelfana. With her developing ease in the language, Jameta was able to discuss her problems with the older woman.

When she had finished her halting explanation of Erlon's strange reluctance, Zelfana smiled. *I know little of this man. He seems kind.*

Yes. He is kind. That is strange in a warrior.

Ah, but what kind of a warrior is he?

Jameta frowned. *Warrior is warrior. What do you mean?*

The Headwoman shook her head. *He is a special kind of warrior. What does he do?*

He guards...oh. I see.

Yes. It takes a certain kind of warrior to guard. It is his nature. That is where the kindness comes from. He wishes to protect. She regarded Jameta. *And above all, he wishes to protect you.*

I do not argue. But why...? She shook her head. It was hard enough to figure out, let alone talk about it in another language.

Zelfana laid a hand on her cheek. *Do you not see, my daughter, that he protects you from himself?*

He what...? And then it all came together. *Oh. He sees him danger to me, and he protects me from danger. But he wants to be with me. Oh, the poor man!*

The Tolbè woman brought her other hand up, and she cupped Jameta's face in her palms. *You are a very lucky young woman.*

I am? How is this so?

Hajira laughed. *Because when this young silliness is over, you will have a wonderful marriage. You are each so concerned about the other's happiness that now it keeps you apart. Once you are together, you will create an unbreakable bond. I envy you.* Her regard drifted across the camp, her eyes unfocussed. *But not much.*

They both chuckled and returned their attention to the bread cooking on a convex pan, upturned over a bed of glowing coals.

Jameta was even invited to observe when emissaries from another tribe were officially greeted in the Headwoman's tent. When she asked how she should dress for this occasion, Zelfana was firm. *Do not wear the dress your mother made.*

But that's all I have that is appropriate. She was proud of that dress. It held its own next to the clothing of these women who wove all their lives.

No. That dress says 'Samnia' too strongly. We do not need that kind of trouble.

I see. She wore her Galesian dress instead.

She was also surprised when she went to sit in her usual chair to find that it had been replaced by a larger lounge, such as that which Hajira used.

Zelfana, as yet unveiled, grinned at her. *Today we bargain for the year's water and grazing rights. We present our most powerful face to our allies.* Then she became serious. *This is a year of import to all our tribes. The menace of the Ferbodeans must be dealt with, and conditions for this are ripe. The tribes need strong leadership, and the Aine Tolbè are willing to provide it. With help from special friends.*

The visitors were announced, she and the Headwoman put on their veils, and Jameta was left to mull over what kind of leadership the old woman meant.

It soon became apparent that she had a place in the discussions. Hajira took the role of hostess, and she introduced Jameta immediately after Zelfana. Their guests, the Headwoman and Headman of the Aine Tmassa and several of their advisors, settled back on their heels at the mention of her name; heads turned and eyes met.

After the introductions were complete the bargaining began. Most of it was not of great moment, involving the restatement of certain age-old rights, privileges and access routes along the shared boundary of their grazing lands. As Jameta was beginning to realize, the boundaries were fluid to the point of not existing. Land that was used by sheep herders in the spring might be occupied by horsemen in another season. Precise and diplomatic discussion was crucial, if incidents of the type Jameta had been thrown into were to be avoided.

It took two days to cover all the details, with more convivial arrangements like inter-tribal marriages and family alliances taking up most of the second day. And night. Two lucky Tolbè youths had been accepted as husbands for two prominent Tmassa girls, and the betrothals were celebrated with great joy and quantities of fermented mare's milk.

The discussions on the third day began late in a more serious mein. There was but one topic: Ferbodin. All parties were aware of the problem. Ferbodean soldiers were patrolling deeper into tribal lands than ever before. The mines were spilling slag over grazing ground and fouling scarce water supplies. Jameta listened as the talk ran on, and she could feel the building frustration. No one wanted war, but the drought had pushed the tribes to the brink of trouble. Older heads, for once, were not the cool ones. Land overgrazed this year might be an eroded mess in five years time.

Finally the Headwoman of the Tmassa looked directly at Jameta. *Zelfana of the Tolbè, there is one aspect of this situation we have not discussed. What does your esteemed visitor have to contribute?*

Zelfana nodded to Jameta. *My granddaughter speaks when she will and has the wisdom to hold her opinion until she has one.*

Jameta regarded the old woman. Her new position as granddaughter was very convenient. She considered her reply. This could have diplomatic repercussions, all the way back to the King of Galesia.

She bowed her head in respect. *I would not presume to instruct the Dry Land People in how to conduct their affairs.*

The Tolbè Headwoman nodded. *But you may have knowledge of the wider affairs of the world due to your education and your upbringing that could be of use to us.* And then she spoke in clear Galesian, "Speak strong and speak true, my daughter."

Jameta concealed her surprise, satisfying herself with a warning glare at the devious old woman. Then she turned her mind to the matter at hand.

People of the Dry Lands. Members of the Tmassa and Tolbè. I have information to consider. I know the realms to the west: how they think and act. Regard my words.

*The Ferbodeans are trouble to Galesia as well. Always they push boundaries. Always they push their ideas. Always their "People's

Government" is only government. All others are wrong. All others must fall. Do you know of Pavenkov?*

The Headman of the Tmassa rose from his seat onto his knees. *We know Pavenkov. He has lured foolish young men into following him. They do ill to all the tribes, and ill to their own souls.*

Jameta nodded. *Pavenkov is the worst of the Ferbodeans. He would use power and ideas of Ferbodin to profit himself. He is worst of all problems in Ferbodin.*

She turned to speak generally to the group. *You know of Galesia, my country, to west of Ferbodin. Do you know Domaland?*

Uncertain nods.

Domaland is very powerful realm. Much business, many factories, much money. Much salt. Make guns, swords, cooking pots. Mines very important to Domaland. Mines here are not Ferbodean. Ferbodean's earn salt from mines. Domaland owns mines.

There was a buzz of comment at this, and Jameta sat back, satisfied for the moment. But the Headwoman of the other tribe wanted more. *Can the Warrior Woman tell what these realms will do?"

Jameta glanced at Zelfana to see how she would react to the name, but the old woman just looked smug.

*Who is to know what any man will do? Realms are many men. Do many things. But I will make prediction. Ferbodeans want land. Ferbodeans want all to live like them. Ferbodeans will take your land. They will push you away, and they will destroy your ways of living. If you stay, you must become like Ferbodeans. Live in cement houses.

Galesians want trade. Galesians will let you live as you will, if you trade with them. But... She held up a cautioning hand, *...goods and ideas Galesians bring change your life. When Galesian things are important, tribal things are not important. Change comes.*

Zelfana brushed this aside. *The river makes a different course every spring. What will the Domalians do?*

The Domalians want money. Salt. They don't want land. They want metals and jewels from underneath. They protect mines with Double-S rifles and cannons. If you let them be, they let you be. Do not attack Domalian businesses.

But they destroy our grazing lands and our water! This came from a younger man who had sat through all the meetings and said little. His tribesmen frowned at him, but Jameta could tell they wanted a response.

Domalians are traders. You bargain with them. They will pay what they must.

The Tmassa Headman frowned. *Can they change their mining?*

I do not know mining. But they will not try if no one tells them to.

The man nodded with a grim smile. She knew what he was thinking.

If you chase Ferbodeans away, you deal with Domalians. If you chase Domalians away, Ferbodeans angry, attack you stronger. Domalians attack with many guns. This is truth.

Zelfana nodded and reached for her veil, the signal that the meeting was over. *We must think on these things. We must talk to our allies.*

The other women put on their veils, and everyone rose. When the guests had left the tent, Jameta rounded on Zelfana. "You speak Galesian!"

The Headwoman shrugged and tilted her hand back and forth.

"Medlili was right. You are a sly old woman! And I hope you understand that!" She switched to Samnian. *And I am granddaughter, now? When you need me?*

The old woman brought her hands together and made a pulling motion. *Family power is strong. Your power and my power together is stronger.*

There was one thing they had to get straight. *If you and I agree, we are strong. But what if we do not agree?*

Then we must talk. That is the woman's way.

That is the woman's way, grandmother.

The corners of the old woman's eyes crinkled, and she laid a hand on Jameta's shoulder. *Good granddaughter.*

* * *

So when the Dalmyn caravan wound its way across the sand to the Tolbè camp, Jameta was in the front of the official greeting party, resplendent in a Tolbè robe, complete with translucent veil. Levan, in his usual outrider position, rode up first.

"Jameta. Have you gone native? I hardly recognized you."

"That's the general idea. Mind your manners and talk to the Headman."

Erlon was right behind him. He jumped from his horse and swept her up in an engulfing hug. "You can't fool me. I'd know that posture anywhere."

She gripped his neck, revelling in the smell of him, the strength of his arms around her. "And you don't have to greet anyone else. I'm already happy."

The rest of the party arrived, and all was abustle. Erlon managed his duties without letting her out of the circle of his arm.

Finally there was a lull, and he looked down at her. "Has something happened?"

"What do you mean?"

He raised his eyebrows. "Let me try again. What happened? You're wearing a veil, and they're all treating you like you deserve it."

"Yes, something happened." She had an inspiration. "I'll tell you all about it one day."

He frowned, but he couldn't keep it up. "I deserve that, but it won't work. Everybody seems happy about it, so they won't be able to keep their mouths shut."

She shrugged. "Then wait until tonight, and whatever you haven't found out by the end of the feast, I'll tell you."

"A feast and the answers to all my questions. This is even better than my fondest dreams as I struggled through sandstorms and bandit attacks to reach you."

"Was it a tough trip?"

"Well, I exaggerate about the bandit attacks. That last day across the desert is a scorcher, though. Wells are getting low. Good thing we knew the route. Medlili is worth more than her Galesian translations. She knows the lore of the land. Poems and songs about the routes, the waterholes, the dangerous places. Came in handy a couple of times."

"How did she make out otherwise?"

He grinned. "That one will always do fine. The men all do whatever she wants, and the gods help anyone who thinks she's cute and pats her on the head."

"And what about you? Did you manage to resist?"

"Resist what? Do you know how difficult it is to be treated with...what to call it...veneration?"

"Veneration? Whatever for?"

"You'd have to ask her. There's a level of formality she never drops. You can imagine how she is with all the men. She has a certain level of flirting that never steps over the line, but automatically assumes you're going to do whatever she wants, just because she's the one that's asking."

"But not with you."

"Oh, no. With me she's always deadly serious, as if I'm a very important person. Like a revered old uncle. Positively unsettling." He grinned and tightened his arm around her. "And then there's Lavan."

"What's she done to him?"

"That's it. Nothing. You know what he's like. If she snapped her fingers, he'd be grovelling at her feet."

"I think you're underrating Lavan, but I admit he would be tempted."

"But she didn't. She doesn't flirt with him, either. She treats him like a younger brother."

Jameta nodded. "That's very thoughtful of her. People are very fragile. When you have the ability to destroy them, you have to be careful."

He glanced down at her and frowned. "And where did that come from?"

She shrugged. "An observation."

"Hmm. You definitely have changed. Perhaps I should start asking questions."

"If you will ask them with your arm around me, go right ahead."

He dropped his arm. "Well, maybe that's not such a good idea either. I suppose I have work to do."

She looked up at him, and his face reddened. He forced a smile. "Save me a place at the feast, will you? If a mere soldier may sit beside whatever it is these people have turned you into?"

She sighed. "Oh, I'm sure you can sit wherever you like. Away you go."

He stood there.

"Go! I understand."

"You do?"

"Oh, yes. Life is unfolding exactly as I should have expected." She reached up and touched his cheek. "And if you won't go, I will."

She allowed her finger to trail down his chin as she turned away, prolonging the contact as long as she could.

* * *

She was quite wrong about her story. The feast went on for hours, and there were tales from those who travelled and from those who stayed behind, but never once did anyone mention Jameta's part in the proceedings. Both Aleria and Roeble commented on her new mode of dress, and Lavan casually mentioned the healing wound on the Roan's leg, but that was all. In fact, Lavan didn't say anything all evening, sitting by himself with a cloud on his face. She noted him for further attention when there was time.

When the party was over, Erlon took her hand and led her out of camp, saying nothing. They reached a rock that stood out from the sand, a few small bushes growing in its shelter. They stood there for a moment enjoying the moonlit desert, then he put his hands on her waist and boosted her up to a sitting position on the rock, holding her there until she had her balance.

"Now. You're going to sit there until you tell me the whole story."

"What story is that? I think you pretty well heard everything, tonight."

"Everything except how you and the Roan got in the middle of a tribal war."

"We were hardly in the middle of it."

He took hold of one of her forearm guards, lifting it and running a finger over the dents. "And you got those falling off your horse, did you?"

"Well, no."

"And everyone in the camp treats you like royalty. Those two girls that always hang around with the old lady? Their eyes follow you wherever you go. They never look anywhere else. Now you tell me. What the hell happened?"

So she told him. From beginning to end. The battle, the baby, the horrible sound of breaking bones.

When she had finished, he reached up, lifted her down from the rock and held her in his arms again, because she was crying. The tears ran down in silence, soaking his shirt. He stood there, pressing her head against his chest with one hand, stroking her hair.

When she had calmed, he released her. "How are you handling it?"

She shrugged and sniffled. "Until now, just fine. The people are wonderful. They treat it like the most natural thing in the word. Like having a berserker from an ancient legend is rather nice but nothing out of the ordinary."

"That's because they believe."

"They believe what?"

"That the legends are true. For them, it is nothing out of the ordinary."

"I suppose. And I was able to go along with them. Until you came back. And then I realized how strange it was. Is. For these people, I'm part of their culture. I'm not a stranger anymore. But to all you people, I'm different. It's all backwards."

He took her in his arms again. "Not it isn't. Everyone has always known about you."

"They have?"

"Of course. It was unavoidable. Think about what Ferian said. Now we know what it is. No problem."

"Only that I'm some kind of crazy, likely to go off my head at any moment."

He put a finger under her chin and tilted her head up. She could see his teeth in the moonlight as he smiled. "I don't think so."

His arm around her shoulders, he steered her back to camp. "Now, I've had a long day, and I'm sure Aleria is going to quiz you before she allows you to go to sleep, so you're off to bed. My Gran always said that in the morning light it would all go, 'Poof!' And it always did."

But Aleria said nothing. At least, nothing about any problems. When Jameta came in the Caravan Master was in her cot, a lamp burning. She put her arms up, her fingers locked behind her neck. "So, it looks like you really fitted in. I've been listening to you. You sound like you speak the language fluently."

"I'm not fluent." She sat on the edge of her cot. "My grammar is pretty basic. But I have remembered a whole bunch of vocabulary, and the tribesmen's version of Samnian is mostly a matter of accent. A couple of weeks ago my head made a flip, and I found it much easier."

"Well, that's good. I think the same thing happened to Medlili. She stopped looking so tired all the time."

"How did she manage?"

"She was invaluable. I suppose Erlon told you about the trail poetry?"

"I already discovered that, myself. It's an easy way to remember important lore."

"It was very handy a couple of times."

"And her brothers?"

"They're rather sweet but a little scary. I don't believe their minds work much past horses and killing enemies. But they have very good manners and they treat Medlili like a princess."

"Which she is, I suppose. Sounds like you all did well."

"We did."

"Except..." She looked at Aleria with raised eyebrows.

"Except what?"

"Except Lavan. He's walking around as if the world is on his shoulders."

Aleria chuckled. "Lavan, the man who can prepare himself for anything? Including the horrors of war and the stench of battle?"

Jameta leaned forward, staring at the Caravan Master. "He didn't...run away or something, did he? That would destroy him."

"No, no. He's still brave, at least as far as he has been tested. No, he ran up against something else."

Relieved, Jameta grinned. "Don't tell me he's fallen in love."

Aleria's eyebrows rose. "Good guess. But it's worse than that."

"Unrequited love."

"Worse than that."

"Ah. A challenge. Let me see...I've got it. She played him for a sucker."

"Right again."

"Don't sound so satisfied. That hurts. Was there any damage done? Other than to his pride, I mean."

"He gave our new partners a bargaining edge we were counting on them not having. It may have cost us, but not seriously. No, most of the damage is, as you say, to his pride. Will you have a talk with him?"

"Me?"

"Yes, you. Who else?"

She ran down the list in her head. "Nobody within a few hundred miles."

Aleria lay back. "Thanks. It'll do us all a favour. We thought he was bad when he was cheerful!"

Jameta swung her legs onto her cot. "Well, it sounds like the trading went well."

"Oh, yes. No complaints on that score." She turned to look at Jameta. "But it was good you didn't come. Things are unsettled in Samnia, and we heard a lot about religious differences and riots and things like that."

"Well, things worked well for me, here, so that worked out for the best."

"Tell me all about it once we're on the road again. Plenty of time."

"Good to have you all back, though."

"Good to have the group back together. One short detour to the Horse Fair, then we pick up Vracha and Rogas at the river and head for home."

"Home. That sounds good."

Aleria grinned and blew out the light. "A good journey is one that you're eager to start out and eager to get home at the end."

Jameta refrained from commenting that a bad journey could go the same way. She rolled over and went to sleep.

29. Honey Trap

The following morning, Jameta caught Lavan at breakfast. "Want to take a ride?"

He glanced up at her, then back to his plate, which he had barely touched. "If you want."

"Don't sound so enthused. I've been starved for good company, lately. Especially of the Galesian-speaking variety."

"I'm not much good as company, lately."

"We can deal with that as well. Come on. Eat up. This isn't an easy ride."

"Where are we going?"

"I'm going to show you the scene of my great battle."

He frowned. "Your battle? There's something going on, isn't there? Nobody's saying anything, but everybody seems to think something great happened. Mystical experience and all that." He put a bite of food in his mouth, chewed without enthusiasm. "These tribesmen tend to be superstitious, don't they?"

She took his knife and stabbed another piece of mutton, placed the knife back in his hand. "I wouldn't be too dismissive, if I were you. Something did happen, and it wasn't to them."

His head came around, a small gleam in his eye. "What do you mean, 'it wasn't to them'? Who did it happen to?"

She pointed to the food on his knife. "Finish your breakfast, and let's go."

Later, they sat their horses at the top of the ridge where she and the Headman had watched the beginning of the drama two weeks ago. By the time she described the situation, up to the point where she had decided to act. Lavan's lethargy had retreated.

"That must have been frustrating, to have to watch our allies be ridden down. What happened then?"

"I couldn't just sit up here and watch. I had to go down."

He nodded in sympathy. "Of course you did. I would have. But that's me. What did you think you could possibly do?"

"I didn't think. I had to do something. So I went."

"How did you get there?"

She pointed. The traces of the Roan's slide still showed in the raw earth.

"You slid down there? That Roan is a better horse than we thought."

"Oh, much better."

"So...?"

"So...I..."

Lavan reached over and laid a hand on her arm. "This is hard for you to tell, isn't it?"

"Yes, it is. But I have to tell it and I'd rather it was you, out here with no one else listening, all right?"

"Any way you need. What happened?"

She looked out at the horizon, blue fading into grey. "That story they told about my family? The berserker warriors?"

"Yes..."

She glanced at him and shrugged. "That's it."

"You went crazy?"

"I guess I did. It didn't seem crazy to me. I felt calm and in control. Except the Roan was galloping down the mountainside at twice the speed he should have been, and both of us were screaming at the top of our lungs. My throat was sore for days afterwards."

"Wow! What happened when you got to the enemy?"

"Well, they were about to attack that nice old woman with the striped headscarf."

"The one with the granddaughters that follow her everywhere?"

"That's right, there were five of these idiots galloping at the women with their swords drawn. There wasn't any doubt what was going to happen. So the Roan and I took them out of the battle."

Lavan looked at her a long while. "I'd like you to explain how an unarmed girl on a cart horse took five armed tribesmen and their horses out of a battle. If you could. If it's too difficult, don't, but..."

She sighed. "I don't remember all of it, but he's twice as heavy as any of them and both of us were very, very angry. I remember him shouldering the first two completely off their feet, and then it was all spinning and kicking to the front and the back and grabbing horses and riders in his teeth and throwing them around.

"Once we finished with the first five the others tried to attack, but by then Sfisef had shown up with our men and their muskets, so we charged them, all down the line out towards the flat, there. I remember at one point we seemed to fly, right over top of another horse, but I don't think that could have really happened."

He reached out and twisted the guard on her arm, examining the dents and cuts. "So now we know why the Roan is all carved up. Also how you managed their swords."

"Yes. These work well. I'm so glad Erlon made me wear them." She regarded the dented metal. "They're a bit light, though. I had bruises on my arm underneath."

"How did you get yourself stopped?"

She grinned. "No trouble. A crying baby."

"A what?"

This is easier. I like this part of it. "Their Headwoman was out in front, foraging like they do. I came roaring out of the brush, and there she was, protecting herself with a digging stick, her baby on her back. The Roan threw up a bunch of dust when we stopped, and it got in the baby's eyes. He started to cry. Snapped me straight back to reality."

He grinned. "We'll have to remember that for next time."

"I sincerely hope there's never going to be a next time."

He shrugged. "Maybe not. But I gather it only happens when you need it, so..."

"So, let's hope I never need it. And that was my little adventure."

"Feel better after you've told it?"

"I do. I'll have to tell Roeble and Aleria, and it will be easier, now. I already told Erlon. That was fine."

He grinned. "He'd understand. And be so proud."

"It's nothing I'm proud about. It's like it wasn't really me, you know? Like another woman took over and did it all while I watched."

"Nonetheless. You saved a lot of lives."

"And took a few."

"Hmm. I can see that might bother you."

She glanced at him. "And now it's your turn."

"Me?" He dismounted and walked to the edge, picking up a rock and tossing it down the hill.

"Yes, Lavan. There's a twist in your saddle girth, and everybody knows it. I gather from a comment Aleria made that you bungled it, but that's all. Give."

"Well...it's not so important..."

She dismounted as well and stood beside him. "It's bothering you more than my story bothered me. Tell." She gave him no room to refuse.

"Well..."

"Come on. Start with the girl. What was she like?"

He sighed. "It's difficult to talk about her. She was sort of...well...like you. Slim and dark and pretty..."

"Why, thank you, Sir." She dropped him a curtsey.

"Very funny. Anyway, she knew a little Galesian, and she said she wanted to learn more. So I obliged. It wasn't hard, believe me. We were in the final city before the Samnian border, the one at the end of our planned route?"

"Yes, I remember. Agadez."

"Beautiful place. And Uncle Roeble and Aleria were in heavy negotiations. It was peaceful, and we were there as friends, so everything was pretty relaxed. Timia showed me around the city, and we had a wonderful time together. She has...had a great sense of humour. Didn't mind laughing at herself when she made mistakes."

"You said 'had.' Is she dead?"

"No, but I need to think of her in the past, that's all."

"I understand. What happened?"

"Well, after a week or so we got to be good friends. In fact, it looked like it might get to be more than that. Much more, you know?"

She nodded.

"And she started to ask me about Galesia. She said she wanted to know all about it. Said she would love to go there. In fact, I got the impression she might want to go there..."

"...with you."

"Well, yes. And so I told her all about life at home: the people, the countryside..."

"...the economics, the politics?"

His head dropped. "You put your finger on it there. Then one day we were all sitting around in our hostel after everyone else had gone home, and Uncle Roeble was complaining. He said these people seemed to know a whole lot more about Galesia than we thought they did. He was amazed that they even knew the price of silk in our markets."

She nodded. "And you remembered..."

"...that I had told Timia all about buying silk a few days before."

"Did you tell him?"

"Not at first. I couldn't believe it. But I could test it. I fed her more information, waited a couple of days, then asked Uncle Roeble about it. He said, yes, they knew that as well. So I had to tell him."

"What did he say? What did he do to you?"

Lavan's head drooped. "He was nice about it. Aleria laughed. That made it even more difficult. And then they made me pay."

"How?"

"I had to string her along. I had to feed her information that they wanted to give out."

"So there the two of you were, each trying to play the other. That must have been terrible!"

"It was. I liked her. Sometimes I still did, and I felt that she liked me, too."

Jameta nodded. "There's no reason why she wouldn't. It's easier to be convincing if the lie is mostly true."

"That's a fact I'll never forget."

"And what happened in the end?"

"Somebody figured it out. She just stopped showing up. I asked around, but they said, oh, she'd gone. Very vague, and since I had to do it all through Medlili, I couldn't push. Medlili was nice about it, but still..."

She clapped him on the back. "So you've experienced your first honey trap. Couldn't happen to a more deserving fellow."

He pushed her arm away. "Don't you start laughing at me, too. Aleria is bad enough."

She put her arm back, but in a gentler way. "Don't be so glum. Deal with the problem."

He stood up and walked away, throwing his hands out. "But that's it! I don't know how to deal with it. I've messed up badly, and I can't see any way to make it right."

She got up and went and stood beside him, looking out into the emptiness before them. "You know how you always try to prepare yourself for things, so that when they happen, you can deal with them?"

"Yes." His head dropped. "I've told everybody about it often enough." Then he turned and looked at her. "Does it sound stupid? Do you all laugh at me?"

"No, it doesn't sound stupid. It's your way of dealing with a problem we all have. Everyone has his or her own way. Nobody laughs at you, especially since it seems to work. For you, anyway." She put a hand on his shoulder. "Although it might be better not to tell everybody about it quite so often."

"Hmph. Obviously, since it doesn't work so well as I thought."

"But I once heard you say that what you're afraid of is finding something you're afraid of."

He stared at her, head to one side. "Do you always remember what everyone says?"

"Only the important bits. But now you've found it. You've come up against something you don't know how to handle. It's the next stage, don't you see?"

His brow knitted. "The next stage of what?"

"I don't know what to call it. Maturing. Getting better. What we're all trying to do. You didn't think you'd stay the same all your life, did you? Preparing yourself for everything, being right all the time?"

"Well, I thought I could cope pretty well that way. Guess I was wrong."

"You were. And that's a lesson in itself. But now you have a challenge. How are you going to deal with the things you didn't know were coming, so you couldn't prepare yourself?"

"I see." He thought about it for a while. "So how do I deal with this one?"

She shrugged. "You're asking the wrong person. My solution to problems lately is to go screaming crazy and throw a large horse at them. I don't recommend it for everyone, but you could try if you like. It's your life."

His mouth twitched, then he let go and grinned. "Thanks for putting me back in perspective, anyway. This doesn't seem to be a 'screaming horse' type of problem."

Their chuckles faded into silence, and they stood looking out at the view.

"You know, I really like you, Jameta."

Oh, no! I have to deal with this, now?

"No, you don't have to worry about it." He raised his palms. "You're never going to love someone like me, and I know that you and Erlon are in love with each other. But that makes it easy."

"It does?"

"Yeah. Back to my old idea of preparing yourself. Sometimes you prepare yourself for the inevitable, you know?"

"Not really."

"Well, I think that a man and a woman who like each other can never be the kind of friends that, say, two men can, because there's always a certain attraction between them, that in different circumstances can turn into something more. Do you agree?"

"I think so." *But where is he going with this? I don't like the 'in different circumstances' part.*

"Good. Because there are times when, for some reason, you simply can never have any other relationship. Like with your sister- or brother-in-law, for example. And that makes it rather easy,

201

because you wall that part off and never think about it. It's not that a sexual attraction can't exist. You have to believe that it must never exist and you don't want it to exist. And then it doesn't. See?"

"I suppose."

"So, take you and me, for example. You're too different from me for us to ever have a life together. So that's out of the question. You're in love with a man I respect. So that puts it even further out of the way." He grinned. "Not even counting that sword of his. So we can be friends with no problem. That's no small thing. Having a friend you can trust."

"I hate to sound negative, but isn't this approach subject to the same caveat as the rest of your attitude? You can prepare yourself for anything, a trick that works until it doesn't work. And then where are you?"

He turned to her in glee. "At a changing point in your life, where you have a challenge to accomplish, and some growing to achieve."

"Well, at least you were listening. Does this mean we're still friends?"

"I hope so. That was the whole point of the conversation, wasn't it?"

"Since you started it, I guess you get to say."

"Great. Let's go back to camp. I've got people to talk to."

"What are you going to tell them?"

He shrugged. "Depends who I'm talking to. The important thing is to talk to them."

"Me, too."

They swung up on their horses.

30. Horse Fair

Leaving the Aine Tolbè was difficult for Jameta, but her enthusiasm to prove herself useful to the caravan prodded her on. After two days of meetings and feasts, they left the encampment – this time with all sorts of appropriate gifts in both directions – and headed back up the caravan trail. Zelfana did Jameta the honour of coming out to see her off, Medlili at her shoulder.

Jameta didn't know the protocol, and she didn't care. She gave the old woman a firm hug, which was returned with more strength than she expected.

Zelfana pulled aside her veil to stare into Jameta's eyes. "We will meet again, Granddaughter."

"I hope we do, Grandmother. I learned much from you."

The old eyes twinkled. "I learn, too. Much Galesian."

Jameta switched to Samnian. *Sly Grandmother.* She had never figured out how much Galesian the old woman spoke.

The sly grandmother teaches her granddaughter to be wise.

And the other granddaughter becomes wise as well. She turned to Medlili for an embrace.

"I wish I went with you."

"Caught the travel bug, have you?"

Medlili smiled. "I enjoyed work with your people."

"Well, some day you must come to Galesia."

The Tribeswoman's eyes widened. "You mean that?"

"Of course I do. If your people are to deal with the modern world, you must come and experience it. You have given me the opportunity to learn your world. I must do the same for you."

Medlili made a graceful gesture, bowing her head over open palms. "I will come, then."

"What does that movement mean?"

"It is most solemn promise."

Jameta mimicked the move. "Then I promise I will receive you as I was received in your tents."

Medlili's eyes sparkled. "Perhaps not with a battle."

"Whatever you wish." Jameta glanced around. Her people were all mounted, patiently waiting for her. "And now I must go."

After another round of embraces, including Hajira, Jameta dried her eyes and swung up on Doe. With another longing gaze at the tent encampment, tucked securely against the foot of the mountain, she reined her mount around and nodded to Aleria.

The caravan pulled out.

* * *

They were three days on the trail to the Horse Fair, situated where the secondary caravan route crossed a smaller branch of the Bel River east of the junction. Once again it was an easy slope down to the water, although the river banks were dryer and there was no sign of permanent habitation.

The Dalmyn caravan wound its way down the hill at a sedate speed, and Jameta had a wonderful chance to see the whole Horse Fair spread out below. It covered a wide flat along the river, with pens and corrals on the outside surrounding a row of tents closer in. The Market itself was in the very centre, a mass of dark tent roofs with narrow alleys between them. A haze of dust rose in leisurely drifts above it all, wafting aside with the breeze.

She glanced up at Erlon, riding beside her. "This is wonderful. It's so huge!"

"That's why we came."

They ambled closer, and finally Erlon raised a hand. "I'll trot ahead and find out where we're supposed to camp."

He kicked the Roan to a lope and pulled up to the gate that blocked the road. As far as Jameta could see, the entry was firmly closed, and several soldiers with muskets and metal breastplates stood in formation in front of it. Erlon rode up to them. *I wonder why he didn't dismount?*

After a short conversation he turned and trotted back towards the caravan. The wagons stopped, but Jameta continued, reaching Aleria's wagon at the same time as Erlon.

"What's the matter?"

Erlon shrugged. "They won't say. They don't speak Galesian, but they won't let us in."

"They what?"

"All I got from the officer in charge is that the Fair is closed or full or something. No entry. He was very clear about that."

Aleria turned to Roeble. "Any ideas?"

He shook his head. "I didn't get the impression that there was anybody who had the authority to make an order like that. The Fair isn't run by anyone. It just happens, like it has for centuries. Either someone has taken control of it and wants a bribe, or they really doesn't want us here."

Aleria loosened her sword in its scabbard and checked her pistol for ammunition. "Perhaps we should try a little gentle persuasion."

Roeble shook his head more firmly this time. "No point in forcing our way in. If they don't want us, they won't trade. I wish I knew what's going on."

"Maybe we should go and talk to them."

All eyes turned to Jameta.

"Well, what other choice do we have? Perhaps it's the same as the Tolbè. All we have to do is discover the problem, figure out the rules. At least find out how much the bribe is."

Aleria shook her head. "I don't think it's that simple, Jameta. I figure a show of force would be appropriate. We'll push on up to the gate with a few Double-S rifles showing. I think they'll see reason."

Erlon cleared his throat.

"What?"

He pointed a thumb back toward the gates. "I doubt if a Double-S or three is going to impress them a bunch."

Four soldiers were wheeling a cannon out and pointing it towards them.

Jameta looked down on Aleria from the back of her horse. "Well? Shouldn't I try?"

"Oh, all right. Take Erlon and a couple of the guards with you."

"I don't think so. As Roeble says, I'm not trying to force anyone. If there's a person or group running this show, that's not going to impress them, either. Besides, having my own soldiers there makes it much more difficult for me. When a bunch of men are bristling and waving their weapons at each other it's very hard to figure out what the real problem is. Let me go and have a pleasant chat."

"A pleasant chat?" Aleria stood. "You must be joking. Those are armed guards in front of us with a cannon pointed our way. You're being a little naïve if you think a pleasant chat is the solution."

Jameta glanced around at the other faces. "All right. It's your choice. I'm only offering."

Roeble swung down from his horse. "It could work, Aleria. I've never made any progress with traders by trying to out-muscle them. These men are salesmen, talkers. They're always playing five different games with your head. They look down on people who use force."

"You think she should go?" Aleria stepped down onto the hub of the wagon wheel and stood beside the merchant, regarding the gate, the cannon, and the soldiers.

He shrugged. "Can't hurt."

"We're sending a non-fighter out all alone to confront a half-dozen soldiers. I can see all sorts of chances for hurt."

Jameta dismounted and stood with the two leaders. "It's not like that, Aleria. I'm no threat, and they won't take me seriously enough to bother me. If they won't talk, I'll come back." She grinned. "Doe runs pretty fast."

Aleria finally nodded. "All right. I'm just worried."

"Of course you are. I am too. I'll be careful, just like always. Any suggestions?"

"There's a nice flat spot over to the right of the gate." Roeble pointed. "That would be a great place to set up."

"I'll do my best. Bribes?"

He shrugged. "Find out the going rate. Tell them we'll discuss it."

"Sounds good." She turned towards the gate.

Aleria still had a frown. "You be careful, now. Those aren't choirboys out there, you know."

Jameta felt the anger boil, and she tamped it down, as usual. Then she stopped. *I tried to be polite. Some people need to have their faces pushed in it.* She faced Aleria squarely, unclipping her vambrace. "Pull up your sleeve and look."

Aleria bared her arm, frowning.

Jameta pushed her arm beside it, brown against white. "Do you notice the difference?"

"What difference?"

"The colour."

"Jameta, what are you talking about?"

"I am drawing your attention to the fact that all the evidence points to me <u>not</u> being your little sister. Nor am I one of your employees. It shouldn't need saying, but I am my family's representative in this enterprise, and entitled to an appropriate degree of respect for my opinions."

Once the words started coming, they tumbled out, and she jabbed a finger towards the gate. "In case you need reminding, I have spent my life with men like those over there. I read them like I read my horses. I can tell what they're thinking before they do, I act appropriately and I <u>never</u> have any trouble with them. In fact," she stepped closer and stared into Aleria's startled eyes, "I have a much better record than you do in that respect."

The other woman's face paled, and pang of guilt shot through Jameta, but she kept on.

"Now, I will go out there and talk to those men, and the chances are I will persuade them to let us into the market. If they will not, I will come back and inform you. If I need the backup of half a dozen rifles, then the discussion will become your territory. I will give a fainting, ladylike squeak, and you can come charging in as you always do, with all weapons blazing."

She snapped her wrist guard into place but instead of mounting Doe, she strode towards the Roan. Erlon was off the horse and handing her the reins as she got there.

He grinned and spoke softly. "You <u>are</u> just going to talk to them, aren't you?"

She awarded him her sweetest smile. "Of course I am." She stepped into the saddle and trotted her horse away, leaving a stunned silence behind her.

The familiar feel of a horse moving under her was calming, and she turned her mind to her task. As she approached the group of men confronting her, she could read the signs. *Only the leader wants to be here. The rest are hesitating. I can deal with that. And he's not as brave as he'd like me to believe.*

By the time she reached them, she was cool and prepared.

Good afternoon, lads. Is problem?

You have no right of passage here, foreign woman.

Matter of opinion, yes?

There is no room. You foreigners go away.

Is Horse Fair. All are foreigners. Is plenty room. She pointed to the flat area beyond the gate. *We camp there.*

That is not a camping spot. You go back where you came from!

She swung off the Roan's tall back, walked up to the man and stopped a little too close to him. *My Headwoman, she sends me here because I am polite and small. Not to frighten you.* She poked a thumb over her shoulder and spoke to the other men as well. *My Headwoman is tough lady. She says, 'Run them over. Kill them all.' I say, 'Do not kill men who do their duty. It is not polite. We talk.' So she says, 'Fine. Pretty Horse Woman is soft. Go and save lives.' So I come.*

You are the Pretty Horse Woman? I don't believe it!

She patted the Roan's cheek. *In Dry Lands I am Pretty Horse Woman.* She shrugged. *Other places? Other names.* She smiled at a smaller man to the left of the leader. *I save your life, yes?* Looking less than enthralled with the idea, he sidled away. She glanced at the soldiers on the leader's right. *Smart men. Make good choice.* She allowed her face to relax into a cold stare. They all stepped back.

A movement at the corner of her eye brought her spinning back to confront the leader, face to face. Her jabbing finger directed his attention towards the Galesians. *You see big man? Man with long sword? My husband. He is not happy man. Bandits shoot his horse. You draw sword one finger more, he comes and cuts off head. One swing. Splat!* Her hand brushed past his throat so fast that he had no time to flinch. The tips of her fingernails left a red line.

His hand fell from his sword hilt.

She smiled at them all. *Good. Smart men. Open gate, we camp there.* Her gesture swept towards the chosen campsite. *Kill goat, big feast. You come, yes? Celebrate saved lives?*

A tentative grin softened the growing desperation on leader's face. *A feast?*

Big feast tonight. Trade tomorrow. Tonight, eat, drink, dance. Tomorrow, make money, yes?

The leader spun to his men, speaking more rapidly than she could follow, but the words *trade,* *feast,* and *money* were all in there. They grinned and stepped aside, two of them springing to the heavy gate and throwing their shoulders against it. The cannon was wheeled out of the road, its muzzle pointing along the fence.

Jameta swept her arm in a forward motion, and Aleria's whistle signalled the wagons forward. As they passed, Erlon strolled up beside Jameta. She ducked in under his arm, her hand slipping around his waist, and grinned at the leader of the guards.

The man looked up at Erlon, then gave her a weak smile and rolled his eyes.

She winked and nodded. *Feast. Sundown.* She tugged Erlon away.

"What was that all about?"

"He just realized how big you are."

"And this helped?"

"I may have mentioned the head-chopping thing."

"Ah, I thought you might have." He reached down and took her hand, brushing his fingertips across her nails. "Did I see a fine red line on his neck?"

"I left a mark for you to aim at. But he got the message."

"What, exactly, did you say to them? I was a little worried about your state of mind. Not very diplomatic, as it were."

"I told them that Aleria, out of the goodness of her heart, allowed me to come out and save their lives. The leader thought about pulling his sword when he saw that I was isolating him from his men, but I persuaded him it was a poor choice. He wasn't sure about it until he stood in front of you."

Erlon sighed. "You've been spending too much time with Aleria."

"And why is that?"

"Because you're harder on your friends than your enemies. That was an underhand hit, back there."

"It was. Perhaps I could have found a calmer way to let my feelings be known. But I have tried."

"I noticed. No, you found the way to get through to Aleria. She spends too much time in charge of everyone and she starts to think that her way is how the world works. Safe to say, you changed that today."

"Huh! For the next five minutes, anyway."

"Celebrate your little victories when you find them, my dear. They don't come that often."

"That's a depressing thought. You need cheering up. How about a stroll through the biggest market I've ever seen?"

"Perhaps I should go and see about the camp setup."

"Perhaps you should keep Aleria out of my path while she thinks things over."

He looked down at her. "You mean that, don't you?"

"I do. She doesn't want to see me right now. At least, she may think she wants to see me, but she has to get over the urge to continue the fight. Once she thinks it through she'll calm down. Then I'll apologize for being mean to her and hurting her feelings, and all will be well."

"You just dressed down one of the leaders of our expedition. In front of everyone. And now you'll apologize for hurting her feelings, and you think that will solve it?"

"Probably. If it doesn't, what happens? She'll sulk for a while and then she'll get over it."

He shook his head. "Do you realize that you're talking about Aleria as if she's a pouting teenager?"

She turned to him. "Do you ever get the feeling that all the people around you are acting like pouting teenagers, and most of them need to be patted on the head to make them feel better?"

"Can't say that I have."

"Well, that's why I like your company so much. You're one of the few people I don't have to be polite to."

"I think I've received a compliment but I may not be happy with the results."

She took his arm and pulled him farther into the market. "Celebrate your little victories when you find them, my dear. Now, winning battles makes me hungry, and after two in a row, I'm ravenous. What do you think that man is cooking over there? It smells delicious."

They strolled further in, nibbling something involving shaved meat rolled in a pancake, the sounds, smells and sights washing over them; not every odour was pleasant, but all were exotic and wonderful.

She was admiring the weaving on a rug when Erlon's hand caught her elbow. He leaned in to speak softly. "Don't worry too much, but there's something strange going on."

She leaned back against him, keeping her voice casual. "What is it?"

"Move on, but look around as we go."

She smiled at the vendor and shook her head. As they strolled along the street, she regarded the area. "I see what you mean. Where is everyone?"

The market was as crowded as before, except for the space near them. As they moved, the crowd parted naturally, flowing in behind. The only change was that there was a space about the length of Erlon's extended sword around them in all directions.

"I think we should wander back to our camp."

"Good idea." They turned and strolled back the way they had come. Their little bubble of privacy moved with them.

"What's going on?"

He shook his head. "They're being respectful."

"Which means they're afraid. You haven't been cutting off heads while I wasn't watching, have you?"

He winced. "I'm sorry, Jameta, but this kind of thing doesn't happen to me. I don't think I'm the one they're afraid of."

She stopped and spun to face him. "Well, it certainly hasn't happened to me, either. What did I do?"

He glanced left, then right, then took her arm and urged her on. "Word gets around fast. Legends travel even faster. These people are looking for an avatar of a god to step into their midst. You walk in and act like one. I'm not saying they've made the connection. They're being careful, just in case. That's why they're so leery about strangers."

"Great. Does this mean I have to leave?"

"We're nowhere close to Samnia. Zelfana said these people were never under your ancestor's rule, so they shouldn't have anything against you. But we better be careful until we figure this out."

"We're careful all the time. Can I stop and look at that silk?"

He shrugged. "Better if we try to look natural."

"What could be more natural than a little tiff about how much you're willing to spend to buy me that scarf?"

"I'm not exactly rich."

"I know exactly how rich you are. I know what your wage is and I see what you spend. Which is almost nothing. You can afford this. Feel that texture. It's almost as good as my mother weaves." She brushed the silk across his cheek and smiled up at him. Out of the corner of her eye she could see the merchant grinning. *I guess he hasn't heard the rumours.* She made a note not to bargain too hard.

31. Feeding the Rumours

The feast needed two goats.

Fortunately, the language spoken at the fair was a babble of several different dialects, including pure Samnian and a pidgin Galesian that was probably better at trade terms than Jameta's translations. So Roeble and Aleria were able to contact the important traders without help, and the guest list grew. By the time Erlon and Jameta returned with the new scarf the goats were already roasting on spits, a band was tuning their instruments, and a circle of curious onlookers was keeping casual watch on the camp.

There were few children in evidence, but those that were wandered freely, weaving in and out of the adults along with a few herding dogs, which slunk along at their masters' sides, amber eyes peering at everything.

Aleria returned soon after and sought Jameta. Her face was serious, and Jameta opened her mouth for her apology. The Caravan Master held up her hand.

"Don't worry about that. You were in a tense situation and you took it out on me. This is more important."

Jameta closed her mouth. *If that's what she needs to believe…*

"I've been hearing interesting things."

"You have?"

The Caravan Master nodded. "There's rumours flying all over. Same as we heard in Agadez, but worse. Big uproar in Samnia. Might even be a revolution."

"What has that to do with us?"

Aleria grinned. "Religion and superstition. Apparently the downtrodden Aissa population is chafing under their Beni Ksabi masters. Now they have an icon to lead them back to power."

Jameta's heart sank. "What are we going to do?"

"Nothing. Samnia is far to the south, and these people care very little about what's happening down there. The news around here is more interesting. They've heard about you. Nobody is sure, but rumour says there's a berserker wandering around the desert, and the usual exaggerated stories are circulating."

"Will that cause us any trouble?"

"No, but it means you might have to play a bigger role in our negotiations."

Jameta tried to absorb this. "That's fine. But maybe we can do one better."

"How is that?"

"Let's learn from Zelfana's people."

Aleria looked at the new scarf. "You mean...?"

Jameta pulled the silk over her nose. "The more powerful you are, the less you show."

"That is classic. We'll stuff those rumours full and roast them over every fire in camp."

"And I have another idea."

"I can't wait."

"You've seen Erlon training with me."

"Yes, it's pretty impressive."

"Perhaps it's time for another go." She indicated the line of watchers. "With his real sword."

Aleria frowned. "Are you..." She stopped herself. "Whatever you think is safe."

Jameta made a moue of resignation. "Whatever Erlon thinks is safe. I just dance."

When she returned from her tent in the dress her mother had woven, Erlon was not so enthused. "Against my real sword? That's too dangerous."

She looked up at him. "When was the last time you touched my skin with the practice wand?"

"A long time ago."

"Well, this is more show than training." She slid the veil across her face and tied it behind her head. "Watch."

She began to dance, her veil flowing with her dress, slipping over her arms and shoulders as she twirled. She stopped and looked at him. "What do you think?"

"Won't it get in the way?"

"I assume you've never seen Samnian dances."

"Except for you, no."

"We always wear veils. It's part of the old costume." She twirled again. "See?"

He shrugged. "I suppose so. You haven't been wrong, yet."

"It's a new weapon, Erlon. We have to find out if it works or not. If I get sliced a bit, I'll learn."

"You get 'sliced a bit' and there will be a dozen people from this caravan in line to chop pieces off me. No matter whose fault it is."

She laughed up at him. "Then you'll be careful, won't you? Listen! The band has started."

She pulled him along until they reached the edge of the circle where the sand had been smoothed for the dancing later on. Then she left him and spun out into the middle. The band picked up their tempo to follow her. She remembered the moves she had learned from Hajira's dance, and began to tempt Erlon, sweeping close to him beckoning, then away across the sand again, laughing. He stepped forward, drawing his sword. A sigh ran through the watchers, and the Dalmyn people slipped in to form an inner audience, seated closer to the dance area.

Now Erlon moved, circling as he always did, sweeping his sword in big, slow arcs, edging closer and closer. She knew when it was coming, because he always shifted his feet...*just...so!* The blade swept in and down, and she slipped aside, reaching out with a descending hand to guide the weapon aside with her palm. He countered with a quick backswing that she avoided by dropping below it, her foot sweeping out to contact his shin.

He hopped back, feigning agony, and the crowd laughed. She kept low, creeping up behind him. He recovered and jabbed at her, and she exploded upward over his sword, her hands reaching for his face. He twisted away, spinning a complete circle to come back at her with a horizontal sweep, a dangerous move because she was behind his back and he could not see her, could not be sure she would avoid him.

She crossed her guards and blocked but did not brace herself, allowing the force of the blow to send her backwards in a somersault. She recovered and stood, beckoning again, her hips undulating.

Now the musicians were with her, and they slowed as well. She began a fluid stalk, circling in on him where he stood, his sword threatening her from a defensive position. They had worked this before, and she knew that soon he would start the quick jabs that she could block with her guards. Sure enough it came, and the clatter of steel on bronze brought the musicians up to tempo again. He made the final lunge, and she spun down the sword towards him. This time she got the balance right, and he was still falling forward with the force of his thrust as she crouched, her hips hitting him above the knees. It took little effort to boost him up and over, and he dove into a forward roll, his weapon out to the side, coming up with his back to her.

214

Again he put on an act, pretending not to know where she had gone. She tiptoed up and touched his shoulder, slipping inside as his sword swept around, ending in the circle of his arms, tweaking his nose and then ducking away before he could reverse his swing. The crowd was aroar, now, the nomads slapping each other on the back. As she circled enticingly outside his reach she caught a glimpse of money changing hands.

So this is a contest, is it? Guess it's time to cheat.

Now Erlon came at her with a standard swordsman's attack, chopping down, then using the momentum to come around for a backswing. She stood still, deflecting his blows with her guards, her hands flowing around her in the gestures of the dance. The music quickened, and he increased his tempo, making moves that should be too fast for such a big sword. But these had little effect, because she was faster, and they were too quick to have much force. Again the rattle of attack and defence rang out.

She knew how this was supposed to end. She watched for his weight to shift to his back foot. Then he made the big lunge, straight for her heart. She crossed her guards and guided the blade upwards, gliding towards him and spinning around to bring her hands up between his wrists, following with her head and body.

But instead of stopping in his arms as she usually did, she reached up and slid her right hand along his cheek, hooking it behind his head and pulling him down for a kiss that she held until he relaxed and began to enjoy it.

Then she reached her hand high so everyone could see it. It snaked down, grabbing his hair, and pulled his head erect. She brought up her left hand and slapped his cheek lightly. Then, one finger on his nose, she pushed him away, straightening her veil and turning to regard her audience with her arm outstretched, holding him there.

Nearby in the crowd of nomads she caught a man in the act of doling out coins to another man. She pointed and signed "money" by brushing her thumb across her fingertips. Then she beckoned him.

He stood, frozen.

She strode forward, taking the money from his hand. She counted a third of the coins into the other man's hand and a third into the owner's. Then she swept her veil up and tucked the remaining money down the front of her bodice, returning to Erlon with a satisfied twitch of her hip.

He made a move to push her veil aside, but she slapped him lightly, took him by the ear and towed him towards the nearest tent, which they slipped behind.

Roars of approval followed them.

"Well, that was fun."

He turned to her and shrugged. "I may have been made a proper fool, but at least I got a kiss out of it."

She grinned. "As Aleria would say, 'Most envied man in camp right now.' I doubt if anyone thinks you're a fool."

He reached out, realized that he was still holding his sword, and sheathed it. Then he took her in his arms for that long hug that he sometimes needed. But this time his hands moved, sliding further down her back, pressing her body against his. She responded, moulding her form against him. She freed a hand and ran it through his hair, pulling his face down as she lifted her lips towards his.

He responded with a soft kiss and a brief opening of his lips. Then he shook his head gently and raised a hand to push her head against his chest. After a while, he sighed. "This is getting harder."

She pulled back and looked up at him. "I know. I mean, I don't know why, but I'll take your word for it. Look. We're going to settle all this once we're on the road home, right? We'll make a time and sit down and talk it out. Until then, I won't play any more 'come hither' games. I didn't plan for the dance to end that way. It just occurred to me in the middle."

"Well, I have no idea what effect our little act will have on the trading. Unless it's to distract everyone's attention from making good deals. I doubt if any of those men will be able to look at you the same, after seeing you dance like that."

She grinned. "Don't worry, they found out about you and your sword, too. I think the trading will go fine." She raised her head. "Is that roasting goat I smell?"

"Since there's been two on the spit in plain sight for several hours, you could be right. All that work has made me hungry."

She grabbed his hand to pull him forward. Then she stopped. "Sorry." She put her arm through his and paraded decorously at his side.

He snorted and strode along at his usual pace.

32. Long Ride

The trading was profitable, although Jameta's bubble of privacy followed her everywhere. She gave up trying to work the tables, because few customers dared approach her, and most that did had no intention of buying anything. So she had a rather relaxing three days, and was bored to distraction and ready to go when Roeble declared himself satisfied.

Against everyone's judgement, Lavan had spent a great amount of his profits from the trip on a fiery desert steed, a white stallion with flowing mane and tail. He was determined to buy it, in spite of the fact that the seller did not seem anxious to sell. For good reason. It was taller and leaner that most, and Jameta suspected it would give even Brownie a good race. *Of course, Doe would be another matter.*

She was the only one to agree with Lavan on the purchase. The night before they left the fair he had finished listing, to a disbelieving audience, all the wonderful qualities of the horse. He turned to her in desperation. "Jameta, tell them. Why should I buy him?"

She shrugged. "I like him."

Aleria burst into laughter. "You like him? Lavan should be spending half his pay on a horse because you like him?" She turned to the young rider. "You have to remember; she's the one who likes the Roan."

Lavan nodded. "Yes, and look where that got her. I'll take Jameta's hunch over a merchant's opinion any day."

Aleria grinned. "Well, she's the horsewoman and I'm no merchant, so that's a pretty safe bet."

Jameta smiled at Aleria. The other woman had never mentioned their problem again. However, she had been cool but polite for the last few days, and it was good to see her friendly again.

After that the razzing died off, and when the others watched him ride out in the morning with the departing caravan, they had to admit that Al Blanco was a beautiful horse. What Jameta didn't say was that the main reason the lad should buy the horse was that their personalities suited perfectly. *He thinks he's making an investment. He's just found a lifelong friend.*

* * *

217

They were about two days from the river and had overnighted in a pleasant valley with a small creek. As they geared up for the day's travel, everyone was feeling relaxed and comfortable. Except Erlon, who, as usual, had taken an extra look around, on their back-trail this time. They were finishing the dregs of the coffee when he rode into camp, his face white. He dismounted and stood there, his mouth working.

"What's wrong, Erlon?" Jameta stared up into his eyes. She had never seen him shaken like this. It terrified her. She looked back down the trail, but there was nothing that threatened.

Finally he broke from his reverie. "I don't suppose it's much use, but we need a meeting."

"Everyone is ready for the road. Come on over."

As they approached the last small fire, the usual chatter fell away. Erlon looked around the circle and shook his head.

"There's no use running. There's nothing we can do. We'll wait and see what happens."

Aleria was on her feet in an instant. "What? Who's coming? What's wrong, Erlon?"

He flapped a hand over his shoulder. "There's an army coming. Desert people. Their scouts will be here soon."

"An army?"

"That's right. About a thousand of them. Fighting men only. No baggage, no women."

Roeble nodded. "Living off their horses, then."

"Looks like it."

"Where could they be going?"

Aleria paced away, then turned back. "Who could they be after? Us?"

Jameta had a sudden thought that brought her heart to her mouth. "They're not Samnian, are they?"

Erlon gave the ghost of a grin. "Let's put this into perspective. They aren't going to gather a dozen tribes together to wipe out one trader's caravan. And the chance that the Samnians would or could find you in all this desert is ludicrous. There's only one enemy worth attacking. The Ferbodeans."

Thoughts bubbled in Jameta's head. "The mines."

"Oh, by all the gods." Aleria put a hand to her mouth. "That's it. The mines."

"Somebody has to warn them." Jameta stood. "I have to go."

Erlon put up a hand. "You don't have to go anywhere."

She pushed his arm down. "We have to warn the miners that this army is coming. I ride the fastest horses. In fact, I'm the one least likely to be bothered, for obvious reasons. You stay here and meet with them. Tell them I've gone on reconnaissance. Hold them up as long as you can." She looked around the circle. No one spoke.

"We're two days from the river, right? And the mine was four days past that, but two of those days we were holding up because of the injured horse and the rough road for the wagons. So it's only five days travel for the caravan. If Doe and Brownie and I can't do that before sunset tonight, I'm going home to be a barge captain." She shrugged. "And if I'm slower, then we did our best, and they'll have that much less time to get away."

She pushed past Erlon, then turned back to him. "Tell the Tribes that the Warrior Woman says they must wait. When I return, I will lead them to victory."

"Victory? What are you talking about?"

Aleria nodded. "That's the best way, Erlon." She sent a twisted grin to Jameta. "Let the women handle this. The tribesmen will appreciate that."

Jameta saddled Doe and threw the light packsaddle on Brownie.

Lavan was there with an extra canteen of water. "I guess you don't want me to come."

"This is one for that Other Woman to solve. Too much danger for a mere mortal. I don't know how She will manifest, but She's our only chance to save those miners."

He slapped Doe's shoulder. "Or the speed of your horses." Doe turned her head and nuzzled his hand. He scratched under her chin.

Erlon stood watching, an unhappy frown on his face. She went over to him. "I have to do this, no matter what."

"Of course you do, but I don't have to be pleased about it."

"I'm not dancing a jig myself." She rested a hand on his shoulder. "Get to Sfisef. He'll be leading."

"He will?"

"Yes, because of me. The Lariba will support him. I have no idea about the others, but I'm their only chance to win this. Oh, they can massacre a bunch of miners. But that will just get them all killed and their people decimated, and I'm sure they know it. I can do better."

"If you say so."

"Off I go. I only have to warn the first mine. After that, it's up to them to spread the word. I'll come back, meet you wherever you are on the road." She kissed him, and he enfolded her in his arms. She leaned against him, gathering strength. Then she pushed away and mounted her horse. "Wish me luck."

"You've got all I can give, Jameta. Please come back."

She leaned down to look into his eyes. "You realize how much I need to have you to come back to?"

"Yes..." He nodded, once. "I'm beginning to realize that. And once this is over, we're going to have the talk I promised you. I promise."

She looked up into his eyes. "By that time it may be too late."

"Too late?"

"That's right. The time for me to boot you out is passing. In fact, I think it's too late already."

Expressions warred on his face. "Oh..."

She slapped his arm. "Stop trying to look like you're sorry. I don't believe it." She found a grin. "We can talk about it once this is over."

She ran a finger down his cheek then turned away and swung up on Doe. She reined the horse around and waved to the others, who had held back to give them a moment of privacy.

And then she was out on the road.

It was strange, this time. *This is how I always do it. Me, alone with my faithful horses. The long road ahead: freedom and power and a sense of purpose. I always feel happy, right about now.*

I'm not happy.

She thought of the caravan and all her friends, back there in danger as well. *Who can tell what those tribesmen will do? We have friends, but if there's a thousand of them...*

She concentrated on the road and tried to get her mind into the ritual of watching and riding and changing horses and moving on. Gallop and trot, then walk. Gallop and trot, then walk. Water the horses. Feed the horses. *Don't forget to feed myself.*

The road flowed by beneath her galloping hooves. *There's where we camped the night Brownie had the stone in her hoof. How many days was that?*

She splashed across the river, noting the wagons on their island, untouched. There was no sign of Vrasha and Rogan. She went on.

Gallop and trot, then walk. Gallop and trot some more. The road smoothed as they came out of the pass where the first ambush took place. She changed horses and rode again.

Now the ride was beginning to have its effects. Her legs were tired, and when they trotted she found herself allowing the saddle to hit her instead of lifting her weight with each stride. Soon her butt began to hurt, and she hoped she hadn't started blisters.

There was a light wind blowing at her back, which cooled her but carried the dust she stirred up into her nostrils, and they felt dry and sore. Every time she changed horses she sponged their noses out with water from her canteen, using the tail of her shirt.

She was sinking into her misery, trying to block out the heat and the dust and her pain, when she realized that Doe was slowing. She tried to think back. *When did I change horses last? Dammit, I have to concentrate.*

She stopped and changed the saddles over, taking a moment to inspect both horses, persuading herself it wasn't just because she needed a rest. Hauling herself back into the saddle was a chore, with the thought of the endless miles still to ride. *Have to keep my pace up. Minutes saved now might mean lives saved later.*

As she got closer to where the mine was, her memory started playing tricks on her. *It's just around the next bend...no it's not. I've still got a mile to go. Or more.*

Jameta was tired and sore and greatly relieved when she finally rounded a corner and there was the mine in front of her. She trotted down the final incline and pulled up. The gates were closed, and armed men stood at the sentry boxes.

"Is Gwaller Rees here?"

"He's busy. What do you want?"

"I want to talk to him. I have about a thousand desert tribesmen in a battle mood on the road behind me. Is that enough to make him less busy?"

"A thousand? Surely..."

She pushed her horse nearer to the fence. "You're aware that there's something wrong or you wouldn't be guarding the gate like this. Whatever you think you know, I have much worse news. Now get your butt into the compound and get Mister Rees out here. We're wasting valuable time!"

He stepped back, his gun lowering. "Yes, Ma'am. I'll get him." He turned to his companion. "You better let her in."

He strode away, and the other guard unlatched the gate, swinging it open only far enough to let her horses slip in, then closing it again and shoving the bar home. "A thousand of them? We knew the tribes were on the prod, but..."

She dismounted. "They're coming up the caravan route behind us. You'd better be thinking of how to get out of here, because they'll smash this place flat."

His face white, the guard returned to his post. She led her mounts forward to meet Gwaller, who was striding across the compound towards her.

"What's this? A thousand nomads? Surely you're exaggerating."

"Erlon saw them, and I'd take his guess any time. They're a day's ride behind me. I've left instructions with Erlon to try and hold them, but it's anybody's guess if they'll listen."

There was a group of concerned people gathering, and he took her arm, leading her aside. He spoke quietly. "Is that woman with them? The one they're all jabbering about?"

"What woman is that?" *If I didn't already know.*

"Their mythical Warrior Woman who's going to lead them to victory over the nonbelievers. We keep our ears to the ground out here. We know all the rumours. Did you hear anything about her?"

"Yes, and she's not with them, right now." *Well, that's the honest truth.* "But she is part of the picture, and the effect she'll have is difficult to determine. They see these mines as the symbol of everything that's wrong about the Ferbodeans in this area. They aren't going to just ride on by."

He straightened his shoulders and turned back towards his people. "You're right. We have to shut this place up as tight as we can and get our people out of here."

"Do you have enough transport?"

"Oh, yes. We have an evacuation plan."

"Well, I'd use it as soon as possible. Can you send warning to the other mines? I have to get back to my people."

"Yes we'll take care of that. But you'll be coming with us, won't you? You can't go back there with that mob of heathens coming. Once we get to the army we'll be safe."

"What army is that?"

"The Ferbodean one. They didn't send us out here without support."

"How big an army do they have?"

He shrugged. "That Pavenkov that's been lording it over us for the past year is in charge. He says he's got enough men and guns to take care of any little native uprising."

"Any guesses? A hundred? Three hundred?"

"I've never seen him with more than about thirty of those tame nomads he runs with, plus his usual escort. But there was a company of infantry crossed the border a few days ago. That's a hundred men."

"So he might have a hundred and fifty. Well armed, but that's not enough. Yes, you'll be better forgetting about him and hotfooting it to the border."

"We will. We have families to think of." The mine manager shook his head. "But I still don't think I can let you go out there."

She made her lips smile. "Don't worry about me. I'll be fine. I got here, didn't I?"

"But you're only…"

She swung up on her horse and looked down at him. "My caravan is back there. The nomads like traders. We'll be fine. They don't like miners. You won't be fine. Get moving." She turned Doe and, with Brownie following as usual, trotted towards the gate. The guard got it open before she had to stop.

She didn't go far. Darkness was falling, and now that her race was over she felt exhausted. She pulled off the caravan route at a spot she had scouted on the trip east, and followed an animal trail down a small gully to a dale with decent grass and a spring oozing out of the ground. She picketed the horses, ate a cold supper, and curled up in her blanket.

Jameta didn't sleep well, and once the light returned she couldn't fight it. She ate, packed and was back in the saddle, headed east into the face of the sun as it topped the mountains. The day was warmer than yesterday, and her horses did not move with the same alacrity. She found herself dozing as she rode, trying to maintain that balance between relaxing just enough to ease the ache and a deeper sleep that would dump her on the ground.

She knew it was dangerous, but in her fatigue, she couldn't dredge up the energy to care. *I have to get back to the caravan. They need me.* She tried to think of a plan, and that roused her for a while, but soon the same ideas ran circles in her head, and she dozed again.

She awoke to find Brownie – *Am I riding Brownie? Oh, yes, there's the notch in her left ear* – with her head down, grazing. The sun was past noon. Giving up, Jameta pulled off the trail again for a nap. This time she slept deeply and awoke with a dry mouth and a dozy feeling. Gritting her teeth, she switched saddles and was away again on Doe's back.

After the river she met no one and she began to hope. If the nomads would wait for her, it might mean life for the miners and their families. The plan she had been thinking of had matured in her dreams, and she thought it through again.

As she left the river she increased her attention towards the surrounding desert. She was being scouted, but they were very good, and she only caught fleeting motions out of the corner of her eye. *If they came this far it's perfect. Save me another few hours' riding.*

An hour past the river she came around a corner and there sat her greeting party. Five men dressed in their most splendid robes and mounted on fine desert steeds. Calming herself, she kneed her mount forward.

To her great relief, Sfisef greeted her. *Warrior Woman. What does the enemy?*

There is an army, Headman of the Tolbè. To the north and west. Few men but many guns.

He shrugged under his robes. *We are not afraid.*

She rode past him, and he turned in beside her. *Fear is for men to worry about.* She glanced over at him. *This war is for women to decide.*

I bow to your wisdom, Warrior Woman.

I meet with your leaders.

They will be at your camp when the sun has dropped one hand-span. He grinned. *Your Voice will be there.*

Medlili? She came with the army?

Zelfana chose her envoy well.

Send her to me now!

The Warrior Woman speaks.

She reached out and slapped his arm. *Do not be silly. Get her over to my caravan. We make plans.*

Around the corner the next valley she met her army. Herds of horses grazed up the mountainside. Tents, row on row in a haphazard scatter filled the valley floor, cooking fires glowing. And down in the middle, in a prime spot beside the small stream that meandered along, was a small pocket of canvas tents.

As she reached the caravan campsite, Erlon strode out to meet her, Stilet and Lavan right behind him to take the reins from her hand and lead her horses away. She was too busy gripping Erlon's neck, burying her head against his chest, revelling in the safety of his arms.

He murmured something in her ear and held her against him.

Finally she relaxed and tilted her head back. "Missed me?"

He shook his head, just once. "I tried very hard not to worry. I performed all my duties to the required level. But it's hard to keep busy when your mind says you're supposed to be asleep."

"You didn't sleep?"

"Not much. That's a long, dangerous road you were on. I kept thinking of ways you could defend yourself."

She laughed. "Now you sound like Lavan. I was doing the same thing. Well, not on the way back. I didn't sleep much either."

"But you made it. How are the horses?"

"Stood up better than I did. They're in wonderful condition."

He ran a hand down her back. "So are you."

She spun out of his arms. "Keep your mind on your duties, guard Captain." She stepped closer. "Difficult as that may be."

She stood on tiptoe and kissed his cheek. Then keeping his hand safely trapped in hers, she looked around the camp. "We have a small crisis to manage."

"And I hope you have a plan."

"I do, and here comes the newest part of it."

"Do you need me?"

"No, this is girl talk."

He nodded. "Girl talk? Somehow I don't think so." He turned and strode away.

The figure who approached the caravan was not what Jameta expected. Medlili was fully covered, head to foot. A fine, gauzy veil covered her lower face. Her brothers strode, silent, sober and well armed, at either shoulder.

Lavan slipped up beside Jameta, shaking his head. "She's been promoted. Too bad."

She nudged him with her elbow. "Stop sounding like a stupid male for a moment. Go out and bring her into camp with all proper respect."

He glanced at her. "And when do I get proper respect?"

She grinned and shooed him away.

He strode out over the sand, greeting Medlili with a dignified bow, offering his arm in the Galesian manner. She took it without hesitation, handing him a parcel.

"It is your custom for young man to carry package for weak woman, yes?"

"I am at my Lady's service."

The formality broke down when the two girls met with a long hug and joyful laughter.

"So, you have gained in stature."

Medlili shrugged. "I am the envoy of Zelfana of the Tolbè. I must demonstrate proper dignity."

"We need to talk about that. Come to my tent."

As they walked, the Dry Land girl waved a hand in the direction of the army. "They all started gathering out of nowhere. First there were fifty Lareba with Outoul in the front, desperate to retrieve his lost honour and the confidence of his Headwoman. Right behind them, forty Hassisna, who had heard about you from the Lareba. And they kept coming as word spread. We had to move out because we didn't have the grazing for all of them."

"Are they living off their horses?"

"Not yet. They are saving the mare's milk and blood for the battle drink."

"Well, let's hope we can save the horses their pain. What does Zelfana say?"

Medlili glanced at Jameta sideways. "She says that the Warrior Woman has new ideas. She says you will fix all this without death."

"Without death? I've got a thousand tribesmen in a battle frame of mind on a collision course with a heavily armed bunch of modern Ferbodean soldiers, with several mines full of Domalian civilians in between. Not to mention a Galesian caravan. Oh, yes, and a Ferbodean bureaucratic snake stirring it all around."

Medlili frowned. "What is...bureaucratic?"

"Be thankful you haven't developed bureaucrats yet. It's a person who does nothing, but spends his life making other people do things they'd rather not."

"Ah. I knew a Headwoman like that."

"Too bad for you." She sat outside the tent door and motioned Medlili to do the same.

Lavan laid the package beside her and disappeared. The two brothers stood silently just out of hearing, their eyes scanning everything, like wolves alert for prey.

"So, how are we going to solve this problem without killing?"

"I have no idea."

"I didn't think you did. I'm thinking out loud. The first thing we do is take control of this army. How do we do that?"

Now Medlili grinned. She held out the parcel. "First step my grandmother already knew. Present from my mother."

Jameta opened it and lifted out a beautiful robe, complete with hood, in a deep blue shot with lighter flecks. "This is wonderful!"

"Put it on. It is of my mother's finest weaving. It will cover fully, as befits your honour. But it must not impede your beauty and your youth."

Jameta stepped inside and slipped the robe over her head. Medlili adjusted it. She turned, and it spun out around her. It was tighter in the upper body than the usual women's robes and flared to a full skirt lower down. She found she could shrug the hood back and free her arms.

"I could dance in this!"

"And fight."

She swirled once more and then sat, clipping her vambraces over the dress sleeves. "All right. Fun over. With my veil, this will do the trick. Now. I will not talk, right?"

"Correct. I will Speak for you. This is good, yes?"

"It is. I don't want them to hear how bad I am with your language. What will I say?"

Medlili shrugged. "They want you to say that you will lead them to victory against the nonbelievers. They expect you to say that if they do not obey you, then their souls will be forfeit to the Outer Frosts for eternity. They hope you will say that they are brave and worthy of your leadership."

Jameta grinned. "Well, I guess that about sums it up. I have a plan, and if they follow it, we have a good chance of packing this whole thing up and delivering it as expected, with no deaths. Anybody who messes it up will be the first one to die."

"You have a plan already?"

Jameta shrugged. "I had two long days on the road. All I need is a chance to run it past my advisors," she rose, "who are at this moment waiting in fear and trembling to see what I have cooked up." She stood, stretched her aching legs and composed herself.

Aleria, Roeble and Erlon were attempting to look casual, lounging in their canvas chairs on a big carpet in the shade of Roeble's tent as the sun sank. They all rose as she approached.

Aleria looked her up and down. "The Warrior Woman speaks." She bowed and indicated a chair.

Jameta nodded to Medlili.

"The Warrior Woman greets you. She would speak to you of her plans."

Roeble grinned. "That's considerate of her. How has she planned to get us killed off?"

"Warrior Woman will solve this problem with no deaths. That is her promise. Anyone who denies her plan will be the first to die."

Erlon nodded. "That sounds like the Warrior Woman we know and love, all right."

Aleria frowned. "Jameta, we don't have much more time. The tribesmen are getting antsy. This demonstration has been very instructive, but are you going to come out and talk with us?"

Jameta flung her veil aside to show her grin. "Aleria, you are a spoilsport. But you're right, as usual. This is how the tribesmen expect their Warrior Woman to act, and Medlili is in the ideal position to guide me."

"And do you have a plan?"

"I've been thinking." She sat, and they all joined her. Medlili made a graceful swoop to the carpet. "We have to meet Pavenkov and his army as soon as possible. If we can get rid of them, we can send our many friends home with victory in their pockets. At that point, they will trust us to take care of the damage the mines are doing to their lands."

Aleria nodded. "That sounds good. There is one small difficulty, though..."

"How to get rid of Pavenkov's army without killing anyone. Do you remember how I dealt with the guards at the gate of the Horse Fair?"

Erlon nodded. "You hit each element of the group with a different threat or inducement. That divided them up and made it easy to conquer them."

"That's right."

Aleria jumped up and began to pace. "And Pavenkov's support is diverse. He has those tribesmen, and his toadies from Ferbodin..."

"And his main body of troops, who are regular Ferbodean Citizens' Army. Who we hope are under the command of the main government, not his cronies in the capital. Roeble, is that possible?"

The merchant frowned in thought. "It's hard to tell because the power situation is so fluid. It's possible that his bloc got a sympathizer to lead the troops, but he's still an officer in the Army and has to report to his superiors, who are not in favour of battles of this sort. Too much chance of getting wiped out by a horde of screaming savages, and for what? To protect a bunch of Domalian businessmen on foreign soil."

Jameta stood and replaced her veil. "Good. Let us meet our forces. I see the leaders approaching."

The troop of riders dismounted at a polite distance from the caravan camp and came forward on foot. There were fifteen of them, dressed in similar robes, but of vastly different patterns and colours. They filed in and sat on the carpet in a circle. Jameta kept the only

228

chair, and Medlili stood beside her. When all were silent, Medlili stepped forward, removing her veil. *I speak for the Warrior Woman. She greets you, and thanks you for heeding her call. There is a blight on our land that affects all tribes. Thus all tribes must aid in dealing with it.*

She flung out her hand. *But though you come of your own will, the free men of the Dry Lands who bow to no man or woman, you have come at the call of the Warrior Woman. She speaks with the voice of all the Tribes, as I speak for her. And as it always is with our people, the freedom of each man to go his own way must be tempered by the needs of the Tribe.*

In this case, you must all bow your wills to the Warrior Woman, that she might speak with a powerful voice against our enemies.

Heads turned, and a quiet hum of conversation began to build.

Jameta held up her hand. There was silence. She pointed to Outoul, who had been sitting silent, cradling his bandaged left arm.

Medlili nodded. *You will listen to Outoul of the Lareba, who speaks wisely on this matter.*

The young man's face reddened, and he settled himself firm and straight before he spoke. *My friends and kinsmen. There is much learning to be done if one wishes to be a leader among our people. The biggest learning is that fiery desires of young men do not always show the perfect path to honour. In fact, giving in to that passion can lead one to the brink of dishonour and death-of-the-soul.* His head came up. *So it was with me, and only the courage of the Warrior Woman stopped me.*

It is the way of our people to listen with respect to the words of the Headman and the Headwoman, who encompass the wisdom of the years of the tribe. Much though I yearn to take my gun and my horse and my sword and attack those who defile our lands, I know that this is merely selfishness and greed for glory, and will not accomplish the goals of our people. In fact, it could lead to our destruction.

If the time comes, and the Warrior Woman says, 'Fight!' then I will attack with all the strength of my body and fire of my soul. Until that time I will be guided by my leaders, so that they may work for the good of the tribe and all our people.

There were judicious nods around the circle. Medlili smiled. *Now, listen to the words of the Wise Woman. She tells you to remember that you are not dealing with the brave and honourable tribesmen of the desert. You are dealing with the Ferbodeans. And the

Ferbodeans do not fight like men. The Ferbodeans fight like women, and you all know what that means.

Yes. The gruff voice came from a heavily bearded tribesman on Jameta's left. *It means that a man hasn't a chance, no matter how straight his gun shoots or how sharp his sword.*

You are a wise man, and you understand what the Ferbodeans are now up against. We have the power and the wisdom of the Warrior Woman, backed by the largest army of tribesmen that has ever been collected in the history of our people. If we use our strengths well, we cannot lose. She glanced at Jameta, who nodded.

And now to the plan. We all would like to wipe the Ferbodeans and the miners from the face of our land, but then the Ferbodeans would come with their thousands of soldiers and their quick-firing guns, and slaughter every one of us: our families and our cattle and our horses, and take our sheep and goats to feed their men. So this is not the solution the Warrior Woman will pursue.

When you come to your Headwoman with your arguments and your quarrels, she solves them cleverly and fairly so that none are injured, all are treated with respect, and the tribe prospers. Thus the Warrior Woman speaks. We will deal with these Ferbodeans using clever woman's ways. If they are as wise as our people, they will listen to the women and go back to their own lands and leave us to manage ours. They will accept that we have the right and the power to tell the Domalian miners what they may and may not do on our lands.

Nods around the circle, especially from the northern tribes.

And if your young men are not allowed the chance to prove their valour, then perhaps instead they can prove their commitment to the good of the tribe, and thus advance in maturity and power.

There was a general muttering of, *That I'd like to see,* and, *We might be lucky,* and words to that effect, but they were spoken with smiles.

Medlili now took a stronger pose and swept the circle with her glare. *The Warrior Woman says she has been gifted with the bravest and strongest army our people have ever created. She will lead you to victory over the nonbelievers.* Her voice dropped. *And she has not said so, but any man of all these tribes who disobeys and causes dishonour to our people,* her voice rose, *will be consigned to the outermost, coldest circle of Purgatory forever! We will meet at sunrise to plan the battle.*

She held that pose for a moment, then swung back to Jameta, to sink to the carpet at her side.

The men's heads were nodding slowly. They began to rise, bowing and backing to the edge of the carpet, where they turned and strode to their horses. Soon there was no evidence of their presence but blowing dust.

The two women rose, watching them go. Then Jameta caught Medlili in a firm hug. "You may congratulate me."

"Of course, then I congratulate you, Warrior Woman. For what, in this instance?"

"For all the wise and powerful things I said today."

Medlili's face reddened, then she tossed her head. "Yes, you were...el-o-quent, weren't you?"

Aleria stepped forward. "Well, I hope you're going to tell us what that was all about. Medlili, you certainly had them twisted around your fingers."

"The Warrior Woman inspires great thoughts."

Roeble raised a finger. "Who was the young fellow you picked on? He didn't seem the type to swing much political weight."

Jameta laughed. "The day I met him the Roan knocked his horse flat and stepped on his sword. He has learned the folly of attacking those he should not. The Headwoman of the Aine Lareba is young, but she is strong. She will not let a fool get away without learning his lesson. I thought he demonstrated it very well, didn't you?"

Medlili's face darkened again. "He seems to have grown from his experience."

Jameta grinned at her discomfiture, then decided to let her go for the moment. She turned to the Galesians.

"And now I turn the battle over to more experienced hands. Our objective is to meet Pavenkov's army in a place we can trap them and demonstrate our power. Once we have them, I will do my best. But first we have to arrange the meeting. Erlon? Aleria? This activity suits your talents."

Roeble gestured. "And such a discussion requires food and drink. Jameta has put in a long day, and the sun has set. I believe I smell the delightful aroma of roasting goat. Shall we sit?"

It came in a rush to Jameta that her legs were weak and her stomach was empty. She swayed, and only Erlon's steadying hand turned her fall into a not-too-clumsy drop into a chair.

Soon the food was served, the drinks poured and the planning started. She was happy to let Medlili speak for her again, and she listened with half her brain and slept with the other half, as she had done on her horse that morning.

33. Confrontation

One thing Jameta learned in this war was the importance of scouting. According to Erlon, the tribesmen were nonpareil. Tireless, reliable and subtle, they rode with three horses, switching often, drinking mare's milk if their food ran low. They opened a small vein and drank the blood if they needed sustenance, but then the horse had to be rested a few days, so they used that technique rarely.

So the scouts brought the Ferbodeans south, herding and enticing them by turns. Erlon suggested that the meeting place should be close to the Bel river. "If we were trying for attack, to win the battle, we would be best to handle them in the open desert, with no supplies, no water."

Roeble nodded. "But that's not what we're after. We don't want a fight. We want to take the pressure off. Let them think they have other options. They won't be so keen to fight if their backs aren't against a wall."

Aleria chuckled. "Can you imagine war run by merchants? Wouldn't work very well."

Roeble gave one of his rare smiles. "And now we've got a war run by women, and we hope this one won't happen at all."

Aleria nodded. "I'll buy a big chunk of that."

So the Nomads moved their camp to a mile short of the river, and their scouts pushed anyone who tried to cross back into the water. The enemy still had no idea what they faced.

One rider did make it through. Just after dark, two Tolbè tribesmen rode up to the camp, followed by a light-skinned rider on a familiar horse.

"Vracha! How did you get here?"

The teamster swung down off Rogas. "I kept saying your name, Aleria. Didn't mean a thing. They had their rifles pointed at me, real serious. Then I tried Jameta's, and they all got happy. Slapped me on the back, brought me straight in."

Erlon stepped up to take the reins. "How's the head?"

Vracha turned his ear to the firelight. "Healed fine. I was never pretty before..." He shrugged. Then he turned to the horse. "What do ya thinka Rogas, here?"

The Captain was already running his hands along the horse's shoulder. "He's got a bit of a scar."

"Aye. Dirt got into it when he fell, I guess. Puffy and oozy for a coupla weeks. The horse doc gave me some stuff to put on it. Seemed to work."

"Horse doctor?" Erlon was at the back of the leg, now. "There seems to be a scar here, too."

"Aye. They got a travellin' horse doctor come through about a week after you left. Onea the tribesmen here talks a bita Galesian, 'n' I told him what happened. The doc prods around, finds the bullet and takes it out, no problem. Morea that gunk on it, and it healed up real quick."

"How's he moving?"

"Like a dream. He ain't fast, but he's got all his old stamina back. I bin keepin' him exercised."

"What's the situation at the river?"

"I dunno, Sir. I saw that army comin' and I took to horse."

"What did you see as you were riding away?"

"A troop a infantry, stridin' in good form, from what I could see. Supply wagons, the lot. A mob a tribesmen. Buncha guys in grey coats."

"Where did they go?"

"Sorry, Sir. I wasn't hangin' around to find out. I was too worried about the lot aheada me."

"I can imagine. Well, you can sling your bedroll with the others."

"And Rogas, sir?"

"Oh, I'll take care of Rogas. Thanks for looking after him."

"Best I could do, sittin' around doin' nothin' while you lot did all the work."

"You paid your share, Vracha. You deserved a holiday."

The teamster slung his bag to his shoulder to leave, but then he turned back. "That's a fine buncha people, livin' there at the river."

Nobody answered, so Jameta stepped forward. "What do you mean?"

"They aren't from any tribe. At least, they're from all tribes. Some'ud call 'em misfits. But they look to their own and they got their pride. Good bunch. I liked 'em."

"That's interesting." She glanced at Aleria.

The Caravan Master nodded. "Thanks, Vracha."

"No problem, boss." He turned away.

Aleria looked at Jameta, her head to one side. "What did you have in mind?"

"Just thinking. This river crossing is a key spot, and it's interesting that it isn't under the control of any tribe. They have contact with lots of tribes, in fact."

"Ah. The Dennal angle. Water transportation."

Jameta nodded. "I wonder what the river's like in the wet season."

Aleria grinned. "I guess you'll have to come back and find out."

"I might do that."

* * *

The following morning dawned clear and cloudless, which was not remarkable for the dry season, although this late in the year that could change in a moment. The tribesmen all appeared in their battle best, their muskets shiny, their swords sharp, and their tribal pennants flowing with the breeze. Jameta was resplendent in her Tolbèan robes, her guards and advisors likewise attired, although the seven Double-S rifles sparkled with a sharper shine than the blued steel of the muskets. Lavan had insisted she ride Al Blanco, as appropriate to her station.

She didn't disagree. "Since Pavenkov knows my horses, it wouldn't do for the Warrior Woman to show up on one of them."

He glanced over at the remuda. "Plus they're so bunged up they still can't walk properly. That was a hard ride you took them on. How are you doing?"

She stretched her back. "The last two days gave me a chance to heal up. I hope that horse of yours is easy on my aching muscles."

"I think you'll be surprised."

The stallion had a fine gait, though he required more handling than her own mounts. *Good thing I've been practising on the Roan. This one's a sweetheart compared to old Hammerhead.*

According to the scouts, the enemy had forted up in one of the old compounds in the ruined city and were safely dug in with a clear field of fire for their modern rifles. And they would have been safe. If three or four hundred tribesmen had attacked, it would have been a massacre.

Jameta had a thousand men and a different plan. *And if it doesn't work, we'll still have a massacre.* She shuddered at the thought, the sounds of dying men and horses echoing in her memory.

She kneed Al Blanco forward. Her personal guard rode bunched around her, bristling with rifles, her honour guard spreading out to each side, standards swirling. She glanced right and left. She had no idea how they did it, but the tribesmen kept pace with her in a line as far as she could see in both directions.

Just behind the edge of the drop-off to the water she stopped. The riders positioned themselves even with the riverbank. She nodded to Erlon, and he slid ahead, keeping below the skyline, looking over. He turned back to her. "They're still there. They have the local people all grouped together on the bank."

"That doesn't sound good."

"That bastard would kill them all just to make a point."

"How many men does he have?"

He grinned. "About a hundred and fifty. One-seventy-five at most."

"Shall we make an appearance?"

"I leave it to you."

"Then let us appear." She glanced back to Aleria, who nodded.

Jameta started Al Blanco moving, pacing slowly. As one, the line of a thousand desert warriors copied her. When the valley spread out below her she stopped. They stopped. As Sfisef's men had that day on the dunes, the whole army sat their mounts immobile, only the horsehair tassels on their tribal symbols sweeping gently in the breeze.

Down in the river village all heads turned and stillness reigned.

"Sfissef."

Yes, Warrior Woman?

Take men down there and talk to them. Tell tribesmen I am very displeased with them. You know to say it better than I do.

Oh, yes. I can talk to the tribesmen. I will tell them that they have disgraced their heritage, and Warrior Woman will flay them and send their souls to purgatory wrapped in their own skins.

Is good. Then return. We see what happens.

He bowed in his saddle and rode off. A troop of standardbearers followed him down the bank, splashing across the ford in fine display. He stopped, and his words wavered on the breeze. Then he turned and rode back across the river and up the bank.

All eyes were on the robed men in the compound, who gathered together, ignoring the soldiers. After a brief discussion they began to mount their horses: first one, then two or three, then the whole troop. She could see the man on the big bay reining his horse back and forth in anger, his shouts echoing. The tribesmen ignored him and turned their mounts to ride away.

She could not make out what the leader said, but every rifle in the Ferbodean contingent snapped around to aim at the departing tribesmen. They turned their mounts, and their long-barrelled muskets fell to firing position.

"Time to intervene." She gestured. *Move forward, Sfissef.*

At Sfissef's signal Jameta's tribesmen began to walk their horses along the riverbank, filing down to the water wherever there was access. There they lined up again and stood, still and threatening.

Jameta and her honour guard stayed where they were, motionless above it all. She knew the effect they had: the dark figure on the beautiful white horse, the barbaric panoply around her. They were close enough for Pavenkov to see the gleam of modern rifles among her attendants.

She glanced towards Aleria. "He'll be a bit frightened, right now."

"Especially since a bunch of his troops took advantage of the distraction to ride away."

"And the locals seem to be enjoying the water." Small dark heads were swimming towards the islands.

Jameta watched the enemy troops, now. She could see them swirling like spawning salmon. And like the salmon, their movements had purpose.

"He still has a divided command."

"He does?"

"No surprise. His toadies circle around him, their fortunes tied to his. Outside that are the soldiers of the Ferbodean Army and their officers, who have been ordered to support him. Their orders should come from the Army. If Pavenkov takes actions counter to what the officers feel is government policy..."

Aleria frowned in thought. "Can we divide them?"

"We can try. Time to make an appearance." She turned to the front. "Medlili!"

"Always here, Warrior Woman."

"How would you like to have a conversation with a snake?"

"I could think it a learning experience, I suppose."

"Good. Because I do not wish to speak to this man. You will Speak for me."

"Of course, Warrior Woman. This man does not deserve to hear your voice."

"Also, he would recognize it, which would spoil our little deception. Away we go."

She heeled Al Blanco forward, and he took the bank with ease. When she reached the ford she did not pause but splashed through at a dignified pace. Her army crossed with less decorum, the wings racing ahead to surround the enemy. Then they all paced forward, tightening the circle.

Pavenkov and his men had chosen the largest compound, and modern rifles bristled along the walls. She stopped outside the gate and nodded to Medlili, who rode forward.

"The Warrior Woman will speak. Where are your leaders?"

There was a command, and the rifle barrels pointed skyward. An officer in the uniform of the Ferbodean People's Army strode out the gateway.

Jameta pitched her voice low. "Wrong man."

Medlili danced her horse forward. "You are not the leader. You are a lackey. Send the real leader out."

The man bristled, his spine straightening, his shoulders squaring. "I am Lieutenant-Colonel Samur Kazan of the Ferbodean People's Army, and I am in charge of the soldiers here."

Medlili circled the man, inspecting him like an object for sale in a market, then trotted back to Jameta, who gave her the next instructions. The girl moved ahead again.

"The Warrior Woman greets you, soldier. You may form your troops and march back to your border. Your real border. You will have escort."

The man's shoulders lost their stiffness. "You're serious?"

"Dear Lieutenant-Colonel. You have one hundred men. A thousand warriors surround you. Is that not serious?"

"But what about the mines? I was sent to protect them."

Jameta spoke quietly. *We deal with the Domalians.*

Medlili turned. "The mines are no longer the affair of Ferbodin. The Warrior Woman will deal with the Domalian government."

"Will you guarantee the safety of the miners and their families?"

Medlili did not wait for prompting. "Did your miners guarantee safety of our herds and our waters when they set up stinking mines? This is the domain of Dry Land People. Who comes here, comes at our invitation, at our command. But Warrior Woman does not fight businessmen. That is your guarantee." She pointed. "You have until the shadow of the gatepost covers that bush."

"And if I do not?"

Medlili swept a hand around the circle. A thousand muskets rose and pointed inward.

"I understand." He bowed in Jameta's direction, made a parade turn and marched back into the compound. He snapped a word to his officers; soon orders were ringing out, and the men were swinging packs on their backs.

Pavenkov had been watching all this from the safety of the bay's tall back. Now he swung from his horse and stormed up to Kazan, his face red. There was an intense conversation in hissing voices. At the end, the bureaucrat stamped back to his horse and threw himself into the saddle. He jerked the reins and drove the horse forward, vaulted the low mud wall and rode away from the compound, his lackeys scrambling onto their own mounts and straggling after him. Jameta counted twenty-three of them, mostly armed with rifles, two or three of them Double-S.

At Sfissef's whistle the encircling nomads parted to let him through. The soldiers formed up into columns and marched out, their supply wagons creaking behind them. Sfissef gave orders, and a contingent of riders followed at a reasonable distance.

Jameta turned to Erlon. "Well! That was too easy."

"You think so?"

"Of course it was. We had all the power and we gave him no choice. He had to comply."

"So, why did we let him go? We have a thousand men. We can hardly send them home without even a little massacre."

Jameta pulled her veil off to show her grin. "But we didn't want to give the handsome Lieutenant-Colonel an excuse to turn around and fight us, did we? Consider political implications."

Erlon absently caressed the barrel of his rifle. "Yes, we still have to go back through Ferbodin."

"That we do. But for now, we have a celebration to prepare." She turned to Medlili. "How many goats does it take to feed a thousand men?"

"I don't know, but Uncle Sfissef does."

"Then we will ask him. And Medlili?"

"Yes?"

"The expression is 'My dear Lieutenant-Colonel.' If you say 'Dear Lieutenant-Colonel,' it sounds as if you are writing a letter to a friend."

"Thank you, Jameta." Then she grinned. "But perhaps I was not wrong. He is handsome man, Samur Kazan. I think he would make good friend. Perhaps I write him a letter."

* * *

They camped in the river valley that night, decimating the local people's goat and sheep population but filling their salt bins. After supper, the caravan leaders held a meeting with their allies.

"Medlili, do we assume that the nomads will go home, now?"

The Tolbèan girl nodded. "I have told them that the Warrior Woman has declared a truce between all the Tribes until they reach their tents. Then they can start all their usual male feuding and fighting until She calls them again."

Roeble nodded. "And what about you?"

She glanced around the circle.

"I must go to the mines. I will tell them new arrangements. They must wait for you talk to Domaland rulers."

"That's right. And I'm sure you'll talk to them about the water and the slag."

"Oh, yes. I need no help, there."

"And then?"

"What does the Wise Man suggest?"

He shrugged. "It will be very difficult for us to speak on your behalf in the meeting rooms of the big realms. It would be much better to have a representative of the Dry Land People with us."

"Then I should come with you?"

"That's your choice. Would you be allowed to travel alone with strangers?"

She twitched a finger under his nose. "No one tells the granddaughter of Zelfana of the Tolbè to go or not to go. And I am not alone. I have my brothers and the Warrior Woman to protect me."

"Your brothers would come?"

"It will be a great adventure for them to come with us."

"They would be a welcome addition to our strength."

Aleria regarded her. "Only the three of you? Emissaries of all your people?"

"I can speak for the Aine Tolbè. Other tribes must speak for themselves."

"We can't take a representative of every tribe with us."

"Of course not. We save those talks for the time of negotiation."

Aleria turned to Roeble. "Do you think this will work?"

Jameta grinned. "You're forgetting the other half of her duties."

"What half is that?"

"She Speaks for the Warrior Woman."

Roeble's face lit up. "Who can make deals for all the Tribes."

"Exactly."

Aleria frowned. "You mean you're going to let this young woman go into meetings with top officials of three realms and pretend that she represents all of her people?"

Jameta shook her head. "There is no pretense. Medlili Speaks for the Warrior Woman. Whatever she says, the Warrior Woman will support."

"So you go along with whatever she says."

"No, Aleria. I don't go along. The Warrior Woman goes along."

"Who is you."

"No, who isn't me. When I wear the veil of the Warrior Woman, I represent all the Tribes. I no longer speak as Jameta the Galesian. My Voice speaks for me. It wouldn't work half so well if my Voice didn't have a far better idea of what is good for the Tribes than I do."

Aleria shook her head. "If it wasn't you, Jameta, I'd be worried about all this."

"Ah, but it is me. And it's Medlili. And you and Roeble take your turn as well. Between us, we will make all this come together."

Medlili bowed her head. "The Warrior Woman has spoken. It will be so."

Aleria shrugged. "Why should I object? Go get your gear. We're pulling out in the morning."

The young tribeswoman bowed and then, with a flash of a grin, hitched her veil into place and strode out to gather her belongings.

34. Setting it Straight

After all the excitement, they tired early and headed for their tents.

Aleria lay back on her cot. "How do you think Medlili will handle all this?"

Jameta grinned as she slipped into her nightgown. "I'm sure she'll be a better traveller than we are."

"It won't be as easy when we get home. When she's in Kingsport, she can stay with me, if you like."

A pang of anger shot through Jameta. "No! She's my Speaker. You can't have her!"

Aleria sat up. "Whoa, there. What's the matter? What do you mean I 'can't have her'? I don't want her for anything. I was just trying to be helpful." The older girl looked at Jameta. "What's got into you?"

"I'm sorry. I guess I've let my power go to my head. I start thinking about the Tolbè as my people."

Aleria canted her head to one side. "No, there is more to it than that. I let your little tantrum at the Horse Fair slide because...well, because you were partly right, and it wasn't the place to divide our forces. But I haven't forgotten it. Why are you so worried about me?"

"I have the feeling that there's an unspoken contest going on between us, and I don't know the rules."

"A game where Jameta anDennal doesn't know the rules? I doubt it. You always know what's going on. It must be marvellous."

"Not really."

"Well, it's a talent I could use more often. How do you do it?"

Jameta turned away, thinking. "Maybe you don't want it." She spun to face Aleria. "Can you imagine a world where everyone thought they were living behind stone walls, and you were the only one that knew that they were living in tents?"

Aleria thought about that. "They would go about their lives, thinking everything they did was private..."

"But you could hear it all."

"That would be wonderful. Think of what you'd know!"

"It's also terrible. Think of what people didn't think you knew. Think of spending your whole life being careful because you couldn't let it slip."

"I see."

"Yes."

"And you're telling me that your life is like that?"

"Oh, not all the time. But until I saw how people who live in tents deal with it, I didn't fully understand how I deal with it."

"And how do you deal with it?"

"With understanding. How can I condemn people for doing things I see other people doing all the time as well?"

"You see more of the foibles of human nature, but instead of being cynical, you're more understanding?"

"Yes. How can I be cynical? All those people are being normal. I'm the one that's different."

"Ah. So you hide it."

"You're damn right I do. You haven't seen the look on someone's face when I slip and they realize I know something I shouldn't. They shut off. They have no idea where I got the information, so they determine never to give me anything again, just in case."

"I can see how that might be a problem."

"Because I do slip. I can't help it. And often it's with friends. I get with a person I respect and look up to, and then I relax too much and forget to be careful and, bang! I mess up."

"Like with Roeble."

"Like with Roeble. He handled it very well."

Aleria regarded her for a moment. "Have you ever thought that this talent of yours runs in both directions?"

"What do you mean?"

"I hear you being so forgiving and mature because you understand that the foibles of others are only human. Have you ever thought that others might feel the same way about you?"

Jameta stopped dead.

"Well?"

Her mind was whirling. *How could I...oh, no!* A vision of Lavan came into her mind.

"What are you laughing about?"

Jameta shook her head. "I'm laughing at myself. I have been so stupid."

Aleria grinned. "Much though it cheers me to hear that, I would be the last person to agree. Of all the people I know, "stupid" wouldn't be you."

"Oh, you haven't been in my thoughts. You have absolutely no idea how stupid I've been."

"I'm glad you can see the humour in it."

"I'd better. If not, I'd be out banging my head against the nearest rock." She turned to face her friend. "Do you realize, I have been acting and thinking as if I was the only smart person in the world?"

"Oh. You, too?"

"Aleria, that is the nicest thing you could have said, right now."

"There you are. And now you're back to normal again."

"What do you mean?"

"That was a very Jameta-like jump of logic. You just took a step back and looked at this conversation from a distance and could tell what was happening, where it was going, who was contributing what. It's what I'm learning to do in a battle. Erlon does it, but much better. You take an objective viewpoint, see what's happening all over, and then make the best decision based on much more information than most people have."

Jameta shook her head. "Once again proving how stupid I've been."

"How is that?"

"Because I never thought of other people doing the same thing in their own specialties. But of course they do. That's what leadership is all about, isn't it? Taking the long view, the bigger scope."

"Well, I wouldn't say that's all, but it is a big part of it."

"Then I'm glad nobody is asking me to be a leader. I obviously have a lot of learning to do."

Aleria reached up and slapped her on the shoulder. "And you made a great jump today."

Jameta shook her head. "I shouldn't tell you this, but do you know what I did to snap Lavan out of his funk?"

Aleria held up a finger. "Let me guess. To prove my leadership abilities, let me show off."

Jameta entered the game. "Show me, O wonderful Caravan Master."

Aleria looked at her. "I'll bet you told him that this was another stage of life he was going through, another challenge to be met."

"And your bird flies first."

Aleria laughed, an explosion of sound that resembled the crow of a rooster. "You have no idea how good that makes me feel."

Jameta frowned. "Why?"

"Can you imagine how it feels to be a leader, but to have someone looking over your shoulder? Someone you suspect is far smarter than you, who could do a far better job of your duties? Someone who couldn't possibly look up to you because she seemed to know all your weaknesses?"

There was a long silence. "You actually thought that? About me?"

"Sometimes." Aleria grinned. "Sometimes not. I have to admit, watching you fumble around with Erlon ..." The grin faded. "And now I've made one of your mistakes, haven't I? I've relaxed too far, and hurt your feelings."

Jameta shook her head. "Hearing it from you only confirms my worst fears. I'm making a hash of it, aren't I?"

"You are."

"Thank you so much."

Aleria chuckled. "Oh, I love being superior. Don't worry. If I didn't have a handle on it, I wouldn't be so mean about it."

"What? You have a solution?"

"Not a solution but an approach. Diffidence. Have you heard that word before?"

Jameta growled. "If I hear it again, I'm going to brain somebody."

"So you already understand? So much for my intelligence. I'd better go back to being polite."

"It's the second part of my problem. Not much point in knowing what people are thinking if I can't make them think something else."

"That one isn't unique."

"And it doesn't help me deal with Erlon."

"And I'm no help, either. I'm sorry, but I'm going back to doing what I'm good at, which is running a caravan."

"And I'll go back to trying not to mess up your caravan by causing a distraction."

"I do thank you for that. I have no complaints." Aleria looked at her, head to one side. "It's unfortunate, isn't it? Your most valuable contribution to this caravan is to figure out what people's problems are and to help them deal with them. But there's nobody to help you."

"Story of my life."

* * *

The next morning Jameta changed back into her Galesian clothing, and the men harnessed their horses to the wagons and lined out along the road north.

It felt strange to be back with the wagons again. Jameta's eyes kept turning to where the nomads were filing out of the river valley, roving along at their own speed back to their lives in the desert. And here she was in her denim pants and swordsman's vest, riding back to civilization. *Well, to my civilization.*

Medlili, still in her tribeswoman's robes and veil, rode a fiery little desert pony that needed a few hops and bounces before he settled down for the day's work. The tribeswoman shouted at her brothers, who whooped and galloped alongside, doing nothing to help. Once she had her horse under control, she scolded them while they grinned at her. Then she flicked a thumb towards Jameta and rode off to curve in beside Aleria's wagon.

The two trotted over to look expectantly at Jameta. They looked identical, although Talat, who rode the pinto, had a thinner face, while Zagor, the younger, had a wider smile. His palomino was taller and longer of leg. Jameta had it pegged for speed.

Erlon glanced at them. "How's the Galesian, Talat? Any better?"

The boy grinned, rocking a hand from side to side. "Better, Erlon."

"Good." He circled a finger over his head. "Close patrol like before. Stay in sight." He touched his eye.

Talat nodded. "Stay to see."

"Right. One patrol, one stay close."

"Right, Erlon." The two boys played a quick game with their fingers, and Talat laughed and punched his brother's shoulder, then lifted his reins and galloped off.

Erlon nodded. "Lavan, take point. I don't expect trouble yet, but you never can tell. Jameta, sweep both sides behind us. Up to the ridge on either side. I'll stay close for a while, keep an eye on things."

They spread out to their duties, settling back into their former roles. Jameta found that the two boys were invaluable. They covered a lot of ground and always seemed able to find her no matter where she was patrolling. Every time she met one of them she taught him a different word in Galesian. It was essential they learn the language as quickly as possible.

The bad news came the following day. A contingent of tribesmen had continued their scouting duties, escorting the Ferbodean soldiers to the border and keeping an eye on Pavenkov and his lot. They were led by Outoul, one of the few tribesmen who knew Jameta's double role. He had a long face when he came to Jameta that morning.

They are gone, Jameta. My men cannot find them.

Pavenkov?

Yes. Most Ferbodeans went home with the army. The other six met with a group of local tribesmen. Perhaps the ones from earlier? My men were not familiar with them. Thirteen men. They camped, and our men left them there for the night. In the morning they took to the road early, and a herd of horses covered their tracks. When our scouts caught up with the horse herd the Ferbodeans and their allies were not there, and their tracks were not on the trail in front. They must have slipped aside along the way. We are searching, but they have many hours start.

Jameta glanced at Erlon.

He frowned in concentration. "I think he's after us. Specifically, you."

"Me?"

"Well, after the Warrior Woman. We tried to disguise our role in the battle, but he seems to be able to find allies. He has to know by now that the caravan travelled with the nomad army. If he has good information, he might even have noticed that you disappeared for the whole time She was there. He may not be that smart, but we have to keep it in mind."

"So, what do we do?"

He shrugged. "We watch and wait. We have good scouts, and if he wants to get at us, he has to come out in the open." A dark frown marred his features. "And then we kill him."

"Yes. I have fulfilled my promise to the nomads. This is a new battle, with different rules."

"And our first problem is Medlili and her trip to the mines."

"Yes. It's dangerous for the three of them, with Pavenkov and his mob roaming around."

Erlon considered. "We can't take the caravan that far out of the way. We can't strip the caravan of its defences to protect them. Any other ideas?" He glared at her. "And you can't go with them alone."

She sighed. "No. Of course, we could always handle it properly."

"Properly?"

"Yes. We could ask Medlili what she plans."

"Oh. I suppose we could."

Medlili was unconcerned. "I do not fear the Ferbodean. Oh, I fear him enough to stay out of his way. But he will not even notice three nomads travelling along."

Jameta snorted. "Everybody notices you."

The tribeswoman grinned. "Nobody notices an old woman with her grandsons."

Jameta turned to Erlon. "We can't do any better than that. It's her choice."

Erlon grinned. "I'm getting used to women who run off and do whatever they want, no matter what I say."

Aleria was likewise amenable. "She knows the land and the people. The more normal they act, the better their chances."

On the third day after leaving the river Medlili, dressed in her darkest and most concealing robes, trotted off to the east, her brothers in line behind her.

Aleria and Jameta watched the little party ride away, tiny and lonely in the vast, arid expanse around them. "How do you think she'll do with the mine managers?"

"If they haven't returned to their mines yet, maybe she'll find a bunch of them together. Which will be convenient, but will create its own difficulties. We have discussed strategy for the past few days. She knows what her tribe wants, what her people want, and what kind of support she can expect from Galesia. Which isn't much. She has to take it herself from there. I have confidence in her. Better than that, her grandmother has confidence in her."

Aleria sighed. "Well, it couldn't go better for us. Responsibility taken out of our hands."

"I think that's a good way to look at this situation. We're a tiny part of this whole swirl of people and politics. A key part, but only a part. The rest of the situation is going the way the people allow it to. I have little faith in the theory that one person can change a whole lot."

"Unless she happens to be the Warrior Woman, avatar of some god or other."

Jameta shrugged. "But that only works if there is a great deal of need in the population for whatever the individual brings. Look at Samnia. If the situation there hadn't been boiling already, the story of a weird throwback to ancient times would have been a ho-hum item of gossip from the fringe fanatics."

"I'd have to agree. But since we have the chance, we can use it to our advantage."

"As long as it's to the advantage of the Tribes, we can."

"Once again, no argument. If we wangle anything to their disadvantage, it will all fall apart anyway. Oh, we might make a bunch of money for a while, but we could lose a lot in the end. It's not worth the risk."

Jameta clapped Aleria on the back. "Spoken like a true merchant. These trips have been good for you."

Aleria swung up on the wagon seat and glowered down at Jameta. "You're starting to sound like my father."

"A wonderful man. I could take worse models."

"Yes. Me, for example." She signalled to Cavick, and he started the caravan off up the trail towards Ferbodin and home.

Jameta mounted Brownie and trotted off to scout their path.

35. Sandstorm

The caravan rolled west and north, following in the path of centuries of travellers. And the path of Tamdjert, the hero of the ancient song. Jameta amused herself by recognizing the landmarks as they appeared out of the haze ahead.

Until the third day. Then, nothing seemed to fit. She found the right landmark, but it was in the wrong place. Then she spotted what could be the next landmark, and it was even farther astray. The feeling of wrongness increased as the day progressed, and she wished for Medlili's greater knowledge.

She was humming the appropriate stanza over to herself when Erlon reined in beside her. "What's wrong?"

"The trail isn't going where it should be."

He looked around. "This is the way we came."

"Yes, but the caravan trail is supposed to pass to the west of the divided hill."

"I don't think so. I remember we curved by it to the left on the way here."

"Yes, you're right. Do you mind if I take a little side trip?"

"Part of your duties, I'd say." He looked up at the sky. "Take extra water. The weather's unsettled."

She did not question his order. Erlon's reading of the weather was another one of the skills that made him so valuable on the trail.

She steered Brownie off at an angle to the west, heading for the distinctive hill with the split in it that she knew from the Saga of Tamdjert. It was less than an hour's ride, and she took care to scout all the surrounding terrain as she rode. The split made it easy to approach the hilltop unseen, and she paused at the top, only her head above the ridge.

When her search of the next valley revealed no one moving, she slipped off her horse and stood higher. Sure enough, a faint trail wound off to the west, heading towards the higher ridges where the bandits had attacked the wagons. She even thought she could make out the next marker, a mountain of darker rock with a big slide down one side.

Satisfied, she turned back, sweeping north beside the modern caravan trail and meeting the caravan as it settled for the night.

Erlon was still ahorse and trotted out to greet her. "Have a nice ride?"

She grinned. "All is as it should be. The old trail goes the other side of the mountains."

He nodded. "That's a great relief."

"Why is that?"

"I was considering how to tell all these nomads they've been using the wrong road for the past three centuries."

"They have been." Jameta shrugged. "But something changed the route, and we'll never know what it was. What's for supper?"

"I could guess. Goat stew and sour beer."

"The man's a genius. I can't wait."

They kicked their steeds to a canter and headed for the picket line.

* * *

The following morning the clouds piled higher on the eastern horizon, a strange brown tinge to them. Aleria frowned over her coffee. "Ever seen anything like that, Roeble?"

He glanced up. "Dust storm."

"Do you think we're in danger? The prevailing weather comes from the west, here, doesn't it?"

"And storms come from the south and east. Yes, we should take basic precautions today. Extra tarps on the wagons, spare ropes handy, water topped up."

"What do we do if we get hit?" Aleria was staring around as if looking for an unseen enemy.

"Get the wagons together with the horses on the downwind side. If there's time, we fill under the wagons with anything that will stop the wind. Cover the horses' heads with sacks, cover our own heads with scarves and sit it out."

"How long do they usually last?"

"A real sandstorm is only a few hours. Dust storms can go for days, but they aren't as dangerous."

Jameta remembered. "And wrap your guns tightly in fine cloth. Sand gets into everything."

Roeble glanced at her. "A good idea. Did they teach you anything else?"

She thought. "Nothing that works with wagons. Higher is better because the sand is heavy and flows along the low ground. Unless there's thunder and lighting, in which case the sand is the less dangerous problem. Make sure you've got high boots and heavy pants on. Your legs and feet get it the worst. That's all I can think of at the moment."

Erlon frowned. "Why is it different with wagons?"

"Horses don't do well in sandstorms. If you can get them into shelter, they're much better. Otherwise it's best if they lie down, like camels do. A tribesman puts his horse on the ground in the lee of a rock, throws a blanket over both their heads, and waits it out."

Lavan found this interesting. "But our horses don't lie down on command."

"Mine do."

"They do?"

"I wasn't just lolling around in the shade for the past month. I was taking lessons on desert survival." She tossed her hand out towards the mountains. "And the tribesmen don't consider this desert. This is only dry country. They call themselves Dry Land People. The true Desert People use camels."

Aleria stood. "Well, if we get hit by a sandstorm, maybe something you learned will help. What I hear so far is that those hills ahead of us would be a better place than this prairie to sit one out. Do you agree?"

"Everything they told me says so."

"Let's move."

Nobody argued, and the wagon train was on the road in record time.

As the day wore on the wind picked up, and soon a fine haze filled the air. At noon Aleria gave orders to slow down so the stock could breathe easier.

"We have water for two days and a good well on the other side of the mountains, so we can afford a dry camp if we have to. Any comments?"

Jameta noted with approval that the tougher the situation was, the more the Caravan Master asked their opinions. *Despite the fact that we don't have any.*

"What are you grinning at?"

Jameta shrugged. "Thinking it was nice to be asked and wishing I had an answer. Why?"

"When you get that smile I always want to check to see that I don't have my boots untied or a crumb of dinner stuck to my teeth."

"Come on, Aleria. If you had dinner stuck to your teeth, I'd tell you."

"Aye. One way or the other."

The others chuckled and moved to their duties.

In the middle of the afternoon, Erlon pulled up beside Jameta. He had a bandana across his face because of the increasing dust. "I don't like what I'm seeing back there."

She had switched to Brownie to keep the workload even and pulled her kerchief over her nose. She glanced back for the tenth time. "I don't either. According to the nomads, a dust storm is brown, a sandstorm is more yellow."

"That's rather a brownish yellow, I'd say. Doesn't help much."

"A sandstorm is lower. Dust is lighter and goes up."

He glanced back again. "That doesn't look high to me."

"It doesn't."

He grimaced. "You get out on the trail ahead and see if you can find shelter. I'll talk to Aleria."

She didn't waste time, lining Brownie out beside the wagons at a slow canter. Ahead the ground rose, and the trail wound between low hills, which seemed a good thing, as far as she could tell. She noted the first possibility, a flat spot protected by a pile of rocks to the east, and moved on. There was a short, steep pitch in the trail, leading through a ridge that shouldered the desert soil aside. Here was a better spot, in the lee of the ridge with boulders strewn around. *Anything to make the wind swirl will let the sand drop out. This would be perfect.*

She turned and ran Brownie back down the road, giving Aleria the details when she reached the lead wagon. The Caravan Master nodded. "Good. This dust is getting thicker. Run down the train and tell everyone to close up tight."

"Got it."

She trotted along, giving the order to every teamster. They were hunkered down on their seats, the guards likewise. She reminded them about the guns as well. *These tribesmen don't consider a sandstorm to be more than an inconvenience. They might attack.*

As she neared the end of the train, she got the feeling of wrongness. *By now I should know how many wagons we have. This is the last wagon, and I haven't passed the remuda.*

She gave the message to the tail teamster and rode over beside Erlon. "Where's the remuda?"

"Behind the third-last wagon as usual."

"No it isn't." She heeled Brownie into a gallop, Erlon and Rogas thundering behind. When they reached the third wagon, there were no horses tied to the tailgate. There was no sign of Stilet.

Erlon peered around. "Which way?"

She said nothing. Swirling dust hid the landscape.

Then they heard a shot.

Erlon's head came up like a hunting dog's. "That way. Keep pointing."

She held her hand steady, wondering what he would do. He ranged up beside the driver. "Give me your extra water. You'll be camping in a moment. Close up tight so you don't get lost. Tell Aleria somebody stole the remuda, and Stilet's in shooting trouble. Jameta and I have gone after him."

He glanced at Jameta's arm and started off. "You stay there. Keep pointing."

When he had almost disappeared in the dust, he stopped and motioned Jameta ahead. Now she was catching on. She kept pointing in the right direction, and as soon as she came near, he moved on. They picked up the pace, with Jameta desperately trying to remember where she had been pointing, and Erlon looking back over his shoulder for her guidance.

Finally shadows appeared around them, and rocks loomed out of the murk. Now Erlon had objects to guide himself by, and he sped up to a trot.

There was another shot. Close by, this time, off to their left. Another in quick succession. "A Double-S. It's him."

They cantered toward the shots, Erlon with his rifle drawn. Jameta put a hand on her pistol inside her coat. No sense letting the dust get at it yet.

Stilet's voice came from close ahead. "Over here. Go to your left."

They slowed and cut sideways. Nearby, they could make out a rocky ledge. Then Erlon pointed. The vague shape of a horse stood against the ledge. "Keep with the horses." He vaulted out of the saddle and clambered up the rocks.

She reached out to take one of Rogas's reins and pulled Brownie alongside the other mount, which carried Galesian rig. Now she identified the single white rear foot. Stilet's horse.

She listened and waited, and for a long while, nothing happened. Except the sound of the wind was increasing, and the murk behind her looked darker than the murk in front. *Maybe it's because I can see the rocks in front. I hope so.*

Her head snapped around at a clatter up the slope, her gun pointing. A figure materialized out of the haze. A large figure with a distinctive bandanna around his face.

"Got them. Stilet's bringing the horses around."

She pointed back. "He better get here soon."

Erlon looked and said something in another language. It sounded like a curse. "We've got to get into shelter. We're on the wrong side of the ridge. Let's go right." He stayed on the ground, leading the two horses, and she followed.

Visibility was getting worse, and she kept Brownie tight against the other mounts.

There was a shout ahead, and a figure appeared. She heard the murmur of voices, and then they started moving again, going uphill, now, weaving between the rocks. Once when the going was rough she lost sight of the horse in front of her, and was about to shout when she saw a white hoof lifting and dropping ahead. She pushed Brownie closer, and on they went.

The back of her neck stung. She put her hand up to find that her scarf had separated from her coat, and the sand was scoring her skin. The wind was howling now, and swirls of brown eddied around the rocks. She jerked her collar higher and hunched her shoulders.

After what seemed an age, the Stilet's horse stopped, then moved on, then stopped again. "What's going on?"

Erlon's voice came over the roar of the wind. "Found a spot. Keep coming."

His shadowy arm reached up to lead Stilet's mount ahead. She followed. They cut left behind a large boulder, and the force of the wind lessened. It was possible to make out the forms of the horses, huddled with their noses in tight against the rock. Stilet was tying cloth over their heads, leaving it drooping down. Some of them tossed against the cloth, but he calmed them.

She dismounted, pulled the sacking out of her saddlebag and did the same for Brownie. Then she led him forward and got him to lie down with his head almost underneath the muzzles of the other horses. She found Doe and got her down as well, then pulled out her spare blanket.

She knelt by Doe, looking up "Joining me?"

Erlon glanced at the wrangler. "Want to flip a coin to see who gets closest to her rear legs?"

Stilet shrugged. "Doe ain't gonna kick nobody." He looked up. "Him, on the other hand..."

The Roan's size was a giveaway. He stood over Doe and Brownie, his head down to snuffle at the other horses.

Jameta laughed. "He's being a very good boy, right now, because he's still hoping for a treat."

Erlon's head was close enough that she could feel him shaking it. "I doubt if he's ever been called that before. Plenty of other things, but 'very good boy' isn't in there."

The wrangler snorted. "I'm of the first opinion m'self."

"Why's that?"

"Because without him, I'da never found them."

Erlon turned to regard Stilet in the dim light. "What did happen? I didn't think you'd leave the train."

"Well, I thought they just got away. I looks, and I sees the rear end of the last horse disappearin' into the dust. I gotta admit, I figured the Roan finally got his rope free, and I was right peeved 'cause I tied him real good, as usual. So I went chasin' after them. Figured it wouldn't take no time at all.

"Well, I gets to the front and I sees there's a guy leadin' 'em. Then I realize I'm in trouble. He kicks his horse into a gallop, and they all go peltin' past me. I looks back but I can't see the train and the only thing I can do is follow the horses. When they slow down, I circle wide and come up on the thieves. There's three of 'em. I took a shot, but the light's bad. Prob'ly missed. They duck into the rocks. The Roan, he stands there, cool as anythin'. So I cut left, leave my horse, and come in from above. Sure enough, there they are. So I take a couple more shots at 'em, and they disappear. Then I hear you behind, and here we are."

"And where are they?"

Jameta stirred. "The sand came in strong while you were ahead of me. I doubt if they're moving. That's what they do when there's a storm. They hole up and wait it out."

He sighed. "If we weren't dealing with Pavenkov, I'd be happy with that. But we won't be going to sleep and waking up in the morning when it's over. The moment the storm dies down, day or night, we have to be up and moving. Everybody got that?"

They murmured their approval.

"So now we sleep. Jameta, you take first watch."

"Sure. How do I know when to wake you up?"

"When your watch is over."

She extricated her hand and reached over Doe's leg to slap Erlon. "When we're on watch at the wagons we use the clock Aleria carries. I have no idea how long two hours is."

"Hmph. I used to own a pocket watch. Can't have one in Galesia, though. Mechanical. Sinful."

"Where did you get a watch?"

He was silent.

"Or is that part of the story you're going to tell me one day when you get around to it?"

He stirred. "I suppose."

"Fine. Go to sleep. I'll wake you up before dark."

He wriggled around, and his hand came over to stroke her head. "Thanks."

"My pleasure."

Her watch was long and boring and uncomfortable. The wind howled and the blanket over their heads blew around, allowing swirls of sand in. Soon every part of her body felt gritty. After what she thought was an hour, she fumbled around and sponged out the nostrils of the horses with a damp cloth, dismayed at how much sand she found.

Then back to waiting, with even more sand in her clothes and in every crevice of her body. Finally, when it could be getting dimmer, she nudged Erlon. "You awake?"

"I am now. Anything happening?"

"Mostly sand. Wind's about the same. I'll clean out the horses' nostrils with water again. A lot of dust in there. I think they need it about every hour or so."

"Trust you to do the right thing. If we get out of this with our stock in good shape, we've got an advantage."

"Except that the guys we're after have a lifetime of the same training."

"We have other advantages. Don't worry. We'll get back to the wagons, then we'll see."

"I believe you. And now, despite the early hour, I figure the best solution to boredom is sleep."

"Sleep well. Stilet will wake you around midnight."

"Can't wait." She dealt with the horses, then curled up against Doe's neck. Earlier she had been too hot, but the temperature had dropped, and it was nice to be against the warm hide. In spite of the discomfort, she drifted off.

She awoke, shivering, to the feeling that she was being smothered. She moved her head and heard the trickle of sand. The pressure on her face lessened, and she pushed the blanket away from her face. Sand poured into her clothes. She lay, listening. The noise of the wind seemed less. She lifted the blanket, but all she saw was inky blackness. Doe stirred beneath her. She reached out and patted her cheek to calm her.

There was a stirring beside her. "You awake?"

"Yes. Sorry. Doe's restless."

"I think the wind has dropped. Maybe she can stand up if she has to."

Stilet's voice came from farther down the horse. "Just give me some warning."

"Stay where you are." She felt Erlon moving around. Then the blanket shifted, and sand ran everywhere again.

"Stop dumping sand on me."

"Shh. If the wind is down, the enemy could be about."

She peeked out again. "I can't see a thing."

"Let's hope they can't either. I need to move."

"Me, too."

They rose, shaking sand from their clothing. She got her horses on their feet and checked their nostrils. "Somebody wash them out recently?"

"I did it 'bout a half hour ago."

"They're looking chipper. Think we can take the hoods off?"

Erlon took a deep breath. "Yes, the sand has pretty well stopped. Dust is much less, too."

Fumbling around in the dark, she freed the horses. They shook their heads but made no other sound. The Roan nuzzled her arm.

"Oh, all right." She reached in her pocket, brushed the sand away. "One for everybody, and no more."

Once the horses were munching happily she located Erlon's shadow. "I can't see any use in blundering around in this darkness."

"I suppose not. We'd make so much noise, anyone would hear us coming. All right. Back to bed, folks. Jameta's on watch again. Wake me up the moment you can see anything."

Again she tried to keep track of the time, but the fact that she couldn't keep her eyes open decided her. Erlon took over, and she slept again.

But not for long enough. She was still bleary when he shook her gently awake. She looked up and saw his figure clearly against the sky. "Morning?"

"Soon. I think we can move."

They roused, stretching. Jameta felt like hell. She checked Brownie over, tightened her girth and put the bit back in her mouth. Then she helped Stilet go over the other horses. Soon after they finished, Erlon returned from a brief reconnaissance.

"I can see well enough. Let's head back towards the road. There'll be a fire going in camp, so we shouldn't have much trouble finding it."

She looked up. The sky was still black, but glows of dim light drifted through rifts in the cloud. Over to the east, there was the faintest flush of dawn.

Erlon mounted and led out, Jameta following with the Roan's lead in her hand. Stilet brought up the rear of the remuda. They wound down through the rocks, moving slowly.

Suddenly Erlon reined in. His voice hissed back to her. "Off your horse. Now!"

She slipped off Brownie's back and pressed herself against the horse's shoulder. There was silence.

Erlon loomed over her, handing her Rogas's reins. "Hold him. There's someone out there."

She stood, immobilized by fear, while he melted away, not a sound showing his progress. In the growing light she could see that Stilet was down as well, but she couldn't see where he had gone. The wait seemed endless, and she longed to swing onto her horse and gallop away. She squashed that thought. *I'd probably get shot off his back after three steps.*

She started when Erlon appeared, leaning close to whisper. "They're in front of us. A line of them."

"How many?"

"At least five. We'll have to go back up."

He took his reins, and they turned the line of horses around, retreating up the hill. Again she followed, glancing back anxiously, but the increasing light only showed her Stilet, looking back as well, his rifle at the ready.

She could now see the top of the ridge ahead, and as they approached it, Erlon stopped again, going back along the horses and disappearing. He returned and brought the wrangler to the front with him.

"They haven't moved yet, so they don't know where we are. But we can't go down the hill. I don't want to get too far from the caravan in strange country with enemies around."

"We could take the old caravan route."

"The one you scouted?"

"That's right. The two routes join on the other side of the ridge." She ran the song through. "There's a stream comes out of the hills, there. Remember where we camped the last night before the mine?"

"I remember. Good water."

"The old trail comes in along that stream."

"Can you find the old trail?"

"I could see it from the top of the notched hill back there. It might be harder to find once we're down in the bushes."

"It sounds like our best chance. We'll cross the ridge over by that boulder and hope they don't notice. Lead on."

Visibility was good enough, once they were over the ridge, to see the faint lightness of the old trail. She pointed it out to Erlon.

"People must be using it, keeping the brush down. Don't really like that idea, but it's still our best option."

He led the way again, and they descended, taking advantage of every bit of cover they could.

36. Chase

Jameta looked around. "I don't like this."

Erlon looked at her over his shoulder. "Neither do I. Why don't you like it?"

She tossed a hand back towards the pass they had just descended from. "When Pavenkov's men find we're not there, they'll come over that rise and see us."

"And we'll see them."

"And then we have a chase where we get to the caravan first if we're lucky?"

"I haven't seen them yet. We will have a good lead."

"Pavenkov still has five of his Ferbodeans, as well as the thirteen locals Outoul saw. What if some of them are in front of us as well?

He pressed his lips together. "That's always a possibility. We need information."

"Do you have a solution?"

"If we were a caravan, we'd have outriders."

"Away you go."

"Which side?"

"We are more interested in what's between us and the rest of our crew. Check out the east." He pointed. "If you get to that dip in the hills, you might even see the caravan."

"Right." She switched saddle to Doe's back. "Take care of Brownie for me. And the Roan."

"Huh! If he causes any trouble, I'll turn him loose. He'll find you, if we're lucky."

"Good enough." She reined Doe away from the trail, trotting through the sparse forest towards the hills that separated their path from the new caravan route. She kept to the thicker trees along the lower part of the hill. The scant forest might slow her down, but would keep her hidden from spying eyes.

As she gained altitude she lost the cover of the trees and could catch a glimpse of the remuda now and then, out on the old caravan trail. Erlon still led, Stilet bringing up the rear. They were loping, now: not wasting energy, but covering ground. Far back along the trail she could see a dust plume rising from the pass.

The race was on.

She scrambled up the hillside more quickly, aiming for the swale Erlon had indicated. It was bare, and she slipped along beside it, trying to stay hidden and raise as little dust as possible.

On the other side of the hills the land sloped away smoothly, and she could see the dust of the caravan, not as far ahead as she had hoped. Lining up the last place she had seen Erlon, she made a rough calculation. *Once we hit the junction we'll have to turn back to meet them. Unless they see us and pick up their pace.* There was a barren hillside up ahead, sloping down to the east, and she noted it as a route that was visible from the caravan.

Cutting back to the west, she crossed the height of land in a clump of trees and headed north again, making quicker time to stay even with the remuda. The pursuers were not catching up. *This could work out fine. If only we knew where Pavenkov and the other five men are.* She scanned the valley before her, but nothing else was moving.

She cut back up the hill for another sweep of the valley. No change. Remuda in front, tribesmen pursuing. On the east side of the ridge again, she ran Doe out onto a shale-covered avalanche path, sliding down to create a dust storm in full view of the caravan. *Maybe they'll be watching. If someone else is, too bad.*

The ground was more open east of the ridge, and she kept just below the skyline, galloping ahead as fast as possible. The next time she found a low spot and popped over the ridge to the west she halted in dismay. Erlon and the remuda were gone. No sign of them, no dust cloud. *They must have stopped. Why?*

She watched the approaching enemy. Her people did not appear. There was only one conclusion. *Something is wrong. If those tribesmen catch them, they won't be able to fight them off. I have to decoy them. Down on the flat, Doe is the fastest horse in this desert.*

"Let's go, girl. Race time."

Her plume of dust was now an advantage, and she pushed down the hill, cutting across the old caravan route close enough in front of the trailing party that they had to see her. Then she turned northwest up the opposite side of the valley, praying for smooth ground. Doe surged under her, pleased at the chance to run. Glancing back, Jameta could see the mob urging their little desert horses to better speed. When she was sure they were all behind her she picked up her pace and opened a lead.

From the best of her estimation, she was now passing the spot where Erlon must have stopped. She pushed Doe harder, glancing back to gauge the speed of her pursuers. Soon they were lost in her dust. She galloped on, working her way back to the trail.

Now she started paying attention to the road surface. When she found a stretch of bare rock she slowed, swung out onto the trackless stone and turned away, leaving no evidence of her passing until she was out of sight behind a stand of brush. She reined the horse in, allowing her to blow. *I don't think that lot will be listening very hard.*

Sure enough, soon the sound of galloping hooves swept past her. She waited until any stragglers would be long gone, then pulled out and trotted back down the trail, every sense alert.

She was rewarded by the sound of clopping hooves. She pulled into a handy copse to wait. Stilet rounded the next bend, the Roan pulled in close beside him, the other horses strung behind.

Jameta kneed her horse forward. "Where's Erlon?"

The wrangler winced. "Gone. There was a waystation in the trees back a ways. Five horses. He figured Pavenkov was there with five men. He sent me roundabout to the east and went in alone."

"Great. Well, I took our pursuers roundabout to the west. They're storming away to the north right now. Soon they'll figure out that they missed me and come back."

"What's the best route to the caravan?"

Jameta was busy switching her saddle to Brownie. "They're pretty close. Just the other side of the ridge, now, and a bit behind us. If you cut over the hill up there, you'll see them."

"And what are you going to do?"

"Go after Erlon, of course."

He frowned at her, but decided not to interfere.

"Don't worry. I've got a fresh horse, the fastest around. Nobody will catch me. I'll go back and see what Erlon's doing. What side of the trail is the way station?"

"East side."

"Fine. See you at the caravan."

She swung into the saddle and headed back down the trail, her heart pumping, every sense on full alert. Stilet cut up the hillside and disappeared into the trees.

All too soon she heard what she had hoped not to: trotting horses behind her. The tribesmen had turned back. She looked over her shoulder. Stilet and the remuda had not yet cleared the top of the hill. She peered ahead down the trail. Nothing. Wherever Erlon was, and whatever he was doing, the last thing he needed was a dozen riders storming down at him.

In spite of her fear, she grinned to herself. *And here I am on a fresh horse. They won't have counted on that.*

Listening closely, she trotted down the trail. There was a shout behind her. She looked back. A horseman had come around the corner and was yelling to the others.

Pretending to be startled, she heeled Brownie into a gallop, but not too fast. Sure enough, they all pelted after her. There were two musket shots, but she wasn't too worried about their accuracy from the back of a running horse. *Of course, someone could be lucky. Hope it's me.*

As soon as she had them moving well, she cut right into the forest again. It was a risk, because she was giving up the advantage of her long-limbed racer, but she figured he was up to it. The desert ponies had already carried their riders several miles. Brownie was just getting warmed up.

Ducking and dodging, she wound through the trees. The tribesmen followed, silent now, saving their breath for riding. She began to cut to the right, hoping to circle around and lure them up the road again. The steeper mountainside, rough with boulders, was closing in on her left, and she didn't want to compete in that terrain.

She had completed her turn and was heading back up the valley again when Brownie stumbled. It wasn't serious. He recovered and galloped on. She focused on his pace, and it seemed to be even.

Then he stumbled again. *Something's wrong.* She could feel it, now. He was favouring his off hind leg. She slowed, but she didn't dare give up much distance.

What do I do now? She was aware of the irony of her situation. *My only courage was based on the speed of my horses. Now I've lost that. What do I do?*

She rode on, half her mind on Brownie's pace, half on her predicament. *Don't give way to fear. What does Lavan say? Keep thinking. Plan. I can outrun them if I can get them on foot as well. If I can get them to chase me, they might not catch up with Brownie, either.*

Glancing left, she assessed the mountainside. It was thick with boulders, here, and ahead a steep bluff stood out. *If I went up there...*

There was no time for thought. Whipping off her scarf, she reached forward and knotted it through Brownie's bridle. "Sorry, girl, but you've got to keep running for a while." She skidded to a stop at the foot of the boulders, jumped off and slapped the horse's rump. Startled, Brownie skittered ahead. The scarf flapped, and she tossed her head and turned away from it, jumping sideways and bucking. Then she settled down to outrun this flapping demon, springing through the trees even faster than before, curving to the right.

Jameta took no more time to watch. She started up the rocks at a good pace, listening for her pursuers to catch up.

They did, in a frighteningly short time, shouting and leaping from their horses. She had no time to see if they all came after her, but it didn't matter. Muskets fired from below, and bullets whirred off the rocks around her. She tried to hide herself better, making the best time she could up through the thickening boulders.

She paused. All she could hear was the scrabbling of feet and the crashing of loose rocks.

Her breath was coming in deeper gasps now, and she knew she had to slow down. Gritting her teeth, she forged upward.

She came to the top of the rocks, and the open ridge stretched before her. *What now? Am I far enough ahead to make it? Should I cut down the hill again?* She turned back, listening. Her decision was made for her. They had spread out, coming up the hill from several directions.

Taking two deep breaths, she sprinted. Up the rock she bounded, her breath coming in great, tearing gasps. Her legs burned and her head reeled. But she kept on, spurred by shouts behind her. She had time to hope that the riflemen were panting as hard as she was. Musket fire exploded, and another bullet whined over her head.

The footing was smooth, here, and she risked a backwards glance. They were coming on, now. Two of them were far in front, the rest strung out behind. There was no more shooting; the front runners were in the way.

Jameta turned and ran on. She aimed to the left, down the valley. She had given Erlon plenty of time to deal with Pavenkov. Now she needed his help, and she was bringing the enemy in exhausted and on foot.

She glanced back again. One of the pursuers was smarter than she thought. He had cut wide, and she was curving towards him. She cursed to herself and turned the other way.

Can't make mistakes like that. Every turn lets them cut the corner.

The two leaders sprinted after her, waving their swords. *No guns. I can deal with swords.* She slipped her hand into her vest. The little pistol rode there safely.

Her next best chance was Brownie. If she could get down off the mountain and find her horse, and the enemy afoot, his limp wouldn't matter.

It didn't really matter. She'd be better running through the trees, now that she had them spread out like this. She angled slowly to the right, leaping down the mountainside, now, her boots slithering on the smooth spots.

There was a cry behind her, and she glanced back to see one of the men down. *Learn a lesson from that, girl.* She watched her footing more carefully. Only one close behind her now, but he was gaining. *He can risk it. If he falls, the others can keep chasing. There's only one of me.* She forged ahead, thinking furiously. *I have to deal with him.* Reaching into her vest, she drew her gun and cocked it. Now she ran more carefully, looking for the ideal spot...There!

She slipped behind a rock and plastered her back against it, trying to breathe quietly. *If only he goes by. I'll have to get very close for this little bullet.*

Footsteps pounded towards her, sliding and crunching in the gravel. The man stormed past and slid to a halt, looking around in confusion. She jumped forward, her left arm up to deflect his sword before he had a chance to swing, her right hand bringing the gun to his face. There was no time for better aim. She pulled the trigger.

He fell without a sound.

Jameta sprinted on, the yells of her pursuers driving her. But now she had more time. On a smoother slope she fumbled another shell out of her pocket and loaded the gun, setting the safety and tucking the weapon away. *They know I have a gun. I wonder what they'll do?*
She ran. Down the mountain she bounded, leaping from rock to rock, her arms out to steady herself, her body writhing in a desperate dance of balance and speed. Slowly, ever so slowly, she pulled away from them. She was gasping in the pain of each breath, but her enemies sounded in worse shape.

She began to think again. *Where would Brownie go? She'd follow Doe. She always does. Brownie's smart enough to get rid of that scarf. She'll rub it off against a bush or tree. Then she'll follow the remuda. All I have to do is find her.*

Jameta jogged down the mountainside into the forest, her breath easing, but her eyes scanning. *I have to remember my lessons. Mess up their minds. How can I do that? Could I go back and steal their horses?*

A few seconds of thought ditched that idea. In fact, the slower runners would have turned back. Might be coming after her on horseback...

Galloping hooves. She slipped behind a tree trunk and watched the rider sweep past. As the sound faded, she trotted on, stopping every once in a while to listen. Sure enough, soon another rider passed her, farther west this time. She continued to circle back to where the remuda had crossed her path.

A third horse burst upon her before she had a chance to hide. She saw his grinning face, grotesque in the shadow of his burnoose, his eyes staring, his sword raised high. Ducking behind a tree, she avoided his swing, sprinting off to the east. He hauled his horse around and came after her. Again she used a tree to good advantage.

He pulled his horse to a sliding stop and jumped off, sprinting towards her, sword raised again. As he ran, he gave a triumphant cry.

She readied her pistol and braced herself. As he swung, she guarded with her left like last time and fired at the leering face.

Somehow, she missed. His free hand grabbed for her, but she twisted free and spun to face him.

His smile widened as he stalked forward, his sword swinging slowly in front of him, left, then right.

Jameta watched him come, her mind frozen. *Now is the time. If I'm ever going to need help from my heritage, this is it.* Nothing happened. Her ancient curse had deserted her.

The enemy slid forward, his sword swinging back...

Wait a minute. He doesn't know that. She took a deep breath and stood up tall. Then she hooked her fingers into claws and threw herself forward, the loudest scream she could summon up tearing from her throat.

His eyes widened and he threw his sword up, but in a purely defensive move. She tossed it aside and struck at him again and again, her fingers clawing at his eyes, her vambraces pummelling his body.

The tribesman broke and ran, his sword flying into the bush. He flung himself aboard his mount and pounded away into the forest, his fearful face staring back over his shoulder.

She glanced once at the sword, discarded the idea and turned and trotted across the old caravan trail. Once in the brush on the other side, she stopped and listened. Not a sound.

Where did the remuda cut off? Aha. There's the tracks.

Jameta took a moment to read the sign. Horses in a line, trotting quickly. Then on top another set. Smaller, with the rounded shoe of the Dennals. Trotting along, but not in such a straight line. *Brownie!* She gave a low whistle. Then she waited. After a while she moved on, trotting up the trail, stopping to whistle and listen. *The crackle of sticks. Yes, there it was again.* She called softly. *There she is!* Relief coursed through her.

Brownie stepped cautiously through the trees, her head up, her ears flicking in all directions. Jameta moved into the clear, a biscuit in her hand. The horse trotted up, nickering, to take the treat.

Jameta checked the horse's hooves were clear, then took the reins and led her along for a few steps. There seemed to be no limp. She mounted and heeled her to a trot, heading south. *Yes, there's the limp again. She's got a strain or something. Hope we don't have to run again.*

They made their way through the trees, staying within sight of the caravan trail. Soon, far ahead, she spotted a building through the sparse pines that lined the valley bottom. She reined off to the east and moved ahead at a walk.

There was a little ridge that overlooked the old waystation, and there she found Rogas tethered to a tree well back from the edge. Elron's rifle was still in the saddle scabbard. *Gone back to his old tricks.* She left Brownie with Rogas and slipped up to the top of the ridge.

The waystation was built of rock, but the roof beams had long ago rotted away, leaving an open shell. The walls were too high to see down into the main building from her vantage point. A ragged drystone wall surrounded it, allowing scant forage for the six horses that grazed there. *Five desert ponies and a large bay. So the rest of his toadies scurried home safely with the soldiers. Appropriate.*

A sentry stood at the entrance to the ruin, leaning against the rocks and staring at the mountains to the west.

Wait. What's that?

Slipping along the stone fence behind the sentry was a blond head. She watched in tense silence as Erlon glided closer and closer. A flurry of motion and the guard was gone, tucked motionless behind the wall where anyone leaving the building would not see him. Erlon regarded the doorway, then slipped over to stand outside, still and silent.

After an endless wait, another man stepped out the door. The moment he moved away from the building Erlon was on him, his hands wrenching the man's head sideways.

There was a call from inside, faint from Jameta's distance. Erlon resumed his ambush.

The next man was more careful. He came out with his sword drawn, and the guard Captain was forced into a quick fencing match. This ended with his enemy dead at his feet, but the soldiers inside couldn't help but hear. Erlon charged into the building. There were two shots, almost together, then several cries, then silence.

Jameta headed down the hill. She came in from the opposite end of the ruin, reasoning that all the attention would be drawn towards Erlon's attack. A low window pierced the wall on that side, and she slipped over the sill, flattening herself against the stones. Careful of the twigs and brush growing from the dirt floor, she crossed to the doorway and peered out into the main room. Then she ducked back. Pavenkov was there, a multi-shot Third pistol in his hand. Erlon faced him, his sword at the ready, the last two Ferbodean soldiers at his feet, rifles scattered, limbs spread in the graceless pose of death.

The bureaucrat did not look good. His uniform coat, usually dirty, was now in tatters. His boots paid no pretense to being shiny, and his lurch forward revealed that one was missing a heel. But the gun in his hand looked clean and deadly.

The Ferbodean smiled. "So the man with the big sword doesn't win the battle anymore." He gestured with his pistol. "Drop it."

Erlon knew she was there, but his eyes did not stray, challenging Pavenkov's gaze. His sword stayed in his hand. "Your time is over, Pavenkov. You picked the wrong side, and it's too late to switch."

The bureaucrat's lips pulled back in a grimace. "That may be, Blond-and-Handsome. But I'm not going down without a fight, and I'm taking a few with me. Starting with you, and next will be that Samnian harlot you hold so dear."

Erlon will attack. He knows I am here, to his left, so he will go right to protect me. She felt a rush of warmth for the dear, predictable man who was preparing to sell his life as best he could so that she could get away. *I'm really going to have to marry him. Because we will get out of this.*

The Ferbodean motioned with his gun. "So go to your death, Galesian, realizing that it is futile. She will die next, and I will have my way with her before she does."

Erlon will attack while his enemy gloats. She watched the gun hand. *He will lift it just before he fires. Right...*

"NOW!" she screamed with all her might and lunged forward as Erlon dove for the enemy's knees. Pavenkov wavered between the two targets, then chose her as closer and more dangerous. As the barrel swung her hands fell into the pattern of the dance, reaching out in the familiar move, her right arm sweeping the gun aside, hand turning to grasp. Her knee rose of its own volition, cracking against the wrist of the opponent. The blast of the shot in the confined space overwhelmed her for a moment, the whine of the ricochet screaming away.

Then her thinking mind took over. She smashed her left vambrace into the enemy's teeth, yanked the pistol from his limp fingers and hammered the butt of it between his eyes.

He dropped to the floor and lay, unmoving.

"You're right. It is a fighting pattern."

Erlon was just regaining his feet. He sheathed his sword and took the gun from her hand. "Told you it was."

There was a thunder of galloping hooves on the road. "His tribesmen." She aimed a shaky grin at Erlon and intied the scarf from his neck. "Not much of a veil, but it will have to do." She turned and went out the door, knotting it behind her head.

The ten riders sat their panting horses, frozen at the sight of her. She strode forward. *You have dishonoured yourselves and betrayed your people. How will you redeem yourselves in your eyes and the eyes of your tribes?*

One of the men reached for his sword, but Erlon appeared with the pistol ready. The tribesman moved his hand away.

You will make this act of atonement. You will ride to all the tribes of the Dry Land People and tell what happened here today. You will tell how the Warrior Woman and her consort defeated the Ferbodean and his armies yet again. You will remind all the tribes that the Ferbodeans must stay behind their borders until I give them permission otherwise. Do you understand your mission?

Their heads bowed as one.

She swept her hand to the south, and they galloped away.

Erlon was cleaning his sword. "Medlili's brothers have been helping me with my Samnian."

She turned to him. "And?"

"I could understand a few words in there."

She gave him a sweet smile. "Which words were those?"

"Have I been promoted?"

She shrugged. "The Warrior Woman has no husband. It doesn't fit the image. Consort is the best you get."

He reached out for her. "I'll take it."

She clung to him, her body shaking as her mind relived the dangers she had just been through. He held her gently, his hand stroking her hair, a finger tracing her nose, her lips. She looked up into his eyes, warm with concern. A glow of peace filled her, and she burrowed her face against his chest again.

A long while later, he released her and leaned back to look down. "What privileges come with the appointment?"

She squeezed him one more time, then broke away. "I've been travelling with merchants long enough to see when I'm in poor position to bargain. Let's get the horses."

He glanced around the scene of the battle. "Yes, the vultures will find an appropriate use for the bodies. The locals can have the gear."

"What about him?"

The figure on the ground began to stir.

"He's got a horse and water. He's not our problem any more."

"I suppose it's better I didn't kill him. He's worth more to Druzhba discredited than dead."

Erlon grinned. "No diplomatic incidents. Roeble and Aleria will be so pleased."

She cleaned her vambrace with the corner of her scarf. "Not half so pleased as I am."

As they rode at a slow pace up the valley, he looked over at her.

"I had a question."

"Mhm?"

"You did very well."

"Thank you. That's not a question."

"Delicate subject. Your...what do we call it? Talent?"

"Oh. You mean, we were in a life-or-death situation. Why didn't I go over the tongue and break them all into little bits?"

"Eloquently put, but that's the question. Did it happen?"

"No."

"You're sure?"

"You suggest I couldn't tell the difference?"

"I hope you don't think I'm being nosy. Your talent is one of the assets of the caravan. I need to know as much about it as I can."

"I wouldn't consider my 'talent' much of an asset."

"Why wouldn't you?"

"There's not much use having a berserker who can't go berserk when she needs to."

He nodded. "Now, that idea we can talk about. You were assuming that in an emergency your inner nature would take over. And it didn't happen?"

"That's right. And I'm not sure how to handle that."

"I can't say I'm unhappy."

She glared up at him. "You mean I'm not so likely to go and do something stupid, hoping that my inner self will save me. Because it might not."

"Exactly. If you'll take the advice of someone with experience?"

"If this is about warfare, I'm listening with every pore of my body."

"I've seen too many people with a new weapon who thought they were invincible, only to discover its limitations too late."

She nodded. "You're right. Now that I know my rage won't take over on command, I have to ignore it, don't I?"

"Consider it a piece of good luck when it happens and assume it won't happen for the rest of the time."

She grinned up at him. "Which still puts me safely under your wing."

"That's right. Which means that we're going back to camp for a little dance practice before supper."

"Fair enough." She glanced up at him sideways. "When do I get to hold the sword?"

He just laughed.

* * *

Two days later Jameta was riding beside Aleria, talking about nothing in particular, having a pleasant chat to pass the time on the road. It was nice to be doing normal things again.

They were distracted by a cloud of dust moving in from the east.

"One rider."

"Lavan's out there."

"He's not in a rush, but he's got news."

As Lavan pulled closer they could see a grin on his face. "Three riders, over the hill."

"Anybody familiar?"

"One's on a palamino. The leader's got a lot of clothes on."

Jameta grinned as well. "When will they get here?"

271

He pointed. "There's a break in the ridge up ahead, there. They'll cut through."

"Any trouble? Enemy dust clouds on the horizon? Sandstorms looming? Officials needing bribes?"

"Nothing. Only three simple nomads, wending their leisurely way to wherever they're going."

Aleria snorted. "And trailing a wake of unrest and political unhappiness behind them."

"Ah, you're jealous." Jameta kneed Doe to a lope and called back over her shoulder. "A couple of years ago, that would have been you."

She was gone before the other woman had a chance to answer.

Medlili and her brothers did not look their sharpest. They pulled up beside the caravan and slowed to a walk, their horses' heads low.

"Tough trip?"

Medlili nodded. "Many miles every day."

"How did it go?" Aleria passed over a canvas water bag. "Anyone listen?"

The girl took a deep swig before answering, then handed the bag along. "They were very polite. All knew about the massacre that did not happen. Most were unhappy about the new mining rules, but did not want to offend a person as important as myself." The dark eyes sparkled above the veil. "I was polite in return. I did not threaten anyone with the Warrior Woman's revenge."

Jameta laughed. "That was a good idea."

Medlili's head came up. "I am learning diplomacy from the best of teachers."

Aleria looked around the group. "Then you've come to the wrong place. The most diplomatic person in this bunch is the big guy with the sword over there."

Medlili nodded. "Easy to be nice when you are strong. So I was very nice."

"Do you think they got the hint?"

The voluminous garments moved in a shrug. "As time moves, we will see."

"That we will. Now you can ride at our speed for a few days and rest up."

"We are happy to do that. And our horses." She spoke to her brothers, and they pulled out on the upwind side of the caravan, ambling along at a wagon's pace.

37. Return

Their return across Ferbodin was more of a procession than a caravan journey. They were met at the border by a respectful honour guard, who escorted them into the capital city, fending off all visitors and providing the best spots in the campgrounds, with fresh meat roasting on the spit each evening as they arrived.

On the way, they were enticed into two bazaars, much too clean and well organized to be "People's Markets," but full of a decent variety of goods, nonetheless. Business was brisk, and the other vendors seemed pleased to see the Galesians, dropping in to check their new Dry Lands goods and discuss prices.

Roeble was in his element. Jameta was glad to drop her translation duties and hone her trading skills, although she couldn't help but notice that the poorly dressed women always came to her to buy their trinkets. Mindful of Roeble's clever trading techniques, she bargained with them more for fun than profit. Medlili worked with her and proved devastating to the male customers.

"I don't know how you do it."

Medlili turned from sliding a handful of coins into her money pouch. "How I do what?"

Jameta gestured with her hand. "Here I am, dressed in my normal working clothes, and all the old women come to bargain with me. There you are, covered in veils and full nomad getup, and you've got the men slavering over you. You have nice eyes, but I'm sorry, they don't look pretty enough to explain it."

The tribeswoman's laugh demonstrated one of her other attractive qualities. "It's not how they look. It's where they look."

Jameta regarded her. "I'm not even going to ask."

"Better you don't. It takes a lifetime of training and an attitude towards men you don't have."

"Are you telling me I'm not desireable?"

Medlili dropped her eyes and bowed her head. "If the Warrior Woman demands, I must answer."

"You'd better." She looked down at her own meagre curves, revealed enough, she thought, by her snug-fitting embroidered shirt. "Why not me?"

The other girl shook her head. "I'm not saying that certain men won't find you attractive. Erlon does, and he's all that counts. He doesn't find me desireable at all."

"He doesn't?"

"Not by any evidence I can find. He treats me like Uncle Sfisef does. Or like a little sister to be tolerated. It's rather disappointing." She held up a hand. "But only in a general way. I help him all I can."

"How do you do that?"

The eyes crinkled, and Jameta knew the girl was smiling. "By acting like barely tolerable little sister. But for the rest of them," Medlili swirled around and Jameta caught the shape of her hip, sliding under the cloth, "those pants of yours don't show off anything."

* * *

Roeble paused at the big double doors of the concrete administration building and glanced at Medlili, fully covered in her traditional costume. He shook his head. "How are we going to persuade these hard-headed politicians that Medlili is as powerful as she is?"

Jameta shrugged. "It all depends on them. I can raise my hand and there will be war across the East. If they can't understand that, then they are going to cause a war, and there isn't anything I can do about it."

"That's rather fatalistic."

"We may not be able to stop the war, but we can do our best to persuade them to stop it."

He regarded her until the same official appeared to lead them through the corridors. "I hope you do some fast talking."

Jameta forced a smile. "Oh, Medlili doesn't talk fast. Just with feeling."

He tilted his head and strode on. Jameta caught the Tribeswoman's eye and gave her a reassuring smile.

There were two empty chairs at the table in the meeting room; when three of them showed up there was a ripple of consternation through the assembly. Jameta solved their problem by bowing Medlili into the seat and plopping herself on the closest bench behind her.

The usual welcoming speeches began, but when it came time for Roeble to introduce his companions he deferred to Jameta.

She stood forward to the edge of the table, embroidering her tale with the gestures she had learned from the storytellers of the Tolbè. "Citizens of Ferbodin. A situation with dangerous potential has arisen on your eastern border. Your leaders have noted huge areas of empty space in that direction and considered it profitable to occupy it. Scientists from Domaland have discovered ores and gems in the area and have taken steps to extract them.

"But that terrain is not empty. It is the traditional grazing ground of the Dry Lands Tribes. The reason it looks empty is that it will not support more people and animals than you see on it now. It will definitely not support any enterprise the Ferbodeans might wish it to bear."

She looked around the table. "You are aware of these facts. I merely repeat them to put us all on the same footing. I repeat them to assure you they are true. The wishful thinking of the businessmen who see profit at no cost is a false path that skirts destruction."

"And so the People of the Dry Lands have sent an emissary to you to discuss these problems. Medlili of the Aine Tolbè is here in two separate roles. First, she is the ambassador of the Headwoman of the Aine Tolbè, one of the most powerful tribes in the area. As such, she does not speak for the other tribes, but she is a representative with the power to persuade the others to follow her lead, if only she leads them correctly."

Jameta paused to stare the main leaders in the eye, ending with Druzhba. "And in her other role she is Speaker for the Warrior Woman of the Tribes. Medlili communicates the wishes of the entity whose word can wipe the Ferbodeans and the Domalanders from the face of the desert. For your own good and the survival of your people, please believe this. When Medlili Speaks with the Voice of the Warrior Woman, she represents every tribesman: Dry Land and Desert. And that is a large number of ferocious fighting men."

She gestured with a flowing, open palm. "This may sound threatening, but think of the advantage. If you make a pact with Medlili, it is as if you have dealt with King Otta of Galesia. She Speaks for all the Tribes. Listen well, O men of Ferbodin."

Medlili gestured, and Jameta removed the Speaker's veil. As she did so, she glanced up to see the looks on the men's faces. *She's doing it already.*

The Speaker for the Warrior Woman rose gracefully, her sweeping hand including all present. "My Headwoman, Zelfana, bids me greet you from the Tribe of the Tolbè. My Mistress the Warrior

Woman bids me greet you from all Her people. It is the command of two most powerful women that these small problems are solved. Thus they will be solved. One way or the other. It is you who sit in this room, you of moderate thought and reasonable mein, who have the choice of method."

She nodded her head to Druzhba and sat.

There was no attempt at games this time. He rose and bowed to Medlili. "This group of Citizens of Ferbodin welcome the opportunity to deal with one so well connected to the power of her people. It makes conversation simpler. But how can my fellow Citizens and I believe that this semi-mythical Warrior Woman exists? We hope you will pardon a lack of faith in hard-headed politicians, who must deal with the realities of the world." He sat and leaned back, waiting.

Medlili smiled, and every face in the room brightened. "My Mistress raises her hand and the Tribes rise. You have the report of your Lieutenant-Colonel Samur Kazan. How many men did he face?"

Druzhba glanced over his shoulder. A uniformed man stood. "The report was uncertain. Well over a thousand."

She nodded. "A small exaggeration. In seven days my Mistress raised an army of 973 horsemen, every one a fighter. At the rising of one hand." Her fingers moved in fluid gesture. "An open hand, not yet made a fist. She allowed your people to see their mistake and leave our lands. Think of that fist, future allies of the Warrior Woman. She is a reality."

Druzhba nodded. "That is well spoken, Citizen Medlili." A dry smile crossed his face. "When you speak of numbers to men of numbers they carry weight. What would your Mistress, the Warrior Woman, say to us?"

"It is simple, Citizen Druzhba. Our boundaries are our boundaries. We are happy that you use your land as you wish. We use our land as we wish. The Domalander mines do not use the land as we wish. They do not pay us for what they take. You know of this." Her head turned to glare at the mining contingent across the room.

Eyes turned aside, and no one argued.

"Good. Then all is simple. We deal with the Domalanders about mines. You deal with the Domalanders about the transportation of the ores across your lands." She shot a glance at Druzhba. "Your people make good roads. Perhaps we want your skills on our lands as well."

The leader nodded. "We understand. I must say, your requests sound eminently logical. However, we are only a group of Citizens.

We have no official status, and no power to make agreements with you."

Her graceful fingers tossed the objection aside. "I did not think to speak to your Headwoman the first day. I did not think to make official meeting at all. I come to ease the path for discussions that will follow, with your leaders and many, many of my people's leaders. That is the way of the People of the Dry Land and the Desert."

"We...um...do not have a Headwoman."

"I have been told this strangeness. How do you get anything done?"

"We seem to manage."

She glanced around. "Yes, I see this. The men must talk with bared faces for many days before anything is decided. It is the same with our Tribes. Do not worry, men of Ferbodin. Our leaders are women of experience and open mind. They will deal with your leaders, whoever they are. As with women of all peoples, our desire is peaceful agreement."

She stood. "And now I have spoken. You know of my people's desires and my Mistress's requirements. Perhaps you would like to speak of this among yourselves and determine how to present these ideas best to your leaders?"

"That would be useful. And how shall we return our answers to you?"

Medlili gestured, and Jameta replaced her veil. "I continue my journey to Galesia and Domaland to make my people's wishes known there. You may contact me through my Galesian allies." She included Roeble in the elegant sweep of her hand.

He nodded in wry acceptance of his role.

After that, several important people had to express their appreciation for Medlili's people and their position, and to promise their support in whatever situations should arise. Then the emissaries were escorted with all ceremony to the busy street where Erlon and the Brothers waited, a small circle of uneasy calm around them. They formed up in their usual travel pattern and strolled back towards the caravan.

Roeble smiled at everyone. "That will work to our advantage."

Medlili shrugged. "Of course it will. They had no chance. You do not send men to deal with such as me. They should have sent for a woman the moment I appeared."

Roeble shook his head. "You had the bunch of them eating out of your hand, but don't underestimate Druzhba. He is a formidable mind."

"He is." Medlili's smiled twisted. "It is not happy to lay out your weapons and discover that your opponent finds you – what is the word? – amusing. Without the support of the Warrior Woman, I would have been quite unsure."

Roeble slapped her shoulder. "Well, that would have been an interesting sight, but in the circumstances, I'm glad to forgo the opportunity to see you looking unsure."

Medlili looked startled, her eye's widening and seeking Jameta's. Then she glanced quickly at her brothers, who were scanning the crowds around them.

Jameta smiled in reassurance, she didn't quite know of what.

When they reached their caravan and separated to their tents, Medlili looked around to see that no one was near. "Jameta, what happens with Roeble? Does he not know that he is never to strike a woman? It is good that my brothers were looking outwards for danger. Either one would kill him if they saw him strike me."

Jameta regarded her friend. "Then your brothers must learn. That is the way of Roeble's class in Galesia. The blow to the shoulder is a sign of equality. Perhaps of condescension to an inferior, but always a gesture of friendship that breaks the barriers of touching, and as such is rare, but important."

"So his act in striking me is an acceptance of my position?"

"More an acceptance of your equal relationship as individuals."

The tribeswoman frowned. "I find it rather...unusual to be offered equality by a man."

"Yes, I suppose it's a bit of a joke to you. But in Galesian society it is an important step."

Medlili sighed. "I have much to learn, Jameta. I am happy you are here to guide me."

"Don't worry. If anyone laughs at your mistakes, the Warrior Woman will straighten them out."

"I was surprised that they dared to question Her power."

"Don't be. The farther away we get from the desert, the less important Her power will be. In fact, when we reach Galesia, we will have to discuss our approach carefully."

With that sober thought, they joined the others.

38. Setting the Scene

"Ferbodin is a beautiful country."

Erlon raised his head to regard the farmland that stretched away from their camping spot under a copse of trees atop a hill. Small villages dotted the valley, columns of smoke rising from the chimneys, straight up into the still evening air. A castle loomed from a nearby hill. "If you could ignore the people."

"It's not the people's fault." Jameta swung her arm out. "Look at this." They were sitting above camp on a rocky point that overlooked the whole scene.

"What am I supposed to see? It's a beautiful valley with picturesque villages and a very scenic and functional castle."

"That's right. A grim and useful castle, a symptom of the situation that existed before the Revolution. Poor serfs under the strict control of all-powerful lords. No wonder they rose up and killed them."

"But look what they replaced them with."

She shrugged. "They were a bunch of poor, uneducated serfs. How would they know anything about government?" She leaned against him. "You know where they got their ideas?"

"A useless philosopher with a warped slant on human nature, as I recall."

"Who happened to be Galesian."

"He was?"

"That's right. Educated in the university in Kingsport eighty years ago." She waved a finger at him. "Don't be so confident about the superiority of our government. Given the right influences, we could end up like this."

"What circumstances?"

"A collapse of our economy."

"Which will not happen, because you and your cohorts are going to solve all our problems with trade to the East."

"Which this expedition has made rather satisfactory progress towards."

"Yes." He smiled. "It has been a successful trip, all round."

"And we are not far from home."

"Oh."

"And you promised me."

"I suppose." He looked out on the scenery again. "And here I thought you brought me out to enjoy the sunset."

She squirmed around so she could face him. "Erlon, here's your problem."

"I quiver in anticipation."

"Your problem is that you're a friendly person. You like people. You don't like to be alone, right?"

"I like other people."

"Right. And you're lonely."

"I am?"

"Of course you are. You have no family. No brothers, no sisters. Your mother is far away. So you make friends."

"Is there anything wrong with that?"

She grinned. "With the men, no."

"But with the women?"

"It's not the same."

"But surely I can have friends who are women."

"Yes, but not close ones. Most women aren't looking for brothers."

"I see. So, when I make close friends with a woman, I'm looking for a sister..."

"And she's looking for something different."

"That might be a problem."

"Which is your problem with me."

"It is?"

"Yes. I've been watching you tear yourself in half. For whatever terrible reason that you're going to tell me in a moment, you don't want our relationship to go past the brother-sister-good-friends stage. But you're lonely, and maybe a little in love with me. So you keep making the wrong moves. That wonderful hug, for example."

"It's wonderful, is it?"

"It would be for a sister or a wife. It isn't for a would-be lover who wants a whole lot more."

"I'm...sorry. I try..."

"But not hard enough." She slapped him on the shoulder. "I hate to tell you this, but you're only human." She grinned. "And I've been pushing you."

"You have...? Oh. That dance back at the Horse Fair..."

"Yes, I did rather take advantage of that, didn't I?"

He tried to frown, but it didn't take. "I should say so. And in public!"

"A situation where you couldn't refuse."

He frowned for real and looked at her. "Have you been playing me along?"

"The man finally figures it out!" She looked into his eyes and became serious. "I have been honest with you. I like you. I think we make a great couple. But this terrible event from your past that comes between us is skewing the relationship all over the place. We don't know how much of anything is honest attraction, and how much is challenge to win who-knows-what. Right now you're suspicious that I've been cheating, right?"

"Aye. Well, sort of…"

"That's my point. Cheating at what? Is this a game? Love isn't supposed to be a game. It's too serious for that."

"I see."

"I'm doing my best not to make it a game. And you're not trying to make it a game. But despite all our trying, it is a game, and you're not playing fair."

His shoulders slumped. "It's happening all over again. And it's worse this time."

"Ah. This has happened before. Is that the problem?"

"Yes, this has happened before. But not the same. It's a complicated story."

"I have…" she looked at the angle of the sun, "…until nightfall." She leaned against his chest. "Talk. I'm listening."

"That will be a pleasant change."

"No insults. No ducking out. Tell the story."

He nodded three times, slowly. He interlaced his fingers, twisting his hands back and forth. Then he leaned back against the rock and looked up into the evening sky. "All right. This is how it happened…"

39. Erlon's Story

"I came to Galesia from Domaland."

He did not continue, so she decided on a prompt. "I thought you were from Shaeldit."

"I am. I was. But I'm most recently from Domaland."

"So far, so good. Is that a problem?"

He shrugged. "Perhaps. But it's not the real problem." He stared into the fading sunset for so long that she wondered if that was all he would say.

"It's a very complicated story, but basically I got itchy feet when I was twenty and went to Domaland."

"Can you do that? Pack up and walk into Domaland and say, 'I want to stay here'?"

"You can if you have money."

"You had money?"

"I'd been mining and I saved up my share of the finds. Instead of selling it to the merchants, I kept it."

"What were you mining?"

"Diamonds."

"You got together a bag of diamonds and took it to Domaland to sell."

"That's right. People always said that the merchants paid us a trifle and took all the profit for themselves, so I decided to find out. I hired on to guard the diamond train going out to Domaland, and presto! There I was in Walhampton.

"I took one of my stones to a merchant and got an amazing price for it. At least it seemed amazing to me. But I wasn't sure. So I deposited the rest in a vault at a bank and took the money from the first one, bought new clothes and a haircut and rented an apartment on a decent street. I hung out in fashionable spots, watched everyone and found out how to talk, how to act." He grinned. "It's not that hard. If you're already from a different country, they can't tell what's ignorance and what's a cultural difference."

"And you're a personable, friendly type."

"And I'm twice as big as most of them. People don't tend to laugh at me."

"And what did you do, then?"

"I was running short of cash, so I took the second stone to another merchant that was recommended to me. This one was in a different street, and I refined my approach. I dressed better and I carried the gem in a little cedar box I bought in the market. On black velvet. The whole show."

"And you got twice as much for it."

"Almost three times. It was amazing. I could make a good living, working in the Shaeldit mines for a year or so, then selling my findings in Domaland and living there for two or three years on the proceeds. And I could make even more if I contracted a diamond cutter to polish them up before I sold them. It would be a useless life, but I could do it.

"However, things didn't work out that way. Domaland has the same kind of people as we do, here. There are feckless young men who make the wrong friends and get into trouble. Serious trouble."

"And you were one of those?"

"No. I met one of those. In an alley, trying to fight off three thugs who were a lot bigger than he was."

"And you had to step in."

He grinned. "My natural sense of fair play. I had the advantage of surprise. I took the first one's sword away and used it to put the others to flight."

"So, you made a friend."

"A very good one. Brear took me home, introduced me to his family, his friends, the whole thing. And they took to me. I spent three years with the Wiske family." He twisted to look down at her. "Like you predicted. A new family."

"Go on."

"His father was a manufacturer but he had an academic bent. He owned a huge library, both technical and literary. Hence the vocabulary. I moved in with them for their protection while we extricated Brear from his troubles. It wasn't that difficult. It required someone with a bit of..." he wiggled his fingers.

"...courage?"

"Well, fighting experience always helps. After I'd thrashed several of them, they got the message he was serious about...dropping their acquaintance, shall we say?"

"Did he owe them money?"

"No, it was more his knowledge of their operations that worried them. I persuaded them to move to more salubrious climes."

"Now you're showing off. Who uses 'salubrious' in normal conversation? You mean you ran them out of town."

"Something like that."

"And his family were very grateful. So they knew about his problems."

"It was impossible to hide them. Yes, they were grateful and very happy to have their son going about town with a noble of good reputation, foreign or not."

"You told them you were Ranked?"

"I told them nothing, but I knew what they thought. I...didn't like to lie, but I was young and stupid, and I thought maybe..." He shrugged. "Once you get started..."

"And then there was the sister."

He stared at her. "How did you know about Tarvie?"

"You said it was happening again, remember? So there has to be a girl involved. I suppose she fell in love with you, and everyone thought you made a perfect match, but in the end you had to come clean."

He turned away. "Why was there such a fuss about telling you my story? You knew it already."

"Oh, stop pouting. You mean I'm right?"

"In essence. The details don't matter. But it wasn't only Tarvie. Mr. Wiske spent a lot of time with me, and he's a good judge of people. He knew that Brear didn't have the right personality to take over the family business. But he decided that if I was there to help him, I would fill in for what he lacked."

"I decided it would be better if I left, but I didn't have the guts to tell them about my charade. So I invented an emergency. I told them my family was in financial trouble and I had to go home to support them."

"Which didn't work, because Brear's father insisted on helping you."

"I still don't know why I'm telling you this. How do you know these things?"

"Because I have an education, too. Part of it comes from reading books, which repeat the same stories over and over. The other part is from reading people, who tell pretty much the same tale. So, what did you do?"

"I politely refused his help and left the city. They weren't stupid. I'm sure they knew something was going on." He frowned at her. "Like other people I could mention. After a while they stopped pushing me to stay. They were hurt, but they wanted what was best for me. Which made me feel even worse."

"I know how they felt. And what about Tarvie?"

"Don't you want to tell me?"

"No, Erlon. That's one area where I can never be sure. I know what I hope you did, but it's impossible to be certain."

"So this is a test, is it? If I did right by her, I pass and I'm in. If I didn't, I'm a cad, and you give me the heave-ho?"

"Not necessarily. You didn't do right by her because you're here and not there. What happened?"

"I did right by her; I left. It was the best thing I could do. It's like you said. I liked her a lot, and I liked what she represented, but I didn't love her. Oh, sure, I'm supposed to tell you that, no matter what, but it is the truth."

She sat up tall to put an arm over his shoulder. "People always believe what they need to believe, so I'll be happy to take that as the truth."

"Thanks for the heartfelt vote of confidence."

"So you left. Where did you go?"

"I left Walhampton to wander around Domaland for a while. Aimless travelling got boring, so I went looking for a job. It was easy to get hired at an arms factory because of my experience with weapons."

"Aha! Hence the custom-made sword and the shooting skills and the ability to lead a team of fighting men."

"That last bit came later. Because of my job with the factory and the contacts I made, I used to take short-term contracts with people who needed guarding. Merchants, jewelry and bullion shipments, that sort of thing. I was big and strong and a good fighter, but also I could dress up and fit in. So I was pretty successful."

"But how did you end up back here in Galesia?"

His mouth twisted. "As my old Gran used to say, 'The gods listen to the tales we tell.' I had a real emergency. My mother got word to me that she was ill, so I had to come home. By this time I had enough money to make a difference. I got her out of the old village and took her to the main hospital in Kingsport, where she recovered. Then she went back to the mountains, the place she loves and will never leave. There I was in Galesia and I realized that I wanted to stay there, too. Partly to see Mum more often, but partly..." Again he shrugged.

"But you were in need of a job."

"Well, no and yes. My investments were paying off pretty well. But I need work. I have to feel I'm doing something useful."

"Investments?"

"Yes. When I sold my diamonds I invested the money in places like the arms factory where I worked. And they are doing rather well, wars being popular entertainment these days. But I wanted to work, and I started looking around for interesting employment. I heard about a position with the Dalmyns, who were said to be a good bunch. Kensel didn't see my time in a factory as a detriment to my morals, as many Galesians did. Then I got involved with Roeble, and then Aleria..."

"And now, me."

"There you have it. The story of my life, up to the minute. And it's all happening all over again. Once more, I can fulfill a role that would be perfect, but I'm not perfect for it. So here I am, about to disappoint a bunch of people I like and admire." He turned away, his hands on his knees, his head bowed.

She looked at him.

His head came around. "What? Why are you staring?"

"I'm trying to figure it out. It's a good story, but why was it so difficult to tell?"

He shrugged. "Because I'm not proud of myself. Yes, I was young and stupid, but I wasted a bunch of my life, and I made mistakes and I hurt some very nice people. It puts a rather different slant on my personality, and I don't want to put someone else through that. It's not fair to do that to people. You don't know what it's like to be so...strong, and to have to be so careful of everyone else because of it."

"Don't be so sure. And don't be so hard on yourself. You were young and stupid...well, you were young. I doubt if you've ever been stupid."

"Exactly. I can't even claim that excuse. But I did it anyway, because it was the best for me. Not for them: for me."

She shook her head. "The only thing you've been stupid about is feeling bad about how you acted. Think of what the Wiske family got out of it."

"What did they get? They got hurt."

"They got their son back. What could be better than that?"

"Oh, Brear is a good lad. He would have come to his senses."

"If he survived. He could have been injured for life. Either his body or his reputation. No, they got a bargain, and they got to enjoy your wonderful company for a few years. That's a bonus!"

"Glad you think so."

"Ask me again in five years, and we'll see."

"How will I find you in five years?"

She grinned. "Roll over in bed in the morning?"

His face reddened. "Jameta!"

She lifted an innocent face to him. "Yes?"

"You can't talk like that."

"I don't talk like that. Not in public. I may have mentioned before that I don't consider it necessary to be extra polite in your presence."

There was a long silence.

"So…"

She turned to look at him. "So…?"

"So now you know what kind of person I am."

"I already told you what kind of person you were. Was I wrong?"

"You were putting a very pleasant interpretation on my flaws."

"Erlon, I'm going to agree with Ferian. You are far too diffident."

"What makes you say that?"

She stood and turned to lean over him, staring into his eyes. "Because that was the weakest, soppiest, reason for keeping a girl at arm's length that I have ever heard. I can't believe we spent a whole year separated by the idea that someone fell in love with you and you didn't love her."

"It was more than that."

"What do you mean, more? Did you bed her? Get her pregnant?"

"Of course not! What do you take me for?"

"It's a matter of what you take you for." She shook her head, then looked up into the evening sky. "What a weak excuse! A whole year wasted. And here I thought we were holding back until we knew each other better."

"Well, we were." He glanced at her sideways. "Maybe I'm only looking for a sister."

She laughed. "Erlon, you're twenty years late to get a sister. What you're looking for is a close relationship with a woman. And at this stage of your life, there's only one option available."

"You're sure about that?"

"Oh, yes. Very sure."

"I see." He looked up at her, then he looked around. Then back to her. "I'm not sure of the rules. Is this when I get to kiss you?"

"It's our game. We make up the rules as we go along."

He stood, holding out his hand.

She stepped into his arms. The time for talking was over.

* * *

When they reached the Galesian border, there was a different officer in charge. Aleria suppressed a smile as she came back to the wagons after arranging entry papers for Medlili's party. She tossed the Double S rifle she was carrying up to Cavick and swung aboard.

Jameta raised her eyebrows. "Is that feather on your nether fang?"

Aleria wiped her mouth. "Thought I destroyed all the evidence."

Roeble glanced at the border station. "I don't see anyone coming to receive our weaponry."

Aleria's lip curled. "I no longer have confidence in the Royal Army to protect our equipment, no matter their protestations of how they have dealt with the offending parties. They have returned our repaired rifle to us and they will henceforth find their own weapons."

"We're keeping the rifles?" Erlon's eyes were wide.

"We're taking responsibility for them while they are inside the realm. When we camp tonight we will seal them in crates." She grinned. "Not too firmly." She pointed ahead, and Cavick started them rolling.

Aleria's mouth turned down. "They weren't interested at all in my offer to return their rocks to them."

When the laughter died, Erlon pointed at Jameta and Lavan. "We're not home, yet. Each of you take one of the boys and clue him in on procedures inside the realm. They've got learning to do."

"May I ride patrol, too, Erlon?"

He glanced at Medlili: up, then down. "Dressed like that? It would hardly be safe."

She regarded her all-encompassing robes. "What do you mean? How is my clothing a danger to me?"

He laughed. "It's not you who would be in danger. I think you'd best stay with the wagons."

"Whatever you say, Captain."

He turned Rogas away, then glanced back at her as if expecting to catch a smile. She looked innocent.

He winked at Jameta and rode off down the pass towards Kingsport.

40. Folk Dance

Jameta peeked out through the curtain. The small audience sat in comfort around the Dennal formal lounge, the furniture pulled back to clear an area in the centre of the room. The three-man orchestra looked at her, expectant.

"All right, girls. Do you remember the steps?"

Hana shrugged. "Drilled into us all our lives."

"But now we are performing for a highly skilled dancer in her own right." She signalled to the musicians. "Let's do our family proud."

As they went through the patterns of the Path of Light, Jameta was pleased to see her cousins become more enthused. By the time they hit the final series of moves their actions were as powerful as hers. And at the end they were sweating harder.

"That was fun."

Gita regarded Jameta. "I didn't know you were such a good dancer. I've never seen it done like that."

"You dance like you mean it. Like it had more significance than just an old folk thing."

Jameta smiled. "That I do, Hana. And now you're about to find out why."

She walked over and picked up her vambraces, snapping them on as she moved to the centre of the room. Erlon drew his sword and handed over her Tolbè veil as he took his place to the side and behind her.

Her cousins sank into their chairs, their eyes wide. As she tied on the new veil, heavier and longer than her Samnian one, she glanced at Lord anDennal. He was leaning his chin on his hand, his elbow propped on his chair arm, regarding her with an unflinching gaze. Medlili smiled behind her gauzy veil. She knew what was about to happen.

Jameta motioned to the musicians. They began to play, but she snapped her fingers, quickening the tempo. When they reached the perfect pace, she began to dance the "Path of Light" with a new partner.

She and Erlon had practised this, adapting it as necessary. He had to hurry in some places, because attacks were supposed to be coming from different directions. But since this was only a family demonstration there was no hurry; they ran through the dance for the enjoyment of the movement and the work together.

When they reached the final throw, where her enemy lay at her feet with her "weapon" at his throat, they froze as one powerful chord of music faded to nothing.

Applause rang out.

She reached down and helped Erlon to his feet – a rather symbolic gesture, considering his weight – and they bowed like street performers. She sent a worried glance at Lord Dennal, but he did not seem disturbed. In fact, he was speaking to a servant, who hurried from the room.

The Twins jumped up and rushed to her.

"So that's why you're wearing those guards." Hana fingered the bronze.

"Yes, I had to adapt the dance for the vambraces. In the original, the girls would have been holding farming implements, like a short hoe or stick, and you use that to protect your arm from the sword." She demonstrated.

"But why are they all scratched? That cut looks deep." Gita turned a disapproving frown on Erlon. "You don't practise that hard, do you? That could be dangerous."

He raised defensive palms, looking to Jameta.

"No, I got that one in battle. I don't exactly remember when. Battles are so mixed up."

A new voice rose over the babble, and everyone turned to face Lord Dennal. "I gather there is a part of this story we have not heard yet."

Jameta felt her face grow hot. "Yes, my Lord. I'm...afraid that dance isn't the only heritage handed down to me from our Samnian ancestors."

He nodded. "I am sorry to hear that."

"As was I. Except at the time, when it came in quite handy."

"I imagine it did. How many did you kill?"

"I...I didn't kill anyone. It was the Roan..."

"You were horseback when it happened?"

"Yes, I was out riding an injured cart horse to see if his leg had healed up." She forced a smile. "It had."

The lord shook his head. "You went into battle unarmed except for those things, on the back of a cart horse?"

"He's a powerful animal, my Lord. He killed one horse and one man for sure. Broke several bones in others. At one point, I gather he smashed a horse into the ground, jumped off its back and leapt clean over the next horse, throwing the rider away with his teeth. That's what they told me afterwards."

"Hmm." He nodded. "And has this state come over you since?"

She shook her head. "Not even when I needed it."

"That is unfortunate."

"I don't think so. Erlon and I have discussed it. He says a new weapon can be very dangerous until you learn its limitations. In this case, I don't have any choice. I can't count on it, because I can't use it at will."

Lord anDennal heaved himself up out of his chair. "You have been counting on it all your life. You just didn't realize it."

He turned to his daughters, standing there with their mouths agape. "There is a part of the family's history that is not widely spread around. I suppose it is the time to tell you. But not now. We have guests, and they are in need of your social skills."

Hana turned a wry glance at her sister. "Well, it's nice to be useful for something."

Jameta held out a restraining hand. "Never think that way, Hana. We all contribute to the family and the realm in whatever way we are able."

"I'm glad you think so." The taller girl sighed and straightened her back. "Well, at least we can tell everyone we told them so."

Gita made a sour face. "Except we won't be allowed to, will we?"

"I'd rather it didn't get spread around, if that's what you mean."

Hana laid a hand on her shoulder. "Don't worry. We would never..."

"...but you have to come to the tea with us on Feastday. There's this woman...Marcé anLangon. You have to meet her. She never stops talking, and some of the things she says are..."

"...they border on vindictive. She needs to be put in her place..."

"...and you're the one to do it. Will you come..."

"...please?"

"...please?"

Jameta held up her palms in protest. "Are you sure you don't want to invite Erlon with is sword? That's a good solution to people like that."

Hana giggled. "Oh, no. We have to pretend to be civilized. If you and Gita double up on her, she won't know what hit her."

She sighed. "Oh, all right. I'll show up at your tea. But I guarantee nothing." She leaned towards them. "What if I like her?"

She glanced over at Medlili, who was sitting in a demure pose, taking this all in as best she could. "I think it's time for a real dancer."

Eyes swung to the tribeswoman, who stood, shrugging off the shawl that had covered her dancing dress. It was not so revealing as her usual costume, but Medlili needed little help.

The musicians struck up a tune, and she glided to the centre of the room and began. Since it was a family occasion, she did not perform one of the solo numbers for which she was famous. This was a folk dance of the same style as "Path of Light," involving the movements of husbandry and the farm. However, she carried it off with such grace that everyone sat, silent, as she finished.

Then the discussion began. Her moves had to be compared to the Samnian dance, her costume material felt and discussed. Medlili was gathered into the conversation of the other girls, and Jameta sat back and watched, satisfied.

Finally Gita paused to regard the tribeswoman. "That dress is rather revealing. Do you have any more...interesting dances you might teach us?"

Medlili glanced at Jameta, who laughed. "Sorry, ladies. Medlili is here as an ambassador of her people. She is not going to stray from that role by the kind of performance you're talking about. It might distract those she deals with from their concentration on her real message."

Gita started to pout, but then her face brightened. "You mean she really does have dances like that?"

Jameta cocked her head and raised her eyebrows, but said nothing.

At that moment the servant arrived carrying a dark wooden chest. At his master's signal, he placed it carefully on the low table. Lord Dennal opened it, and they craned forward to see inside.

There, lying on a bed of velvet, lay a pair of vambraces. They were shorter than Jameta's, and far more ornate. They, too, were scratched and dented, but the craftsmanship was superb.

Gita glanced to her father for approval and picked one up. She fiddled with it, then clipped it on. "It's the right length for my arm!"

AnDennal nodded. "We are bigger than we used to be. Better nutrition, I suppose. That was a man's set, two or three hundred years ago. Family heirlooms. They come down to us from long ago, but their story was lost in the migration. Perhaps for the better."

Gita ran her finger along one deep cut, then removed the guard and put it back. She did not speak.

Hana's face grew sad. "And your horse killed a man. That must have been terrible."

"Yes, and our tribesmen came and killed more. The difficult part was having to watch the other tribe pick up their dead and put down the injured horses." Even now she shuddered when she remembered that. "Those nomads love their horses."

"But they attacked you?"

"They attacked a bunch of defenseless women." She shrugged. "They were just tribesmen carrying out one of those senseless tribal battles that make life so difficult and trading so dangerous. The good that came of it is that we're hoping for more peace in that region. Now everyone is treading a soft path around our allies, the Tolbè, who have strong leadership, so they're not likely to take military advantage."

Lord Dennal cleared his throat.

"Yes, my Lord. They're also treading softly around me. When I go back, I will have to play a very subtle game."

"If you go back."

She shrugged. "There are other situations in that area that need our attention."

"Our?"

"Yes. Roeble's family is rather pleased at how this expedition turned out. Besides all the new opportunities, he brought back a huge profit in spices, cloth, gemstones, and handworked silver...well, you saw how much our portion was."

"Yes, they were generous with the shares. So your contribution was more important than we expected. And the new opportunities?"

"Well, my Lord, you sent me out to find ways for the Dennals to aid in the operations. I found a river."

"Yes, the Bel. And...?"

"And...nothing at the moment. But where there is a river, there is a place for anDennal. Aleria and Erlon think so, too."

"Then we must consult with our partners. What do you suggest?"

"We must sit down with our partners and make a plan to use the river. First we need a survey, north and south from El Sibh. I don't know how to manage that, because we have to work from the shore to get upstream, but we need a boat to do soundings from. I haven't figured that out, yet."

Erlon smiled "A steamboat would be nice."

She spun to face him. "A steamboat?"

He shrugged. "A boat powered by a steam engine. The Domalian Navy has several, and they're making more all the time. All sizes. You need a steam powered boat that is fast enough to navigate the river."

"And they build those?"

"I have no idea."

"But you can find out? Will Brear know?"

"If he doesn't, he'll go looking."

"Good. Write to him immediately. Ask where can we get plans for one of these boats. We need a very shallow draft for the river. Do they make those?"

"I'll ask him."

"Great."

Jameta was aware of silence in the rest of the room. She turned away from Erlon to see her uncle regarding her with a bemused look. "Oh, I'm sorry, my Lord. We didn't mean to leave you out. But the ideas come so fast…"

AnDennal smiled. "Yes, it seems that they do. We must meet with our partners even sooner. Until then, I must ask you to keep these thoughts to yourselves. We are not the only ones having new ideas. Who is this Brear person you are contacting?"

"He's a friend of Erlon's in Domaland."

"You trust him?"

"Most definitely." Erlon shrugged. "I have a close relationship with his family."

"Ah. Well, try not to give any more information than you have to. The businessmen of Domaland are reknown for their ability to sniff out a good idea. And steal it."

"But I may write to him?"

"It sounds advisable, if Jameta's plan is to go ahead."

"Are you approving my plan, then?"

He smiled again. "Not yet. Put it together and present it at the meeting."

"Right. I'll do that!"

41. A Businesslike Proposal

Before Erlon left to go back to the Dennal yard she pulled him aside for a walk in the garden. The weather was getting cool, and they strolled slowly, his arm pulling her close.

"Erlon, I'm afraid I've dumped you in the same old situation again."

"And how did you manage that?"

"It was easy. We need you, Erlon. I need you. Everyone needs you. And you don't need us. It's just like before."

"In what way?"

"You're footloose and self-sufficient. You come and go as you please. We're stuck trying to make the best of...where we're stuck."

He laughed. "That is the silliest thing I've ever heard you say. You just got back from a journey farther from Galesia than anyone in the realm has ever dreamed of going. You could get on your horses and be a hundred miles from here by sunrise. And you're stuck?"

She laid her head against his chest. "This is a different kind of stuck. We're trapped on the path to what we desire. In order to succeed, we must follow that path. Once you want something badly, it limits your choices."

"And you think that doesn't apply to me?"

"It didn't last time."

"But this time there is something I want." His arm tightened around her.

"Ah." She snuggled closer. "That makes a difference."

"I have a plan. If we get married first, we can go to Domaland as our wedding voyage, and find out about boats." He frowned as she stopped and pushed away. "What are you staring at?"

"I'm staring at you. You stole my idea!"

"What idea?"

"Getting married and going to Domaland. That was my idea."

"But I haven't asked you yet."

"No, you haven't asked me. But you will."

"No, I won't."

Her heart fell. "You won't?"

"What's the point? Rather anticlimactic, don't you think, after all this kerfuffle?"

"But how are we going to manage it, then?"

"What is there to manage? We know we're getting married. So we get married."

"I must say, that's not very romantic. What happened to the flowers and the jewelry…"

"You're already wearing it."

She looked down at her vambraces, scratched and dented, gleaming in a brief shaft of sunlight. "What are you talking about?"

"Why do you think I gave them to you?"

"To keep me from getting killed, perhaps?"

"To give you a chance to go on the expedition. I kept hoping that if you got to know me you could overlook my…well…"

"You mean you were in love with me even then?"

"How could you think otherwise? You're the one that always knows what's going on."

"Am I? And you've been in love with me all this time, through all these arguments?"

"Of course."

"Then I don't see how we can get married."

"You don't?"

"How can we? It would make me the first woman in history to get married when she was already her fiancée's widow." She raised her fists. "Because I'M GOING TO KILL YOU!"

He laughed, restraining her wrists easily. "No, you won't. You're trapped on the path to your desire. It restricts your choices. No husband, no wedding. So, no killing. Sorry."

"No killing, no romance, no suspense." She sighed. "This will be a very boring marriage."

"I don't think so."

"Why not?"

"Because I love you more than I can say. And I want to be married to you more than anything I have ever wanted in my life. And because I will keep on loving you, no matter how wealthy and powerful you become. Because I loved you when you were only a girl, swinging on my arm down a beautiful mountain valley, and I'll never forget that moment."

She remembered to close her mouth. "Even then?"

"Especially then. I remember how brave you were. How much in awe I was."

"You were in awe of me?"

"Oh, yes. It's easy for me to be brave when I'm the best fighter in the battle. But you did all the dangerous things when you had no way to defend yourself. It didn't matter, you went out and did them anyway."

She shrugged. "Trapped on the path to my desire."

"And what was your desire that was so important? Before I came along, I mean."

"To be useful. To be needed."

He shrugged. "Well, I don't find you so useful, but since I need you, I'll have to make do with that." He twisted her arm guards up to the light. "How about trying to be ornamental?"

She freed her fist. "I don't think this marriage is going to be boring after all."

Epilogue: New Business

As Jameta's carriage pulled up at the Dalmyn mansion a footman opened the door and handed her down. She thanked him, bemused. *Must be an important meeting. I wonder...*

She entered the ornately carved front door and Aleria appeared, taking her arm and shooing the footman away. "Come on. Everybody's waiting."

"For what?" She regarded her friend.

There was more than the usual bounce to the Caravan Master's step, and a spot of high colour marked each cheek. "For us to tell them where our enterprise is going next year."

"And we know this?"

"Of course we do. Just follow my lead." Aleria glanced at her and then away, frowning to herself. Then she smiled at Jameta. "And be ready to take over when your time comes."

Jameta shrugged. "Improvising as usual, are we?"

Aleria copied the shrug. "Works most of the time." She pushed open the door to the formal sitting room. There, rising from their seats around the central table, were three very important men: Duke anCanah, Lord anDalmyn, and Lord anDennal, the last with a quick grin for her.

Why didn't we ride here together? Ah. They've already had a meeting.

Once everyone was seated again, Duke anCanah looked around the table. "We have all been talking informally about the East but we need better information on where we stand. Aleria, will you give us a rundown of the situation out there right now?"

Aleria shrugged. "I gave you the gist of it, my Lord. If you want the details, you know who to ask."

Eyes turned to Jameta, who frowned. "I may not be the right person. I am too heavily involved. I started a revolution in Samnia merely by existing."

"Merely existing?"

"Lord Dennal can give you more details, but our family dynasty ruled there for centuries. A hundred years ago one of my ancestors was such a tyrant that the realm rose up and slaughtered him and his family. My relatives were the only ones to escape.

"Now the wind blows the opposite direction. My family's sect was looking for an excuse to rise up. The rumoured return of a semi-mythical berserker of their old ruler's line was all they needed. So there's warfare and mayhem in Samnia. If you want to sell a lot of guns, I'd get down there fast. You may be too late already.

"The nomad tribes to the north of Samnia won't have anything to do with it. Their problem is the Ferbodean government, which claims uncertain title to about half their traditional grazing lands, and wants them all to stop roaming around and settle down like good little Citizens so Ferbodin can take over the rest. They also disagree with the mining interests in the area, run by companies from Domaland with permission from Ferbodin, which is not theirs to give. The mines are covering grazing land with slag and polluting water, which is scarce. This doesn't make them popular with the Dry Land People, who aren't peaceful types to start with.

"So, business opportunities: arms, mercenaries, ammunition as usual. Transport of ore and equipment to and from the mines. The usual flow of trade goods: metal and technology south, spices, gems and fine fabrics north.

"But transport is the problem. The caravan trail doesn't have a durable enough surface for wagons. I could see the difference on our way back. By the time we had travelled that road twice, the wagon wheels were already digging ruts. No telling what this fall's rains will make of the gouges."

She looked around the group. "I miss anything?"

Aleria shrugged. "That you're the one person who could go in there and set the whole desert ablaze."

"Unfortunately, my only talent seems to be causing large amounts of trouble. Hardly useful to merchants."

"Oh, I don't know." Aleria grinned. "I've often found it convenient."

Duke Canah held up his hands. "We already have one of you, Aleria, and that's quite enough." His look went around the table, but no one had anything to add.

"I find that a reasonable analysis from which to work. If we want to get an oar in that profitable water, we have to solve their transportation problems for them." He looked at the two women. "Tell us about water transport."

Aleria shrugged. "The Bel is a big, wide, river. It's just that it flows south into Samnia."

Jameta leaned forward. "But what about north?"

"North?" the Duke regarded her. "What good would that do?"

She put up her hands helplessly. "I'm only tossing out ideas." Then it occurred to her. "We Dennals are the worst people to ask about this. We do all our barging down the river. In fact, the whole of Galesia is mentally fixed on using water to carry goods downstream.

"But what about carrying goods upstream? The Domalian Navy is converting its ships to steam engines. I don't know how far the Bel River is navigable to the north, but if we could move that ore up to the foundaries in Aesmark, we could move iron, steel and finished products back downriver to the whole East, and perhaps down the Channan to Kingsport and even to Domaland."

She looked around the table. There was dead silence. Looks were going back and forth. "Have I said something I shouldn't?"

Lord Dennal cleared his throat. "I'm sorry, my Lords. Jameta had absolutely no idea of our project. She thought all this up on her own."

Duke anCanah frowned. "Good for her. But if she can figure it out, others will. We'll have to push our schedule."

Jameta looked from her uncle to the Duke and back again. "Is it permitted to ask what I have been talking about?"

Lord anDalmyn had not spoken yet. Now his cultured tones slipped in and stilled the rising chuckle. "I suppose I should explain, Jameta, since this is my project. Along with Lord Dennal, of course. We're having a boat built. A paddle-wheeled steamboat. The engine is coming in by wagon in pieces. And the boat is being built..."

"...at the Trus sawmill in Hymnos...! Oh, I'm sorry, my Lord. I shouldn't interrupt. But it all came together..." She dropped her head, her face burning.

Lord Dalmyn chuckled. "I imagine that happens rather regularly."

Her head snapped up. "Oh, no..."

"I mean the sudden inspiration. I'm sure you don't usually let it run away with your manners."

"Thank you, my Lord."

"So, if I may continue...?" he grinned, and she knew she was forgiven. "One of the main problems with barging is getting the hulls back upriver. At the moment, we can't. Building new ones for each trip is the only solution, and it is wasteful. And they always leak."

Jameta caught his eye and wiggled her fingers.

"Yes, Jameta?"

"Isn't this rather counter to your carting interests? If Dennal Shipping could run cargo in both directions..."

"Very true. Hence your presence on the last expedition to the East." He raised his eyebrows and looked at her.

She gave him a tiny glare to let him know he wasn't getting away with anything. Then she turned her mind to the test he had set her.

"Right. Diversification. You need to work on water transport. We need to learn land transport. Both families need to get into more trading. There's no sense in making a small percentage by moving the goods when the merchants who make the deals are taking the major share of the profits." Then she remembered. *Diamond cutting.* She raised a palm to stop his response. "And we'll make even more profits if we manufacture the goods we're hauling and selling. But...no family has the expertise or the capital to do all those things, so we need a...a...I don't know what you call it. A group. Pooling resources, knowledge, and capital..." She looked around the table. "Who's the manufacturing expert?"

The room was still. They were all staring at her.

Except Aleria. The Caravan Master's chuckles burst into laughter. All eyes turned to her.

"What are you gawking at? She isn't saying anything you haven't been jawing about for the past year. Jameta, the word you're looking for is 'consortium.' But they don't know where to find their manufacturing expertise. But we do, don't we?"

"You do?" Her father frowned. "You never said anything about this before."

"I didn't know before." Aleria nodded to Jameta. "Tell them."

Jameta glanced at Lord Dennal, who nodded, so she began. "What would you say to an agent proven loyal to one of our families, bound to another of our families by marriage? An agent with strong contacts who are mid-level manufacturers in Domaland. An old family with a small but strong manufacturing base, who consider themselves deeply in our agent's debt and trust him implicitly."

Kensel anDalmyn grinned. "Lord Dennal, have you finally managed to marry off one of your daughters?"

Her uncle looked at Jameta for a moment. "No, I suspect it's one of my nieces. I'm sure she'll tell me when she's good and ready."

Kensel anDalmyn slapped his hands on his knees. "Well, gentlemen, that's the last piece of the puzzle. Do you think it's time to retire into our dotage and leave our enterprises in the capable hands of the next generation?"

"Oh, no, Father. You're not getting out of it that easily. I still need you for all sorts of little jobs for the next twenty years or so."

He lowered his brows. "And you still need me to cushion you from the falls you're going to take."

Aleria shrugged. "So life rolls on as it always has." She turned to Jameta. "And you?"

Jameta shrugged. "Back to wherever I'm useful."

"Which happens to be on the Bel River, right next to your new family and allies?"

"Convenient, isn't it?"

Lord Dalmyn cleared his throat. "Do I assume, then, that we are building another ship?"

Jameta shook her head. "Not yet. We have to make a survey. We need to chart how deep the water is, what parts of the river are navigable what parts of the year. It's too low to take a decent-sized boat up right now, but it's the end of the dry season. We have to spend time on the river. Talk to the people. We can get a good idea of the depths and the currents. Then we need..."

She turned to Lord Dalmyn. "What we need is a smaller boat, one that only carries a few people. I'll bet you could ship the engine for that overland. The fall rains are starting, and the river ought to be navigable in about three months. Of course the roads will be bad by then..."

"Jameta," Duke Canah raised a cautioning hand, "what are you planning?"

She turned to him. "I can have a report on the navigability of the Bel River from the ford at El Sibh to Aesmark by the middle of next summer, my Lord. Without that, any planning is idle speculation."

Lord Dennal nodded. "And where are you getting the money to buy or build this little ship of yours?"

"From the consortium. Look, Uncle, I don't have the experience or contacts to manage that end of the business. I'm better off out in the East, smoothing our way with the people, learning the land and its rhythms. There's also the matter of the mines themselves. We have to deal with the Domalian government and the companies that own the mines. Their refining techniques are destroying the nomads' land, and we won't stand for it."

"Oh, we won't, won't we?"

She turned to Duke anCannah. "No, *we* won't. We have to remember where our power comes from in that area. From the Dry Land People. If we fail them we might as well give up and come home and let our economy flounder until the Domalanders come in and swoop us up at ten cents for every dollar's worth."

The Duke pretended to consider, though she could tell he was playing for time.

"We support your tribesmen or we turn our bellies up and die?"

"I doubt if it's that simple, but you've got the idea. Are you in?"

"Am I in?"

"Yes. This has little to do with your logging interests in the North. But would you like us to manufacture your new logging Mechanicals in Aesmark, or do you want to pay top dollar plus huge shipping fees to bring them upriver from those robbers in Domaland?" She regarded him. "What about the king's objectives for the economy?"

"What do you mean by that?"

"You don't fit in at this meeting, my Lord. And I ask myself. Why is an outsider interested in our business? You're here to represent the King, aren't you?" Her heart quailed, but she held him with a level stare.

"You do make a persuasive argument. In that case I'm in." He raised a cautioning hand. "For the survey of the river. If that doesn't work, then where will we be?"

She shrugged. "After eight months out there, we'll have a dozen more ideas. There's always downriver into Samnia."

"Samnia! I thought it was too dangerous for you to go there."

"It all depends who wins the present revolution, doesn't it? If the Assisa side wins, we're back on top again."

Lord Dennal shook a finger at her. "Jameta, you will stay out of Samnia. If you go down there, we'll never get you back. They'll either crown you or assassinate you."

"Well, then. You'll have to come and visit my throne or my tomb, won't you?"

AnDennal sighed. "I suppose having the ruler of a country in the family would increase our value to the consortium."

"Thank you, my Lord. Now." She slapped her hands on the table like Aleria did. "What's the plan? Erlon and I have to go to Domaland to re-establish his contacts there."

"Have you thought of buying your boat in Domaland and shipping it around to the south by water?"

"That will depend on who wins in Samnia...no, I suppose it doesn't. I don't have to go with the boat."

Lord Canah looked around at each of his partners. Then he smiled at her. "I gather traders profit more when there is peace in the region. So I believe the consortium will wish their agent restricted to the northern part of the river."

She pretended to wipe sweat from her brow. "Much the way I would prefer it, my Lord."

"Fine. I'll write you some letters to contacts in Domaland. You have three months to get a boat on that river. I'd suggest you get cracking. If you'll take my advice," his eyes twinkled, "I always find that this sort of operation takes about twice as long as you think it will."

"Thank you, my Lord." She stood. "In that case, I suppose I must take my leave."

Aleria rose as well. "I'll go along. I have to keep reminding her that she has a wedding to organize first."

"Oh. My wedding! I forgot about that."

They stood in the doorway, grinning at the three stunned faces. Then they burst into laughter and turned out the door together.

* * *

Watch for the next book in this series, "Queen of Mischief," coming next year.

About the Author

Brought up in a logging camp with no electricity, Gordon Long learned his storytelling in the traditional way: at his father's knee. He now spends his time editing, publishing, travelling, blogging and writing fantasy and social commentary, although sometimes the boundaries blur.

Gordon lives in Tsawwassen, British Columbia, with his wife, Linda, and their Nova Scotia Duck Tolling Retriever, Josh. When not writing and publishing, he works on projects with the Surrey Seniors' Planning Table and is a staff writer for <indiesunlimited.com>.

More from Gordon A. Long

"Out of Mischief" World of Change Book 1
"Into Trouble" World of Change Book 2
"Mountains of Mischief" World of Change Book 3

"Zoysana's Choice" Book 1 of the Petrellan Saga

"A Sword Called...Kitten?" Romantic Comedy with an Edge
"The Cat with Many Claws" Sword Called Kitten Book 2

"Why Are People So Stupid?" Social Humour with a Point

Look for Gordon's books, selected reviews, poetry and short
stories at <airbornpress.ca>

Gordon's opinions on humanity are at the
"Are People Really That Stupid?" blog

Find his weekly reviews and his ideas on writing at
"Renaissance Writer"

www.ingramcontent.com/pod-product-compliance
Lightning Source LLC
Chambersburg PA
CBHW070222260626
47160CB00002B/647